25.00

THE FORTUNE TELLER

by MARSHA NORMAN

Second draft, revised

Copyright 1986 Marsha Norman

1:00 A.M.

* * *

Fay Morgan never had any money. Had never had any
money, in fact. But then, she'd always <u>known</u> she'd
never have any money, and that helped, really it did.
More than you'd think.

The other thing Fay had always known, was what was
going to happen. Where things were. Who was coming
into who else's life and when. And why.

What little money Fay had, she had earned by
selling these powers of location. The police department
would pay five hundred dollars to find a suspect.
Widows would pay half that much to discover their little
doggies asleep under the porch. Then, of course, there
were ordinary people, brokers and teachers, lovers and
clerks, who would pay fifty dollars an hour for Fay to
read the Tarot cards, or their palms, or the looks on
their faces and tell them where <u>they</u> were.

It was a good life, and a good enough living to
raise a daughter. A daughter who wouldn't have to tell
fortunes for a living. A daughter who would have a
better life. A girl named Lizzie, who was nineteen now,
lithe and lush-haired.

Lizzie had asked about it one night, how it worked.

"All I do," Fay had said, "is tell people who they
are."

"Don't they know that?" Lizzie asked, getting ready to go out.

"They like to get a second opinion," Fay said.

Lizzie bent over to brush her hair. "But what about fate?" she asked, upside down.

"Fate is just. . . fate is what happens to people like you," Fay answered, amazed that the child could bend in those jeans.

"Like me?" Lizzie asked, from under her hair.

"No, hon," Fay smiled. "Like them."

Lizzie straightened up. "Don't I have any fate?" she asked.

"You're a teenager," Fay said. "What happens to teenagers is they grow up."

Lizzie nodded. That suited her fine. She threw the brush on the bed, left for the dance, and never asked about it again.

But the work would always be something of a mystery to Fay. People were rarely surprised by what she told them. In fact, the less surprised they were, the more impressed they were by her genius.

But, Fay would say, it doesn't take a genius to know what's going to happen. The same things happen to everybody.

Our children grow up and leave us, and our friends die. Our families hurt us, then help us, then hurt us again. We find our work, we lose our selves, and we spend what little time we have wondering where it went.

It takes a genius, Fay would say, to live in spite of what we know, to be, despite our friends and families and our own best efforts, alone.

Most days though, Fay would counsel, it will be all right to be alone.

This story is about one of those other days, when it wasn't all right at all. The day the Devil came and took Fay's daughter away.

* * *

There are seventy-eight cards in a tarot deck.
Four suits of fourteen cards each, Swords, Cups, Coins
and Wands, and twenty-two picture cards called the major
arcana, the big mysteries. Fay's mother told her she
could learn these picture cards by associating them with
people she knew, but it had taken nearly forty years to
meet them all.

The Juggler was a boy she loved and lost when he
kept going to school and she didn't. The Hanging Man
ran the mission at the corner, the Pope ran numbers for
the mob. Naturally, she'd married the Fool, Lizzie's
father, and though Fay didn't know where he was today,
she was sure he was <u>still</u> a fool, God bless him.

Justice was Arnie Campbell, just about the best
detective on the force and Fay's lover now for years.

But she'd never met the Devil. Oh sure, she knew
mean people, liars, schemers and cheats. But it takes
more than mean to be a Devil. The Tarot's Devil is a
special horror. He is the leering genius of evil. He
is willful and proud, vengeful, haughty, greedy, and
cruel.

What does he care if everything goes to hell?
Suits him fine. He lives there.

The exact picture of the Devil depends on which
Tarot deck you're using, but the basic elements are
always the same. He has a hog's body, a crocodile's
head, wings, hooves, horns, and a snake coming out

of his stomach.

But he also has luscious breasts, and a stiff penis. Which is exactly how you know he's the Devil. He can do it all himself, thank you. He doesn't need anybody for anything. He is endlessly and successfully self-absorbed.

The five-cent version of the card's meaning is destruction through black magic. But, depending both on where the card appears in a reading, and the skill of the reader, it can mean evil forces are gathering. Or maybe you're just believing anything anybody tells you these days, and, honey, they're all lying.

A generous reader, trying to make you feel better, might caution you about being seduced, or tell you not to make any decisions right now. Not Fay. She'd find out who it was who wanted your soul, and ask if you wanted to sell it. Then at least, she could make sure you got a decent price.

The card has, however, another meaning. Yes, the Devil can come after _you_, but you can also go to the Devil. In the classic portrait, he is pictured with two slaves, lesser beings, humans maybe, although they look like goats.

These slaves are the card's way of warning that if you use magical powers for selfish ends, you will wind up enslaved by those powers, chained securely to some whipping post in the underworld.

Magical powers like spells and chants? No.
Magical powers like somebody trusts you and you betray
that trust, or somebody tells you something in good
faith and you use it against them, or somebody loves you
and you lock them up and refuse to let them go when the
time comes.

The Tarot is very clear on this. Not for spells
and chants are you damned, but for ordinary abuse of
extraordinary things.

* * *

Fay had been about to close when they came. At one
o'clock in the morning, anybody else would have seen
three college boys in tuxedos, all pretending to be
drunk. But Fay recognized The Devil right away. He was
the one in the middle. Glossy black hair, a smooth tanned
face, and a carefully witheld smile. He was easily the
best looking man she'd ever seen outside the movies.

The boys were having a great time. They'd probably
told themselves they were doing the town. What they
really wanted to do was get laid, but in the meantime,
they'd get their fortunes told. Maybe the fortune
teller would know whether they got laid or not.

The Devil leaned against the window while his
friend Phil, brave with brown hair and glasses, sat
down at the table.

She handed him the cards to shuffle. "What do you
want to know, Phil?"

The cards were too big for him to shuffle
comfortably. But then, he wasn't going to be real
comfortable here anyway.

"I don't know," he sat up straighter. "You tell
me," and laughed.

"Cut the cards in three piles to your left," she
said.

He could do that.

"What's the matter with your neck?" she asked.

"Nothing!" he said, grabbing the sore place.

"It's all right," she said, wishing he would relax.
"It'll go away in another day or two. Why don't you try
sleeping on a different pillow?"

"It never bothered me before," he said, massaging
his neck now, and wondering what else she knew about
him.

She collected the three piles and dealt seven cards
off the top in an arrangement known as the Magic 7
Spread.

"Maybe if you didn't go to bed drunk," she said,
"you could find a more comfortable position before you
passed out."

"Good idea," he mumbled.

The Devil was standing by the record cabinet now.
"Who's this?" he asked, pointing to a picture of Lizzie
at the piano in a blue satin dress and straight brown
hair, five years old.

"One of the kids in the neighborhood," Fay said and
looked down at the cards.

But he'd found the other pictures, so he knew Fay
was lying. There was Lizzie on the first day of junior
high, Lizzie on the debate team, Lizzie on the black
stallion at the riding stable, Lizzie going to the prom,
Lizzie at graduation, and Lizzie on the beach.

Lizzie on the beach was the one, of course. Fay knew
what he was thinking. Marry me, be my wife. Big house.
Lots of servants. Take you away from all this. Show

you the world.

He picked up the picture of the little girl at the
piano. His laugh was haughty and mocking. "Who made
the dress? You?"

Of course she'd made the dress, but what damn
business was it of his? It fit, didn't it? The seams
were flat and smooth, weren't they? Nobody else at that
recital even had a long dress.

Lizzie hadn't wanted to wear it. Cried about
wearing it. Fay had told her the reason nobody else had
a long dress, was their mothers didn't care how they
looked.

"No, Mother," Lizzie had said, "their mothers all
know what you're supposed to wear. Just regular
clothes, Mother."

Well how was Fay supposed to know that? She
thought Lizzie should look nice, that's all. The lessons
had cost a lot of money, and the trips to the lessons
had taken a lot of time. Lizzie was good on the piano
and Fay was proud.

O.K. So the dress was Fay's celebration. The
dress was a dress she, Fay, would want to wear if she
could play the piano. What of it? It was a nice dress.
And no, Lizzie didn't play very well that day, but it
wasn't the damn dress, it was just too hot in there.

"I can't concentrate with you standing there," Fay
said to the Devil. "Do you mind sitting down?"

"Yeah," Phil said, turning to his friend, "I've got
my life on the table here."

"Where would you like me to go?" the Devil asked.

Fay didn't know what she could use on him that
would work, that would drive him away, but there had to
be something. Why wasn't her mother still alive? She
would know exactly what to do.

Phil was getting anxious. "What do you see?" he
asked, tapping the table.

Fay was grateful for the interruption. She laughed
and looked at the cards. "Not much," she said.

Phil didn't like that. "Not much future?"

Fay looked up at his face, but it was there too.
"Sorry," she smiled.

But Phil wasn't going to settle for that. He knew
he had a future. If worse came to worse, he could buy
one.

"You're lying," he said. " Tell me what you see."

"O.K.," she sighed. "You'll do all right in
school, not great, but good enough to get out, then
you'll go home and work for your Dad. You won't like it
much, but it pays well."

She pointed to the Queen of Wands. "Then you'll
marry Joanie and have two boys. They won't look a thing
alike, but that's because," she paused, "one of them
won't be yours."

Phil played dumb. "Who's Joanie?" he asked.

Fay looked up at him. "She's tall, athletic-looking, nice teeth, bad feet." She paused. "Right?"

He tried to laugh again. "You're just making this up," he said.

"No," Fay said, "I'm just making a living."

Phil couldn't stand it any longer. "O.K.," he said, "so I already know Joanie. Who's the guy she has the thing with?"

His friends laughed.

"Phil, that's years and years from now," Fay cautioned.

"I want to know," he said.

Fay picked up the Valet of Cups. "Joanie's a runner, right?" Fay asked.

Phil nodded. "Cross-country," he said.

Fay was sorry to have to tell him. "She joins a running club. It's the man she gets her shoes from."

He was a lot sorrier than she was. "Like a coach, maybe?"

Fay picked up the deck again. "Maybe," she said. "I really don't know. What's the matter with her feet?"

"They're flat," Phil said, his anger rising. "I'll call her as soon as I get back to the dorm."

"And say what?" Fay asked.

"And break up with her!"

"Don't do that!" she said, and she dealt three more cards for a little more information.

He twisted in the chair. "Why shouldn't I call

her?" he asked. "You want me to waste the next 40
years of my life?"

She winked at him. "It's not a total waste,
hon."

Phil bounced back fast. "You mean something good
happens to me?"

Fay smiled at the new cards on the table. "Well,
of course it does. One of your boys wins a spelling bee
in the 5th grade."

Phil's mouth dropped open. "That's the good news?"

Fay picked up the cards and put them back in the
deck. "No," she explained. "The good news is you work
during the day. You don't have to go."

Phil stood up, buttoned his coat, grinned, and
looked around the room. What a lark, huh? He took a
deep breath. He couldn't believe how sober he was all
of a sudden.

The Devil slapped Phil on the back, walked over to
the window, pulled back the curtains, then turned to
face Fay.

"Do you know what's going to happen to you?" he
asked.

Fay stood up. There was no point in kidding
herself about it. "I get robbed," she said.

His black eyes glistened. "When?" he asked,
letting the curtains fall from his hand.

"Later on tonight," she said.

Phil was beginning to recover from his future now.

He didn't like the sound of this robbery business.

"What you sitting around for?" he said. "Get out of here! Lock the place up tight, take all your money and go."

Fay shook her head. "So they can catch me with all my money in my purse? So they take my keys too, and my credit cards, and my picture of my mother?"

"So they don't hurt you," Phil said.

"No," Fay said. "I've been fooling with the future for a long time. It doesn't help to run from it."

Phil didn't understand.

"You run right into it, that's what you do," Fay said.

"So you just have to sit here and wait for it?" he asked.

"That's how the future works," she said easily. She liked this boy.

"I don't know," he said slowly, putting his hands in his pockets.

"You haven't been there," she finished.

"That's what I was going to say," he laughed.

She laughed with him. "No kidding."

* * *

Fay wanted them to leave now. Lizzie was due home
any time. Actually, she was due home some time ago, but
you didn't have to read the tea leaves to know your
child would come home later than she said.

Actually, reading the tea leaves was the only thing
Fay had never tried, though she knew if that's all she
had to go on, she could probably come up with something.
She wouldn't charge you for it, though.

The idea of charging for any of this was
uncomfortable for her. It wasn't really a skill, not
something she learned, or worked hard to get good at.
She'd just always had it. By the time she was in the
fourth grade, none of her girlfriends would play cards
with her. It wasn't fair, they said. Fay always knew
who had the Old Maid.

By the time she was in high school, she had learned
that not everybody wanted to know their boyfriend was
standing them up, or they were going to choke on their
driver's test. Everybody did want to take her to the
local trotting track, but she almost never had a date
for the movies. Even if the people were made up, Fay
knew what would happen to them.

So, because she wanted to make friends, and wanted
to keep them, she dismissed it, this talent of hers,
until one other August night, hot like this one, and
about this time of night too. Lizzie was about a year

old then.

They'd buried Fay's father that afternoon. Everybody
had gone to the country for the funeral. Fay's two
sisters, their husbands, their babies, and Fay's
husband, Lizzie's father, Ed.

The service, late that afternoon, had been fine.
The preacher gave the details of her father's life,
raved about how he had served his country in World War
I, and explained that he'd met his bride in someplace
called "the old country." Then he said how kind he was
to his animals, how proud he was of his moustache, and
how sick he had been for so long.

Fay looked at her sisters, both of them wearing
hats, and suddenly knew what was going to happen.

They would all go home to dinner. But after the
dinner, all the aunts and sisters would leave. Then
Ed would tell Fay it was time for them to go too.

Fay would say, "We can't go. I can't leave Mother
by herself."

Ed would say, "Well, she can't live with us, if
that's what you mean."

They'd argue about it until two o'clock, but
neither of them would give in. Ed would leave, go back
to their apartment in the city, and Fay would never see
him again.

Fay and Lizzie would stay with her mother, pack up
the house and sell it. Then the three of them would

move back to the city together, where her mother would tat and crochet for four more years until she died of pneumonia which would set in after she broke her hip falling on the sidewalk. Fay wouldn't marry again, and her mother would always be a lot more mad at the others for leaving, than she ever would be grateful to Fay for taking her in.

At the time, as Fay was sitting there in the church seeing all this, she simply couldn't believe it would happen. It was too crazy, too contrived, too detailed to be true. So she put it out of her mind, looked over and smiled at Ed, then squeezed Lizzie's hand.

But four years later, when her mother died, and everything had worked out exactly as she had seen it that day, Fay rented the little apartment down the street from the police station, and hung up the sign that said FORTUNE TELLER.

                          * * *

     Fay was worried about Lizzie now. Not that the girl
had ever given her any reason to worry, but then, she
wasn't home, so there wasn't any reason not to worry
either.

     Phil had asked if he could use the bathroom, the
Devil was looking at the show clock in her afternoon
paper, and the third boy was scratching his palm.

     "It's almost two o'clock," she said, when Phil
came back into the room. "It's time for you to go."

     But they didn't know where they were going next, so
Phil just walked over and joined the Devil who was now
trying to find a nightclub that had a late late show.

     Rudy, the third boy, sat down at her table.

     "No, no," she said, "no more. I'm closed."

     "I used to play the flute," he said quietly.

     "You still do," she said, turning around to check
on Phil and the Devil.

     He looked up at her. "I don't like it," he said.

     "I know that," she said. "Please," she said,
grasping his shoulder lightly, "I'm tired, hon."

     "Should I quit?" he asked, turning his palms up for
her to see.

     This boy had a problem all right. A big one.
Wearily, she sat down across from him and reached for
his left hand.

Fay actually preferred reading hands instead of
cards, but the good paper for the prints you could only
buy in China. Why nobody imported it, she didn't know.
But she did know she wasn't in China often enough to
keep herself supplied with the stuff.

"You play well," she said, feeling for the mounts
and the overall strength of the hand. "How can you be
so good at it and not like it?"

Rudy didn't answer.

She looked up at him. "You need to call home," she
said.

He was alarmed. "What happened?"

"How long has it been?"

"I don't know. A month, maybe."

She found his eyes. "Do they send you money?"

He was really worried now. "Yeah, they do. But I
got it yesterday."

"Good," she said, and smiled. "Call them up and
thank them."

But he didn't want a lecture on family courtesy, he
wanted the answer. "I want to quit," he said.

"Your father wouldn't like that," she said,
picking up his other hand.

"He wants us to go on tour."

"And you can't figure what's in it for you, is that
right?"

The boy nodded. "Right."

Fay was studying the hand for real now. "Look

here," she said, "see this space between these two
lines? See how small it is in your right hand?"

She looked up at him, just to see if he had his
eyes open, which he did. She was genuinely puzzled.
"You had the makings of a real ham, but you're not. How
come?"

His hand started to shake. "I don't know."

"What did he do to you?"

"Who?"

"Your Dad," she said matter-of-factly.

And then she saw it.

And he saw she saw it, and tried to pull his hand
away, but Fay held on.

"I'm so sorry, hon," she said, much more softly.
"What happened to him? Something terrible happened to
him."

"It was an accident," the boy said.

"But you were driving?" she asked.

"Yeah," he whispered.

"But he's not dead, Rudy," she said. "I can see
he's not dead. What's so bad if he's not. ."

"He's in a wheelchair," the boy said. "And he has a
bag, you know, a colostomy thing. But he plays every
day. He's still good, you know, still feels it and all,
but. . " Rudy couldn't finish.

"I see," she said. "You don't want to be the other
half of his freak show."

It hurt him to hear it, but she was right. "Yeah,"
he swallowed.

Fay rubbed the top of his hand, patted it,
actually. "He's good, isn't he, your Dad."

The boy smiled as his eyes watered. "He's great."

She turned his hand over, this time knowing exactly
what to say. "How many months is the tour?"

He was relieved to answer a question with a number.
"Six," he said.

She traced the life line to its base and showed
him. "See here? You have to go. I see. . . trouble
ahead if you don't." Then she squeezed his hand and
placed it back on the table. "What's six months, huh?
Not very long, really."

He spread his fingers wide and stretched his hand.
"I guess not," he said. And then he made a fist and
stared at it. "Hell, the army could take more than that
and they wouldn't even ask."

Fay stood up. Where was Lizzie, anyway? She wanted
these boys to leave before the girl got home, but she
did want her home.

"So!" Rudy turned to his friends and clapped his
hands. "What's up?"

Phil showed him their choices in the paper, while the
Devil took one more look out the window. Fay wasn't the
only one who wondered where Lizzie was.

Fay stood perfectly still and tried to send a
message to her daughter. "Stop at the police station,"

she said to herself. "Go see Arnie." She didn't really expect it to work, but she had to try something.

When Lizzie was little, Fay had worried that someone might just walk in the door one day and scare her, or hurt her, or take her away. So she rigged a sort of alarm system on the door. She sewed hundreds of tiny bells on red felt strips, then hung them on either side of the door. When it opened, there was no missing it. This was not the wind. This was somebody there. Not a frightening sound, you understand. More like, well, hundreds of little bells ringing.

"And when you hear these funny bells start to ring," she told Lizzie, "you run like hell and lock yourself in the bathroom." Fay didn't know if other mothers taught their daughters to lock themselves in the bathroom, but it made the little girl feel better, so who cared.

Just then, as the Devil was folding up the paper, and Phil was counting how much money he had left in his wallet, as Fay was watching every move the Devil made, and Rudy was wondering if there were a Burger King on this street, the doorknob turned, and hundreds of little bells started to ring. Lizzie was home.

* * *

Fay rushed to the door. She knew what she had to
do. Catch Lizzie before she walked in. Send her up the
street to get Arnie. Arnie had to get a look at this
Devil so he'd know who they were chasing when Lizzie
left with him.

"Hi," Lizzie chirped.

"I'm not through yet, hon," Fay said quickly,
pushing the girl back out on the sidewalk. "Can you go
get Sergeant Campbell for me?"

Fay blocked the Devil's view with her body.

"Who's in there?" Lizzie asked.

The Devil moved to the window, and pulled back the
curtains.

"I tried to call Arnie," Fay said through the crack
in the door, "but they keep putting me on hold."

Lizzie craned her neck to see who pulled back the
curtains. He didn't look so dangerous. He looked
pretty good, in fact.

"What's going on?" Lizzie asked.

"I'm all right," Fay said. "Just go, huh?"

"Sure," Lizzie said, shrugging her shoulders. "No
problem." She liked Arnie. Maybe it was some kind of
party for him.

"Thanks," Fay said, closed the door, then watched
the girl as she walked up the street.

Fay didn't like this solution, but it was her only
choice. If she forced the boys to leave, Paul, the

Devil's name was Paul, would just forget his scarf and
come back for it sometime later when Lizzie was there
alone. Then they'd disappear together and Fay would
never find them. No. She had to watch this meeting and
find out where Paul was taking her. Then, of course,
she had to find a way of stopping it.

2:00 A.M.

                            * * *

     When Lizzie got to the police station on the
corner, she found Arnie on the phone to his bookie. She
was glad to see him, a rough-edged, handsome man
slouched over his battered desk, the racing form spread
out in front of him. He looked a little used this time
of night, but not used up, not by a long shot. Arnie
Campbell could be tired, hungry, mad, beat up, and
broke, and still get the job done, whatever it was.

     "What's the spread on the Cubs?" Arnie asked the
bookie.

     Lizzie took off her Yankee baseball cap and shook
out her mass of black hair.

     He covered the mouthpiece with his hand. "Great
hair," he smiled. "Where's your Mom?"

     "At home," she whispered, pointing down the street.

     She kicked off her old sneakers, pulled off the
baggy black jumpsuit, and stuffed it into her dance bag.

     "Nice," he mouthed, as the silky black dress she
was wearing underneath slipped over her hips and down
her long, slim legs.

     "Thanks," Lizzie said, then retrieved her stiletto
black heels from the bag and stepped into them. Owing
to years of dance class, she could change from a black
cloud to queen of the night in less than thirty seconds.
Or go the other way if she was coming home late and

didn't want any trouble on the street.

"O.K.," Arnie said into the phone, "I'll take the Orioles and 4, the Mets and 8, and 500 on Thunderhead to place in the fifth."

Then he hung up the phone, shoved the racing form and reading glasses into his desk drawer, stood up, and reached for his cigarettes.

"What's up?" he asked, sensing, somehow, that it wasn't a murder or anything serious.

"I don't know," Lizzie said, taking his arm. "Mom wouldn't let me in. She told me to come get you."

Suddenly, his whole manner changed. Apparently, anything having to do with Fay was serious. "Was somebody with her?" he asked.

"All I saw were three guys in tuxes," she said.

He held the door open. "So what is it?" he asked, trying not to frighten the girl. "You think they stole the tuxes?"

"Maybe they did," she laughed.

"Where'd you say you went?" he said, as they started down the street.

"I didn't," she said.

"But you had a good time, right?"

"It was O.K.," she said.

Actually, it had been more than O.K., but she knew better than to tell him about it. Arnie Campbell didn't know Mozart from Moby Dick, and didn't want to either.

Lizzie wondered if her Mom was still screwing

Arnie. She didn't mind, either way, but she would like
to know. She probably was. Lizzie figured if you once
loved this man, nothing on earth could make you stop.

Arnie took her hand, and gave it a gentle squeeze
and they walked the rest of the way without talking.

* * *

Before Lizzie and Arnie got back, the Devil had
picked up, looked at, and laughed at every doodad, knick
knack and whatnot in the room, including her jar of
clear glass marbles.

"Crystal balls," Fay explained, then watched
carefully to see that he didn't steal one.

He thought the lampshade made of post cards was
maybe the ugliest thing he'd ever seen. He asked if
she'd been to all those places.

She said the lampshade was there when she moved in.

He played with the fringed black shawl on the table
and wondered what happened to the fringe.

"It's just worn off over the years," she said.
"People. . you know, sit there and braid it while I
shuffle the cards," she paused, "like you're doing."

Then, he asked about the bears. One hundred onyx
bears, sitting on chessboards, also onyx, which had been
given to her by a client who had paid her in onyx.

The client had told her he had a garage full of old
schooldesks, a fabulous collection of geodes, and a safe
full of green stamps if she'd rather have those, but she
wouldn't. Lizzie liked the bears.

"What I'd like to have," Fay had told the man, "is
some of the cash you buy this stuff with."

"But I never have any cash," he said.

But she knew he had money coming. He had the

longest, deepest fate line she'd ever seen. She could wait.

The Devil asked where the bears came from, but Fay didn't want to tell him. He said they were funny. She said yes, they were.

And then Arnie opened the door, and walked in flashing his badge.

The boys stood up, scared to death. This was a man who got what he wanted.

"Fay?" Arnie said, "It's a little late for you to be open, isn't it?"

"I've been telling them to go," she said, looking at the boys. "But they haven't been hearing me."

"Let's go, folks," Arnie said, "fun's over," and opened the door for them.

Lizzie slipped in behind him as quietly as she could.

Phil spoke up in their defense. "She said she was going to be robbed," he said, pointing to Fay.

Lizzie couldn't help laughing. "And you thought you could protect her?"

"No," the Devil said to her.   "We were waiting for you."

Lizzie stopped laughing. They weren't waiting for her. He was waiting for her.

"How did you know I'd show up?" she flirted.

"We prayed," he said, in his softest smirk.

Fay was right. It was all over. All they'd had to

do, these two, was see each other.

Lizzie backed away and started rearranging her bears on the chessboards. She had nothing more to say to anybody but him. The Devil took Phil's arm and walked toward the door. He had to get rid of these kids and get back here.

"It was great talking to you," Phil said over his shoulder to Fay.

"Yeah," Rudy said. "Thanks."

"If I were you," Arnie said, catching the Devil's sleeve as he walked through the door, "I'd take those cufflinks out of my shirt and put them in my pocket."

The boys stepped out onto the sidewalk, and Arnie closed the door behind them.

But as soon as he saw Fay's face, he knew the boys weren't the problem.

"What was that all about?" he asked.

"I'll tell you later," she said, and then turned to Lizzie.

"Where have you been?" Fay demanded.

Lizzie was still fooling with the bears. "You tell me," she said, and laughed like it was a joke.

Fay looked as if she'd been slapped.

But Lizzie was right, of course. Fay did know where she had been.

"Come on, Lizzie," Arnie said, trying to stop this squabble before it got started. "Answer your Mother, huh?"

Lizzie turned around. She hated it when Arnie corrected her, but he was usually right about it. "I went to hear Ashkenazy at the Philharmonic. Want to see the stubs?"

"Til two o'clock in the morning?" Fay asked.

"I met some friends," Lizzie said.

"What friends?" Fay pushed.

"Mother," Lizzie pleaded. "You don't know them, so what difference does it make?"

Arnie wanted out. Fay could be such a witch. So the kid went to a concert. Isn't that why Fay paid for all those music lessons all those years, so the girl would go to concerts? Lizzie was ready to leave home. Why didn't Fay, who knew everything else, know that?

"You girls don't need me for this," he said. "I'm going back to work."

Fay grabbed his arm. "Please don't go," she said.

"Have to," he grinned, leaning down to kiss the top of her head. "I need the money."

"Isn't there somebody else down there?" she asked.

"Oh sure," he said, "but he's answering the phone."

"So can't he call you if he needs you?"

"Sorry, love," he said. "I have to listen to the radio." He waved to Lizzie. "Night, angel," he said.

Lizzie blew him a kiss and Fay walked outside with him.

"I'm sorry," Fay said.

"It's O.K.," he said. "Just let her alone. She'll
be all right." He put his arm around her. "She's a
good kid."

But it would take more than a hug to comfort Fay.
"She's going to leave me, Arnie."

"Honey," he said, as gently as he could, "she's got
to. She's all grown up."

Fay looked away.

"You did a great job. You should be real proud.
She's going to do great things out there. Make you even
prouder."

"No, Arnie," Fay said. "She's going to leave me
for that boy in the black hair, Paul. She's not going
to do anything except what he tells her to do."

"Fay," he reached into his pocket for a cigarette,
"she just met the boy!"

"You don't believe me."

"Sure I believe you," he said, staring at the
building across the street. "I believe everything you
say. But she could do a whole lot worse, Fay. He's got
some money anyway. Let her go."

"Arnie, I'll never see her again!"

"You'll see her."

"She'll be ashamed of me. She'll never come back."

"She'll be back."

"He's the Devil."

That did it. "Good-night, Fay," he crooned, and

walked away. He wasn't mad, but he walked as though he might be.

He shouldn't have stayed this long. He really did have to listen to the radio. He hadn't wanted to tell Fay yet, but there was something real strange going on out at the Fairgrounds. Something that could involve her, before it was over.

* * *

When Arnie first made detective, they moved him downtown, but he didn't like it there. The coffee was made by somebody who thought coffee was bad for you, and the water cooler burped. Arnie liked his water out of the faucet, so he came back to this neighborhood and stayed. The deli was cheap, the shoe repair was fast, and the firehouse was a good place to pick up extra cash playing cards. Then, too, Fay Morgan lived here.

The street was dirty, but it was hard to keep a busy street clean. Alfred slept on the sidewalk outside the mission, and there was a girlie show next door. Alfred had a bed inside the mission any time he wanted one, but he slept outside because if he couldn't pay to see the girls in the show, at least he could see their legs when they came to work.

When he worked days, Arnie would go down to Fay's for lunch. She was never busy at lunchtime. At lunchtime, people were still trying to figure out the future for themselves. Only after work did they give up, and see a professional.

The first summer that Lizzie went to ballet camp, Arnie took Fay fishing. He had a little cabin, and a little boat, and a big sweater for her to wear at night. He liked fishing well enough, but that's not why he went there. He kept this cabin, year after year, because he liked to catch rainwater in a tin bucket, take the bucket to the porch, and shave outside.

"Always get a better shave out here," he said.
"Good water. Good light. Fresh soap. Makes a big
difference."

She nodded.

He liked her to watch. He had thought about
marrying her. But he knew he'd never be as important to
her as Lizzie was. That was the way it should be, but
it wasn't how he wanted to be married. So he never
asked. And she never said anything about it.

Their first job together was almost fifteen years
ago now. Arnie's brother owned the butcher shop next
door to Fay. Middle of the day one day, somebody came
in and shot him. Fay would've seen the whole thing, but
she'd taken Lizzie to the pediatrician.

Father June, from the mission, had gone down to the
butcher shop to borrow some bratwurst for lunch. He saw
the blood, found the body, then ran back to the station
house and grabbed Arnie out of his chair.

The killer didn't take any money, didn't even mess
the place up. It was weird. Arnie couldn't tell
whether the blood on his brother's apron was from the
bullet wound or from the steaks and chops he'd been
cutting up when he was killed. The crime unit would
know later it was lamb's blood, but Arnie wouldn't ask
them.

Arnie went in the back room and threw up. He
would've checked this room eventually, of course, but as

he raised his head from the sink, and wiped his mouth on
a spare apron, he saw the bloody hand print on the back
door.

Apparently, the killer had slipped on a wet spot on
the floor, and grabbed hold of the meat-bloodied cutting
table to keep from falling. When he pushed open the
back door to escape, he made one perfect blood-red print
of his left hand.

The department ran a check on it, but came up with
nothing.

Arnie hadn't met Fay before, but he'd seen the
palm-reading sign in her window. It was worth a try, he
figured. So he walked down to her parlor, knocked, then
opened her door. Fay was reading. Lizzie was in her
playpen.

"Are you Fay?" he asked.

"Yes," she said, standing up and smoothing out her
dress.

"I'm Arnie," he said.

He still wore a uniform then, so he didn't have to
say he was a cop.

"I'm Jack's brother." He motioned toward the
butcher shop. "Next door?"

Fay already knew who he was. She had seen the
crowd when she came home, and another detective had
already been in to see her.

"I'm so sorry," she said. "I've just been here a
couple of weeks, but he seemed so nice."

"He was O.K." Arnie said. "He was my brother."

"I'm sorry," she said. "Is there anything I can do?"

He was a little nervous. "I saw your sign," he said, hoping she would read his mind.

"Yes?" she said, having not a clue.

"I'm sorry," he said, turning around. "This was a bad idea."

"No, no," she said, standing up. "You saw the sign and you thought. . ."

"Well, look," he said, not knowing how to say it, "this sunuvabitch who killed my brother left a palm print on the back door."

"Was it his left hand?" she asked.

Now he was really nervous. "How did you know that?"

"Just a guess," she said, trying to make it seem like one. "He probably held his gun in his right hand, that's all."

He wished he hadn't come here, but he couldn't leave now without insulting her. "O.K.," he said. "Come on." He started for the door. "Bring your stuff."

"I don't need any 'stuff,'" she said, "but I can't leave Lizzie.

Arnie stopped cold. He was a detective. His brother was dead. What was he supposed to do with a three year old?

"Bring her with us," he said. And he walked over
to the playpen and picked Lizzie up, picked her way up,
Arnie was a big man even then, and followed Fay out onto
the street.

Next door, they walked through the police barricade
and into the empty shop. He stopped in front of the
meat cases, where steaks and chops were turning gray.

"Somebody ought to eat this stuff before it
spoils," he said.

"Why don't you call the mission," she said.

"Good idea," he said, walking to the phone. "I'll
call them right now."

He shifted Lizzie slightly in his arms. "Go on
back," he said, pointing toward the back room. Arnie
didn't want to go back in there just yet. So he called
Headquarters and told them to call the mission.

When he came in, she was staring at the palm print.

"Well?" he asked. Lizzie asleep on his shoulder.

"It's pretty messy," she said. "You didn't see his
other hand anywhere, did you?"

He didn't think that was funny. But on some other
day he might.

"O.K.," he said, turning around. "Thanks anyway."

"No," she said, motioning for him to come look.
"He was real short. Does that help?"

"Well he had to be short," Arnie grumped. "Look
where the hand is on the door." He turned back toward

the front room.

"And lazy," she said.

Arnie stopped. "Lazy?"

"And young," she said. "A kid, maybe. He's either
not lived very long, or not lived very much. He's been
sick though, so that could account for it."

Arnie took a step toward her. "He's a kid?"

"It's the fingers," she said. "See how short they
are?"

He came close enough to see for himself now. "That
third finger's not so short."

"Well, it's longer than the rest of them, but
that's because he's a gambler."

"Come on," he said. "You can tell from his hand
he's a gambler?"

"I'll show you," she said. "Put your hand up
beside it."

He shifted Lizzie to his other arm and put his left
hand up beside the killer's print. She had to laugh.
Arnie had that same long third finger.

"You're a bit of a gambler yourself, aren't you?"

"Well," he said, "I'm not getting through life on
my looks."

"You could," she said, turning back to the hand.

He didn't want to hear that. He cleared his
throat. "So we're looking for a sick, kid, gambler."

"Yes," she said. "Know any?"

He didn't answer.

"How old was your brother?" she asked, just to keep him talking.

"Older than me. 40, I think."

"Did he have any children?"

"Just one," he said. "Bobbie."

"I'm sorry," she said. "This must be awful for him. How is Bobbie doing?" she asked.

Arnie knew he shouldn't tell her, but for some reason, he wanted to. "Bobbie doesn't know it yet," he said. "We can't find him. But he's not home much anyway."

"Neither was this one," she said, and pointed to the hand. "See how straight that life line is? This kid doesn't know where home is. A real drifter."

Arnie nodded.

She went on, almost as though she could see the boy. "He's real emotional, though. He has terrible crying jags, then fits of hysterical laughing. But he gets all out of breath and you think he's going to die right there in front of you. Like. . " she stopped, and looked again. "No, not _like_ anything. Asthma. The boy has asthma."

"Are you sure?" Arnie asked. "Asthma?"

"I'm sure," she said. "And I could probably tell you when he got it, but that would be showing off."

She expected Arnie to laugh, but he didn't.

"What else?" he asked.

She bent down for a closer look. "He's careless.
He drops things." She paused. "But this is the problem
right here."

She pointed it out to him, but he wasn't looking.
"See how little his little finger is?"

Arnie didn't answer.

"He thinks nobody loves him anyway, so what's he
got to lose? My mother used to say you could stretch
fingers like this, just by pulling on them whenever you
thought about it. Even if it was you that loved you,
that would be better than nobody, she'd say. The
future's not over yet, right?"

When Fay stood up and turned around, Arnie was
staring out toward the front room and stroking Lizzie's
hair. She didn't know when he had stopped listening.
He was lost in some other day. Any other day.

"I guess we should go," she said.

"I'm ready," he said blankly.

Arnie walked her back to her house and took Lizzie
into her bedroom to finish her nap.

"Can I make you some coffee?" Fay asked, when he
returned.

"No thanks," he said.

But he didn't seem to be in a hurry to leave.

"She's a sweet kid," he said, motioning toward the
room where he'd left Lizzie.

"She better be," Fay said. "She's all I have."

"Do you have plans for dinner?" he asked, sitting down, without even realizing that he had.

Fay didn't think he'd make it to dinner. If he closed his eyes for even a moment, he'd be asleep in that chair. But far from being nervous about a stranger in the room, she felt quite safe, suddenly. She even liked the apartment better with him in it.

"Why don't you go in and lie down," she said, nodding toward her bedroom. "I'll wake you when it's time for dinner."

He stood up. He knew he should leave, but his feet just wouldn't move.

"It's all right," she said quietly. "I won't bother you."

He rubbed the brim of his hat between his fingers. "How do you know I won't. . ."

"Won't what?" she asked.

"Won't sleep through dinner," he said, looking down at her.

"I'll wake you," she smiled.

He nodded, turned and walked into the bedroom. Fay followed him at a respectful distance and closed the door.

Inside the bedroom, Arnie sat down on the bed and took off his shoes. Jesus God.

He took off his pants and coat and hung them over the chair. Bobbie had killed his dad.

He folded up his holster and put it on the seat of

the chair. He couldn't believe it, but he wasn't
surprised. Maybe he'd even seen it coming, but nobody
thinks things like that will really happen. Not even
policemen. Not in their own families, anyway.

He eased back onto the bed. But what could he do
about it now? Nothing. Nothing, that is, except catch
the kid, and put him in jail for the rest of his life.

He closed his eyes. Arnie had never done this,
collapsed like this. He didn't know who she was out
there, or where he was in here, or when he'd ever wake
up, and he didn't care to know any of those things. He
only wanted to sleep.

He slept straight through Lizzie's nap and Lizzie's
dinner and after Lizzie was back asleep again, this time
for the night, Fay opened the door, just to check on
him.

She knew too, that it was his brother's own son
who had killed him. She didn't know how she knew, but
she was glad she hadn't said anything. That was his to
say. He was the detective.

Now, standing there watching him sleep, she
remembered seeing the sign on the door of the butcher
shop. The funeral was tomorrow. Suddenly, she felt
such love for him, this man in her bed. What was his
name? Arnie?

The room was dark, except for the night light she
left on for Lizzie. She closed the door quietly behind

her, tiptoed over to the bed, and leaned down to wake

him, though by now, he was fully awake and watching the

whole thing.

"Arnie," she whispered, "do you want some dinner?"

She leaned over and kissed him on the forehead like an

old love.

He took her face in his hands and pulled her mouth

gently down to his.

It was a sweet kiss.

She sat down beside him.

"Where did you come from?" he whispered, stroking

her arm.

"Oh, you know," she smiled, patting his chest.

"The front room."

"I guess we're not very busy tonight, are we," he

said, finding her hand and squeezing it.

"I guess we're closed," she said.

Then he reached up to kiss her neck, then her

mouth, and then together, they sank back into the bed.

There was no small talk. There was no talk of any

kind. Nobody asked for directions, nobody gave them.

There were common courtesies, yes, but no modesty to

speak of. This was simply necessary.

He took hold of her like life itself. He wanted

some answers here, some proof that it was worth it, some

proof that it was possible. That he could go on. Live.

Start over. Have something besides all this goddamn

pain all the time. See something besides how ugly

everything was. Love somebody.

She reeled from his desperation, but clung to
him. She found the rhythm of his rage and lost herself
in it. This was not a man she knew, and Fay was not a
woman he'd spent years learning to love. This was a man
fighting death itself, and a woman who was not afraid to
watch.

When it was over, he lay beside her, still without
speaking. In a few moments, the tears came from behind
his eyes, where they had been hiding, and crept down his
face, hoping to get away before anyone saw them.

When Fay heard them, she got out of the bed and
left the room, giving him all the darkness she had for
cover.

A little later, he came out of her bedroom. And
though he was fully dressed, he wasn't quite ready to
talk yet.

"I'm sorry," he said.

"For what?"

"I promised you dinner."

"I ate with Lizzie," she said.

And then he saw the cheese sandwich she had made and
left for him on the table.

He picked it up and took a bite. "Please don't say
anything," he said.

"About what?" she asked.

"About Bobbie," he said. "About Bobbie killing his

Dad," he nodded toward the butcher shop.   "I have to find him.   I don't know where he is.   But I want to be the one who finds him."

"Your bookie might know."

"Yeah," he said as he swallowed.   "He probably would."

He lifted the sandwich to his mouth for another bite, then stopped, and put it back on the plate.

"What's the matter with me?" he asked.   "What do I mean, I want to find him?   I don't want to find him! What am I going to say to him?"

He put on his hat.

She picked up the sandwich, walked him to the door, opened it, and handed the sandwich back to him.   "You'll say you're sorry," she said quietly.   "You'll just say you're sorry."

And a month later, when Arnie found Bobbie down in Valdosta, Georgia, playing the only video game in town, that is exactly what he said.

                              * * *

     Inside her bedroom, Lizzie had already changed from
the silky black number she had worn to the concert, into
a bare-backed pink sundress, in case Paul came back.

     Fay found her there and stood in the doorway. She
wondered what Lizzie was wearing under that little
sundress, but she also knew the answer. Not much.

     "You don't need a sundress," Fay said. "The sun
went down a long time ago."

     "I'm just trying it on," Lizzie lied in a cheery
voice. "How does it look?"

     "You better take a sweater," Fay said, leaning on
the doorjamb for support. "It's cool on the river."

     Lizzie was never really surprised when her mother
knew where she was going, but she liked to pretend she
was. It was a game they had played for a long time. So
long, that it was almost fun.

     "Am I going out on the river?" Lizzie asked.

     Fay nodded. "Paul is coming back for you," she
said. "He has a boat."

     "That's great," Lizzie laughed, changing into her
crepe soled flats. "A boat is great on the river."

     Fay clasped her hands in front of her. "I'm sorry
I screeched at you a while ago," she said. "I was
worried, that's all."

     "You weren't worried," Lizzie said. "You just
don't like me to go out."

"I want you to go," Fay said, "I just want you to come home when it's over."

"No," said Lizzie, "you don't want me to go at all."

Fay was quiet a minute. "The dress looks great," she said.

"Thanks," Lizzie said, putting a rubber band in her pocket in case she needed it to control her hair in the wind.

Fay took a few steps toward her, hoping to make up.

"Mother," Lizzie took her hand, "if he were going to hurt me, you'd know, right?"

"Right," Fay said.

"So he's not," Lizzie said. "So don't worry, O.K.?" She reached out and stroked her mother's hair.

Fay didn't like for Lizzie to do that. It made her feel like a pet, like a cat. She backed away and made herself talk.

"He's very smart," she said. "Very smooth. And he's going to be wild about you."

"Thanks," Lizzie said, wondering if her mother knew when Paul was coming.

"There he is right now," Fay said, feeling his presence at the front door.

Lizzie walked past her and into the hallway, but she didn't see him.

"Where?" she asked.

"He dropped his car keys," Fay explained, following Lizzie into the living room.

And then they both saw him. Standing outside the window, putting his keys back in his pocket. He was alone now, and even better looking, Lizzie thought.

"See you later," Lizzie said, kissing Fay lightly on the cheek.

"Have a nice time," Fay said, as pleasantly as she could.

Then Lizzie turned, flashed Paul a ready smile, and left.

As Fay locked the door behind them, she was proud of herself. She hadn't said one wrong thing. Well, all right, maybe she had said a wrong thing. She didn't always know what the wrong things were. But she hadn't screamed, anyway.

She went to the record cabinet for the deck of Tarot cards she used for family matters. She sat down at her table and shuffled them.

"What's going to happen to us?" she asked, cutting them three times.

"To Lizzie and me," she said, reassembling the deck and dealing seven cards off the top.

In the Magic 7, the first card indicated the past. It was the 7 of Coins. Oh boy. Coins never meant money when Fay was reading for herself, so it was some other valuable thing she was about to lose. Guess what that might be, huh?

Next card. The present. The Valet of Swords, a
young person. Boy or girl? Girl. Lizzie. Next card.
The immediate future. The 6 of Swords. She already
knew that too. Journey by water. Why was she even
doing this?

Quickly, she turned up the other cards. The fourth
card was the 3 of Coins. A sale? She was selling her
child? Come on. So maybe it's the other
interpretation, an old association can help now, but
who? Arnie, maybe. Her mother?

She turned over the fifth card.

"Jesus Christ," she whispered.

It was the 9 of Cups. The wish card. There was
only one meaning to this card. You get your wish.

Fay was very cold, suddenly. What wish? That
Lizzie not leave? No, the girl was already gone. That
the Devil died? Yes, she'd probably wished that, all
right.

"Calm down," she said, talking outloud now. "Turn
the cards."

The sixth card would show her who was against her,
or if not who, exactly, what their qualities were.

The Knight of Swords. This was too much. A
dashing young headstrong man? No kidding.

She hesitated a moment before turning over the last
card. This was the end of it, the outcome of the
situation, and there it was. The King of Coins.

"So his Dad's a banker," she said. "So I'm beat.
Lizzie goes off to count his father's money."

She looked at the spread as a whole now. Coins and
Swords. Money and Conflict.

The wish card bothered her. Could it be something
she had wished for in the past, maybe? Like for Lizzie
to have everything she never had? Sure. What was wrong
with that?

She picked up the 3 of Coins. Had she wanted her
daughter to be rich? Wanted it so that she, Fay, could
be rich? What if she did? If there was that much
money, what was wrong with sending Mom some of it?

She turned to look out the window.

What if the cards were talking about Lizzie and not
Fay? Was Lizzie about to lose something, have some dark
and secret wish come true? Lose her self, maybe, a self
she didn't know what to do with anyway? To a headstrong
young man and a banker?

Suddenly, Fay felt the same fear she'd seen on the
faces of her clients over the years. If there's bad
news, and I can't do anything about it, don't tell me.
If there's bad news, and I can do something about it,
but I blow it, so it happens anyway but now it's my
fault, don't tell me.

Fay wished Arnie would come back. But he'd come
when he was ready, she knew that.

Should she call Gail?

She started for the phone.

No. She stopped. Gail and Marvin had taken little
Beth to the fairgrounds tonight, so they'd be exhausted
by now.

But then, Fay looked at her watch, it was almost 3
A.M. Anybody in this time zone would be exhausted by
now.

She stared out the window. The building across the
street had been condemned last week. The windows were
boarded up, and people were being evicted. The sign on
the front said the wreckers were coming at the end of
the month.

The place is already a wreck, Fay thought. What's
left for them to do?

And then, just as she was wondering if anything in
the refrigerator would help, Arnie's face appeared on
the other side of the glass.

3:00 A.M.

* * *

"Let's walk," Arnie said, as she opened the door
for him.

He wasn't taking a break. She knew it. Something
was going on.

"Are you still on duty?" she asked.

"I sure am," he said. "And so are you."

She waited while he stopped to light a cigarette.
There was something he had to tell her, but he didn't
know where to start. If it was a new case, she'd have
to turn him down this time. She could hardly go looking
for some suspect while her daughter was out with the
Devil.

Arnie threw the match in the trash can, then picked up
the lid from the ground and jammed it back on the can,
as hard as he could. The garbage men were going to
have trouble with that lid in the morning. They might
have to take the whole thing, can and all, or leave it
here, trash and all.

"Looks like we've got a strange case in the works,"
he said finally.

She knew that someone was missing. "Who is it? "
she asked.

He took her hand. "It's Gail's little girl," he
said. "Gail Wilkins."

Fay stopped cold. "My Gail?"

"Your Gail," he said. "Her Beth. Come on. Keep walking."

Fay couldn't keep walking. Gail was the only friend she had.

"Arnie!" she protested. "We can't just walk around the block while Gail. . ."

"She isn't home yet," he said. "She's still down at headquarters. There isn't anything for us to do now but walk."

She turned back around to look at Gail's building, but all the lights were out.

He grasped her hand, more firmly this time, and pulled her around beside him.

"I'll tell you what I know," he said. "But it isn't much. I stationed one of our guys at the apartment in case Beth shows up there."

"Beth couldn't get home by herself, Arnie. Beth is five years old."

"That's what I told the Chief," he said. "But you know how he is."

"Just tell me what happened, hon," she said, forcing her feet to move.

He shook his head. "It's real simple," he said. "Gail and Marvin took Beth to the fair. Gail paid for the cotton candy, but when she turned around to hand it to Beth, Beth wasn't there."

"When was this?" Fay asked.

"Gail thinks it was about nine o'clock. But it was

midnight before all the other parents were standing at
the information booth."

Fay stopped. "All <u>what</u> other parents?"

He nodded. "I told you it was strange."

"How many parents are we talking about, Arnie?"

He took a long drag on his cigarette. "Twenty,
thirty, maybe. And the last count on the kids was
somewhere in the twenties. Twenty-four maybe. I
forget."

"You forget?"

"O.K.," he admitted. "I didn't listen. It's a lot
though."

Fay was frantic. "So what are you doing?" she
asked. "The police, I mean."

"Checking," Arnie said.

"Checking with whom?" she demanded. "There isn't
anybody left at the fair now except the freaks and the
farmers."

"Right," he said. "They're waking up all the
freaks and farmers, and asking if anybody saw anything."

"I think we better go over there," she said.

"I think we better just keep walking," he said.
"Did you get all patched up with Lizzie?"

"Gail's Beth is gone?" Fay asked, still not quite
able to take it all in.

"Beth is gone," Arnie said.

She shook her head and walked on. Fay knew better

than to try to <u>see</u> where Beth was. That was the movie
version of what psychics did. Real psychics needed real
information first.

And the only real information this psychic had was
about her own lost daughter.

"So did Lizzie leave with that boy or not?" Arnie
asked.

"Yes," Fay said, "she did."

"Did they say where they were going?" he asked.

"They didn't have to," she said.

Arnie knew what that meant.

Fay had seen it, all right. As clearly as if
she had been there, as plainly as if it had been
projected on a billboard in front of her. Full color
like a billboard, too, plus wraparound sound like a
film. Faster though. A flash forward.

"They're on a boat," she said. "On their way to
another boat, a big boat. The biggest boat I've ever
seen."

"A ship?" he asked.

"A yacht," she said.

Then she saw the flags on the big boat. Weather
flags maybe, but another country's flag too. Fay
didn't know which country, though. Fay didn't know much
about flags. Lizzie's dress was whipping around her
legs, her hair was blowing wildly in the wind. She was
wearing the Devil's tux jacket and eating a bagel.

Fay had to laugh. The girl had stopped for a bagel.

The Devil was smiling. The moon was out.

"Why did you come with me?" the Devil asked Lizzie.

"Oh, I don't know," Lizzie said. "I wasn't ready
to go to bed yet."

"Well," he caught her hair in his hand, "you just
let me know when you are."

Fay turned her head and they were gone.

Arnie put his arm around her shoulders. He didn't
know what to call these trances of hers, these
sightings, but he knew when she was having one. He
thought, though he wasn't really sure, that when she saw
something, something happening somewhere else, there was
a slight drop in her body temperature. Her hands became
very limp, her whole body grew still, her breathing was
very deep. The real sign, though, was that the part of
her he liked to think of as her, as Fay, was gone.

When she came back, he tried to speak very softly.
"Lizzie will be all right," he said.

"We'll see," she said.

He laughed. "I just wish I had a boat to take you
out on."

Fay was lucky to have this man, and she knew it.
"I like these walks," she said.

"I do too," he said.

She particularly liked these walks this late at
night. She liked to catch the night changing into the
morning. She could feel it turn. Clocks had nothing to

do with it. Clocks had it all wrong, in fact. So did
the calendar. The way Fay saw it, the day should begin
at 4:00 A.M. and the year should start in September.

                              * * *

     Lizzie's first day of school had been the first and
only day Fay had used the 8 mm movie camera one of her
clients had given her. She learned that day, that
however annoying it was to see the future before it
actually happened, it was even more irksome to see the
past the way it really was.

     She'd taken Lizzie to the school for registration
the week before, presented her birth certificate, and
proved she'd had her shots. Then she found Lizzie's
classroom, and introduced the girl to her teacher.

     "You're a single mother, Mrs. Morgan?" the teacher
asked, looking at Lizzie's papers.

     Fay didn't like that question. "Do the other kids
have more than one?" she asked.

     The teacher didn't like that answer. But then she
saw Fay's address, and that was really something to
worry about. Only welfare people lived on that street,
hookers, robbers and bums.

     "And what do you do?" the teacher asked.

     "I'm a fortune teller," Fay said, wondering if that
was above or below stripper in this woman's view of
things.

     "I see," the teacher said. "How interesting."

     Fay looked at the woman's signature on the
blackboard. It wasn't that the teacher lacked

imagination, just that she only imagined the worst.

"I'm not a prostitute," Fay said, "if that's what you're thinking."

The teacher coughed. Lizzie dropped Fay's hand.

"Of course not," the teacher said. "But even if you were, that wouldn't affect the quality of instruction your daughter will receive here."

Lizzie walked to the door. She was ready to go.

The teacher smiled at the little girl, promising to provide a welcome relief from the nightmare the poor thing must live in.

Then she turned back to Fay. "I just like to have as much background as I can on the children."

"Her background," Fay said, joining Lizzie at the door, "is just fine."

Fay was sure Lizzie didn't know what a prostitute was, so she didn't discuss the teacher's conversation on the way home. They didn't talk at all, really, except Fay did say how much fun it was going to be for Lizzie to find out who else was in her class.

But when the first day came, Lizzie said that Fay could walk her to the school, but she wanted to go up the driveway and in the door by herself. She said she remembered where the classroom was, and she was a big girl now.

That's when Fay thought of the camera. If she couldn't actually _have_ the experience, she could at least see it whenever she wanted.

Once they crossed the street, Fay handed Lizzie the
little sack lunch with the pimento cheese sandwich and
the two dill pickles wrapped in wax paper, and said how
nice Lizzie looked. Then Fay promised she could get
back here in two minutes if she had to. For any reason,
she said. When the warning bell rang, Lizzie said she'd
better go because she didn't want to be late and have to
sit in the back.

Fay kissed her, stood back and let her go.

As Lizzie started up the walk, she turned back to
her mother, smiling and waving. That was Fay's cue.
She put the camera up to her eye and pressed the button.

She followed Lizzie all the way to the steps, then
tried to keep sight of her as the other kids, most of
them with their mothers, all of them worried about being
late, crowded around the little girl and pushed her up
the stairs.

By the time Lizzie got to the big wooden doors, Fay
had lost her completely. She took the camera down from
her eye and found herself quite alone at the sidewalk.
The second bell rang, and the custodian closed the doors
from the inside.

Fay looked at the camera, then looked at the doors,
then hoped like hell the pictures came out, because she
sure had missed it if they didn't.

The pictures did come out. But how could Fay know
the batteries were low and the camera was shooting in

slow motion? She couldn't. And neither could the projector, which played the film back at normal speed.

So Fay's permanent record of Lizzie's first day of school was the girl running up the walk with that choppy, old-time flickers motion. Not walking. Running as fast as she could. Lizzie couldn't wait to get away from her, it looked like.

The brave smile and sweet wave Fay thought she remembered, were projected on the screen as the giddy, glad-to-be-rid-of-you gestures of a pint-sized prisoner making her first escape.

Lizzie thought the pictures were funny, and asked to see them again and again.

Fay gave the projector and the screen back to the mission, and threw the camera away.

                              * * *

     Fay and Arnie had walked almost a mile now. As
they came around the corner, back on their street again,
they saw an ambulance with its light flashing, and a
fleet of police cars massed in front of Gail and
Marvin's building.

     When Fay didn't start running toward the ambulance,
Arnie knew she must know something.

     "Well?" he asked.

     She shook her head. "They didn't find Beth," she
said.

     Arnie stopped at the curb to talk to one of the
other detectives, while Fay made her way inside to talk
to Gail.

     "It's more than Beth," Gail said, when Fay finally
found her in the little girl's bedroom. "It's like the
Pied Piper, it's like maybe thirty, forty children
missing. All of them from the fair, all of them about
Beth's age."

     "And you didn't see anybody?" Fay asked.

     "Nobody," Gail said. "She just disappeared."

     "Where's Marvin?" Fay asked.

     "Still at the fairgrounds," Gail said. "I think.
Talking to... I don't know, trying to help or something.
But there isn't anything for him to do now, is there?"
She rubbed her eyes. "I don't know why he isn't here.

He likes to be," she faltered, "where it's happening, I guess."

"Did they talk to the guard at the gate?" Fay asked.

"I don't know," Gail answered. She was going through Beth's closet now, flipping the little dresses quickly, but looking carefully at each one.

"That won't help, hon," Fay said.

"No no," Gail explained. "They need something that smells like her. But. . " and she looked down now, almost embarassed by what she was about to say.

"I keep her things so clean. She doesn't wear anything more than once. I don't know if I have anything here that. . "

Fay finished the sentence for her. "Anything that smells like her."

"Yes," Gail said, grateful for the help.

"Give them a pillowcase," Fay said. "Nothing smells more like kids than their hair."

Just then, Arnie came into the bedroom holding a list of the children's names. He went directly to Gail and put his arms around her tight.

"I'm real sorry, Gail," he said.

"Thanks," she said, patting him on the back and squirming free. Gail wasn't ready to be held yet.

Fay took the pillowcase off of Beth's pillow and folded it into a square. She stared at the picture of

Beth on the dresser, all done up like Humpty Dumpty for
the day care Easter party.

"They didn't find anything at the fairgrounds,"
Arnie said. "Marvin's on his way back right now."

Gail took the pillowcase from Fay and pressed it to
her face.

Arnie turned to Fay. "How can forty kids just
vanish?"

"They can't," Fay said, sitting down on the little
girl's bed. "Somebody took them."

"Yes, I know that," he said, "But who? And for
what?"

Gail sat down in the rocking chair, still holding
the pillowcase.

Fay wished she could talk to Arnie alone, but she
didn't want to leave Gail right now, so she had no
choice. "What did the guard at the gate say? Did he
see anything funny?"

"Like a panel truck rolling out the gate, you
mean?"

"It has oranges on the side," she said.

"What?" he asked.

Fay shifted slightly on the bed. "It's a fruit
truck. The kids are in a fruit truck. There are
oranges painted on the side of the truck."

"Are you sure about this?" he asked. But he knew
she wouldn't have said it unless she was sure.

"Yes," she said, glancing at Gail. "It's a tractor

trailer with oranges painted on the side."

Arnie started for the door. "O.K.," he said,
suddenly feeling new energy course through him. "Good."
He patted her on the shoulder as he passed. "That's a
start."

By the time he hit the stairs, he was running.
Maybe Fay was right, maybe she wasn't. But she was
right often enough to check it out.

Gail got up and walked to the window. "I just
don't understand," she said softly.

Fay came over and put her arm around her. They looked
out the window together, hoping there would be something
to see, but there wasn't.

Arnie was talking to the Chief of Police who had
just driven up. A photographer was taking pictures of
the front of the building. Two police cars were pulling
away from the curb, apparently in pursuit of Fay's lead.
And three girls from the strip joint were leaning on
squad cars talking to the cops.

Finally, Gail spoke again. "Is she going to be all
right?"

Fay waited a moment before speaking. Gail wanted
the truth. "I know she's all right for now," Fay said.
"Does that help?"

"Sure it does," Gail said, nodding, folding her
arms across her chest. "Some."

          * * *

Fay had met Gail one day about five years ago, when
Gail walked in off the street, sat down at Fay's table
and asked if Marvin would ever be any fun to live with.

Fay looked at her palm, showed her the strong
psychic line just above her wrist, and told her she
could make a decent living telling fortunes. But Gail
already made a decent living writing not-so-decent
greeting cards.

She showed Fay one she'd just written. The front
of it said,

"A DAY IN THE LIFE OF A RESPECTABLE MAN"
and the inside of the card was perfectly blank.

So Gail already knew the good times with Marvin
were over, but she had no idea what to do about it. So
she just kept writing the greeting cards, but they were
getting sicker and sicker.

The company that bought nearly everything she
wrote, was beginning to refuse them now. One of the
latest rejects said,

     "LIVING WITH YOU IS NEVER EASY, BUT
         I'M STILL HERE BECAUSE"
and you turned the page,

     "I KNOW HOW MANY MORE OF YOU THERE ARE
       OUT THERE, AND IT WOULD MAKE ME FEEL
    REAL STUPID TO GET A DIVORCE, MEET SOMEBODY
     ELSE, FALL IN LOVE, AND FIND MYSELF STUCK
    IN THIS SAME SHITTY MARRIAGE ALL OVER AGAIN."

Fay had read the Tarot cards for Gail, seen the Moon in a dangerous position, and taken her up to the deli for lunch. They passed the warehouse on the way and it occurred to Gail to buy it.

"Marvin needs a project," she said.

They had had little Beth to save their marriage, but it hadn't worked. Gail said she thought maybe they could save a building instead.

So they had bought the warehouse across the street from the mission and converted it into loft apartments, which were rented to painters, some of whom could paint, but all of whom had to prove to Marvin that they had outside income.

It had all worked out pretty well. Gail and Marvin were still married, and Fay and Gail had become friends. Still, every time Fay read the cards for Gail, the Moon came up somewhere.

The Moon is maybe the unluckiest card in the whole deck. Worse than Death even. Death is a breeze compared to the Moon.

The picture on the Moon card is of two towers, seen only in the dim moonlit shadows. A road passes between the towers, and two dogs, one white and one black, bay at the moon. A scorpion crawls in a small pool of light.

The card warns that the darkness is not empty, that there is someone, something, there. Stop now, it says.

Listen carefully. That is not just the wind you hear.
You may hope those are not footsteps behind you, but
they are.

People smiled when the Moon card showed up. It
didn't scare them, the way the Death card did. People
thought the Moon must be a promise of some romantic
encounter.

But the Tarot held with the old notion of the moon,
which saw it as cold and bleak and dead, compared with
the sun. If you had your choice, you should take the
sunny, rational, right-handed, active, male road to
wealth and power, rather than the moonlit, emotional,
left-handed, passive female route to confusion at best.

Over the years, Fay had realized that people loved
the moon because they were a lot more interested in
deception than they were willing to admit. People do
believe the lies they are told. People do tend to trust
because they want to, not because they have some reason
for it. And people do think that if they avoid the
truth, it might change to something better before they
have to hear it.

Yes, maybe we do want to be seduced, want to be
deceived, Fay would say. Seduction and deception do
require that someone spend some energy on us, notice
things about us, lavish a certain kind of attention on
us.

But we also love the moon because we, too, have
things to hide. Maybe we don't look so good ourselves

in the all-revealing light of day. In the moonlight, we
can be heard and not seen. We can say who we are and
present no physical evidence to the contrary. For this
opportunity to deceive, we willingly pay the price of
being deceived ourselves.

What Fay said about the Moon card depended, of
course, on where it was in the spread. If it showed up
in the past, it wasn't so hard to tell people they had
been deceived. If it indicated the forces against them,
she could simply tell them to double check their
information, or be wary of any advice they received
right now from neighbors or friends. When the moon was
in a position describing their powers, Fay would warn
them that they were fooling themselves about something,
and they would have to pay for it eventually. Rarely
did she say you are lying to me, but that was the case,
more often than not.

When the Moon was in the fate position, or the
final outcome position, well, what was there to say?
Could she say you're not safe? Yes, sometimes she did.
She told people to take themselves out of their situation
if they could, or keep an eye out for an escape, if
they couldn't leave immediately. Whatever you do, Fay
would say, don't put yourself in someone else's powers,
and don't count on being lucky because it's just not in
the cards, O.K.?

Fay had said that to Gail over and over again.

This was not, however, news to Gail.

One time, when Beth was just a baby, Marvin bought an old clapboard house near a big park in the city. It was just an ordinary three-story disaster but Marvin, blind as he was, saw something in it. They spent every penny they had restoring the house, and moved in.

Marvin's experts had told him the furnace in the basement would last one more winter. He believed them because in a year, he could afford a furnace. His geothermal wells would really be gushing by then, wouldn't they?

But one morning, when his milk froze around his cornflakes, Marvin had to admit his experts were wrong. Something had to be done. He consulted his home repair manual and decided to replace just the blower on the furnace. He would do the work himself.

"Save money," he said, "nothing to it."

Gail was too cold to complain.

Marvin bought all the parts, got the thing installed, and came upstairs that night in complete triumph, except for the fact that he looked like there'd been a cave-in at the mine.

The house did seem warmer almost immediately. Maybe this would work after all. They went to bed and slept straight through without having to get up even one time for another blanket.

But the next morning, Gail woke up sneezing. That wasn't so strange, really, she often did that. But that

morning, every sneeze blew great gusts of black powder
out into the room.

"What the hell?" she thought, and put her feet down
on half an inch of black powder on the floor.

"Oh my God, Marvin!" she said, looking around
the room, beginning to understand the size of this
calamity. Every surface in the bedroom was covered in
soot. Walls, curtains, rugs, everything. She turned on
the light, but that didn't help much. The lampshade was
black, too. She shook Marvin and he sat up in a cloud
of dust.

"What's the matter, honey?" he said.

"It's your goddamn blower," she said, getting out
of the bed and wrapping her gray robe around her. "You
didn't clean out the vents or the ducts, did you. You
just went to bed, didn't you. You saved us so much
money, doing it yourself, didn't you. Well,
ccngratulations, Marvin. Your goddamn new blower just
blew two hundred years of soot onto every fucking thing we
own." She picked up her hairbrush from the dressing
table and was beginning to attack her hair when she
remembered.

"Beth!" she screamed. She threw down the brush,
and ran down the black hallway, leaving a trail of
footprints for Marvin to follow if he dared. She opened
the door and by now her hands were black too, just from
turning on the lights. She took one look and stopped.

She put her hand to her heart to stop the pounding. Beth was all right. There she was safe and warm in her crib. There was her little black face, nestled peacefully in her little black blanket, her little black arm around her little black bear.

Gail walked slowly across the room to the chest of drawers, and took out a clean white diaper. Praise God for chests of drawers. She leaned over and carefully dusted off the child's face, then brushed her fine blond hair and wiped off her round little hands. There wasn't any point in waking her up, was there. What was there to tell her? Maybe by the time Beth grew up, they would have forgotten about this morning.

Gail stood back up, and walked over to the window. She had planned to stare out the window and cry, but of course, it was solid black too, so she couldn't see a thing. She took a deep breath, and drew a big circle in the dust on the pane. Then she calmly wrote the word HELP inside the circle, in mirror writing, in the fervent hope that someone, anyone, out there, would see it.

The Moon was Gail's card all right. She was not safe, luck was never on her side, and Marvin always did the wrong thing.

4:00 A.M.

Gail wondered where Marvin was. Not that she
wanted him home, or wanted to talk to him, just that she
didn't want the rest of her family lost too.

She started for the kitchen. She needed something
else to think about. "How's Lizzie?" she asked Fay.
"Want some coffee?"

"She's fine," Fay said. "She's out."

"At four o'clock in the morning?" Gail asked.

Fay followed Gail into the kitchen, hoping they
weren't going to have a conversation about Lizzie.

"Well," Gail said, smiling now, "it's about time, I
guess."

"About time for her to come home?" Fay asked.

"No," Gail said, "it's about time for her to
find somebody."

"Somebody found her," Fay said.

"Good," Gail said. "Decaf or real coffee?"

"Decaf," Fay said.

Gail turned around, terrified. "You can't leave
me!"

"I'm not leaving you," Fay said. "I'm right here."

And to prove it, she sat down and started folding
a stack of newly washed napkins.

Gail was silent.

"O.K., O.K.," Fay smiled. "Real coffee."

Gail was a little ashamed of herself now. She
tried to laugh. "You can have decaf if you want. I
just don't want you going home to bed."

"Real coffee," Fay said.

"No, it's all right," Gail said. "We'll both have
decaf."

She measured the coffee into the filter cone.
"So," she said, "tell me about this boy of Lizzie's."

Fay cleared her throat. "His father's a banker.
They went out on his boat. That's all I know," Fay
said.

"But he's gorgeous, right?" Gail asked, thinking
maybe it would help if she lived in Lizzie's life for a
while.

"Oh yes," Fay said. "Black hair, black eyes, lean,
tan, rich. The works."

"I had a thing with a gorgeous man, once," Gail
said, pouring the water into the coffeemaker. "An
actor. But he didn't work much, so we played all the
time. He made me laugh. Great in bed. You know."

"I know," Fay said.

Gail turned on the coffee machine. "I was so
dumb," she said. "I thought all that fun wasn't
enough."

"I know," Fay said.

Gail got two cups down from the cabinet. "I don't
even know where he is now." She opened the refrigerator

and reached for the cream. "I wish I did."

    "What would you say to him if you saw him?" Fay
asked.

    "I don't know," Gail said. "Just ...I'm sorry I
was so dumb, I guess."

    "How long ago was this?" Fay asked, just trying to
keep the conversation going.

    "A long time," Gail said.

    "So," Fay said, "if you did see him, or run into
him somewhere, he'd look older now."

    "Right," Gail said, and laughed. "Would that make
me feel better or worse?"

    "Oh much better," Fay lied.

    And they both laughed, and shook their heads. And
Gail sat down across the table from Fay and appeared,
for the first time all night, to relax a little.

* * *

The Tarot's name for the ups and downs of fate is
The Wheel of Fortune. It looks a little like a ferris
wheel at a carnival, or a spin-for-dollars wheel on a TV
game show, or a clock, or the paddle wheel of an old
river boat, or the little wheel that hamsters run on
between meals. We say we invented the wheel, but all we
really did was tame it, put it to work, make it look
like fun.

It's almost impossible to be around a ferris wheel
without looking at it. The children scream and clutch
their cotton candy, their feet kick wildly and their
stomachs are suddenly all goofy inside them. It is fun,
yes? It's a ride, right? The Tarot would certainly
agree that it's a ride, all right.

The picture on the Wheel of Fortune card is an
eight-spoked wheel, whose axle is a great column, on top
of which sits a Sphinx holding a javelin. Two creatures
climb forever along the edge of the wheel. The genius
of good, Anubis, in some decks, clutches one side of the
rim and rides to the top, while the bad guy, Typhon, is
carried under by the turning of the wheel. In a moment,
though, all the good in the world will be ground down,
and the evil one will rejoice on top. This is how
things go, the Tarot says. But we all know that.

It is no accident that there are eight spokes in

the wheel. Eight is the Tarot's number for justice.
Justice is done when the wheel turns, and balances
things out. Nor is it an accident that the wheel is
round. Round is the full circle, the completion of an
orbit. Stars come around, and spring comes around. And
human lives, in time, come around.

The ancients believed that time itself was a
circle. A few of the more calculating ancients even
thought the same people were born and the same events
occurred every 36,000 years or so.

But circular time was comforting. If you had an
idea, it was sure to be one you'd had before, so there
was no reason for you to be afraid of it. If you lost
something, you were bound to find it again, and if you
had ever been happy, you would feel that way again
someday, so you might as well relax and enjoy your
depression.

Scientists have proven, of course, that time is
a line, not a circle. Today, they can even prove that
time moves forward. This means that there can be
progress, that humans, as a group, can get somewhere.
But it doesn't make us feel as good as when we believed
we'd have another chance at things, another go-round.

When the Wheel of Fortune card came up in a
reading, Fay would look at the other cards in order to
know where the client was on the wheel, which direction
he was going, that is. She thought the bottom half of

the wheel was submerged in water, so that you really
couldn't breathe under there. She'd seen something like
this in a movie, some torture device, she thought, where
the poor victim was tied to the wheel and turned around
and around until he talked or drowned. Even if it
wasn't a torture device, the Wheel of Fortune was, at
the very least, exhausting.

For Fay, the question was, did the Wheel of Fortune
revolve endlessly by itself, quite oblivious to the
despair and the joy it delivered at every turn? Or
was it more like the ones that hamsters run on, turned
by the action of the people on the edge.

There certainly was something about being on the
bottom that forced you up. But there was also something
about being on the top that pushed you over and dragged
you down. What that was, exactly, she didn't know.

Fay thought the rim of the wheel was more like a
circular ladder, with rungs to grab onto as you climbed
up, and rungs to hold onto as you plunged down. The
figures in the picture on the card do have claws instead
of hands. Is it this clawing that turns the wheel of
life? Is grabbing the only way to get around?

Can't you just walk through life, appreciating what
is there, taking only what comes to you naturally, and
letting things, like years, simply go by? Maybe you
can. People do it. Maybe they are the lucky ones. Some
people can just look at a giant ferris wheel, they don't
actually have to ride it. For some people, it is enough

just to watch other people take a spin.

What the Tarot says, is that once you grasp the wheel, once you reach out for even one rung of it, you are caught. You'll reach for the next one just to stay on, then the next one to get higher, and so on, until you reach one rung too far and over you go. You'll get on the thing and forget it's a wheel.

But it is a wheel, and you're going down. You hold on tight, grasping whatever security you can find. You try not to listen to the squeals of joy from the people behind you, or the agonized howls of those further ahead, and finally, you reach the bottom. Your head is bursting with the blood pooling in it, and gravity is pulling you with a force that seems irrestible.

You are easily five times your normal weight. It would be so easy to let go. But if you let go, then where would you be? Alone, weightless, drifting in the vast empty space that surrounds the wheel. You have no idea when you would ever touch anything, or anyone again.

But even at the bottom, you can't just hang on. If you don't move, the people behind you will crawl over you, trample you. You feel them shoving you already. They will push you off if you don't move. You don't have any choice.

You can let go and drop off, or get on with it. So you force one claw open, you summon a strength that is

made of nothing but fear, and reach for the next rung.
Reach, with some blind faith that the next rung is
there. Reach, out of some vague and distant memory that
this is a circle.

You go. You reach. You feel it. There. You grab
it! You've got it. You bring your other hand up now.
It's a little brighter here. You feel a little lighter
now. It's O.K. Keep going. You're moving easily. You
shake your head. You laugh. You yell back to encourage
the others, you take one hand away and wave to your
mother. You're coming up all right. You're almost
there. It's terrific up here! The view is incredible.
One more step and you're at the top. Nothing to it.
Take it!

You're there! You made it! Everybody sees you. They
love you. They thought you were finished, but you showed
them, didn't you? You can stand up straight now. You
hold both hands over your head in triumph and the crowd
cheers. You did it. You're at the top. Enjoy it.
Everybody in the whole world wants to be you. You try
not to make them feel bad about it, but what is there to
say. You worked hard, and you won. You've got it all!
Everything you ever wanted.

You take the next step with your feet, no hands,
just to show how them how easy it is, and suddenly, you
stop. You keep smiling, of course, but is that foot you
just moved a little lower than the other foot? It is.
Shit. What does this mean?

Put your hands down, that's what it means. Stop
congratulating yourself and get hold of this thing.
Grab the next rung.

And which way are you looking now? Down. You're
looking down. This thing is a circle. You're on your
way down again. Goddamn this thing.

Could you have avoided this fall? If you hadn't
been standing there grinning and having your picture
taken, could you have seen it coming and protected
yourself? Certainly not, if the wheel turns by itself.
And if the wheel is turned by the action of the people
on it, then no, the scrambling of the others behind you,
to stand where you are, would have pushed you over.

The only way to stay on top would be to shrink so
as to occupy as little space as possible, then carefully
take one step backward over and over again, suffering
the knocks and curses of the others climbing by you
to the top.

There wouldn't be much room, and you'd be afraid
most of the time. And although you _would_ appear in all
the photographs of everybody else in _their_ moment of
glory, you would probably be looking at your feet.
People on their way by would ask you what you'd done
lately. Staying on top wouldn't seem like enough of an
answer.

No, hard as you tried, you couldn't stay on top for
long. Somebody would push you, or maybe you'd just give

up and go around again.

Who made it a circle is a good question, but not
anywhere near the point. The point is nobody asked you
to get on it. You wanted something else, right?
Something more than you had. Well, this circle is what
else there is to have. Get off it if you can't take it,
and hang on if you can't let go.

Some people do try to escape by jumping off while
they're at the top. Actually, this is harder than you
might think, requiring a literal jump, instead of a
simple letting go. But they do it, because they think
they can beat the wheel that way. And maybe they can,
for a while. But eventually, they realize the emptiness
that surrounds the top of the wheel is more or less the
same motionless void that surrounds the bottom. And
wherever you are in the emptiness, you can still see the
wheel, towering, gaudy and bright, far above everything
else, like the ferris wheel when you drive by the
fairgrounds on the expressway late at night.

Gail hadn't noticed the ferris wheel when she left
the fairgrounds in the police cruiser. If she had
looked back, she would have seen that it had stopped for
the night. A terrible sight, a dead machine. On the
Tarot's Wheel of Fortune card, there is a warning about
this. The sphinx at the top of the wheel holds a
javelin in his hand. At any moment, he can stop the
wheel, catch you and hold you wherever you are in its
cycle. When the wheel stops, it feels like it will

never turn again.

Fay looked at Gail now, and wondered what good
would be intense enough to seem like the other side of
the wheel from having your child kidnapped. And what
had Gail ever done to deserve this?

Not that anybody ever deserved anything like this,
of course, but what had Gail ever reached for, to trap
her on the wheel, this wheel which had turned and caught
her now. Nothing.

Well, she _had_ wanted a little girl. Was that all
it took to start this wheel moving? One hand, extended
in the direction of one, so far faceless, unborn child?
Yes, Fay admitted reluctantly, sadly, it was. It
happened all the time.

* * *

As Gail was rinsing her coffee cup in the sink,
she heard his footsteps and froze. Marvin was coming up
the stairs two at a time.

"Gail!" he shouted from the front door. He sounded
frantic, as if he'd carried his barbells up the stairs
and was about to drop them if she didn't get there in
time.

"What is it?" she said, running. Fay followed her
down the hall.

"They found the truck!" he shouted.

"Where?" Fay asked.

He was talking very fast. "It's just like you
said!" He slapped Fay on the back. "One of the guards
saw a truck with oranges on the side!"

He slung his jacket over the chair, and flipped off
the John Deere tractor cap he wore at night for fun.

He was so proud to be the one to tell them. "The
guard thinks it left at midnight!"

Gail looked away.

But Marvin moved around so she could see him again.
"Gail, they've got every highway patrolman for two
hundred miles watching for the thing! They're bound to
spot it sooner or later."

Fay spoke for Gail. "So they didn't actually <u>find</u>
the truck," she said.

"No," Marvin said, rubbing his hands on his pants.
"Just a matter of time, though."

Fay shook her head. He was behaving like a
junior varsity cheerleader.

She spoke slowly, hoping to calm him down, get him
to take this seriously. "So all they really know,
Marvin," she said, "is that somebody else, besides me,
saw the truck. Is that right?"

Marvin sunk into the chair. "Yeah. I guess so,"
he said. He thought it was better news than that.

Gail tried to cover her disappointment. "Want some
decaf?" she managed.

"No thanks," he grinned. "I had some coffee and
donuts with the boys," he said.

"What boys?" Gail asked.

"The police."

"I see," Gail said. "The boys." And she walked
back down the hall to the kitchen.

"Is Arnie still down there?" Fay asked, pointing to
the street.

"He went back to the station," Marvin said. "He
said he'd call if he learned anything, and he wants you
to stop by there before you go home."

"Thanks," she said.

He planted his hands on his knees and leaned
forward in his chair. "How did you know about the
truck?" he asked, eyes wide in amazement.

"I don't know," she said, "I never know."

"Well, do you know anything else?" he demanded.

"They're not going very far," Fay said, turning for the kitchen. "I don't even think they're on the highway."

Marvin jumped up and flew to the phone. "That's great!" he said.

Fay left him talking to the police, and found Gail at the sink, her face buried in a wet washcloth.

"If you're all right," Fay said, "I better go."

"Please," Gail said weakly. "Don't leave me with Marvin. He has no idea how. . ."

"You just stay in the kitchen," Fay said. "I'll tell Marvin to stay in there."

"He's having _fun,_" Gail said.

"I know it looks that way," Fay said, "but that's how men handle a thing like this. They run. They make calls. They keep moving so it can't get them. They don't mean any harm by it. They just can't help it."

Fay gave Gail a hug.

"I want him to sit and cry with me," Gail said. "I want him to be somebody else, somebody who could make me feel better."

"I know," Fay said. "If I could change him for you, I would. But I can't. All I can do is go find Beth. O.K.?"

Gail stepped backward and turned on the water. She was mad, all of a sudden. "What are you going to do," she asked, "read the cards?"

"I don't know," Fay said, simply. "I don't know
what it will take."

"I'm sorry," Gail said. "I'm sorry I said that."

"It's all right," Fay said. "You just rest."

In the living room, Marvin was hanging up the
receiver.

"I think you should stay near the phone," Fay said
to him. "Gail isn't in any condition to answer it."

"Good idea," Marvin said and picked up his cap from
the floor.

"And I wouldn't wear your cap," Fay said.

"Yeah," he said, and opened the closet door. "It
looks a little funny, I guess."

"Yes," she said. "It looks like you're having a
good time."

He pitched the hat up on the shelf and closed the
closet door. Fay made him nervous. He was afraid she
would know what he was thinking before he did.

* * *

Fay closed the door behind her. She liked
hallways. Always had. Even when you loved the people
you'd been to see, it was such a relief to leave.

She had to find Arnie now. And maybe Lizzie was
home. But as she grabbed the newel post at the top of
the stairs, she stopped cold. There it was, the whole
thing. She saw it all. She stood there paralyzed and
watched.

Lizzie and Paul were on the big boat now. So were
a lot of other people. All dressed up. Dancing.
Drinking. Paul's mother was in white, beads all down
the front in little roses, with curling vines of beads
wound around her hips. No, not beads. Pearls. Ten or
twenty thousand dollars worth of pearls. Maybe more.

And food. Oysters on ice in a brass cart and a
special waiter with cold red hands from cracking them.
Somebody carving something. Rare, whatever it was, and
black bread to go with it, and a bowl of, well, it
looked like whipped cream. Couldn't be whipped cream.
Horseradish. Whipped.

Paul and Lizzie were dancing. Lizzie looked better
than any of the other girls, no money or not. They
could be skating, they were so smooth together.
Everybody else had to work at it, dancing, they got hot,
bumped into each other, smiled too much. Paul and

Lizzie belonged together. They . . . fit.

They left the dance floor. They were talking with
his parents, now. Lizzie liked the beads, she wondered
if the dress was heavy.

"So heavy," his mother said, "that Pierre guarantees
I'll lose three pounds just wearing it." She laughed.

Lizzie knew not to ask who Pierre was. Chances
were she'd meet him soon enough without asking. Paul
and Lizzie walked out onto the deck.

"Where does he find these orphans?" Paul's mother
asked after they left.

The moon was still out.

Wait a minute.

This boat was moving. Moving fast. Too fast not
to be going somewhere. The other people were gone. The
party was over. This boat was underway.

But where were they going? Atlantic City? Bermuda?
Some island not on the map?

Fay saw Lizzie's cabin. It was already stocked
with the clothes Paul's mother always provided for his
girls. All Paul had to do, Fay realized, was find
somebody the right size.

Where was he taking her?

Paul and Lizzie walked to the back of the boat, the
stern.

"It's the Red Sea," Lizzie said, watching the huge
wake curl and foam behind them.

"What Red Sea?" he asked.

"You know," she said. "Moses. He raised his arms
and the Red Sea parted." She raised her arms and Paul
slipped into them.

"In the movie?" he asked.

She laughed. "And the book."

"I love your hair," he whispered.

"It's mother's," she said. "It's gypsy hair." And
she folded her arms around him.

"Who _are_ you?" he asked.

"Nobody," she said.

He kissed her.

She liked it, laughed and pulled one end of his bow
tie. It fluttered up, all undone, then settled down
smoothly against his shirt.

This is what you pay for in a good tie, Fay
thought, as she watched.

Then Paul lifted Lizzie up to sit on the railing,
stepped between her legs and kissed her hard.

* * *

Fay ran down the steps to the street. The police
would simply have to find these missing kids without
her. She had to find Lizzie, and Arnie had to help her.
Alert the Coast Guard, rent a speedboat, catch up with
the yacht, and get Lizzie away from that boy.

She crossed the empty street and walked quickly to
the police station. She hated to think how she must
look by now, but she was glad she didn't know.

Arnie was alone in the duty room, waiting for her.

"Boy, am I glad to see you," he said, standing up.

"Arnie. . ." she began.

"Look at this," he interrupted, unfolding the front
section of tomorrow's paper on his desk.

The headline read,

        "27 CHILDREN ABDUCTED FROM STATE FAIR"
and then underneath that, in smaller print,

        "LOCAL PSYCHIC ON THE CASE"

Spread across the page, in rows, were the pictures
of twenty-five of the children.

Fay sat down. Thinking about missing children was
quite different from seeing their pictures in the paper.

"Where are the other two children?" she asked. "I
thought you said there were twenty-seven."

"The other two are the mayor's," Arnie said. "He
kept their pictures out because he hopes maybe the

kidnapper doesn't know they're his kids. He doesn't
want the ransom to go up because of them."

"Poor man," Fay sighed. She liked this mayor,
Peter Ewing. She had known him for a long time. "Does
Peter have any enemies?" she asked.

"We thought of that," Arnie said. "Not a one. The
unions are happy, the owners are happy, hell, the
Republicans are even happy. He's a hit."

"Well, then, what about his wife?" Fay asked. "Isn't
Vi on some abortion thing? Some planned parenthood, or
pro-choice committee or something? She's always on TV
about something. Isn't that it? Abortion?"

"I don't know," Arnie said. "But what does that
have to do with. . ."

"Maybe it's Vi they want to punish."

"Who?" he asked.

"The kidnappers."

He shook his head. "You just don't like her," he
said.

"No, I don't like her, but they're her kids too,
aren't they?"

"This isn't abortion, Fay, it's kidnapping," Arnie
said, standing up.

She nodded, but she wasn't at all Arnie was right
about that.

"Anyway," Arnie went on, "Vi is out of town.
Speaking at some convention somewhere."

"Saying what?" Fay asked.

"You're going in the wrong direction, Fay," Arnie
said. "All I wanted to tell you was the Mayor called
here looking for you. He said if there was anything you
needed. . ."

"I can't work on this case, Arnie," she said.

"You have to," he said, folding up the paper and
putting it under his arm. "There's one kid with
diabetes, one who's on an anti-convulsant. . ."

"No," she said, "I can't. All I can think about is
Lizzie and Paul. All I see is the two of them."

"It's not the same thing, Fay," he said, nodding to
the new Sergeant coming on duty. "Lizzie and Paul are
two nearly grown up kids doing what we'd all like to be
doing right now."

He opened his desk drawer and pulled out his
shoulder holster. "These other kids are babies in the
hands of some real weirdo who's doing God knows what to
them."

"Lizzie is my baby," she said. "We have to find
her."

He strapped on the holster. "Lizzie will come home
all by herself."

"No," she said. "That boat is going somewhere.
He's taking her somewhere."

"Honey," Arnie said, flatly, "I can't go find Lizzie
because she's not breaking the law." He picked up his
keys. "This creep, this maniac with all these kids,

<u>he's</u> breaking the law. He's who I have to find, not
Lizzie."

Fay shook her head. He didn't understand.

"I'm glad Lizzie's out with somebody," he said. "I
hope he's the best she's ever had."

"He'd be the first, Arnie," she said, folding her
arms across her chest.

"You don't know that," he said.

"I do know that!" she snapped.

"All right, Fay," he said. "Fine. Do you want her
to be a virgin all her life?" He started for the door.

Fay whirled around in the chair. "Where are you
going?"

"You'll see," he said. "Come on."

She turned back around. "I told you. I'm not
working on this case."

"Fine, then," he said, coming up behind her,
touching her gently on the shoulder. "You're not
working on this case. You're just taking a ride with
me. Remember me?"

She covered her face with her hands.

"Now what's the matter?" he asked.

"It's not a man," she said.

"Who's not a man?" he said.

"The guy who stole the kids. He's not a man."

He sat down across from her. "It's a woman?"

"There's something about a church," she said.

"What church?"

"And girls," she said.

Arnie couldn't keep up. "Is the truck at the church?"

But she didn't answer.

"Girls or women?" he asked.

"Girls," she said.

"All right, then. Let's go," he said, standing up.

"Go where?"

"Go see the man who'd know about a group of all-girl, anti-abortion, religious fanatics," he said simply. "Isn't that who we're looking for?"

She shook her head. He was amazing. Even when he didn't seem to be listening, he never doubted what she said.

She stood up. "If I find these kids for you, will you find Lizzie for me?" she asked.

"Fay," he said wearily, taking her arm and leading her toward the door, "this is twenty-seven kids here. I'll do whatever you want."

"Say it again," she said. "I want a real promise."

He held the door open for her. "You find these kids," he said, "and I'll find Lizzie."

"O.K., then," she said, and stepped out onto the street.

As the door closed behind them, he stopped a moment and looked at the moon. "We're in the wrong business, Fay," he said. "Everybody's in bed but us."

"We'll get there," she said.

He unlocked the undercover car. "I hope you slept
well last night," he said.

"Why is that?" she asked.

"Because," he said, starting the engine and
shifting into gear, "the Chief says the kidnapping
statistics all say the same thing. If we don't find
these kids in twenty-four hours. . ."

"We don't find them," she finished.

"Yeah," he said, pulling away from the curb.
"Ever. We don't find them ever."

5:00 A.M.

Fay had met the elegant, young Mayor during his first campaign. He was walking her neighborhood in a yellow windbreaker, knocking on doors and introducing himself. She looked at his palm, saw his Mount of Mercury and the star on his headline, and told him he would win.

"So I can quit all this walking and talking?" he laughed.

"If you want to," she said.

"But I like it," he said.

"That's why you're going to win," she said. "The other man doesn't want to do the work, he just wants to be the mayor."

"How do you know that?" he asked.

She smiled. "Trust me," she said. "I know these things." She laughed. "In fact, all I do is know these things."

"Can I use that?" he asked.

"Sure," she said.

And he did. He brought a camera crew down to Fay's parlor, and they went through the whole scene again on film for an ad. The mayor won the election, and the ad took the top national advertising award in the political category that year.

Fay met Peter's wife, Vi, at the big victory party after the election. But Vi Ewing was not a woman you'd

ever really know. If you tried to get close to her, all
you would see were the details of the surface.

Fay was a big star at the victory celebration,
entertaining the troups with a little Tarot numerology.
When you add up the numbers corresponding to the letters
in a name, you get a key number, which indicates one of
the Tarot cards, which, she said with a wink, was the
sum cosmic total of everything that ever has, or ever
can happen to you. It's the Perameters of Fate, she
said. Some people laughed at that.

At one point in the party, the mayor's wife flew by
and perched on the arm of Fay's chair, like a parakeet,
chirpy and bright, but not likely to light here for
long. She gave them all a big smile, and said wasn't it
fun to know somebody special like Fay, and wasn't the ad
worth all the trouble it caused everybody.

One of the young volunteers said Fay was doing
numbers and why didn't Vi let Fay do hers. Vi was
trapped, but she was used to that.

"Is Vi your full name?" Fay asked.

"No," she said, "but that's what everybody calls
me."

"All right, then," Fay said. "V is 6 and I is 10.
That makes 16. The Fallen Tower."

"Oh, that's no fun," the mayor's wife said, "do my
whole name. I'm sure I have something better than
that."

So Fay added up all the letters, including Vi's

maiden name, the middle name she never told anybody, and the real first name on her birth certificate, and it still came to 16.

Not wanting to seem afraid of some voodoo nonsense, and not wanting to insult this woman whose endorsement had been so good for them, Vi asked Fay what the "infernal" tower meant anyway.

"But that would take so long," Fay said, knowing what she would have to say if she were forced to.

"Go on," someone shouted from the group. "We dare you." Nobody could back down now. Not at a victory party, anyway.

"O.K.," Fay said. "It's like the Tower of Babel in the Bible."

"I like the Bible," Vi cooed. Then she looked at the group and added quickly, "I like the Torah too, of course." She looked back at Fay. "That's like the Tarot, I guess, isn't it. I like them all, is what I'm saying. Go on."

"Well," Fay said, "there's something in your life built out of lies. Out of nothing but selfish ambition."

"I'm not ambitious," Vi said. "I just want the right people to be where they should be."

Fay tried to be careful. "The people who live in Falling Towers, well, they sit up there and look down on everybody else."

"Not look down," Vi corrected. "Bring people up to where we are. Where we all should be, I mean."

"Right," Fay said.

And the mayor's wife shouted a little Hooray and some of the people in the group clapped.

"The danger is," Fay went on, "that one day while you're looking over the wall and having a great time, you know, throwing things off the wall just to see how long it takes before they hit the ground. . "

"That sounds like fun," the mayor's wife said, "I used to do that from a hill at my old daddy's farm."

"One day," Fay went on, "lightning could strike and the tower could fall, and, because you're up there on top of it, so could you."

"What a wonderful game," said the mayor's wife. "How long did it take you to learn it?"

Fay knew she should stop, but she couldn't. "It isn't just lightning, though. Sometimes, it just crumbles from within. All because of the lies. The lies simply won't stand up."

"I don't lie," the mayor's wife said, defending herself with practiced cool. "How could I lie? The press can find out anything, you know. Anyway, what would I have to lie about?"

"Sometimes it's crumbling already," Fay looked at the group. "People lie about that, you know, like a woman whose marriage is ending, who gets all involved in some social issue. . ."

The mayor's wife stood up now and motioned to someone that she would be there in just a moment.

The group was listening, so Fay went on. "But that only puts more stress on the original tower, makes it crumble faster."

"I wish I could hear the rest of this," Vi said, standing up, "but you know how parties are."

She shook Fay's hand. "Thank you for all you've done for my husband."

Then she turned to the group. "I think this one should have her own TV show, don't you?"

The group applauded, and the mayor's wife breezed back into the crowd standing around her husband.

At the time, Fay felt a little humiliated, a little done in by her own faith in herself, and a lot relieved that there was always the bathroom to go to in moments like that.

But now, as she drove through the sleeping city with Arnie, going she knew not where, she shuddered to think about the Mayor's wife and the Falling Tower. Was this kidnapping what the cards had seen that night? How many of these children would the tower take with it when it crashed?

Fay tried to look out the windows, tried to think of something else, tried to rein in her racing mind. No, she insisted. No. She would rather reject everything she knew about the cards, find other ways to

explain why they had been so right so often, than
believe they actually had prior knowledge of something
as terrible as this.

But it wasn't the cards, was it. The cards didn't
know anything, not by themselves, anyway. It was she,
Fay, who knew things by looking at them.

But that was even worse. Had Fay really known that
night, that this woman, Vi Ewing, was going to fall? It
couldn't be. What lies could Vi have told to unloose a
horror the size of this one? There weren't any lies
that big, were there?

No. Vi couldn't be responsible for this. She must
be an innocent victim, just like all these other
parents.

But Fay knew there was a lie of some kind behind
this thing. Some tower was coming down all right.
Right on top of all of them.

* * *

Something was bothering Arnie too, Fay sensed. He
hadn't said a word since they left the police station.
Maybe he didn't know if he could really find his
informer in the middle of the night. Maybe Arnie was
just tired. Or maybe she'd made him mad making him
promise to find Lizzie.

He pulled into the parking lot of the bus station
and got out of the car, still without saying anything.
She followed him, but there wasn't anything to see.
Just the empty bus lanes and the empty benches beside
them. Somebody had left a suitcase in one of the
garbage cans.

Arnie walked over, picked it up, shook it, then
jimmied the lock with his pocket knife.

"Is this where he lives?" she asked finally.

"Where who lives?" he asked, opening the suitcase.

"The man you're looking for," she said.

"Sure is," he said.

Fay wasn't convinced.

The suitcase was filled with old shoes, a whole
family's worth. Arnie picked them up, pair by pair.
Battered wingtips, ragged sneakers, red pumps, one of
which was missing its heel, four pairs of once-white
baby shoes, and yellow plastic cowboy boots that might
fit a teenage girl.

Arnie shook his head. Something about the suitcase made him feel even worse. He slammed it shut, pitched it back in the trash can, took Fay's hand and led her toward the door of the bus station.

"Is that how you know where he is, that suitcase?" Fay asked.

"No," he said. "That's just somebody's whole life they threw away."

"Is something the matter?" she asked carefully.

"I don't know," he said, opening the door to the waiting room. "Wait here."

He walked over to the restrooms, disappeared into the men's, came out and went into the ladies'.

"It's late," he said, coming back to her. "Let's get some coffee, huh?"

He nodded toward the coffee shop on the other side of the station. But Fay could already see through the glass that it was empty too, except for the man behind the counter. Whoever Arnie was looking for wasn't here.

"We can't just stop and have coffee, Arnie," she said, trying to help. "How about the produce mart? Maybe that's where they stole the truck."

But he didn't want any help right now. "I need some coffee, Fay," he said, opening the door. "I can't go any further til I get some coffee. It won't take long."

Fay didn't like it here. "The produce mart is a perfect place to hide an orange truck," she said.

"I'm a policeman," he said.

"What?" she asked.

"I have to have my coffee when I say so." He opened the door. "And my donut. I want a donut."

"O.K., O.K.," she said. "We'll get you a donut."

But that wasn't all Arnie wanted. "And I'd like to go to bed," he grumped. And get up and go fishing. And fry some catfish in an old black skillet and have a few beers."

"Anything else?" she asked, beginning to understand what this was about.

"Yeah," he said, sitting down at the counter. "I'd like to walk around the lake with you, and hear the birds. I like birds." The words were coming easier now. "I'd like to live outside with the birds. I'd like to spot a blue warbler up in the top of some tree, then take you back to the tent for the rest of the afternoon."

"That sounds good," she said.

"Two coffees, two donuts," he said to the waiter who shuffled toward them.

"Toast for me," Fay said, trying not to watch Arnie too closely.

Arnie unzipped his jacket and reached for the sugar, so it would be ready when the coffee came. He shook his head. He picked at the spout of the sugar jar, scraping away the crystals so it would pour easily.

Then he just sat there, with his hands folded around the jar.

"It's real simple, Fay," he said finally, staring straight ahead. "I don't want to find these children."

"You don't want to find them hurt or dead, you mean," she said.

He took a deep breath. "I don't find people any other way, Fay."

They sat silently, as though they didn't know each other, while the waiter set the coffee in front of them, filled water glasses from the faucet over the sink, and replaced Arnie's spoon, which had something vaguely green on it.

When the waiter left, Arnie took a sip of his coffee and sat up a little straighter.

"I could do other things, you know. I could drive a bus, or teach car repair, or hang wallpaper. I could paint fucking dog houses is what I could do."

"Arnie, Arnie," she said, "it's all right. The kids are all right."

"No, Fay, they can't be all right. Why kidnap them if you're not going to hurt them? Ten dollars says tomorrow we get a message, telling us which garbage can they stuffed the first one in."

This was a conversation they'd had over and over again, and there never was anything for her to say at the end of it. Arnie simply didn't like criminals. He liked that they were off the streets for a while, but he

didn't like being with them on the way to the jail. He
didn't like driving them downtown. He didn't like their
talk. If he'd known he'd have to spend so much time
with them, he'd never have set that first foot in the
police department.

"Let's just go home, then," she said. "You can come
back to my place and sleep for a few hours anyway."

"I don't think I could sleep."

"All right, Arnie," as the the waiter came around
to refill their cups. "What do you want to do?"

"I want you to marry me," he said, lighting a
cigarette.

She turned to face him. She thought he was joking.
But no, Arnie was quite serious. As serious as she'd
ever seen him. If there was any emotion in his face at
all, it was something you'd have to call hope. Why was
he doing this?

He took her hand and stared down at it. "I want us
to move away somewhere. Wyoming maybe. A friend of
mine out there says they haven't had a killing in his
county for eight years, except two cocaine dealers
nobody knew anyway. He told me you never need a key to
your house, and the only time you even have to lock your
car is when you go into town during tourist season."

"Marry you?" she asked.

He shifted in his seat. "O.K.," he said. "You
don't have to marry me if you don't want to. But come

out there with me. Come out of here with me."

"Arnie, what would I do in Wyoming?"

"Don't they have a future in Wyoming?"

"Sure they do, but I don't know anybody there. It
would take me years to. . "

"O.K.," he mumbled. "Forget it, then," and took
out his wallet and put a five dollar bill on the
counter.

But that wasn't what she'd meant. "I don't want to
forget it, Arnie, it's just that I ... "

He tried once more. "I want you with me, Fay."

"I am with you," she said, and stroked his face
lightly. "I'm right here."

He pulled away. "I don't want to live someplace
where they steal children from the fair."

"We'll find them," she said.

"Yes," he said. "We will. And then I'm going
away."

He turned around on the stool. His face was set.
For the last twenty years, leaving the police force had
seemed impossible. In the space of one conversation, it
had become inevitable.

"I can't leave Lizzie, Arnie," she said.

He stood up. "I thought you said he was taking her
somewhere. That boy. Paul."

"He is," Fay said.

"So what are you going to do?" he asked. "Sit here
and wait for her to come back?"

"We're going to find her," Fay said.   "You
promised me . . ."

"Right," he said.   "I did.   We'll take her with us.
She'd like Wyoming."

But Fay knew that Lizzie would never go to Wyoming.
"Can I tell you tomorrow?" Fay asked.

"Sure," he said.   "Tomorrow is fine."

"Where are we going now?" she asked, standing up too.

"I'm going to the men's room," he said.   "Want to
come?"

She sat back down.   "No," she said.

He smiled and patted her on the shoulder.   "O.K.,"
he said.   "I'll be right back."

She smiled back at him.   He was all right.   The
coffee had helped.   The conversation had helped.   He
could go on now.

* * *

As Fay turned to watch Arnie walk away, she saw
that the coffee shop wasn't completely empty. A drunk
was slumped over in the last booth.

What she didn't know was that this particular drunk
hadn't had a drink in fifteen years. He was calling
himself Dr. Goodlife now, and was actually doing a fair
amount of good recycling the neighborhood bums by
teaching them to refinish furniture.

"Wake up, buddy," Arnie said to Dr. Goodlife.

"God bless you, brother," the slicked back head
said as it raised up from the table.

"It's me, Arnie."

"God doesn't care what you call yourself, my
friend. He knows who you are."

"Open your eyes, Doc," Arnie said.

"You open your heart, I'll open my eyes," said Dr.
Goodlife, his hands clamped around his Bible on the
table. "I don't want to see you, son, til you've seen
the last of drink."

"It's Detective Campbell, Doc," Arnie said.

The doctor opened his eyes. "Got a dollar for some
coffee?"

"Sure," Arnie said, and motioned to the man behind
the counter. "I'm looking for some girls," he sat down,
"some church girls."

"How many you need?" the doctor asked, searching his pockets for the paperclips he played with since he quit smoking. "Methodists, Baptists, bowlers, ball players, what?"

"I think it's a new church," Arnie said. "Something private. Weird maybe. Sick maybe. Tough, young. The kind that can drive a truck."

The doctor found a toothpick in his pocket and stuck it in his mouth. "Lot of girls drive trucks now, Campbell," he said. "Farm girls always did, of course. Then there's Army girls. Girl bus drivers could drive a truck easy, I guess. If they had the truck. How big a truck we talking about? Lot of trucks in and out, you know. Gotta get things place to place. It's a big country, America."

"Have you seen a truck with oranges painted on the outside?" Arnie asked him, remembering now, how much work this man could be.

"Maybe I did," the doctor said.

"Where was it?" Arnie asked.

"I guess it was in Florida," the doctor said. "I used to live there, you know. Years ago. Nice place. Gets pretty hot, though. Lot of Cubans. I probably saw an orange truck there sometime, wouldn't you think?"

Arnie thought he was waiting for money, but he didn't know how much money the doctor's information was worth. The coffee arrived.

"Drink your coffee," Arnie said. "There's no rush.

I'm just sitting here waiting for the sunrise."

The doctor took a sip. "You hear about those kids?"

Arnie laughed. Nobody else in the city would know about the missing children til the papers came out. "Drink your coffee, pal," he said and got out his wallet.

Arnie thought about asking Fay to come down here, save him some money and just read the doctor's mind. But when he looked back at her, she seemed to be counting the little boxes of dry cereal. That wasn't something he wanted to interrupt.

"Do you know where they're keeping the kids?" Arnie asked.

"Make it real easy on you if I did, wouldn't it?" the doctor grinned.

"Do you?" Arnie asked.

"No."

Arnie tried again. "Do you know who the girls are?"

"Bad girls," the doctor said.

"Why did they steal the truck?" Arnie asked.

The doctor shook his head. "You ever sit with a bunch of kids in a car?"

"No," Arnie said.

"Never shut up, kids. Got to keep 'em in a truck, I guess, if you're gonna have any peace, you know."

"How much do you want?" Arnie said, pulling out

what money he had.

The doctor waved away the money. "The church is at
9th and Oak," he said. "They've got a sign out front
with Jesus hanging upside down from one foot, tears
running up his face, blood running up his shirt. Not a
xerox or anything. Looks like they did it with
crayons."

"Where's the truck?" Arnie asked again.

"What do you want the truck for? You're looking
for the kids, right?"

"Right," Arnie said.

"Can't keep kids in a truck very long," the doctor
said.

"Yeah," Arnie said. "Thanks. How much do you
want, Doc?" Arnie extended his money.

"I don't want any money," the doctor said, lowering
his voice. "I want you to find those kids. And chase
those girls out of that church."

"Girls or women?" Arnie said.

"Girls."

Arnie stood up. "I want to give you something for
this."

"Uh-uh," the doctor said. "Some other time. " He
opened his Bible. "Some other life, you can buy me a
drink."

Arnie put a ten dollar bill on the table. "You
ever been to Wyoming?" he asked.

"Cold out there," the doctor said, turning to

Revelations.

"Lot of animals," Arnie said.

"Sounds right."

"Well, if you ever get there," Arnie said, tapping
the table, "look me up."

Arnie walked back over to Fay, and lifted her head
off the counter.

"Let's go, love," he said.

"Go where," she said, brushing her hair out of her
eyes.

"You were right about the girls. And the church is
at 9th and Oak. Come on."

Once they were out the door, he walked so fast that
Fay could barely keep up with him.

"Who was that man?" she asked. "Are the kids all
right?"

"He doesn't know."

"Are the kids at the church?"

Arnie opened the door for her. "He doesn't know
that either."

"They can't be," she said. "If that drunk knows
where the church is, then a lot of people know where the
church is, so it wouldn't be a safe place for the girls
to come back to, would it?"

"He's not a drunk, Fay," he said, starting the
engine.

"I'm sorry," she said.

"It's O.K." he said. He knew she was tired, but he
needed answers now. "Doesn't one of your cards have a
a guy hanging upside down from a tree?" he asked.

"Yes," she said, "the Hanging Man. Why?"

Arnie sped out of the parking lot. "This church
has an upside down Jesus in the front yard." He paused
at the red light, then ran it.

"He isn't Jesus in the cards," Fay said. "He's
just anybody."

"What does it mean?" he asked.

"It doesn't mean anything," she said.

"I know it means something," he insisted.

"Arnie," she patted him on the knee, hoping he
would slow down. "It's probably just some old hippie
who burns incense and flips through the coloring books
at the mystical book shop."

"That's right," Arnie said. "It's done in crayons.
Tell me what it means."

"Are you taking me home or am I going with you?"
she asked.

Arnie wasn't sure he wanted her along. With any
luck, this could be dangerous. But he knew he needed
her.

"You're coming with me," he said.

He picked up his radio and called headquarters for
backup at the church. He could see it all. The truck
would be parked in the alley, empty. He'd find the kids
all huddled up in the nursery, tied together maybe, and

the kidnappers upstairs preparing their statement for
TV. He'd arrest the weirdos, rescue the kids, take Fay
home to bed, and quit the force in the morning.

Fay saw it quite differently. Nobody was at the
church. The kids were all split up now, not in the
truck any more. The truck was gone, but not empty.
Somebody was working in the truck, making signs.
Posters. Pictures. Pictures of the kids, and writing.
Like a traveling exhibition, a McDonnell-Douglas van
that teaches school kids about jet engines: the kind you
walk through, look at what's there, and come out the
other end.

She couldn't tell him that, though. It didn't make
any sense.

He turned onto Oak street and slowed down, making
a mental map of the street. Frame row houses, a welfare
hotel, and a deserted foreign car repair with the new
location painted on the window. One new building, mid-
block, something for the Blind. And on the far corner, a
bar with blinking neon martini glasses over the door.

He pulled up in front of the church. It was a
low white frame building. The faded lettering over the
door said it had been erected in 1940 and was, at that
time, a pentecostal tabernacle. It didn't look erected,
though. It looked like somebody lowered a tin roof onto
a double-wide mobile home.

"I think you better stay in the car for now," Arnie

said. "I'll come get you if there's. . ."

And then he saw the backup cruiser pull in behind
him. He got out of the car without finishing his
sentence.

"I'm fine," she said to the silence. And then she
locked all the doors and cracked a window.

* * *

Fay watched as Arnie and the other two detectives approached the upside down Jesus in the front yard, then proceeded to the front door. They found it locked, and split up to find another way in.

Could Arnie really be serious about moving to Wyoming? Could he really be asking her to choose between him and Lizzie?

She couldn't think about it. Not now, anyway. She stretched her legs out across the front seat and folded up her jacket and placed it between her head and the window. Maybe she could sleep a while.

But that was not to be. As she closed her eyes, she saw Lizzie and Paul standing beside his parents at the railing of the boat, saying good-bye to the other guests.

So the boat was docked anyway. That was good.

"I'm glad you could stay," Paul's mother said to Lizzie.

Staying? Staying what, Fay thought. Overnight?

"I hope you found everything you need," the honey-haired woman said.

Fay saw the guest room. There was not a human alive who could actually <u>need</u> all those things. Little lizard pill boxes, tortoise shell trays of dusting powder and perfume, smooth ivory shells of sherbert scented soaps... all indications, Fay noted, of how the endangered species got that way.

"Yes, thank you," Lizzie replied. "It's lovely."

Lovely, Fay thought. Since when did Lizzie say
lovely? By morning she find the stewards divine, and
the air delicious. By lunchtime, she'd be calling
people Darling.

"Will you come inside, or stay here?" Paul's mother
asked them, as the last guest left the gangplank.

"Here," Paul said, laughing at her for even asking.

"Cook will be awake, if you need anything," she
said, and swept off through the door.

There was that word again. Need.

Paul pulled a thin cigarette from his coat pocket,
put it to his lips, lit it, inhaled deeply and passed it
to Lizzie. Fay wasn't surprised. Marijuana, she
thought. Did people _need_ marijuana?

Lizzie took the joint from him happily. Fay waited
for her to cough. When she didn't, when Lizzie seemed
to know exactly what she was doing, on this boat, with
this boy, with that dope in her lungs, Fay opened her
eyes, sat up, and bolted out of the back seat of Arnie's
car and onto the sidewalk.

But then where was she? Staring at an upside down
Jesus stuck in the front yard of some tacky white church
at 6 o'clock in the morning. And, for the moment, that
was exactly where she wanted to be.

6:00 A.M.

Fay walked up into the yard and stared at the hanging Jesus. The Tarot card, on which the drawing was based, did not always mean bad news. Sometimes, when it showed up in a reading, she would simply tell the client, "Oh, you're all right. Your life is just upside down right now." Or she might ask if there was something they'd left hanging. Or if there was something the matter with their left ankle.

If there were other clues confirming some recent escape, she would say, "You caught yourself just in time, didn't you?"

"What do you mean?" they'd ask.

"You know what I mean," she'd say. And they'd laugh, and tell her the story.

Sometimes, she'd get hold of a real martyr, like the preacher who ran the mission at the corner, or somebody's mother. The question was always the same.

Why don't my children appreciate what I did for them? I gave them my life. Why don't they love me?

The answer was always the same too. Nobody likes a sacrifice.

"If you sacrifice everything for your children," Fay would say, "they'll only end up hating you for it. It's an unpayable debt. Sacrifice makes people mad."

Fay didn't know why sacrifice made people mad. But then, nobody had ever made a big sacrifice for her, so

she only knew one side of it. Except for Jesus, that
is. The preacher who ran the mission at the corner told
her Jesus had died for her sins. That would qualify as
a sacrifice.

"What sins?" Fay asked. "Who has time to sin any
more?"

"He died to save you, sister," the preacher said.

"I didn't ask him to die for me," Fay said.

"You didn't have to ask," the preacher said.
"That's how much he loves you."

"He can't love me," Fay said, "He doesn't even know
me."

"Oh, he knows you," the preacher said.

"Prove it," Fay said.

"He died for you, didn't he? Would you die for
somebody you didn't know?"

"He doesn't know me!" Fay screamed.

"O.K." the preacher gave up. "He doesn't know you.
But that doesn't keep him from loving you."

"Well I don't want anybody loving me who doesn't
know who I am."

"You can't stop him," the preacher said.

"I don't want it," Fay said.

"It doesn't matter if you want it or not. He loves
you."

Fay knew when she was beaten. She gave the
preacher five dollars for the mission and walked off.

But now, as she looked at Jesus's face hanging upside down on the poster, she understood about sacrifice. She knew exactly why Jesus did it. For the same reason she did it.

But Fay didn't want to be paid back for her sacrifice. She just wanted Lizzie to love her. No. Not even that, if she didn't want to. Just. . . What?

Nothing, Fay thought. I gave her my life because I loved her. All I wanted to do was show her I loved her.

But did I love her too much, Fay wondered. Tell her too often? Did I make her feel bad because she could never love me as much as I loved her? Maybe I did. Maybe I drowned her in it. Maybe I rained that love down on her so hard, for so long, that now all she wants is to live in the desert, where she has to go out and look for water, where she has to work for it, where, most of the time, when she thinks she sees it, it's only a mirage. She wants to feel lucky to find it, kneel down on the ground and praise the Lord for it. Oh boy.

Fay thought about Jesus again. His sacrifice had backfired too. He died on the cross for the sins of the world, but then the people decided, since it was already paid for, they might as well go ahead and sin some more.

It was true. Sacrifice made people mad.

* * *

Around the side of the church, Arnie had found an open cellar door. Deciding not to wait for the third police car, which was on its way with the search warrant, he took off his shoulder holster and slipped inside.

The cellar was more of a cave, really, more like a hole the church was dropped into. Rocky ooze and muck, with pools of water in particularly low places. It smelled like snakes. Arnie wasn't at all sure that there was a way upstairs from here, but in the beam of the flashlight he saw that, in fact, the only thing down here was a ladder. He sloshed over to it, then saw the trap door directly overhead.

The whole place felt like a rodent playground to him, particularly the ladder, the rungs of which, Arnie was sure the rodents were using as a latrine.

He took his first step up. It seemed solid enough. He held on with both hands and stepped up to the second rung, but not for long. It cracked right in two and Arnie fell seat first into the slime.

"Goddammit to hell," he said, and heard something climb the wall to get away from him.

"That's right, you little bastards, run," he said, drawing his feet up under him, so he could get up without putting his hands in the goo.

He tried the first rung of the ladder again,
then took the big step to the third rung, then the
fourth and hit his head on the ceiling. This was not
what he had in mind when he joined the force.

He braced himself on the ladder and gave the trap
door a hard shove with both hands. It opened with a
loud crack and slapped over on the other side. Arnie
waited a moment, in case anyone was inside to hear this,
and then climbed the next two steps, so that just his
head was poking up through the floor.

The air in the room was stale, and smelled vaguely
of old paper. There was a slight hint of chlorine.
That made no sense at all to Arnie, but he hoped it was
enough to kill whatever germs he'd breathed in the
swamp. He wiped his flashlight on his pants and brought
it up to floor level.

Directly in front of him was a pane of glass. He
took another step up the ladder, turned around and
realized he was in some kind of box. What's a box doing
at the front of a church?

"Ah. O.K.," he thought, "it's a baptismal tank."

Arnie wished, just for a moment, that he was ten
years old, fidgeting in the front pew on some hot humid
night, bored by the sermon and mad at having to sit there,
when all of a sudden, some guy poked his head up through
the bottom of the empty baptismal tank and took a look
around.

There was a painting on the back wall of the tank.

Jesus at the river baptising a little girl. It was
pretty sentimental stuff, but it made Arnie feel better
to see Jesus right side up.

Arnie climbed up the stairs on the other side of the
tank, and out onto the slightly raised floor that was
probably the pulpit. He did a quick sweep of the main
floor with his flashlight.

"What the hell?" he said, under his breath.

There were no pews. There was no altar. There was
only a lecturn, with a projection screen set up beside
it, and tables. Metal tables, maybe twenty of them,
covered with white tablecloths, with some funny metal
pieces attached to the foot of each table.

Feeling a little more comfortable now, he walked on
out to the tables for a better look. The tablecloths
were made of paper, and the tables weren't real
examination tables like in emergency rooms, but they
would do in an emergency, he thought. The metal pieces
at the end were stirrups, for women's feet during
deliveries and pelvic exams.

"Shit," he thought, "Fay is right about this whole
thing."

The last thing Arnie wanted to do was get in the
middle of a war about women's things. Women's things
were too messy for him, the blood, the milk, the
water breaking, the afterbirth, the whole thing. Women
were comfortable with mess, he knew. Not men. Men

liked death better.

There was a knock at the front door.

"Yeah," he called. "I'm all right."

"We've got the warrant," the other detective said.
"Open up."

He walked to the front door, slid the bolt out and
opened it slightly. When he turned back around to the
church, he saw the muddy path he had left on the floor.

"Whatcha got?" Heller stepped inside.

"Tables," Arnie said. "Some kind of clinic."

"Can't be," said Heller, walking on in. "There's
no medicine."

Heller was right. Even if they kept the medicine
locked up, there would at least be trays of cotton swabs
and gauze around.

Fay walked up behind the two detectives. It didn't
feel bad here at all. Girls had been here all right,
but not bad girls. Nice girls. Girls like Lizzie.

"What do you think?" Arnie asked her.

She had to laugh at him. "I think you shouldn't
have gone wherever you went to get whatever that is all
over you," she said.

""Yeah, I know," he said. "Did you see the Jesus?"

"Yes," she said. "It's a Tarot card all right.
Just an ordinary Jesus wouldn't have those coins falling
from his pockets. As far as I know, Jesus didn't need
pockets."

"What do you make of this?" Heller asked.

She backed away. She needed some air. "I don't know," she said. "It looks like a classroom to me."

"Yeah," he said, disappointed. "Me too."

"I have to call downtown," Arnie said to her. "Do you want to stay here?"

"I need to sit down," she said. "Can I sit on the steps out there?"

"Not with the print team coming, hon," Arnie said. "Why don't you come back to the car and. . ."

Fay remembered seeing a rocker on the porch of the house next door. "Do you think I could go next door and sit on that porch?" she asked.

"Nobody there to ask," the young detective said. "I rang the bell. Nobody home."

"Go ahead," Arnie said to her. "We'll be about twenty minutes."

The young detective loaded his Polaroid with a new pack of film, Arnie and Heller left for the cruisers at the curb and Fay stood there quietly, listening to the camera clicking.

There _was_ something else here, some other memory. Not the person at the lecturn though. Someone very small. No, not small. Short. No. Sitting. Someone sitting. Sitting in a wheelchair.

She shook her head. She was too tired to do this. The man in the wheelchair probably came here for the laying on of hands. Then he probably got up and walked home after the service. That wasn't any help at all.

She turned quickly and walked out of the church.

All she could do here was get out of the way.

* * *

When Fay stepped outside, it was morning. She took
her first gray breath of air and saw Lizzie and Paul
asleep on the deck of the big boat, lying on a double
air mattress, covered with a beige comforter. The ocean
sunrise was there too, but they didn't know it yet.

Paul pulled up on his elbows, and turned to look at
Lizzie, her hair shimmering in the early morning light.
He stood up and walked to the railing. And Fay had
to admit, nakedness actually seemed natural in the
morning. She even liked her own body in the morning.
But his, well, his was perfect. It was Apollo, or
David, one of those.

His back was surprisingly muscular for a man who
did no work that Fay knew of. Maybe he got those
muscles by playing all day. Tennis. Something like
that.

He stared out at the water, the light just frosting
the tips of the waves. It was the hour of nymphs and
sea sprites, of lutes and mermaids, when blue and pink
were simply shades of silver.

He climbed out onto the prow of the boat and
unwrapped the flag. It unfurled easily, then flapped
briskly, eager to rid itself of the creases of the night.
Lizzie was awake now, and watching him.

"Nice morning," she said quietly, when he was on the

deck again.

"Nice night," he said, and just stood there letting
her look at him.

She sat up, brushing her hair back away from her
face. Fay hadn't seen Lizzie's breasts for years now.
Paul was remembering them too.

"Don't get up," he said. "I'm coming back."

"Good," Lizzie said, and pulled the cover away to
show him the rest of what he remembered. She rubbed her
fingertips along the inside of her thigh, maybe
unconsciously, maybe not, maybe reminding him where he
had been, maybe just remembering, herself. She shifted
slightly, as if to get more comfortable.

He sat down beside her, eased his hand up to hers
on her thigh, then slipped it up to rest between her
legs.

Lizzie shifted again, and his fingers traced some
invisible line up her stomach to the little hollow
between her breasts.

"This is a sweet place," he said.

"It is?" she said.

"Yes."

"You mean on the sea?" she asked.

"No," he said.

Lizzie leaned back and Paul moved on top of her
with the same smooth motion Fay had seen from him on the
dance floor. Fay couldn't see Lizzie any more now, only
Paul. Only his back rising and falling, Lizzie's arms

around him, her hands pressing him to her, playfully at
first, then settling into a rhythm that was young, yes,
but felt oddly familiar to Fay. Lizzie wasn't a
beginner after all.

Didn't they worry that someone might come up here
and see them? No. Wasn't this what the morning was
for? Yes. Wasn't the sea the oldest lover of all?
Yes. Yes. Yes, Lizzie was whispering.

"You," he said, "you are. ." and he couldn't
finish his sentence. He gave in easily, naturally to
the ecstasy, as though it were his birthright.

Fay wiped her eyes. She hadn't wanted to see this.
Didn't want to know it. But there it was. Paul lay
quietly on his back, and Lizzie nestled up under his
arm, her hand resting peacefully on his chest.

As Fay walked across the yard of the church, Paul
pulled the cover back up over them, and they slipped
back easily into the dreams of the dawn.

* * *

Children, Fay thought, turning back to the church
for one more look. Where are these little children?
Not in that church, she knew that much. They'd never
been in there.

She continued on across the yard and up the cracked
concrete steps of the peeling yellow house next door.
It certainly did look empty. The grass had given up
years ago, the front screen hung from one hinge, and the
cobwebs outside the front windows were more closely
woven than the curtains hanging inside.

But as soon as Fay sat down in the rocker on the
porch, she felt it. Someone was watching her. Someone
inside this house. Her shoulders quivered from their
eyes on her back. It could be anybody, though, or
anything. It could be bats. Or somebody who died here.
Fay had learned long ago, not to jump to conclusions
about these watchers when she felt them.

She sat very still. If they watched long enough,
she would be able to tell where they were, anyway.

The gaze settled between her shoulder blades. She
felt a flush spread over her back. They were alive.

It was hard not to move, particularly hard in a
rocking chair, but just a little longer now and she
would know where they were.

There. She felt it. Just a slight prick, then a

tingle. She caught it, like a fishing line and held it
in her, then she followed the beam back and up to the
eyes behind the blinds in the upstairs window.

She didn't understand. Was this watcher in a
chair? The eyes were barely as high as the window sill.
And then she got it. This was no hermit in a
wheelchair. This was a child.

"Arnie!" she screamed, and tore off down the steps.
"Arnie! Quick!"

The policeman from the church came out of the door,
and Arnie raced up from his car.

"What is it?" he shouted.

She stumbled on the clawing roots of a tree in the
front yard, and fell into Arnie's arms.

"What is it?" he asked.

"There's a child in that house," she said, pointing
behind her. "Second floor. All the way to the right."

The other detective shook his head. "I knocked for
ten minutes," he said. "If there was anybody there..."

"So maybe they're locked up," Arnie said. "You
stay here with Fay. We don't have a warrant for this
place either."

As Arnie ran toward the house, the detective turned
to Fay. "How did you know that?" he asked.

"Let's see if I'm right, first."

"I think I better help him," the detective said.

"No," Fay grabbed his arm. "I think you better do
what Arnie told you."

At the rear door, Arnie slit a hole in the screen
with his army knife, and flipped up the hook. Then he
jimmied the lock on the door and drew his gun, just in
case Fay missed seeing who else was in this house.

The kitchen counters were covered with a thin coat
of dust. There was no food whatsoever, except for a
community of ants on the kitchen table, conferring over
a grape gumdrop.

He made his way to the hall, found the stairs, then
wondered, as he started up, where the hell the ants
thought they were going to take that gumdrop.

They'll give up, he thought. They'll just pick at
it until it's gone. Or maybe they'll each take a bite
and run it home to the kids. But some of them would
probably swallow their grain of grape sugar by accident
on the way. And the rest of them would probably forget
they even had kids and eat it on purpose. Ants can't be
very smart, he thought. With their mouths full, they
probably can't remember a damn thing. And then he
wondered how smart he was to be thinking about ants all
this time.

There were no lights on anywhere in the house, but
as his feet hit the upstairs hall floor, he heard the
little voice.

"Mommy?" It was a girl. "Mommy?" she cried.

Fay was right. Arnie hurried to the door.

"Is somebody in there?" he called.

Tiny feet pattered toward him across the floor and stopped. Arnie bent down to what he guessed was her level and spoke through the keyhole.

"Hello little one."

"Hello," the child answered softly, and Arnie heard her turn around and lean back against the door. From the sound of the hello, she must be sucking her thumb.

"What's your name, love?" Arnie said.

"Shelley," she lisped. "What's yours?"

Arnie guessed she was about three. "My name is Arnie," he said. "Do you know your other name?"

"Yes," she said, sounding so proud.

He had to laugh. "Well, Shelley, my sweet, what is it?"

"Chambers," she said.

Arnie pulled the list of missing kids from his back pocket. She was on it, all right. Shelley Chambers. Only the list said she had a sister, Susan, who was also missing.

"Shelley?" Arnie asked. "Is anybody in there with you?"

"They went away," she said, and Arnie could hear her fumbling with the door knob.

"O.K. now, Shelley," Arnie said, putting away his gun. "You have to listen real close, O.K.? I've come to take you to your Mommy," he said. "But the door is locked."

"When is Mommy coming?" she cried.

"As soon as I get the door open, we'll go see
Mommy."

"It's me, Shelley." she said.

"I know it's you Shelley, and this is me Arnie, and
I have to break the door down now, O.K.?"

"O.K."

"Good," Arnie said, standing up. "Now why don't
you go over to the window and see that lady on the
porch."

Shelley didn't answer, but he heard her mocassins
scuffing across the floor. He only had a second before
she'd return. He rocked back and crashed into the door,
grabbing it as it gave way, ending up on his knees in
the middle of the room, his hands prickling from the
splinters.

But when he looked up, there she was, a curly blond
cupid cowering in the corner.

"You broke the door," she said, and pointed.

"I wanted to see you," he said. "Doors are easy to
fix."

"Where's Mommy?" she asked.

Then he saw the other one, on the bed. Or what
looked like another one. A pile of blankets. Something
like a foot at the end.

"Who's that?" he said to Shelley, jumping up.

"It's Susie, silly," she said. She took her thumb
out of her mouth, padded over to her sister and pulled

the blankets back just enough for Arnie to see that the
sweet face was breathing.

"What's she doing over there?" Arnie asked.

"She's sleeping," Shelley said. "But we don't want
to wake her up, because she'll cry and we'll get upset."

Arnie walked to the bed. "We won't get upset," he
said, picking up the child in the blankets. "We haven't
heard anybody cry in a long time."

"Why not?" Shelley asked.

"Because I don't have any children," he said,
taking Shelley's soft hand.

"Why not?" she asked.

"I don't know," Arnie said, leading her out into
the hall.

"Why not?" she asked.

"I never thought about it, I guess," he said.

"Why not?" Shelley asked.

He was relieved when the sleeping Susan woke up and
started crying and they couldn't talk any more.

When they got to the stairs, Shelley came down them
backwards, then flapped toward the back door as if she
lived here. Arnie knew without a doubt that this was
the best morning's work he had ever done.

* * *

Shelley's parents arrived outside the house in ten minutes, followed shortly by an ambulance, the Crime Lab team, a dozen or so police cruisers, the Mayor, the Chief of Police, and about fifteen neighbors who had nothing better to do than stand behind the police barricades and try to guess what was going on.

The department was checking all the houses on the street now, hoping to find the rest of the children right here. Fay didn't think they would, but there was always a chance. They'd asked her if she'd go sit on every porch, door to door, but she'd said No. There wasn't that much of a chance.

"I wish you could have seen Shelley's face when I broke down that door," Arnie said, as he walked Fay to his car. "I wanted to just grab her up and...No," he paused. "The person I wanted to grab up was you."

"I'm real glad," she said. "I'm real. . ."

"You're real tired is what you are," he said. "But you ought to be real proud too."

"I am," she said, trying to smile. "It's just that. . "

"Fay," he said. "We all know you can't find the rest of them this easy. We're just happy to get started, that's all."

"I don't want to talk to the press," she said.

"You don't have to," he said.

"I don't want to talk to the girls' parents either," she said. "I just want to hide."

He put his arm around her. "You don't have to talk to anybody but me."

"I know that sounds weird," she said, "but. ."

"Who cares what it sounds like?" he said. "You found the girls, so you get what you want."

"Thanks," she said, and tried smiling, but it didn't feel right yet.

"Just lock the doors and scoot down in the seat," he said, putting her in the car. "They won't even know you're here."

But as soon as Arnie shut the door, the Mayor appeared at her window. Peter Ewing was lean and fit, but this morning, he was holding himself up with will, not muscle. He hadn't been to bed either. He couldn't even imagine it until his boys were found.

"Fay," he said, "I can't thank you enough for..." He stopped, seeing the exhaustion on her face. "Are you all right?"

"I'm fine," she said. "I just need to be. . ."

"Do you mind if I come sit with you a minute?" he asked, motioning toward the empty driver's seat.

She did mind, of course, but then she saw his eyes. Always before, they had been eager to see what happened next. This morning, they were shadowed by the fear that they had seen it all before.

"You're sure you're all right?" he asked, getting into the car.

"Yes," she said. "I'm fine. It's just. . ."

"What do you think it means?" he asked. "Are they all spread out, the kids? Hidden away like this all over the city?"

"Yes," she said. "I'm afraid they might be."

"What should we do?" he asked. "What if I went on TV and asked everybody to check the empty houses on their streets?"

"That's worth a try," she said.

"Good," he said. "I taped the announcement as soon as I heard."

She shook her head. "If you'd already done it, why did you ask me?"

"I thought you might know some reason why I shouldn't," he said. "That's all."

"No," she said wearily. "I don't know a thing."

"But you found these two didn't you," he said.

"Yes," she said, turning to look out the window. "But I can't promise that I'll be able to. . ."

"I know, I know," he said. "All the same I'd like to tell you what my sons were wearing."

He couldn't help it. He was trying to be the Mayor, trying to be concerned about all the missing children, but not for one second could he really forget that two of those children were his.

"Let me see your hand," she said.

"You can see my boys in my hand?" he asked, wiping his palm on his pants.

"If your boys are in your brain, they're in your hand," she said.

"Fay," he stuttered, "I didn't mean to put you to work here. I just wanted you to know that if you need anything, even to be left alone. . ."

"This is what I need," she said. "What we both need. Let me see your hand."

It would be rude to resist her now, so he turned on the interior light, gave her his right hand, and hoped one of his aides would come looking for him soon.

"This is your heart line," she said. "This one at the top." She saw the island on the line right away, but she couldn't talk about that yet.

"These little feathers pointing down, are disappointments in love, early in your life. One major one, here, see? How old were you? Twenty?"

"Yes," he said. "You're right." He tried to laugh. "I thought I was over it, though." He was very nervous now. "Not so, huh?"

She smiled. "You like to be in love," she said. "You like to be married."

"I guess so," he said, noticing Arnie's radio and wondering if a police operator somewhere was monitoring this conversation.

"You do," she said.

"That girl I loved," he said, quietly, "she barely
spoke English."

"Where were you?" Fay asked.

"I was in the Peace Corps in Africa," he paused.
"Avoiding the draft."

"You should've come see me before you went," she
said. "I could have told you travel was no good for
you."

He didn't laugh. "I could've died from loving her
I ate what she ate, swam where she swam, slept where sh
slept. I should've died from it, gotten one of those
tropical diseases and died. But I didn't. I escaped.
But I've been sick ever since from losing her. I feel
it every day, somewhere in me."

He tried to get back to the story. "I taught her
what little English she knew," he said, "but the more
she learned," he played with the turn signal, "the more
she wanted to go speak English with somebody else.
Somebody who didn't know how she learned it."

"Yes," Fay said. "That happens."

"Tell me about the boys," he said. "Are my boys
all right? Do you have any idea where they . . ."

"Here they are," she said. "These two little lines
over here, those are the boys." Then she spotted
something else. Good news. "Peter," she smiled,
"there's another child here."

He tried to pull his hand away, but she grasped it
more firmly.

"It's not for another three years," she said, and
felt him relax a little. "But it's . . ." She paused.

"What?" he asked.

"It's somebody else, another relationship, another
woman. Another marriage, I think."

She glanced up at him, suddenly wished she hadn't
gotten into this, released his hand, and tried to make
light of it. "There's nothing to be ashamed of," she
smiled. "You haven't met her yet."

"I can't be married again," he laughed, rubbing his
hands together. "It would ruin my career."

"Peter," she laughed. "Romance is on the way."
She patted his knee. "Cheer up."

They sat in silence for a moment, neither of them
quite knowing where things went from here. She had
already stumbled across more information than she felt
entitled to know. But she had to ask him about that
island on his heart line.

"Look at your right hand," she said. "There's a
little circle on your heart line. Do you see it?"

"Sure," he said, holding his hand up to the light.

"We call it an island," she said. "And islands on
the heart line mean a loss, an emotional loss."

"Not the boys," he said, his eyes wide with fear.
"Please not the boys."

"No," she said, "I don't think so." But of course

she wasn't sure of that. "Is there anything else you know of that could. . ."

"It's Vi," he said, staring out the front window. "It's not the boys. It's Vi. It's over between us."

"I'm sorry, Peter," she said.

He shook his head. "I'm sorry I sat down here," he said. "I was feeling pretty good before. Two kids found, twenty-five to go."

"Feeling good?" she asked.

"O.K.," he admitted.

"I could be wrong," Fay said.

He shook his head. "If I lose Vi," he said, "I'm finished as a politician."

"I don't think so," she said. "Once you get past that island, everything's going to be a lot better. Work _and_ life. I promise."

"Thanks," he said, wishing he could believe her.

She spoke softly, knowing that he was ready to be comforted. "Your hand is like a roadmap of your brain," she said. "An island begins to form as soon as you know you have to protect yourself. If the island is already there, then I'd say you were ready to deal with it, whatever it is. It can't. . . hurt you now."

He nodded, hoping she was right.

"Our brains," Fay said, "are smarter than we are. All they want to do is help. And all we have to do is stay out of their way."

"I didn't know this could be so personal," he said, reaching for the door handle.

"I don't know why you're complaining," she said, grinning, and trying to sound unconcerned. "All I told you was your boys are fine and there's someone new coming into your life. Lot of my clients would pay double to hear that."

"I have to go," he said, and stepped out of the car. He closed and locked the door, then straightened his tie, motioned to his driver, and walked around to Fay's window.

"Thanks again for finding these girls," he said.

"Your boys are all right," she said. "All the children, they're all right. I know it. They're just lost."

"I hope so," he said.

"Trust me," she said, grasping his hand and squeezing it tight. "I know these things."

He smiled. "That's better," he said. "That's what I wanted to hear."

Fay nodded and watched him walk toward his car. What Peter Ewing needed right now, was to be the Mayor again. But what he had to do first, was go pick up Vi at the airport.

Fay took a deep breath. Did she really know the children were all right? Yes. They were sleeping. But would they be all right when they woke up? That, she didn't know.

"Ready?" Arnie said, opening his side of the car.

"I didn't even <u>see</u> you," she said.

"I know," he said. "I waved, but you were. . "

"Lost," she said. "Are we ready to go?"

"We sure are," he said. "It's about time, too, don't you think?"

"I think we're late," she said.

"O.K.," he said. "Then we'll hurry." And he turned on his flashers and siren, and blasted off down the street.

7:00 A.M.

On his way to the car, Arnie had picked up the
special edition of the newspaper. As they drove, Fay
unfolded it and looked at the front page. The banner
headline read,

   27 CHILDREN ABDUCTED FROM THE STATE FAIR

"Want me to read this to you?" she asked him.

"Sure," he said. "If there's anything new in it."

But there wasn't. The main story had quotes from
the Security Chief at the fairgrounds, the Police Chief,
the Mayor and the parents. There was a list of hot-line
numbers and a statement that the city had posted a
reward for information leading to the arrest of the
kidnappers or the recovery of the children.

There was a companion piece in the next column
about two children who got off the school bus a year ago
and never made it home, and a background piece further
down, about missing persons nationwide.

Then across the bottom of the page were the
pictures of the children. She had seen the pictures
earlier this morning, but looked more closely this time.
One little girl was taking a shower under a garden hose.
Two little boys' heads were poking out of their tent in
the backyard, and one chubby boy was sitting in Santa's
lap in a department store. None of them were old enough
to read this page and learn what had happened to them.

She glanced at the weather forecast, found it

wasn't going to rain today after all, rolled the
newspaper back up, replaced the rubber band around it,
and remembered Lizzie's fourth birthday party.

Fay's mother had been quite withdrawn then,
crocheting in her room for ten, sometimes twelve hours a
day, her rocker thumping like a heartbeat, her lap
covered by the ever lengthening white tablecloth.

Lizzie was afraid of Granny and wouldn't go in the
room. There was, the little girl said, a bad smell in
there.

Fay kept asking Lizzie why didn't she go sing for
Granny. Lizzie said Granny didn't know any of her
songs. Fay said, "You could teach them to her," but
that only made Lizzie cry and grab the bottom of Fay's
dress.

In truth, Fay wasn't sure how much the old woman
could hear any more. What she hoped was that her mother
could hear Lizzie singing in the bathtub, but couldn't
hear her say that Granny smelled bad.

Lizzie's birthday was on Saturday that year.
Fay had invited her sisters and their families to the
party. Fay wore a red flowered dress and spiky black
heels, and served fried chicken and mashed potatoes,
Lizzie's favorite.

The cake from the bakery was dry and grainy, but
everybody said it looked good. Fay had asked them not
to put those ridiculous green leaves around the roses.

She said there wasn't a single thing in the whole of
creation that pasty colored green, but the baker forgot
and put the leaves on anyway. More leaves than ever,
Fay thought.

Then came the presents. The sisters brought
clothes for Lizzie, both of them thinking Fay had no
taste in clothes and that's why she and Lizzie looked
like gypsies. The cousins brought doll house furniture
and one of the brothers-in-law promised to build Lizzie
a doll house for it as soon as he got a free Saturday.

Finally, there was only one present left, a long
box wrapped in giraffe paper and tied with a yellow bow.
Lizzie looked up at Fay in wild delight and said she
already knew she didn't have one of these because she'd
never gotten a box like this before. The joy on the
child's face, the sheer ecstasy of anticipation, was
unlike anything Fay had ever seen.

Children are funny. They actually believe they are
going to get something they want. They can't imagine
what they might want, of course, but they know it's in
there. It's something they'll jump up and down
about, something they'll run around the room and show
everybody, something they might feel slightly bad about the
other kids not having one of, but finally, something
that will make them feel loved and understood. Children
think that presents are for them, that their parents
know who they are, and know how to make them happy.

Lizzie tore into the box. She threw off the

lid and ripped away the tissue paper and there it was.
A brown umbrella with a little dog head on the handle.

Fay saw it happen, saw Lizzie pull the shade
between them. The hopelessly disappointed little girl,
crying behind her eyes, stood up, held the thing out for
the relatives to see, and said, "It's an umbrella."

Fay didn't know why she had thought a four-year-old
would need an umbrella, much less want an umbrella.
Lizzie thought it was fun to get wet. What did she need
an umbrella for? So she could be a little grownup?
Lizzie had no idea, until that moment, that she would
ever be a grownup. But now she knew. And from the look
on her face, the idea didn't appeal to her.

Maybe Fay gave Lizzie the umbrella because she,
Fay, wanted a new umbrella. Or maybe because what Fay
knew about life then, was that it rained a lot.

Anyway, it was a bad idea. Fay saw that now.

But then, as they were all diligently admiring the
umbrella, and trying to convince Lizzie what fun it
would be to have one, they heard Granny's door open. No
one had expected to see her, much less to see her walk
into the living room, but walk she did, carrying a
package under her arm.

As Granny creaked into the room, Lizzie backed up
and tried to hide behind the piano.

"This is for her," Granny said, pointing to Lizzie.
"It's her birthday."

"Isn't that nice of Granny," Fay said, prying the child's fingers off the piano bench. "I wonder what it could be."

"Thank you, Granny," Lizzie said, like a well-behaved little robot.

"Open it!" Fay said to Lizzie, trying to show enough enthusiasm for both of them.

"You open it," Lizzie begged.

"No, you," Fay said. "Granny worked real hard to get you something and everybody wants to know what it is."

Lizzie accepted the package. She sank down on the floor and began to open the box. But she was much more careful this time. She worked very slowly, hoping to postpone the sight of another gift until say, next year, when she was older, when she could handle it better.

Granny didn't watch her. She seemed content enough just to sit in the rocker one of the cousins brought out from the bedroom. It was such a shock having the ancient woman with them, that nobody knew quite what to do. What could they say to her? How is your room? No. They couldn't even say they were glad to see her because they weren't at all sure they were.

Lizzie lifted the lid off the box. There was no tissue paper in it, there was only another box, a cheap red plastic box.

"What is it?" Lizzie asked, looking up at her mother for help.

"Well, I don't know," Fay said, in her cheeriest
voice. "Let's lift it out and see."

It was a too big for a lunch box, but it was about
the right shape, Fay thought. But it had some moving
parts inside, some of which were moving by themselves
already. Fay hoped it wasn't broken, the party was in
enough trouble without that.

"Here," Fay said, showing Lizzie the latch on the
side of the box. "You open it."

By now, Lizzie wasn't resisting her at all, but was
simply going along because she was the little girl, and
this was what little girls did on their birthdays. She
popped the little plastic flap open and raised the lid.

And then she shrieked, "It's a record player!"

She jumped up and nearly choked Granny to death
hugging her. "A record player! I've never had a record
player! Now I can listen to records!" And just like
that, Lizzie starting singing one of those songs kids
make up out of sentences. "I've got a record player,
I've got a record player." She danced around the room
holding her skirt out and kicking her legs up as high as
they would go.

"You have records too," Fay said, finding them
taped to the inside of the box.

"I want to hear it!" Lizzie squealed, and went over
to hug Granny again. Everybody clapped and said they
wanted to hear it too. Granny looked up from her

crocheting and said what she wanted was some Bourbon.

So, as Lizzie held onto the arm of Granny's chair, rocking her faster than the old lady had ever gone in her life, Fay started playing the records. They heard the Animal Supermaket, The Three Little Pigs, Little Red Riding Hood, the ABC song and Twinkle Twinkle. They listened to all the records twice, in fact, before the rest of the family remembered wherever it was they had to go that afternoon.

After they left, Granny continued to crochet and Fay sat on the floor with Lizzie until bedtime, wishing somebody would tell her what she was supposed to learn from this.

The next day, Fay subscribed to the record of the month club for Lizzie, and their life was changed forever. Fay's made-up stories had been just fine for a baby. But now, Lizzie could fly with the Eagle and the Thrush and cheer for Dumbo, puzzle over the Grasshopper and the Ants, and imitate the Queen Ant's firm but fair voice.

In another year, Lizzie could identify numbers, so she didn't need Fay to tell her which record was the beginning of Cinderella. And the year after that, Lizzie found books. Night after night, year after year, Fay would see Lizzie sitting across the room in a chair, but when people are reading, you never really know where they are.

Fay didn't know what had happened to that little

record player. But she knew what had happened to Lizzie
that day. And knew that it was irreversible. And she
knew, finally, that Granny could hear absolutely
everything.

* * *

"How long do we have?" Fay asked Arnie, as they parked in front of his house.

"Til somebody needs us someplace else," he said. "We should take a nap if we can."

"Arnie, how can we take a nap?" she asked.

"Easy," he grinned. "Pull the shades." He turned off the engine. "Come on."

Fay yawned in spite of herself.

Arnie lived on the top floor of a white frame rowhouse in an area called Germantown. When he first moved in, he agreed to paint the green shutters once a year instead of having his rent go up. But every year after that, the landlady had added one more chore to his list, reasoning that if he lived there for six years, he would be paying six rent increases, not one. After ten years, the landlady didn't see any reason to keep the ladders, hammers and paint in her apartment, when Arnie was needing them virtually every weekend, so he moved everything up to his place, and now he lived in what looked like a one-bedroom hardware store.

Fay liked being there. She liked the sawdust he swept into the fireplace, and the screwdrivers standing with the knives and forks in the drain rack beside the sink. There was a can of turpentine on the floor in the shower, and in the bedroom, two sawhorses on which his

paint-spattered drop cloths hung folded and serene like
prize quilts.

He unlocked the front door. "When we get
upstairs," he said, "we'll make a pot of coffee and call
Lizzie. If she's not home, we'll get the Chief to post
somebody at your house to watch for her." He collected
his mail from yesterday. "Then we'll drink the coffee,
take a shower and go to bed."

"Have you seen a big Indian anywhere?" she asked,
following him up the stairs.

"A big what?" he asked.

She saw it quite clearly. "There's a big Indian
somewhere, like a sign, only 3-D. A statue."

He picked up the newspaper outside his apartment.
"An Indian?"

"It's plastic, I guess," she said. "Or wood maybe,
like a tobacco store Indian."

He opened the door, pitched the paper on the hall
table and walked into the kitchen. "Sure there is," he
said. "It's that Indian Point Shopping center out in
the south end. Big Indian. Thirty feet tall maybe."

There was no place for Fay to sit down in the
kitchen, so she leaned against the refrigerator as he
filled the old percolator with water. She had given him
a Mister Coffee for his birthday one year, but he never
used it. He said the coffee didn't smell right unless
it perked.

"That's it, then," she said.

"It what?" he said.

"That's where they're going to set up the orange truck," she said.

He lit the burner under the coffee. "They're going to drive the truck to a shopping center?"

She nodded, picking up the phone.

"And do what?" he asked.

"I don't know," she said, dialing her number. "Park it, I think."

He looked at the pot, listened to the hiss and static of the water as it began to feel the heat. He had to have a break here. He didn't want to know about the orange truck. Not now, he didn't.

Fay hung up the phone. "Lizzie's not there," she said.

"I'm going to take a shower," he said. "You watch the coffee. When it starts to perk, turn it down."

Fay nodded, she knew a little about coffee herself, and patted his arm as he passed her.

But just as he hit the hallway, the telephone rang. He looked at it, swore under his breath and picked it up.

Fay looked down at the floor. She had helped him lay this tile one year. They had done a great job. This green and gold tile was the best thing about this kitchen.

"What do you mean, where am I?" Arnie shouted into

the phone. "I came home to take a shower! What's the
matter, did everybody else quit?"

Arnie covered the phone with his hand. "It's the
Chief," he whispered. "He wants to talk to you."

Fay shook her head.

"She's going to cost you plenty on this thing,"
Arnie said to the Chief.

"How much?" the Chief asked.

"She'll do it for ten thousand," Arnie said.

"Ten thousand dollars?" the Chief said. "How about
a hundred dollars an hour."

Fay had never heard Arnie do this before, negotiate
her salary.

"Christ almighty," Arnie said. "She's working
twenty-four hours a day. She'll cost you ten thousand
in four days. Better take the flat fee, Chief."

"O.K." the Chief said, "ten thousand."

"And another thousand for each kid she finds
alive," Arnie said. "You can get that back from the
parents."

"I can try," the Chief said. "Do you know where
she is?"

"No," Arnie said, winking at Fay. "But I know how
to find her."

"O.K., then," the Chief said. "I'll see you both
down here in an hour."

"No," Arnie said. "It'll take me til nine o'clock
to find her. Meet us at the Indian Point Shopping

Center at nine."

"Why there?" the Chief asked. "Does she know
something?"

"She knows everything," Arnie said. "Did we pick
up the orange truck yet?"

"No," the Chief said.

"O.K.," Arnie said.

Fay was trying to get his attention, but he knew
what she wanted.

"Punch up the harbor list for last night," Arnie
told the Chief.

Arnie heard the Chief getting the list up on his
computer monitor. Fay walked over to listen.

"Got it," the Chief said.

"Get to the private boats," Arnie said. "I'm
looking for a big yacht that left last night about three
o'clock."

"Yeah," the Chief said, "here it is. God almighty,
this is a big fucking boat. Miss Majesty's her name.
But it's not scheduled to sail til tomorrow night."

"They could've left early, I guess," Arnie said.

"Does this have something to do with the kids?" the
Chief asked.

"Just check it," Arnie said. "I want to know
everything there is to know about that boat."

"They don't have to tell us where they're going,
you know. It's a private citizen. They can go wherever

the hell they want."

"Find out where they're going," Arnie said. "Find
out who it belongs to. And get a warrant ready."

Fay mouthed a thank-you to Arnie, and walked back
into the kitchen. If Arnie did leave, she would miss
this place. She would miss the morning light in this
kitchen. Not that it streamed in, or flooded the room
or anything. It seemed, well, almost amused to be here,
like what a trick it had pulled to get here, stealing
around the neighboring housetops, ducking under the tree
limbs, jumping to the roof of Arnie's building, then
sliding down and slinging itself in this window right at
the last minute. If Arnie left, she would miss him,
too. But how could she go so far away? Could she go?
She couldn't go. Could she?

"I love you," he said, coming back to find her.

"I know," she said, turning around.

"Come here," he said, opening his arms.

And as the coffee started to perk, they wished, as
neither of them had ever wished before, that everything
would just stop now, that they could hold each other
forever like this, in a space just wide enough for one
embrace, with the cabinets and the appliances standing
guard against time and the world.

"I need a shower too," she said, finally.

Arnie released her, and turned around to the broom
closet. "I think I've got another bar of that, what is
it, Dove soap," he said. "Yeah," he smiled, finding the

soap. "I sure do." He held it out to show her. "I
don't want to force you though."

"Force me to take a shower?"

"Force you to make love with me."

She looked at his face. It was a ragged face,
eyebrows going gray, and eyes a little red around the
edges from the night, but a handsome face, easily and
happily male. He never thought about his face, it was
just another thing he'd always had, like long arms. He
wouldn't know what to think about it. She did.

"You watch the coffee," he said, turning the burner
down to medium. "You'll know when it's ready by the
smell. Just take the basket out and turn it way down.
I'll be out by then."

And he walked down the narrow hallway to the
bathroom, leaving Fay holding the soap.

* * *

Fay stood there a moment, then reached for the phone
to call Gail.

But before she could pick it up, the phone rang.
Was it going to be one of those days, she wondered.
Those days when she knew every goddamn thing one-half
second before it happened? She hoped not. Those days
seemed so long.

"Hello," she said.

The voice on the other end was frantic. "Fay,
thank God I found you," Gail cried. "They called me!
The people who took Beth. They just called me!"

"Jesus Christ," Fay said. "What did they say?"

Gail was hysterical. "They said I would have to work
to get her back. They said there wasn't any other way
to wake people up. They said if I wouldn't help, I'd
never see Beth again. They said they were serious, they
were going to win this thing once and for all, and then
the whole country would thank them."

"Right," Fay said. "What did they tell you to do,
honey?

"Wait for another call, they said. I told them I'd
do anything."

"That's was exactly right, Gail. Did they say what
this thing was they wanted to win?"

"No," Gail said.

"All right," Fay said. "Did you hear anything in

the background?"

Gail blew her nose. "I guess it was a phone booth, but I don't know, I just. . ."

"Breathe, Gail," Fay said. "Nice deep breaths."

"I'm sorry," Gail said. "But that voice just. . I don't know. It made me mad, it made me sick."

"Breathe, Gail," Fay said. "Beth is obviously all right or they wouldn't have called you. They need you for something. So, until they get what they want from you, they're not going to hurt Beth."

Gail wanted to believe that. "O.K., O.K. I'll try." Gail cleared her throat and made an effort at normal conversation. "Did Lizzie get home all right?"

"No," Fay said. "I mean, she's all right, but she didn't come home."

"Did she call you?"

"No," Fay said. "But I've been with Arnie all night, so that helped. You stay by the phone, like they said to, and I'll call you as often as I can, just to check."

"Where are you going to be?" Gail asked.

"I don't know," Fay said. "But I'll call you. Or if you need me, the police can always find Arnie."

"O.K.," Gail mumbled.

"It's all going to be all right," Fay said. "You'll do what they want, and they'll give Beth back."

Gail managed a broken "Thanks, Fay," and hung up

the phone.

By the time Fay got to the bathroom, Arnie was already in the shower, balanced on one foot, his other leg bent up so he could soap his calf, the water beating down on his back and running over his neck and ears in slick streams.

"That was Gail on the phone," Fay said.

"What?" he asked, scrubbing his foot, massaging the big toe that had bothered him since last summer when he had dropped a can of creosote on it.

"The kidnappers called Gail," she said, and sat down on the wicker clothes hamper under the little window.

He turned off the water and opened the door. "What did they want?"

But she waved him back in the shower and shouted over the noise of the water. "They don't want money," she said. "They want the parents to do something."

"Do what?" Arnie asked, rubbing the soap back and forth between his hands to work up a good lather, then squirting the soap back into its greenish metal dish.

"They didn't say," Fay said. "They're going to call them back later."

"Sons of bitches," Arnie said.

A cloud of steam was forming on the ceiling, and Fay could feel her hair frizzing at the ends. Arnie sudsed his chest, under his arms and his neck. Then he reached for the soap one last time to wash his face.

"Would you hand me another shampoo, hon?" he asked, spitting soap bubbles as he talked.

Fay went to the closet and picked out the Head and Shoulders from the tubes of caulking compound and super glue. As he opened the shower door, a puff of steam escaped and swirled around her. She put the shampoo in his hand and a trail of bubbles ran from his arm over the plastic tube and down her arm.

"That the right one?" she asked.

He nodded. "Thanks," he said, and closed the door.

The misty cloud picked up a faint medicine scent.

He called over to her. "God this feels good," he said. "Want to get in here with me?"

She shook her head and sat back down on the hamper. He stood directly under the water now, rinsing his hair first, then turning around to rinse his face and the rest of his body. He held up his arms and twisted slightly from the waist, as though he were showing the water where to find the suds. And when the soap was gone, was only circling around his feet toward the drain, he just stood there letting the water pound him.

"Great," he said. "Just great. Best thing in the world."

"It's seven-thirty, Arnie," she said.

"Christ!" he said, and turned off the water. Then he smiled, opened the door and stepped out onto the rug. "Good morning," he said.

"Feel better?" she asked.

He reached for a towel. "I look pretty good for an old man, don't you think?"

"Why do you think I'm sitting here," she said.

"Don't blame you a bit," he said, and wrapped the towel around his waist.

"Did you try Lizzie again?" he asked.

"No," she said, stepping out of her shoes and taking off her dark stockings.

"Why not?"

"She's not there, Arnie,"

"How do you know unless you call?"

"I know."

"Want me to call, just in case?" he asked.

"No," she said. "Thanks, though." She unbuttoned her blouse and walked out of the bathroom to find a hanger for it. "Lizzie's not a virgin, though. You were right about that," she said.

"Of course I was," he said, reaching blindly for the hand towel.

"How did you know?" she asked, coming back in wearing her half slip and bra.

He dried his face, hung the towel back up neatly, turned to her, and sighed with pleasure. He slipped his hands under her bra straps and eased them gently down over her shoulders. "I know Lizzie's not a virgin," he said, "because she's got your body. And young men. . . ." he let his fingers trail along the lacy edge of her bra

until they came to rest on the clasp between her
breasts. "Young men," he undid the clasp, eased the bra
away and cupped her breasts in his hands. "Young men,"
he whispered, "are not so different from old men."

"I don't know why you keep calling yourself old,"
she said, as she stepped out of her slip and panties.

He opened the medicine cabinet for his comb.
"Because old people don't work," he said, looking in the
mirror. "If I'm old, then I don't have to work." He
ran the comb through his wet hair. "All I have to do is
catch fish and get laid."

"Well, you don't look old," she said.

"Go on," he said, opening the door for her. "Get
in the shower. I'm getting older by the minute."

She smiled. He was getting something by the
minute, that was obvious, but it wasn't older.

Fay stepped into the shower, Arnie blew her a kiss
through the door, and went to the kitchen for his
coffee.

* * *

Fay knew she would never enjoy a shower the way
Arnie did, the way men did. Women, she thought, women
just get clean in the shower. Men play in the water.
It's no trouble for men to get wet. That's the
difference. It's fun. Men and children.

Lizzie was awake now, Fay could feel it. She
didn't even have to shut her eyes, this time. They were
standing in the boat's galley. Not Lizzie and Paul.
Lizzie and Paul's mother. Mrs. . . What? What was her
name? Ah. Honey. God. Honey. Lizzie was watching
Honey crack eggs into a fine old copper bowl.

"What does your father do?" Honey asked, handing
Lizzie a wedge of parmesan and a grater.

"I don't know," Lizzie answered. "He ran off."

"Oh, I'm sorry," Honey said.

"That's all right," Lizzie said. "We weren't all
that crazy about him."

Lizzie was lying. They'd been wild about her
father. Both of them. Wild about him.

"Careful of your fingernails, darling," Honey said,
reminding herself to buy a food processor for the boat.

Lizzie put the cheese down on the counter and
stepped out of the way. Honey was happy to finish the
job correctly.

Fay was desperate to know where the boat was going.

"Where are we going?" Lizzie asked.

"Oh, didn't Paul tell you?" Honey laughed. "California."

"Aren't we going the wrong direction?" Lizzie laughed.

"Darling," Honey said patiently, "you can't go the other direction by boat. It's almost solid land the whole way."

"Yes," Lizzie smiled. "So I've heard."

"How long do you think you'll be with us?" Honey asked, turning the heat on under the omelet pan.

"Is there any way for me to get off?" Lizzie asked.

"If you were desperately ill," Honey said, pressing a buzzer to call the steward, "We could all the Coast Guard for a helicopter. But the last time we had to do that, they said we'd have to pay for it from now on."

"Well," Lizzie said, brightly, backing out of the narrow room toward the stairs, "So far, I feel just fine."

Fay washed herself quickly and turned off the water. That was enough. The girl was gone. Happily gone. Gone off on every girl's kidnap fantasy come true. Somebody will come get me, it goes. Somebody who knows I don't belong here. Somebody who knows what I really want. Somebody who has nothing to do but play with me. Somebody who never says No. Somebody fun.

* * *

Fay walked out of the bathroom and into Arnie's
bedroom.

"Feel better?" he asked from the bed.

"Lizzie isn't coming back," Fay said, opening his
closet and pulling out the blue cotton robe she gave him
last summer. "They've sailed for California."

"The Chief said the boat isn't scheduled to leave
til tonight," he said.

"They left," Fay said. "She's gone."

"Do you want me to call and check?" he asked,
putting the newspaper on the nightstand and reaching for
his coffee cup.

"No," she said.

"She'll be back," Arnie said. "I promise. She's
all right."

Fay nodded. She'd said the same thing to Gail.

Fay had to think about something else. She had to
try anyway. "I don't know why you don't like this
robe," she said.

"I like it," he said. "It's just that I don't wear
robes. But if I'm ever sick, I'll be real glad I have
it, love."

She walked over to the window. "I always give
people the wrong things," she said, wrapping the
venetian blind cord around her finger. "For years I've

given you these . . ."

Arnie was friendly but firm. "Fay," he said "we
love the things you give us."

She turned to face him. "But why don't I know what
you want? I know all this useless stuff, like a lady
shows up for a reading and I know she hurt her back
that morning falling off a ladder in her closet, but I
don't know what Lizzie wants for her birthday, or what
you want for your birthday, or what you and Lizzie don't
want for your birthdays."

"Please. . . Fay," he said, extending his hand to
her.

"What hon?" she asked simply, dropping the cord and
turning around to face him.

"Please come love me. Please don't worry about
birthdays or Lizzie right now. Just let me have an
hour, or half an hour even. You have the whole day to
hate yourself, if you feel like it. I just have this one
hour and then I have to go back to work. Please," he
said, "I need you."

She walked toward him, slipping off the robe to
reveal her nakedness.

"That's better," he whispered.

They had loved each other so long and so well, that
sometimes, like now, just looking at each other was
enough to bring them to an aching readiness. But this
long love had also taught them how to wait, how to

linger in the memories of other nights, other days,
other afternoons. His eyes fell from her face to her
slim neck and smooth shoulders to the brimming fullness
of her breasts. He approved as her nipples rose to meet
his gaze, their tawny coral still a miracle of
coloration to him.

Just looking, he could taste them. It was summer,
there would be a hint of salt this morning, and a trace
of soap, then finally, in the shadows under her breasts,
when he got there, he would find the warm scent of
camellias, a fragrance she had used for so long, her
skin yielded it now, even fresh from the shower.

"What are you looking for?" she asked, easing one
knee up on the bed.

"Oh, you know," he said, accepting her breezy
invitation, his eyes sweeping the widening triangle
between her thighs. "Peace of mind."

She smiled. The list of his answers to this
question was as long as their love. She took his cock
in her hands and stroked it, peacefully, at first, then
more deliberately until it swelled full ripe in her
hands.

He began to float, moored only by his manhood. He
was a boy, a boy in a dream, feeling the sun's pulsing
heat as it began to burn its way through the morning
haze. Her fingers circled him languidly, urging the
flesh to tighten further still.

He reached for her, for something to hold on to,

for her arms, then her waist, and pulled her gently
forward. "Ah," he gasped, the sudden silkiness of her
skin registering in his brain like an electric shock.

"Yes," she breathed, slipping down over him into
the heat and the wet that was no longer clearly his or
hers.

"Please," he said, "I need a few of my brains for
the rest of the day."

"No you don't," she said. "You like this,
remember?"

"I remember," he said.

He knew what she was going to do now, glide up and
then down, her hands planted on his shoulders, her body
luring him away from his mind, his past, his life, and
into his own pulsing heartbeat. He loved the sound of
it, the lapping, tidal rhythm of it.

He opened his eyes to watch. His lips parted
slightly, no longer under his control, and he looked
into her eyes, and directly, he thought, down into her
soul. She knew him so well, how could he not love her?
He blinked, as two quick tears filled the outside
corners of his eyes. He didn't know why that happened,
but he didn't mind it. Just that it was out of place.
We can't cry over this. It's not the last time, it's
just another morning together.

He pulled her down to lie on top of him, then
wrapped his arms around her, rolled over, and lifted

himself high above her. He paused a moment.

"Do you want to start over," he asked, "or shall I go on?" She didn't answer him. She never did. And he always took that to mean he should go on. It was a silly question, but one he enjoyed asking.

Fay felt him relax, heard his easy assured sigh, and knew he was going to take his time here. Sometimes, there was an urgency he made no effort to control, but today, he would leisurely drive her up to the edge and then quite good-naturedly push her over. If there were an accrediting organization for this, Arnie would be a life master.

His was not the giddy agitation she remembered in young men, or the noisy exhortation, the somber preparation, endless narration, or frenzied determination she had, unfortunately, shared with others. With Arnie, it was all effortless, uncomplicated pleasure. He was a born lover, a natural in bed. It seemed like something he'd always known how to do. He never consciously showed off his skills. He may not have even known he had them. He was just perfectly at home between her legs. In fact, he was so goddamn comfortable with it all, that sometimes, Fay half-expected to hear him start whistling.

She shifted slightly under him, and felt a tongue of fire race between them, as her movement forced him deeper inside her.

"God you feel good," he said, and lowered himself

onto her. She wrapped both legs around his waist. "I
could do this all day," he said.

"I know," she whispered, licking the beads of
moisture from his neck.

"I don't know why anybody ever does anything else,"
he said. He brushed his tongue behind her ear, then
skimmed up along her temples, as though nothing were
going on below, as though they were just beginning. And
then he found her mouth, slipped his tongue under hers,
circled around to her throat and dared her to breathe.
She knew there was no going back now, and knew that he
did not want her to wait for him.

For all the things Fay saw in her life, her
visions in bed with Arnie were her favorites. She'd
never told Arnie about these accompaniments, but guessed
he was probably doing the same thing. When he didn't
want to come, he'd told her, he thought about laying
roof tile. So it was reasonable to assume that when he
<u>did</u> want to come, there was also something he thought
about.

She saw herself leaning back against the railing of
a boat. It was night, there was a moon. There was
another boat, a little way off in the water. There was
a man standing at the railing of that boat. He saw her.
She wore a loose gauze robe which fluttered in the soft
breeze to disclose her bareness, which robe was tied
only at the neck, which tie she loosed as he watched.

Her hand stirred, on her thigh, then drifted in open suggestion across her pale skin to comb lazily through her thick chestnut ruff.

Another man, her companion on the boat, emerged naked from the shadows, or the cabin, she never quite knew where he came from, or who he was, even. He brushed the robe away from her hips and spread her legs with his hands.

The man watching from the other boat lit a cigarette, signaling his attention. But her attention was now drawn sharply to the throbbing flesh suddenly thrust into her from the darkness. She gasped from the insistence of the entry, the immediate, the unyielding demand.

She grabbed the railing with both hands. She couldn't breathe, she couldn't see, she could only gulp the black air, and utter sharp cries of surging need, cries that were clearly heard by the man on the other boat. The ringing in her ears pitched high and higher, the pressure coursing from its white-hot center, ripping up her spine, clawing at her neck, and finally stabbing through the back of her brain to find the hair-breadth trip-wire, detonating a massive explosion, blasting and shattering a brilliant blue star into the empty black sky of her mind. Its particles shimmered silently for an instant, then floated weightlessly out into the universe.

Arnie stoked her hair gently, brushing the wet

curls around her temples back into place.

"Was that nice?" he asked.

She didn't answer. She was still trying to get her
breath.

"It was nice to watch," he said.

"It was nice, Arnie," she said, relieved to find
that she could still talk.

"I don't think I'll come today," he said. "I'll
come tomorrow."

"What if we can't be here tomorrow?" she managed.

"No," he said, "I want you to stay til tomorrow.
Stay right here til tomorrow." He rose up on his hands
so she could breathe more easily. "You won't be bored, I
promise. We'll take it real easy, like we're screwing
for charity and we get a thousand dollars an hour."

"Oh you think you can last another hour, do you?"
she asked, with a little laugh.

"I do," he said.

She put her fingers in her mouth to get them wet,
then stroked her nipples, pulled them toward him like an
offering, and watched his brain give way, watched it run
for cover as his eyes were stunned by the sight below
him.

He watched as long as he could, until his eyes
glazed, until his head was spinning, until he released
his appetite from his control, his driving hips no
longer restrained, no longer considerate and masterful,

but loosed to their fury, wild in their unbridled rush
toward the quivering wondrous appeasement of his hunger.

And in the quiet that followed, a cool morning
breeze blew across them. He kissed her cheek. She
smoothed his forehead, then wrapped her arms around him
tenderly.

"How old did you say you were?" she asked.

"I forget," he said.

"Well, that's all you forget," she said.

"Is that a compliment?" he asked, his eyes still
closed.

"It is."

"Thanks."

"You're welcome," she said. "Any time."

"How about tomorrow?" he asked.

"Tomorrow is good," she said.

"All right then," he sighed, easing himself up,
then over to rest beside her on the bed. "It's a date."
He found her hand, squeezed it, and they drifted into a
familiar double sleep they both knew would be the last
luxury of the new day.

8:00 A.M.

The Mayor was waiting in his limousine on the
tarmac when Vi's plane landed. The other passengers
didn't understand why they had to wait while she got off
first. But they'd seen enough movies to be mildly
intrigued by the scene. Through his car window, the
Mayor watched their heads, framed in the portholes, as
they followed her down the ramp and over to his car.
When Peter realized he was watching them instead of his
wife, he wondered what that meant.

An aide opened the car door for her, and she sat
down without saying anything. He leaned over to kiss
her, but before he could get there, she reached for the
button to close the window behind the driver.

The Mayor sat back as the window sealed them in. He
wanted to hold her, he wanted to be an ordinary man in
pain. But she was never very receptive in the morning.
So maybe he'd start off with the good news. That should
make her feel better, he thought.

He rolled his newspaper into a tube and tapped his
knee with it as he talked. "There's wonderful news," he
said, as they drove off. "Fay Morgan just found the
first two."

"You don't mean that fortune teller," Vi said.

"That's her," he said. "One of the other mothers
is a good friend of hers. She got right on it."

Vi was not pleased. "Peter, for God's sake, can't

we do better than a fortune teller?"

"Vi, she found two of the children already."

"What are the police doing?" she snapped.
"Shuffling her cards for her?"

"Vi, Vi," Peter said, "they're doing everything they
can. But Fay thinks. . "

"I don't want to hear what she thinks," Vi said.
"I want you to find my boys." She opened her purse.
"How much money would the city pay?"

"As ransom, you mean?"

"Yes, as ransom," she sighed.

He thought a moment. "I don't think the city can
pay anything. If the kidnappers ask for a ransom, we'd
have to pay it ourselves."

"You're the Mayor!" she said.

He wished he had sent one of his aides to get her.
Let somebody else fill her in on the details before he
saw her. He could've been waiting at his desk, she
could've come in, closed the door behind her, and walked
into his arms.

"The city can't pay a ransom, Vi," he said. "I
wouldn't even ask."

"What about the other parents? Do they have any
money?"

"Maybe the kidnappers don't want money," he said.

"What else is there, Peter?" she asked, wishing he
would wake up about all of this.

They rode for a while without saying anything. The Mayor wanted to ask her how her speech went, or how the flight was, or even if she'd had breakfast yet. He wanted to ask questions for which there were answers. He had been expecting her to cry, but now he was beginning to fear she wouldn't.

Finally, he forced himself to talk. "I have to tell you what Fay thinks because you might get a question about it from the press."

But Vi still didn't want to hear it. "You never should've gotten involved with that woman. All she wants is publicity for herself. It's my boys who are gone, but who's getting all the attention? She is."

"She found two girls!" he said. "Isn't that _worth_ some attention, Vi?"

"All right," she muttered, reaching in her purse for her hairbrush. "What does Miss Fay think?"

"She thinks it's about abortion," he said. "And that you might be the real target of this whole thing. She thinks they want to force you to take back your position on abortion, and admit that it's a crime. Make a public statement or something."

"Well," Vi said quickly. "I could have told you that." She brushed her hair.

"What do you mean?" he asked.

"We've been expecting something like this," she said.

"Who has?" he asked, not following her at all.

"We have," she said, "in the movement. We're
targets. We always have been."

"You haven't been in the movement long enough to
be a target," he said.

"No," she smiled, "but I have a position now."

"What position?" he asked. "Did something happen
at the convention?"

"I'm your wife," she said. "Remember?"

He remembered all right. His staff had talked to
him several times about her pro-abortion stand. It
could hurt him in the next campaign, they said.

But he had known it was no use asking Vi to abandon
it. Sure, he wished she'd adopted some other cause,
like handicapped children, or meals-on-wheels, but he
couldn't ask that either. So he simply told her that he
couldn't go with her when she spoke on the subject, and
he couldn't cosign the letters of appreciation she wrote
to abortion clinics.

He was, in fact, pro-abortion, himself. That is,
he believed it should be available to women who needed
it. He knew there were families who couldn't afford
more children, and teenagers who were too young to be
mothers, and any number of other situations where lives
would be saved by it.

But abortion was a hard thing to fight for in an
election. It was hard to pound the lecturn and campaign
for it. He admired the people who did, but he couldn't.

He just hoped the Supreme Court would stay strong about
it. The truth was, he thought, nobody likes to think
about it, nobody wants abortion to be necessary. It's
makes you kind of sick to think about it. And it makes
us sad that that we don't have enough money or space or
time or love for all the children we make, but the fact
is, we don't. Better not to have them, than have them
grow up knowing there really isn't any place for them.

Abortion is for the Supreme Court to uphold, he
thought. Politicians have to get elected, have to
represent all the people, so they can't always say what
they believe. But the Supreme Court only has to say
what's right. They can protect the option of abortion,
in the name of freedom, in the understanding of human
error, in the faith in a second chance. Only the
Supreme Court can insure the safety of the women of this
country. Everybody else is just too human.

The Mayor's limousine turned off the expressway now
and headed for City Hall.

"Did you fire him yet?" Vi asked.

"Fire who?" he said.

"Fire that aide who lost my boys."

"Vi," he said, "I can't fire him without letting
the kidnappers know that two of the children are ours."

She turned on him in shock and anger. "What did
you say?"

He unrolled the newspaper, and showed her the
twenty-five pictures. "I kept Kevin and Kerry's names

out of it," he said. "We decided it was. .

"Who decided?"

"The staff and I decided. ."

"Why didn't you tell me this last night?" she
screamed.

He tried to talk calmly. "We didn't really decide
til. . "

But she wouldn't let him finish. "You mean I'm
supposed to pretend my boys are in school today?" She
was wild with rage.

He looked at her. "Yes," he said.

She couldn't believe it. She just couldn't believe
it. "Don't I have anything to say about this at all?"

"I could be wrong, Vi, but I just don't think it's
a good idea for the kidnappers to know who they have.
It will be easier to get all the children back if it
doesn't get political."

"It's political already, Peter."

"Well, I don't have to give them the platform," he
said.

"You don't want to give me the platform," she said.

"Or you either," he said. "That's right. I want
to try to keep this thing as ordinary as possible, an
ordinary terrible crime. And the city is going to solve
it, get the children back and punish the criminals, not
because they took the Mayor's boys, but because they
took the city's children." He paused. "I'm asking you

to go along with us as long as you can."

"You're not asking," she said, "you're telling."

"Well," he said, and thought a minute. "Yes. I guess I am."

The car pulled into the alleyway that was the Mayor's private entrance. The guards at the street saluted, the sidewalk was lined with photographers. Two aides opened their doors, and the Mayor and Vi, having nothing further to say to each other, got out of their respective sides of the car.

* * *

Fay was awake, but she hadn't decided what to do
about it yet. Her eyes opened, found they were not
able to stay open by themselves, and closed again slowly.
Arnie was still snoring quietly, lying on his side
facing the wall. She considered getting up, but there
really wasn't anything to do in Arnie's apartment. He
didn't subscribe to any magazines, or have any plants
she could water, or cats she could feed. There wasn't
any juice in the refrigerator, and she couldn't make any
phone calls without waking him, so what was the point of
getting up?

She rolled over and curled around him. He moved
slightly, apparently aware of her presence on some
level, but not, she realized as he resumed snoring, on
any interesting level. So she slipped back to her side
of the bed, opened her eyes again and stared at the
ceiling.

And though she didn't want to see Paul and Lizzie,
there they were, or there he was, anyway, waiting for
her on the deck of the boat, his loose white shirt and
khaki shorts just the thing for a beautiful day at sea.

"You didn't tell me we were going to California!"
Lizzie said, grinning as she came up the stairs.

"You didn't ask," he said. "But once I saw you
last night, I couldn't leave without you. Who knew
where you would be when I got back?"

"I'm kidnapped," she said, picking up her
shirttails and tying them in a knot above her waist.

"A slight deception, I'll admit," he said. "But
I'm weak."

He motioned toward the silver-haired man reading a
stack of telexes which had apparently come through
during the night. "Dad wanted me on board. Maybe
because it's a new boat, but there really isn't that
much for me to do." He stroked her hair. "If they
bother you, we can just let them fly home from St.
John's or someplace, and take it the rest of the way by
ourselves."

"Do you live in California?" she asked.

"They do, some of the time."

Lizzie smiled. She enjoyed this slippery talk.
"Where do you live, Paul?"

"Oh, you know," he smiled. "Wherever."

"Are we going through the canal?" she asked.

"Yes," he said. "But we'll stop in Bermuda,
maybe, and St. John's to see people, and possibly St.
Maarten too, but I doubt it. Dad doesn't like St.
Maarten much any more."

"Why not?" she asked.

"I don't know. Something about a woman, I think."

"What if there's a storm?" Lizzie asked.

My question exactly, Fay thought.

"If there's a storm," he said, leaning over to kiss

her forehead, "we'll go inside." "What does your father
do?" Lizzie asked.

"He reads his mail and makes calls," Paul said.

"Is that what you're going to do?"

"When I grow up, you mean?"

She laughed. He shook his head.

"I'm not going to grow up," he said. "Hungry?"

"Starving," she said.

Paul took her arm and escorted her toward the
stairs to the top deck. His father put down his papers,
smiled at Lizzie, nodded to Paul indicating his approval
of her, and followed them up to the table.

Fay closed her eyes, and felt a little dense for
not seeing the resemblance before now.

Lizzie's father had been another man who wouldn't
grow up. No wonder Fay was afraid of this boy. When
somebody you've lost to once before shows up again, you
can't help but be afraid.

* * *

Ed, Lizzie's father, had been lean, like Paul, and
smooth. He moved like a skiff skimming the water on a
cloudless day. He danced like a dreamer and loved like
the world owed him his pleasure and his only obligation
was to share it.

Fay was not what you'd call popular in high school.
She didn't look like the rest of the girls. Her hair
was wildly out of control and her mother refused to let
her cut it. She already had a woman's body, but it
didn't fit the girl's clothes that were handed down to
her. She was ashamed of it. Ed Conley would change all
that.

The night they met, it was late fall, and she was
seventeen. She didn't remember why she'd gone with her
religious sister to the church youth group's hayride,
but it was probably as simple as not having anything
else to do.

She saw him right away, standing a little apart
from the crowd. The other boys were gathered around a
black Corvette convertible parked in front of the
church. They inspected the tires, and one boy cleaned
the rear view mirror with his shirttail. Two of them
bounced the rear bumper and whistled in awe of something
they called the suspension. They pressed their faces
against the windows and drooled at the black leather
interior. Then stood back up and giggled about how it

wasn't a good car for a drive-in movie, but who'd want
to go to a drive-in when you had that car to ride around
in.

They didn't know who it belonged to. But Fay
guessed it must be his. She watched as he watched them.
He was keeping his distance from these youngsters.

The hayride truck was parked directly behind his
Corvette, but the other kids were staying well clear of it.
They wouldn't even look at it, much lean on it, as he
was doing. The old farm truck waited, mysterious and
forbidden, like something they had to be invited into by
the adults, like some shifting and not altogether
safe bed.

Yes. They were all going to jump into bed
together, but not until the Counselor said to. They
were going to climb up into the hayloft in God's name.
But who knew whose name they would be calling when they
came down again.

Most of these kids had grown up together in that
church, learned their Bible verses together, presented
Christmas pageants together, and given themselves to
Christ as a group when they were eleven. Now, they were
fifteen, sixteen, some of them seventeen, and God was no
longer who they wanted to be one with.

Fay asked her sister who was the dark haired boy
leaning up against the truck.

"He's a hood," her sister said.

"I can see that," Fay said. "What's his name?"

"I don't know," the sister said. "Ask Miss Thompson."

"Who's Miss Thompson?"

Her sister looked at Fay in utter despair. Why had she brought her along anyway? Was she going to ask stupid questions all night?

"Miss Thompson," the sister sighed, "is the head of the youth group. Over there. Wearing the scarf." And she walked away from Fay to join the group of girls who were combing their hair in the reflection from the glass signboard on the front of the church.

Just then, Miss Thompson saw the truck driver come out of the liquor store across the street, where he had gone, he said, to buy cigarettes. She waved to her co-leader, the new young assistant minister, new to the church, that is, but not new to Miss Thompson.

Years ago, when his team won the State Basketball championship, she'd cut his picture out of the newspaper and stuck it in her mirror. Then she'd seen him again during college, when Christian Athletes set up a booth on the beach in Florida. He was beyond her now, having married a girl from somewhere in the East, but she was not beyond asking for his help with this hayride.

With the truck driver assisting, the minister lowered the tailgate of the big old truck. Miss Thompson checked the kids' names off the list, as they climbed up into the hay. Fay managed to get behind the unknown hood, so she could hear his name.

"It's Ed Conley," he said, as Miss Thompson looked at her clipboard. "But I'm probably not on your list."

"Well, you sure are now, Eddie," Miss Thompson said brightly. "How did you hear about us?"

"The preacher knows my Dad," Ed said, grabbing one side of the truck.

"Do you know anyone else here?" Miss Thompson asked.

"No," he said, putting one foot up on the truck. "But it looks like I'm about to."

"Well, wait a minute," Miss Thompson said, turning him around to face Fay. "This is Fay Morgan. She doesn't come with us as often as she should, but we like her anyway."

"Fay?" Ed said. "That's your name?"

"Yes," Fay said.

"I like it," he said, and put his hands around her waist and lifted her up into the truckbed. Then he jumped up himself, easy like a cat, and led her to the far corner, knowing that the minister and Miss Thompson would sit at the back to make sure nobody fell out.

"Are you going to be warm enough?" he said, tugging gently at the thin sleeve of her blouse.

"I don't know," she said. "Is it going to get cold?"

"It might," he said. "You let me know."

"What will you do?" she asked. "You can't give me your jacket because you're not wearing a jacket."

Suddenly, she was shoved into him, as two girls standing in front of them, held hands and flopped down in the hay on the count of three.

"If it really gets bad," he said, putting one arm around her, "I'll steal one of _their_ jackets for you." And he pointed to the windbreakers and junior varsity letter jackets the well-prepared boys' mothers had reminded them to wear. They both laughed. These other people were children, they were not. Ed was comfortable with that knowledge, even casually proud of it. Fay felt very calm, all of a sudden. She'd known she didn't belong here, but it took this hoodlum to show her why.

As the truck pulled away from the curb, the singing started. Neither Ed nor Fay knew any of the hymns or camp songs, but it didn't bother them to listen. When they stopped for traffic lights, people in cars would roll down their windows and clap for this beatup choir truck, and wish they were kids again. Then they'd turn around and tell their own kids to shut up in the back seat and think how much nicer other people's children were.

At one point, the truck took a corner too fast to suit Miss Thompson, and the girls squealed as they were all thrown across the truck onto the boys. Fay's head fell against Ed's chest and he wrapped both arms around her pulling her on top of him under the cover of the pile-up.

The young minister stood up at the back of the truck. "Anybody hurt up there?" he called. Then he saw that the tangle of bodies was straightening out by itself, thanks to good manners and all those years in church. He leaned back against the slatted sides of the truck and decided to ride standing up a while.

Miss Thompson didn't want him to think she was just going to roll around in the hay like a teenager, for God's sake, so she stood up beside him.

"Who are those two?" he asked, noticing Fay and Ed curled up next to each other in the corner.

"He's new," she said, and remembered what the senior minister had told her. "His Dad's a drunk. She's Doris Morgan's sister."

"Do you think I should go sit with them?" he asked, suspecting that some liberties were being taken up there.

"If they like each other," Miss Thompson said, patting his chest to reassure him, "we'll have two new regulars won't we?"

The minister looked down at Miss Thompson. He didn't blame her for wanting to touch him, he just hoped it was all in the spirit of Christian fellowship.

Suddenly, one very thin girl in pigtails asked the new minister if there were any mice in the hay. He said there probably were a few, but they were little ones,

and everybody screamed. Two of the boys shouted that
they saw one and started burrowing through the hay to
catch him. All Miss Thompson could think of to get
control of the situation was to start singing. So she
launched into a chorus of "Since Jesus Came Into My
Heart." She knew they couldn't resist that, and she was
right. Pretty soon, the burrowing boys were doing no
more than sneezing, and everybody else was singing.

The truck bounced off the main road and onto
the gravel path that led back through the truck driver's
fields. Somebody spotted the bonfire, and kids stood up
all along the sides watching as they approached the
glowing spot in the middle of the pasture.

Fay started to stand up, but Ed pulled her
further back into the corner. "I sure am glad you're
here," he whispered.

"Me too," she said. And he squeezed her closer to
him, turned his head toward her, and brought her lips to
his for an easy kiss. Nobody saw because they were all
watching the bonfire. Nobody, that is, except Fay's
sister, who was horrified.

Later, around the fire, while Miss Thompson
passed out marshmallows and the truck driver showed the
boys how to whittle the end of a stick into a point,
Fay's sister let her have it.

"I saw you kiss him," she snorted.

"_He_ kissed _me_," Fay said.

"You liked it. I saw you like it."

"It was your idea for me to come here," Fay said.

"It wasn't my idea for you to start necking with a greaseball," her sister said, full of contempt.

"I'm not necking and he's not a greaseball," Fay said.

"Don't you know what people say about him?" Doris asked.

"How do you know what people say about him?" Fay asked. "While ago, you said you didn't know him. Now you're telling me you've heard people talk about him. Make up your mind, Doris."

"They say terrible things about him," Doris said, "but that's nothing compared to what they're going to say about you."

"I don't care what they say," Fay said. "I don't like them anyway."

"I'm going to tell Mother," Doris said.

"Fine," Fay said. "Tell Mother. Then I'll never have to go to church with you again."

Doris realized there was no point in talking to Fay any more. If Fay wanted to ruin her reputation with a hoodlum, that was fine with her. Fay wasn't aware that she had a reputation to ruin. She was only aware that Ed was waiting for her back by the truck.

"Want to have a smoke?" he asked.

"I don't smoke," she said, "but I'll wander off with you, if that's the idea."

"That's the idea," he grinned.

"Why did you come here?" she asked him, as they headed for a clump of trees.

"My Dad's drunk tonight," he said. "I like to get my car out of the driveway when he's drunk."

"I _thought_ it was your car," she said. "How did you get it?"

"I bought it," he said.

"Well, I didn't think you stole it," she said.

"Somebody else stole it," he said. "I bought it from them."

Fay was quiet a moment, trying to sort out the ethics of that.

"It takes a lot of work to keep it running," he said.

"Is that what you do, work on cars?" she asked.

"It's good work," he said.

"I didn't say it wasn't."

"I'm not used to talking so much," he said.

"We don't have to talk then," she said. "It's all right."

"Do you want a ride home?" he asked.

"Yes," she said. It was easy to say, it was all she could say, all she would say for six years.

On the trip home in the truck they had their spot in the corner again, but by that time, the new minister had had enough of Miss Thompson's fellowship, and sat right down next to Ed, in fact.

Ed and the new minister talked about basketball,
but all the time they were talking, Ed had his hand down
the back of Fay's pedal pushers, between her panties and
her skin, and she didn't dare move or everybody,
including her sister who was sitting directly in front
of Fay, would see it. It wasn't that he did anything,
exactly. It was that he knew where he was. And if Fay
had ever thought that nobody could stay interested in
her round little behind for twenty minutes, well, she
was wrong.

When the truck reached the church, Fay told Doris
that Ed was taking her home, and that was the last
real conversation the sisters ever had. Doris didn't
come to the wedding, even. Over the years, Fay heard
from their mother that Doris was praying for her, but
Fay never knew precisely what Doris was asking for.

When Ed unlocked the door of the Corvette in front
of the church, seven boys gasped. The one who'd cleaned
the rearview mirror nearly fainted. But Ed took no
notice of them. He sat down behind the wheel, reached
across to the glove compartment, got out the gray-tinted
glasses he wore to protect his eyes, handed an extra
pair to Fay, started the engine and tore away from the
curb, leaving the boys and girls dumbstruck on the
sidewalk.

That Fay slept with him that night was a given.
The surprise was that he called her the next day, and

the day after that, and there wasn't one day from that night to the night of her father's funeral, when she didn't want him. Want to be around him, want to look at him, want to go to bed with him. When she got pregnant, they got married. He said he didn't mind. He said he always figured he would marry.

So yes, Fay knew about men who wouldn't grow up, and she wished she could tell Lizzie, warn her. But she knew Lizzie wouldn't listen any more than she had listened.

A man like this is so wildly attractive, so maddeningly alive, that he is absolutely irresistible. In the Tarot deck, he is The Fool, and sits, depending on the deck, either at the beginning or the end of the picture cards. When these Major Arcana, the big players, are placed in a circle, describing, as the Tarot sees it, the journey we all must take, then it's clear we're all going to love at least one fool in our lives, and it's probably both the end and the beginning.

In the picture on the card, The Fool, like a hobo, carries a sack tied to a stick. They leave you, these men, but they never said they were staying, never said they were committed, or purposeful, or responsible even. All they want is to have a good time. And what's wrong with that? Nothing, except you begin to wonder how interested you are in having a good time. You begin to think you might not even be capable of having a good time for very long, and there's plenty wrong with that.

The joy of being with these men is the giddy
return, through them, to a child's world, where there
are no clocks and no claims on your time, no clothes to
be kept clean, and no consequences to be considered.
Days and nights are filled with the silliness, the
spontaneity, the conspiratorial privacy, and all the
breathless secret pleasures of life in a tree house.

Girls, as we know, are rarely allowed in
treehouses. So the invitation, when it comes, can't be
refused. You're curious at first, and then giddy about
the prospect of actually belonging. It can take quite a
while before you realize you don't know what you do up
there all day. When you ask what else there is to do
besides play, well, then you see the other side of these
men.

They don't always come home, and they won't ever
apologize for it. They won't help around the house
because they like it all messed up. They won't work
very hard because they don't want to get trapped by
success. And they won't work at the relationship because
it's not supposed to be work, it's supposed to be fun.
If you don't want to play with them, they don't mind.
But that isn't going to stop them from playing.

Somehow, they make you feel very old, these men.
They turn you into their mother.

On the Tarot card, a cat is nipping at The Fool's
pantlegs, pulling them down to expose his bottom. He is

walking toward a fallen obelisk. When he gets there, the
crocodile hiding behind the obelisk will eat him. You
can see that he's walking blind and bare-assed right
into the mouth of destruction. But he can't. He can't
see the crocodile. You know the outrageous stupidity of
simply following the road. You know he's making a
terrible mistake. But he thinks, God save him, he's
having a good time.

You have to tell him. You have to warn him what's
ahead. But when you do, he leaves you. He strolls out
of your life as aimlessly and happily as he wandered
into it.

This card always troubled Fay when it came up in a
reading. What is a mistake compared to the other evils
the Tarot cautions against?   What's the matter with a
little light-hearted folly now and then? What is life
without it?

Should she try to keep people from making
mistakes, from being foolish? Was it even possible?
Weren't people going to make mistakes no matter what she
said? And what was a mistake anyway?

Was it a mistake to marry that black-haired boy
whose arms were lean and strong? No. She would have
been a fool not to fall for him. Was it a mistake to
get pregnant? Not if the baby grew up to be Lizzie it
wasn't. If it was foolish to love him, then she would
give her very soul to be foolish again.

People could survive mistakes, and Fay didn't want

to face a world without fools. She wished, in fact, she
knew more of them. She wished she had one to call up
right now. She wished Arnie would wake up and say
something silly. She wished she could laugh and laugh
and forget herself and everything else in the company of
one exquisite fool.

* * *

Fay got out of the bed, found a blouse she'd left
in Arnie's closet, and got dressed. She wanted to
believe Paul was just a Fool, but he wasn't. He was the
Devil. He wouldn't return Lizzie when he was finished
with her. He would finish her off and move on.

Arnie stirred in the bed. "What time is it?" he
asked.

"Quarter of nine," she said, going into the
bathroom to brush her hair.

"My God," Arnie said, jumping out of the bed. "Why
didn't you wake me? We have to meet the Chief at Indian
Point at nine."

"What if there's nothing out there," she asked.
Fay wanted to go to the harbor, see for herself if the
boat was there. Find Lizzie.

"Look, honey," Arnie said, throwing on his clothes.
"Nobody expects you to take us directly to these people.
Every cop on the force is on the look-out. They've got
the computer going crazy looking for parking tickets in
front of the church, or anything that could be a lead.
But I happen to believe that your hunches or instincts
or whatever the hell you want to call them, will get us
there faster. If you say there's something about Indian
Point, then we'll go there. And if it isn't there,
then I'll just assume it went away while we were

asleep."

He followed her into the bathroom where she tried
to tame her hair. "I'm buying you breakfast either way,
whether we find something or not, so what have you got
to lose?"

"Lizzie," she said.

"I'll call right now," he said.

But suddenly, Fay stopped brushing her hair, the
brush caught in a thick tangle, her eyes caught by
something in the mirror. "One of the kids is sick," she
said.

He rushed back in the room. "What?"

"Asthma," she said. "One of the kids has asthma."
Fay grabbed the edge of the sink.   "Call headquarters.
Tell them to alert the emergency rooms. He'll die
without help."

Arnie raced to the phone. Fay closed her eyes.
Her head hung limp as she clung to the sink. Why
couldn't she see something good? Wasn't there anything
good to see?

Fay found Arnie at the phone in the hall, and
motioned that she had something else to tell him.
"They'll bring the boy in and leave him somewhere."

Arnie nodded. "He's on the list of missing kids
all right. All I had to say was asthma. His name is
Timmy Willis. They're calling the parents right now.
Anything else?"

"Blue shoes," she said.

Arnie spoke into the phone again then listened and gave Fay the thumbs up sign. "Blue shoes. That's our boy all right," he said.

"Tell them to hurry," she said quietly.

"O.K.," he said into the phone. "That's it for now. Every hospital in the city."

Arnie hung up the phone and reached for Fay's hand. She looked so weary. Whatever she had seen, had hurt.

"They wouldn't let him die, would they?" she asked.

"No, Fay, they wouldn't." He stroked the back of her hand, then something in the bedroom drew his attention. "Death in the course of a kidnapping is murder one," he said.

"Arnie, they're not worried about _that_!" she sighed, and pulled her hand away.

He went to the bedroom and closed the window. "Oh I imagine they're worried about _that._"

She didn't like the tone of his voice. "Arnie," she said, "if they were worried about being punished, they'd never have done this in the first place."

"Well," he said, strapping on his holster, "I guarantee you they're thinking about it now."

"I don't think so," she said.

He stuck his badge in his pocket. "Then they don't know what they're up against," he said.

"The police force rides again," she said.

"You're damn right."

Fay felt a sudden chill. She spoke slowly. "And
what will you do with these people, kill them?"

"If they hurt those children we will. You bet your
ass we will."

Fay forced her head up. "He's not breathing,
Arnie. Timmy Willis stopped breathing."

Arnie stopped cold. "Jesus Christ, Fay, are you
sure?"

She stood up. "I'm sure."

"Let's go then," he said, handing her her purse.
"We don't have another minute."

She wasn't ready to move yet. He took her hand.

"I'm sorry I got a little, you know, whatever."

"Cop-like," she said.

"Yeah," he said.

"O.K.," she said. "Let's go."

Calling Lizzie would have to wait. Finding Lizzie
would have to wait. Maybe Arnie was right. Maybe
Lizzie would come home by herself. She wasn't a baby.
Timmy Willis was a baby. And Timmy Willis was dying.

9:00 A.M.

When the Death card came up in a reading, Fay never
said it meant a death. It did, of course, but if she
said that, people always took it the wrong way, people
overreacted to that word.

The card itself, not so coincidentally numbered 13,
shows a skeleton reaping a harvest of heads, feet and
hands which have sprouted from the earth. He swipes a
scythe across the field and smiles. The smile is
because the Tarot is not talking about death in general,
or about the death of a person, but rather, the death of
a project, a partnership, a way of thinking, a way of
life. This Death, says the Tarot, will be the beginning
of a transformation, the first step toward some new
life.

"Something is coming to an end," Fay would say.
Then she would look at the other cards to see how soon
it would happen, then at the face of the client to see
how much of a surprise it would be.

"Don't be afraid of it," she would say. "Things
have to end. Things die to clear new space for other
things. Just think of death as good housekeeping,"
she'd say. But that never went over very well.

"All right, then," she'd try again. "The thing
about the future, death included, is that it's nothing
new. Maybe, at the beginning, it was just a look on his
face, or a difference of opinion. But it accumulated,

like interest on a savings account, until finally there
was enough of it to do something with. That's when you
started calling it the present. When it keeps growing
until there's so much of it you can't even begin to
control it, then you'll call it the future. But there
was a moment, way back there, when the future was a
speck so tiny, you didn't even notice it, or didn't take
notice of it."

People didn't like that either. It made them feel
guilty, or dumb, for not doing something while there was
still time.

"Well, look," she'd say finally. "Whatever this is
that dies on you, it's going to leave a vacuum. Nature
abhors a vacuum. Something will fill it up."

"Yeah," they'd say, "like pain."

"Maybe," she say. "But maybe not as much as you
think."

"Yeah," they'd say. "Maybe more."

Fay didn't know who said 'Nature Abhors a Vacuum.'
She didn't even know where she'd heard it. Whoever said
it was dead, though, she knew that much. Nobody said
'abhor' any more.

Finally, Fay would give up. "What is it?" she'd
ask. "Your marriage?" That was a pretty safe guess
these days.

"I don't know," they'd say.

Fay knew that meant "Yes."

"When is his birthday?" she'd ask. And when they

told her, she would flip through the big red book of
astrological tables to find out who the husband was.

Fay didn't know why the star tables were as
accurate as they were. And it didn't matter to her.
She used them because they helped. She didn't know why
the cards worked either. But then, whoever said that
nature abhorred a vacuum probably didn't have a clue why
it worked. It just did. And that was enough.

As soon as Fay had some feeling for the husband,
she could see whether the ending the cards predicted was
the end of the marriage, or just the end of this
particular period in the marriage. Sometimes, in a
marriage, people were just going to school, taking an
advanced course in some special area of the
relationship. When the course was over, there would be
a final exam, and then, a vacation. People already knew
this about their marriages. Fay just helped them
remember it.

A Death card just meant a change, that's all.
People don't like change either, but they like it better
than death. What Fay believed, but never dared to say,
was that a change required a death. She would love to
meet the client she could say that to. Starting at that
point, they could really get somewhere.

Fay's mother had understood that. "I'm changing,"
she had said. What she was doing, Fay knew, was dying.
But "changing" was, as far as her mother was concerned,

exactly what was happening. She'd changed before, and
had always liked who she'd become, so there was no
reason to be afraid of this one.

It had been months since her mother had sat in her
rocker, longer than that since she'd crocheted. It was
winter, and lying there on the bed, her mother would, as
she described it, "take little trips." She would leave
her body under the covers and "go places." Fay would
come into the room and nearly die herself, looking at
the seemingly lifeless form beneath the sheet. Her
mother warned Fay to check her pulse very carefully
before calling the coroner. She didn't want her body
carted off to the funeral home, then have her spirit
return to the bedroom and not be able to find it.

Fay asked if that wouldn't be a way to cheat death
after all, to have your spirit on the loose, with its
bags checked conveniently in the locker downtown.

"No," her mother had said. "People don't pay any
more attention to spirits than they do to old ladies."

"I would," Fay said.

"I know you would," her mother said. "But you've
got your own life to lead now. I've taken up enough of
it. It's time for me to go."

"Do you know what's going to happen to me?" Fay
asked.

"I always have," her mother said.

"I know," Fay said. "Will you tell me?"

It was nearly dusk outside. What little light

remained in the day filtered through the lace curtains making rosette shadow prints on the bedspread. The walls receded into the darkness, as Fay sat quietly, her chair pulled up close to the bed.

Her mother leaned back against the pillows. They hadn't talked about the coffin, or what her mother wanted to be buried in. But her mother had never slept on tufted pink satin, and she'd never, that Fay knew of, slept in her clothes. Fay wished, when the time came, that she could slip both mother and bed into a big cedar chest, eyelet covers and all.

Fay reached across to stroke her mother's withered hand. She could see the bones clearly, and knew that the skeleton which had, until recently, been in hiding, was about to shed its skin and emerge. It was waiting patiently for the pumping and gurgling to slow and then cease, for the rising tidal chest walls to fall for the last time, for the blinking electrical circuits to dim, and then flicker out.

And then, the last messages from the world received and filed, its work would be finished. The windows would be closed, and the white skeletal form would lie alone in the silence, in the creeping chill, in the red becoming black. The skeleton's length and form would be the only remaining evidence of the life it had upheld.

"What will happen to me?" Fay asked again softly.

Her mother moved her hand toward the drawer of the

nightstand. "My cards," she said, her hand floating
weightlessly back to the bed.

Fay found them at the back of the drawer, wrapped
in the old blue scarf they had been wrapped in for
seventy years. They smelled faintly of camphor now,
from the little vials and pots of salve her mother liked
to keep close at hand.

Fay placed the cards in her mother's hands, and the
old woman unwrapped them carefully. Then, with deft,
but slow motions, she tied the scarf loosely around her
neck. Fay knew then, that her mother was through taking
her little trips. Her spirit had found whatever it had
been looking for, and was now content to help her over
this next little rough place in the road.

Her mother handed the cards to Fay to shuffle,
which she did, fighting back the tears that formed at
the sight of this nearly bald old wispy white-haired
woman in a long-sleeved white cotton gown, lying
perfectly still with a never washed, never worn but
wearing thin, blue silk scarf looping lazily at her
neck.

"You have a great gift," her mother said, "and
you'll start using it soon." She patted Fay's arm.
"Just be sure to charge a lot of money." She smiled.
"It's the only way they'll believe you. And don't tell
people it's a mystery. Tell them it's a trick. Tell
them they could do it. Tell them anybody could do it."

Fay couldn't answer, but cut the cards and dealt

them, calling out their names. "Death, Justice, The
Sun, The Falling Tower, The Wheel of Fortune, The
Priestess, The Hanging Man."

Her mother thought a minute. "That's good," she
said. "There's a man. I want you to have a man."

"I don't know if I remember how," Fay said softly.

"There may not be a marriage," her mother said,
"but there is a man."

Fay liked the idea of a man. Lizzie was getting
old enough to be left with a sitter for an evening, and
Fay missed the smell of a man. She missed how a man
could pretend to know where he was going, and by
pretending, get there.

"This man will not be the problem for you," her
mother continued. "Lizzie will. But he'll help you
take your mind off Lizzie."

"What about Lizzie?" Fay asked.

"Don't be fooled into thinking you can keep her
safe."

Fay saw the Falling Tower but answered anyway. "I
can try," she said.

"She's not safe, Fay," her mother said. "She
wasn't born safe. If you could find a way not to love
her, that would protect you, anyway."

"None of us is safe, Mother."

"Oh yes," her mother said. "You are. You are
perfectly safe. The world is your home. You know where

everything is, where everything goes. Your only
misfortune, is that so many of the people you love are
not safe at all."

"If they stay with me, will they be safe?"

"No, my love." Her mother made an effort to smile,
as her eyes blinked open, then closed again. "Look at
me."

And Fay's tears fell freely now. Her mother was
right. She had thought that by taking the old woman in,
she could save her, she could keep her from falling on
the ice, or prevent the pneumonia Fay had seen coming
when her father died. And now she saw she couldn't.
Finally, fearfully, she was watching her mother die.
She was, she realized, about to lose her mother's life.

"Are you crying, Fay?" her mother asked, her eyes
still closed.

"Yes, I am," Fay said.

"I'm sorry that you're crying," the old woman said
slowly. "But I hope it makes you feel better."

And when Fay looked up, her mother was dead.

Fay reached for her mother's wrist and felt for a
pulse, but she knew she wouldn't find one. After a
moment, she lifted the lifeless palm to her lips and
kissed it. Then Fay stroked her own face with her
mother's hand. It was what her mother would have done
if she could, what her mother had always done when Fay
was sad. Smooth her hair back from her temples, slip
her hand gently up to her forehead, feel for a fever.

With her mother's hand, Fay brushed her tears away,
accepting the tender consolation granted so freely by
those who are unable to help.

When Fay could stand up, she did. She left the
light off in the room. Soon enough, someone would come
in and need to see. They could turn it on. Fay and her
mother didn't need it.

* * *

Fay's tip about Timmy Willis had gone out to all
the squad cars, all the hospitals, all the walk-in
clinics and directly to the mayor's office. The news
wasn't released to the press, but they knew it anyway
because they monitored the police radio.

Madonna Willis phoned Timmy's doctor to make sure
he was available, and Ted came home from his real estate
office to wait with her. Timmy was Madonna's red-haired
elf son fron a former marriage. Ted had wanted to adopt
the boy, but Timmy liked his real dad, a minor league
pitcher with a fiery temper and a mean curve ball.

The call came in to police headquarters from dusty
old St. Vincent's Hospital way out the Brownsville Pike.
A brown Ford station wagon had driven up to the front
door and deposited Timmy Willis on the steps. Bobbie
Jenkins, who had been sitting behind the reception desk
for forty years, looked up from the Donahue show on TV
in the lobby, saw the stricken boy, picked up the house
phone first, and then activated the new automatic dial
function for the Emergency Medical Service. Even from
the window, she recognized the symptoms. Status
asthmaticus. Her own mother had nearly died from an
attack of it.

She was talking to the EMS, when two orderlies and
a young intern rushed across the lobby. Several people
waiting in the lobby tried to get out the door with the

men in white suits, but Bobbie barked at them to back
off. If they hadn't moved, they would have been run
down by the inhalation therapist pushing his wobbly cart
faster than was safe for either one of them.

What St. Vincent's had in the way of an emergency
room, was not much more than a first aid station for the
staff. All they could do was keep him alive til the
ambulance got there.

The orderlies brought Timmy inside and laid him
down on the wide countertop right in front of Bobbie.
They clamped the oxygen mask over his little blue face,
and Bobbie reached over and squeezed his hand.

The young intern remembered that aminophylline
could cause convulsions in too high a dosage. Or was it
Theophylline. Or were they the same thing? Adrenalin
should be safe enough, he decided, and called for an I-V
hookup.

Bobbie thought Timmy didn't look as blue as he had
on the steps, but she worried it might just be the
light. Then she heard the siren, and saw the ambulance
racing around the circular drive to the front door. Two
police cars followed, and a photographer jumped out of a
black Honda that came in the driveway the wrong way.

The people in the lobby were wild with excitement.
Bobbie had seen enough fear in her life to know that
that wasn't what they were feeling. They felt like
extras in an episode of a hospital show on TV.

While the EMS men transferred Timmy to the
ambulance, the police asked Bobbie to describe the car.
Did she get the license number? No. Could she describe
anybody in the car? No. Well, did she remember how
many people there were in the car? Two, maybe. Which
direction did the car go? That way. How long ago was
that? Ten minutes. Do you remember anything about the
car? It was brown. What color brown? It had a strip
of wood down the side of it. Any bumper stickers? I
don't remember. Anything in the back window? There was
something on the aerial. What? Like a little pompom, I
think. What about the paint? It was dirty. It had mud
flaps on the wheels. All the wheels? Just the back.

Bobbie lit a cigarette. The administration had
asked her not to smoke at the desk any more, but this
was a moment when any smoker smokes, regardless.

The photographer had snapped about fifty shots of
everything, from Timmy on the stretcher, to the begonias
in the concrete urns on either side of the steps. Now
he wanted a picture of Bobbie with the intern. She
drank the last of her grapefruit juice and put her
cigarette out in the empty can. The intern and the two
orderlies stood behind her chair, as the photographer
wanted a good view of the countertop, and they all
smiled.

The ambulance arrived at Duncan Memorial at 9:20,
and Timmy's doctor was there by 9:30. But Madonna and
Ted were caught in a traffic jam caused by construction

on the freeway. It would be the longest half-hour
either of them ever spent in a car, and after this was
all over, the first thing they would do was sell that
Subaru.

By the time Timmy's doctor found him in one of the
treatment rooms, the little elf was not only breathing,
he was crying. But seeing his doctor made him feel a
little better. And the doctor had thought to bring
along the old yellow teddy bear he kept in the office
for the kids to hold onto. The doctor brought the bear
because while he was afraid Timmy might not recognize
him, he knew the child would remember the ragged bear.

In the waiting area, just outside the treatment
rooms, the other patients had no idea why so many police
were hanging around. They didn't seem to be sick. All
they were doing was bothering people for change for the
candy machines.

Fay, sitting in the coffee shop at the Indian Point
shopping center, didn't know Timmy had recovered. But
she did feel a little better. She thought it was the
coffee.

                          * * *

     Their booth in the coffee shop window provided a
perfect view of the monstrous Indian. Fay figured his
loincloth to be at least five feet wide. She doubted
that he was anatomically correct underneath it, but she
couldn't help wondering about that. His nipples and
boots were brown, his eyes were yellow, his hair black,
and the blue streaks on his face were, she guessed,
somebody's idea of warpaint. Otherwise, of course, he
was red. Fay was glad there weren't too many real
Indians left in this part of the country.

     "Who do you think we're looking for?" the Chief
asked Fay when their breakfast came. "Are they here
anywhere? I mean, are the kids hidden in the shopping
center?"

     "No," Fay said.

     Arnie stopped the Chief before he could say it.
"Don't ask her how she knows," he said.

     "O.K.," the Chief said. "Who are they?"

     "It's ordinary people," she sighed.

     "Ordinary people don't steal children," he said.
"It has to be nuts. Religious nuts."

     "Maybe," Fay said. "But they don't look like nuts.
They look just like us. That woman," and she pointed
across the coffee shop to a middle-aged woman wearing a
beige polyester pantsuit, "that's what they look like."

     "But what do they want?" the Chief asked. "Why

haven't they called us with their demands?"

"They will," Fay said. "They've got twenty-five
children to take care of. They're busy."

The Chief didn't like her attitude. "So what do
you think?" he tried again.

"I don't think they'll hurt the kids," Fay said.
"On purpose, I mean. I think if you do what they say
they'll give them back."

The Chief put down his fork, looked at Arnie, and
then at Fay. He tried not to sound mad. "Pardon me,
Miss Morgan, but I'm not paying you ten thousand dollars
to tell me to go along with these people."

"Don't pay me then," Fay said. "I have three
clients today who do care what I think. I'll just go
home and see them." And she tried to get past Arnie in
the booth.

"Fay," Arnie said, easing her back into her seat,
"we have to find these people. If they get away with
this thing, we'll have kidnappings twice a day."

"I'm trying to help you," Fay said. "You're just
not listening."

"Try again," the Chief said, spearing a forkful of
eggs. "It's just morning, is all. I hate the morning."

Fay took a deep breath. "These people are so
clean," she said, "that you won't even find parking
tickets on them. They pay their taxes, they work for a
living, you know, they're regular folks. The only way
they'll do something criminal. .

"Something _else_ criminal," the Chief corrected.

"Right, something else criminal," she said, "is if
you push them into it. If you corner them, they'll
fight you. If you let them alone, they'll do the right
thing."

"If that's who they are," the Chief said, "then I
don't understand why they did this in the first place."

"It's something personal," Fay said. "That's all I
know." And she looked across the room to watch the
woman in the beige pantsuit pay her bill and leave.

As the Chief waved to the waitress for more coffee,
the announcer on the radio in the coffee shop
interrupted the program to say there was a special news
bulletin about the 27 missing children. Fay, Arnie and
the Chief froze in place.

"One of the children abducted from the state fair
is now recovering in Duncan Memorial Hospital from an
attack of asthma which police say caused his captors to
release him."

"Hot damn," Arnie said. "That's my girl," and he
slung his arm around Fay and gave her a good squeeze.

"City detectives," the newscaster continued,
"acting on a tip from the local psychic who has been
retained to help in the investigation, alerted all the
hospitals to watch for the child. Bobbie Jenkins, the
receptionist at St. Vincent's, where the child was
brought for help, said she didn't know he was one of the

missing youngsters. She just knew he was sick. She
said she would have done the same thing even if he
hadn't been famous."

Fay looked up at Arnie. "He's all right?" she
asked, not quite believing it.

"I'm the Chief of Police," the Chief grumped from
across the table. "Will somebody tell me why I have to
hear this news on the radio in a coffee shop."

"Your radio's in your car, that's all," Arnie said.

The Chief turned to Fay. "That's good work, lady,"
he said. "Real fine."

"But is Timmy really all right?" she asked. "Or do
they just not want the kidnappers to know he died."

"He must be all right," the Chief said. "I'm the
only one who could make a strategy decision like that."
He paused. "Or I was when I left the house."

Just then, one of the Chief's assistants rushed in
the door of the coffee shop and over to the table.

"They've got him," the man said. "They've got
another kid."

"Yeah," the Chief said. "We know."

Then the man told them that Timmy's parents hadn't
arrived yet, so the detectives hadn't been allowed to
talk to the child. But the brown Ford described by the
receptionist at St. Vincent's had been found abandoned
about three miles from the hospital, with its license
plates removed.

"They're no dummies, these people," the Chief said,

taking the man's radio and patching into headquarters.
"Give me Sergeant Barnes," he said to the dispatcher.

"Somebody in this city knows who drives a car like
that," he said to Arnie. "We'll put it in the paper
tonight. Offer a reward to anyone who can lead us
to the owner. Not a big reward though," he said. "We
don't want all the crazies in town calling. Just enough
to be worth the trouble. Fifty bucks, something like
that."

The Sergeant came on the line.

"O.K.," the Chief said. "Send somebody back out to
talk to that receptionist. Show her pictures of old
Fords. See if she can pick out what year it was. Then
get DMV to run a list of the registrations for brown
Fords in that year. If these people think we can't find
them just because they took off the license plates,
they're crazy. We're the fucking government here."

The Chief signed off in much better spirits. The
call had made him feel like the Chief again.

"There it is," Fay said quietly, pointing as the
18-wheeler pulled into the huge parking lot. "There's
the truck. Right over there."

Arnie and the Chief jumped up, but the radio in the
Chief's hand stopped them before they could take off.
"Attention all units," the dispatcher said. "A message
has just been received that any interference with the
truck now parked at the Indian Point shopping center

will result in the deaths of the kidnapped children."

"We were sitting right here!" the Chief screamed.

"Are the kids in the truck, Fay?" Arnie asked.

"No," she said.

The three men bolted away from the table, ran
out the door and across the asphalt. Fay sat back down
and watched as the truck stopped on the far side of the
parking lot. Even from here, she could see that the
oranges on the side had been painted out, and replaced
with a huge red cross. She kept her eye on the driver's
door, in case he got out and tried to run away. Later,
she realized she should have been watching the people
passing behind the truck, watching for someone new to
join the crowd walking to their cars.

As a stream of police cars entered the shopping
center and surrounded the truck, Fay ate the last bite
of her French toast and motioned to the waitress for
a glass of water.

* * *

By the time Arnie and the Chief reached the truck,
other officers had climbed up to the cab, found it empty
and locked, and tried the back doors which were also
locked. The Chief talked with the officer in charge,
and Arnie inspected the tires. But they both knew there
was nothing more for them to do here, and so they
started back for the coffee shop. The Chief hadn't
finished his breakfast, he said.

"Fay said they would do this," Arnie said.

"Too bad she didn't know it in time for us to grab
the driver," the Chief said.

"So," Arnie said, "I think we have to wait, like
she said. Wait for them to tell us what they want."

"Wait for them to think it up, is what we're
doing," the Chief said. "Bunch of goddamn. . ."

"Right," Arnie said.

"What's the matter with her anyway?" the Chief
asked. "I thought you said she wanted to do this."

"She's all right," Arnie said. "Any news on that
boat I asked you about?"

"If that Miss Majesty is the one," the Chief said,
"she's still out there sitting in the harbor."

"Are you sure?" Arnie asked.

"What do you mean am I sure?" the Chief snapped.
"The harbormaster saw it. He was right looking at
it while I was talking to him." The Chief paused as a

teenage girl in a pair of shorts took his breath away. "Said she was a real beauty too."

"Who owns it?" Arnie asked.

"It's registered in California," he said. "Orange County. But they took delivery here. Taking it back to California through the canal. New boat. The guy is one of these stock market whizzos. Banker too, maybe. South America. I forget."

"And they're not leaving until tonight?" Arnie asked.

"Right," the Chief said. "They had a helluva party last night, though. Lots of champagne. Limousines up the wazoo at the pier."

"So Fay's right about that part anyway," Arnie said.

"What's this about, drugs?" the Chief asked.

Arnie shook his head. "Fay is convinced her daughter sailed off on that boat last night. Thinks the kid isn't coming back."

"Nope," the Chief said. "The harbormaster said there wasn't one private boat left the harbor last night from midnight on. Not a one."

"O.K.," Arnie said, "thanks," and lit a cigarette.

"Kids are a bitch," the Chief said. "Nothing but trouble."

"I guess," Arnie said.

"I don't have to see mine much any more, though,"

the Chief said.

"Why not?" Arnie asked.

"Why do you think?" the Chief said calmly. "They hate my guts."

Arnie could see the coffee shop window now, but Fay was no longer sitting at their table. Normally, he wouldn't have worried about it. He would've just assumed she was in the ladies' room. But somehow, this morning, he wasn't so sure. Maybe she called the Coast Guard, found out on her own about that boat in the harbor, and called a cab to go there and look for Lizzie. Suddenly, Arnie was afraid that if he let Fay out of his sight just once today, he might never see her again.

That wasn't the kind of thought he was comfortable with. Arnie wasn't a worrier, and he certainly couldn't spend this whole day worrying about Lizzie, and neither could Fay. She _had_ to understand. If she didn't, then she didn't understand much about him, did she.

Would she ever love him the way she loved Lizzie? Would she be this distracted and jumpy if _he_ were missing? Probably not. But Lizzie wasn't missing, or at least she wasn't missing the way Fay thought she was. Maybe Lizzie did go to that party on the boat, but she was bound to be home asleep by now, unless she went straight to dance class. Maybe that's where she was.

Arnie did care about Lizzie. She was as close as he would ever come to having a daughter. But she wasn't

his. He didn't have to put her first. He couldn't. If
anybody came first it was Fay. But since Lizzie was
first with Fay, didn't that mean Lizzie should be first
with him? No. How could it? Then what did it mean?
Was Fay first, or work? Fay. Definitely. But not
today. Tomorrow she would be first again, or the next
day, or whenever they found these children.

But what if it took a year? What if Fay went off
to find Lizzie without him? She would do it, he knew.
If Lizzie were his daughter, he'd do the same thing.
He'd drop this case in a minute and go find her, Chief
or no Chief. What did work matter when your child was
in trouble. What did work matter anyway?

Anybody could do what he did. If he wanted proof
of that, all he had to do was quit. They'd replace him
the next day, and nobody would know the difference. But
if he quit this case and helped Fay find Lizzie, they'd
fire him. He didn't want to be fired. What if he got
to Wyoming and needed a job?

Well, sure, there were things that paid better than
police work, but nothing he knew as well. No. He had
to stay on this thing til all those kids were safe in
their beds, Lizzie or no Lizzie. No Lizzie. Oh boy.
No Lizzie. No Fay. No job. No. Arnie couldn't start
worrying about this. No sir.

* * *

Fay could see Arnie and the Chief walking back toward the coffee shop, but that wasn't the conversation she heard.

Paul and his father were standing on the top deck of the big boat. The breakfast had been cleared, and the boat was moving much faster. The day, the trip, and the father-son conference were all well underway. They leaned against the railing, as two stewards removed the breakfast table and set up an exercise bicycle in its place.

"She's a beautiful girl," Paul's father said.

"Lizzie?" Paul said.

"Yes, Lizzie," his father said. "Do you have another beautiful girl onboard?"

"She's sweet," Paul said, admiring his deepening tan.

"She looks like a dancer."

"Maybe she is," Paul said. "I didn't ask."

"Where did you meet her?"

"Her mother's a gypsy," Paul said, accepting a bottle of suntan oil from one of the stewards. "I had my fortune told. The girl came home while I was there."

"A gypsy?" his father asked.

"The woman is a nightmare," Paul said.

"Does your mother know that? A gypsy?"

"No," Paul said.

Paul's father walked over to the exercise bicycle, and used it to steady himself as he did a few knee-bends and stretches. "Will she be any trouble?" he asked.

"She adores me," Paul said. "She does whatever I say."

"No," his father said, "I mean the mother."

"What trouble?" Paul said. "Has there ever been any trouble? I'm very sweet about it. When we get to California, I'll say thanks, that's all. Then I say good-bye."

"Yes," his father said, mounting the bicycle and beginning to pedal, slowly at first. "That's all one can say, really."

"What she tells her mother is her business. If she were afraid of the old frump, she wouldn't have come. Besides," Paul said, "when's a girl like that ever going to get a trip like this in her life?"

"Oh, now you're the Good Samaritan," his father grinned, and started pumping harder.

"Why not?" Paul said, "It doesn't cost _me_ anything. Why should she have to work hard and be miserable her whole life?"

"Because that's who she is."

"Well a little fun first won't hurt her." Paul poured a little oil into his palm and rubbed it onto his shoulders. "What was I supposed to do all this time? Sit up top and look for whales?"

His father slipped his forefinger into the
pulsemeter on the handlebars and smiled as the digital
readout flashed a figure not much above his normal
resting rate. "Would Lizzie be here if she knew about
Alyson?" his father asked.

"Maybe," Paul said. "And maybe she'd try to take
me away from Alyson."

"When they fight over you, son, you lose them
both."

"Well it's not like they're the last two, Dad."

His father had to laugh. "No, you're certainly
right there." He set the timer for twenty minutes and
turned the odometer back to zero.

"Alyson will never know," Paul said. "She can't
meet the boat in California because she's in Tibet."

"Missing you desperately," his father joked.

"That's what she says."

"Oh son," the trim gray-haired man sighed.

"What?" Paul grinned, as Lizzie came up from below,
saw that they were talking and went to the aft deck for
some sun.

"Not a thing," his father said, as the boy walked
away. "Enjoy."

Paul left his father and walked down the steps to
where Lizzie was spreading the thick white beach towel
across the slatted wooden chaise. He watched as the sun
played in her hair, envying its absorption in the

lustrous mass.

When she saw him, she smiled, inviting him to watch as she removed her cover up to reveal the white string bikini his mother had so thoughtfully provided in the guest room.

He walked across the deck, as she lay back on the double wide lounger, then sat down beside her and stroked the long smooth arm she offered him.

"Why did you come with me?" he asked.

"I wanted to," she said easily.

"And you want to stay?" he asked. "What about your mother?"

"I don't want to talk about mother," Lizzie said. "She'll hear me."

Paul's instincts for human weakness were infallible. "She'll hear you?"

"All my life," Lizzie said, "all my whole life, she's known everything I thought, everything I did, told me every dumb thing I was going to do right before I did it."

Paul had to laugh. "Made it a little hard to breathe, huh?"

"Took all the fun out of it, yeah," Lizzie said. "This," she opened her arms to the sea air, "is the first morning of my life, of a life that's not hers to spy on."

"Spy on?" said Paul, putting on his sunglasses, coaxing the rest of it out of her without seeming to be interested.

"She may know where I am," Lizzie said, "what I'm doing, even what I'm saying right now, but she can't tell me she knows it, and she can't stop me. I don't want to know what's going to happen. Whatever happens, happens. I'll just. . . wait and see," she grinned.

"Dad would like to meet her," Paul lied.

Lizzie laughed. "No, no," she said. "She doesn't like to meet people. She just likes to stay in her little apartment. She doesn't even have friends she talks to. And she can't leave the city because of her clients."

"Not even to come to California to see you?" Paul asked, fully aware of the implications of what Lizzie was saying.

"I don't think so," Lizzie said.

"Even if you invited her? Paid her way?"

"No," Lizzie said. "She wouldn't have, you know, she wouldn't know anybody."

"How did you escape?" he asked. "Why aren't you like her?"

Fay thought about the piano lessons, the dancing lessons, the children's theatre, the book clubs, the arts camps, summer school, the honors program, the school trips, and the money that had bought it all.

"I was quiet about it," Lizzie said. "But I've been gone a long time now. She just thought, I don't know, she just thought I was somebody else."

Fay's heart was breaking. She had waited so long
to hear Lizzie talk, really talk. And this, this was
what she was saying.

"So who are you?" Paul reached for the portable
tape deck.

"Do you like me?" Lizzie flirted.

"Wild about you," he said, opening the box of tapes
under the chair.

"Then it doesn't matter, does it," Lizzie said,
putting on her sunglasses.

He squeezed her arm. "Not in the slightest, babe.
Not in the slightest."

Fays eyes filled with tears, the coffee shop
blurred around her. The waitress asked her something
but she couldn't make it out. If there hadn't been an
empty plate smeared with congealing maple syrup in front
of her, she would have put her head right down on the
table and sobbed.

Maybe the waitress asked if she was through with
the plate. If so, then Fay had understood too late. A
lot of things. Understood a lot of things too late.

10:00 A.M.

When Arnie opened the door of the coffee shop,
Fay was standing at the pay phone.

"I'm calling Gail," she said, dialing the number.

"Good idea," he said, and leaned over to kiss the
top of her head. "I've got some good news for you when
you're finished," he said.

"Anything over there?" she asked, nodding in the
direction of the orange truck.

"Not a thing," he said, and sat down on the edge of
the big concrete planter near the window.

"Marvin?" Fay said, disappointed that he had
answered. "It's me, Fay. Is Gail there?"

"Yeah," Marvin said, sounding lonely. "She's in
the kitchen talking with Lizzie."

"Lizzie!" Fay shrieked. "What's Lizzie doing there?"
Arnie jumped up and came over to stand with Fay.

"Looking for you, I think," Marvin said. "Want to
talk to her?"

"Are you sure it's Lizzie?" Fay asked.

"What's the matter with everybody today?" Marvin
said. "Of course it's Lizzie. She's been here about an
hour, and I'm real glad she came, too. I just didn't
know what to say to Gail after that phone call."

Fay heard an electronic click on the line.

"Wait a minute," Marvin said. "Let me get this
other call."

Fay turned to Arnie. "Marvin says Lizzie's sitting

in Gail's kitchen!"

"That's what I was going to tell you," he said.
"They had a party, but the boat didn't leave yet."

Marvin came on the line again. "Fay, it's the
kidnappers," he said.

Arnie was close enough to hear what Marvin said. He
grabbed the phone.

"Marvin! Don't hang up!" Arnie said quickly. "Did
the men come to put the tap on your phone?"

"Yeah," Marvin said. "About a half hour ago."

Arnie was dialing headquarters on the other phone.
"I just want to patch in so Fay can hear them, O.K.? So
go get Gail, but give me a minute."

"O.K." Marvin said. "Good luck I guess."

"Right," Arnie said, talking to the operator on the
other line. He raised his eyebrows to Fay, as if to ask
if she were ready. And she nodded back, as if she
really felt like doing this.

Arnie handed her the phone and the Chief reached in
Arnie's pocket for a cigarette. He knew it wouldn't
taste good, but he wanted it anyway. He knew he
shouldn't have quit smoking. But what can you do, you're the
head of the force. You're supposed to be fit. You have
to set an example.

Then Fay heard Gail's voice. "Hello?"

"Mrs. Wilkins?" the other voice asked.

"This is Gail Wilkins, who is this?"

"You know who this is," the kidnapper said. "We
have Beth here."

"Can I talk to her?"

"No," the voice said. "Come to the Indian Point
Shopping Center at one o'clock this afternoon and meet
the other mothers in front of the big white truck in the
parking lot. On your way there, stop by the bowling
alley at First and Cedar and pick up the package with
your name on it, but don't open it. When all the
mothers are together, you can open the packages and that
is how you will know what to do next. Good luck, Mrs.
Wilkins, and God bless you."

"I want to talk to Beth," Gail said.

"Mrs. Wilkins," the voice said, "if the police
interfere by picking up your package, Beth will not be
returned to you. Is that clear?"

"I understand," Gail said, and the phone went dead.

Fay motioned to Arnie that the call was over. He
took the receiver.

"Gail, it's me, Arnie," he said. "Are you all
right?"

"No, Arnie," she said. "I'm not all right at all."

"I'll let you talk to Fay in just a minute, but I
want you to do exactly what they said to do."

A recorded voice interrupted Arnie, announcing that
if he desired to continue his conversation, it would be
necessary for him to deposit another five cents which
would buy him an additional three minutes. Arnie swore

under his breath and jammed a nickel into the slot.

"Gail," he continued. "We're not going to do anything to scare these people. Don't you worry about that. We're at the Shopping Center right now. And we'll be here when you get here. We'll do exactly what they say. So you be brave and we'll get this all straightened out in no time. All right?"

"I'm fine," she said softly, but she wasn't really talking any more, she was just saying words she remembered from somewhere.

"Here's Fay," he said, and handed the phone to Fay. He didn't for a minute believe it was going to be as easy as he'd made it sound.

"Gail," Fay said quietly, "you did just fine."

"Are they going to give her back?" Gail cried.

"They're not killers, Gail. They're not. You do your part and they'll do theirs. I promise."

Suddenly, Gail attacked her with a wild fury. "How can you promise me that?" she screamed. "You don't know any more than I do!"

"They don't want to hurt the children, Gail," Fay said. "They're just using them to make some kind of point."

Gail was screeching. "Well, you just tell Arnie and his gang to stay the hell away from that truck!"

"Gail, the only reason the police are going to be there is to make sure nothing goes wrong."

Gail was frantic. "I'm coming out there right
now," and she called out to Marvin to go start the car.

"There's nothing to see, Gail," Fay said. "The
truck is just sitting there. Nothing's going to happen
til twelve-thirty at the earliest."

Gail didn't answer. Fay waited. Arnie gestured
wanting to know what was going on. Fay motioned back
that she didn't know.

"Gail?" Fay said, finally.

"What?" Gail screamed.

Fay knew she had to be very careful here, but she
had to ask. "Gail, can I talk to Lizzie?"

"She left," Gail grumbled. "She said she'd see you
later."

"When later?" Fay asked. "Where?"

And Gail completely lost control. "I don't know
when! I don't care where!"

Fay tried as hard as she could to remain calm.
"Gail, please. I've worked all night trying to find
Beth, and I'm going to keep working until I do find her,
but I have to know about Lizzie. Please."

Something in Fay's voice reached Gail, touched her.
"She went to a big party on a boat last night. She's
madly in love, and they're going out again tonight."

"Thank you," Fay said.

"I'm sorry," Gail said, trying to sound like
herself.

"Don't be sorry," Fay said. "That just means I

still have time to stop her."

"Oh Fay," Gail said, weak from fear, weary with
frustration, "let her go."

"Are you letting Beth go?" Fay asked, then knew
instantly she shouldn't have said it.

"Of all the goddamn nerve," Gail screamed, and
slammed the phone down in Fay's ear.

Fay was numb, paralyzed by the pain she had caused,
and the pain she felt. Gently, Arnie took the receiver
out of her hand.

"I can't believe I said that," she said.

"It's O.K.," he said, leading her back into the
coffee shop. "We don't have to be perfect today." He
sat her down. "Tomorrow. We'll be perfect tomorrow."

"What's the matter with me?" she asked.

"You were scared," he said. "But Lizzie's home
now. She's come back."

"No," she said. "It just means I've been seeing
tomorrow instead of today. I'm losing her, Arnie."

"You just sit here and rest a little," he said.
"I'll go see what the Chief wants us to do." He grasped
her shoulder and gave it a hang-in-there squeeze. "And
if the waitress comes by, order me a coke float, O.K.?"

As he walked away, she envied his assured, easy
progress through the world. She had no idea how it must
feel to be a man like Arnie. Wherever this basic
comfort came from, Fay knew she'd never have it.

* * *

When the woman in the beige pantsuit came back in
the coffee shop, Fay looked up. Why was she back here?
Had she forgotten something? There was a young man with
her now, a brittle looking cowboy wearing black jeans,
hiking boots, and a blue shirt buttoned all the way up.
Even the collar button. If this woman were involved in
the kidnapping, this man could certainly have driven the
truck, Fay thought.

But there was something else about the woman.
Where had Fay seen her before? Somewhere, she knew it.
In the neighborhood? For a reading? Where was it? Was
she that stern typist at the Driver's License Bureau?
Or how about a Christmas bell-ringer for the Salvation
Army?

No, no. Fay had it now. It was Edith Masters, the
receptionist at Lizzie's dentist! That bloodless,
efficient Mrs. Masters who had no patience with the
children's patter, and no sympathy for their fears.
Edith Masters. With the daughter. Oh boy. Now Fay
remembered the whole thing.

She'd met the daughter just briefly one day in the
office. But Mrs. Masters must have told the girl that
Fay was a fortune teller, because about six months
later, Colleen, or Coreen, which was it, Colleen, right,
Colleen, showed up at Fay's parlor. She said she was

pregnant and wanted Fay to read the cards for the baby
to see if she should have an abortion.

Fay was startled, but tried not to show it.
"Abortions are illegal," Fay had said.

"A girl at school gave me the name of the place,"
Colleen said.

"Has she had an abortion at this place?" Fay asked.

"I don't know." Colleen paused. "I've got the
money, if that's what you're worried about."

"It's not safe," Fay said, now genuinely alarmed for
the girl, who couldn't be more than seventeen. "Those
places are dirty, Colleen, anything could happen. No,
child," and Fay reached over to squeeze her hand, "you
don't need me to read your cards. You need to go tell
your mother about this, and see what she thinks."

The girl shook her head. The excitement of coming
to a fortune teller had worn off now. She sat
forward in the chair, her head drooping, her arms
bracing her body, her hands clasping the edges of the
seat for support. "I can't tell my mother," she said.
"I already know what she thinks."

"I've known your mother a long time," Fay said. "I
don't know her well, I'll admit, but she seems like a
good woman. Let her help you."

"I've got the money for the reading," Colleen said.
"I just want a reading. I didn't come here to talk."
And then, afraid she had offended Fay, she looked up and
tried to smile.

"Fine," Fay said, but she didn't mean it. She didn't like to expose her cards to such wild fear. She didn't even like to sit in front of it herself. Nevertheless, this little girl needed somebody, and Fate, or whatever you call it, had appointed Fay. So there she sat.

Fay asked Colleen to shuffle the cards, and then cut them in three piles to her left. "How far along are you?" Fay asked.

"Two months," the girl said.

"Have you been to a doctor?"

The girl didn't answer.

Fay collected the cards and dealt the first seven onto the table. "Well," Fay said smiling, looking at the Three of Cups, "at least it wasn't a rape."

"No," Colleen said, and managed a smile.

Fay pointed to the Emperor. "_That_ we already know," she said.

"What?" the girl asked.

"The law is _not_ on your side," Fay said.

"No," the girl said.

"You don't want the child at all?" Fay asked, pausing at the next card.

"I want to grow up," the girl said, and the tears appeared at the edges of her eyes.

Fay looked out the window while Colleen wiped her eyes. She was angry suddenly, thinking about the laws

that are supposed to protect children. They can't drive
til they're sixteen, vote til they're eighteen, or drink
til they're twenty-one. But we'll let a girl have a
baby any time she gets pregnant. In fact, we'll force
her to have that baby.

We make those other laws to protect us, Fay
realized, not them, to protect us from their driving, us
from their drinking, us from their ignorance. But their
mistakes? No, no. We can't protect them from their
mistakes. Those they have to pay for.

"I think it should be against the law for girls like
you to have babies," Fay said.

Colleen nodded, but remained silent.

Fay looked the next card, the ten of swords. Total
defeat. Oh, terrific, Fay thought. Just terrific.
That was the best possible outcome of the situation?
The client's goal? Fay decided to pass over that one
and go on to the seven of wands, the past.

"It looks like you've been up against it for quite
a while already," Fay said.

"It's not so bad," Colleen said. "Mother's getting
better. She'll be back to work in another three months
or so."

"What happened to her?" Fay asked.

"Just some surgery," the girl said. "She had
insurance and everything, so the money wasn't a problem,
but I had to do all the house stuff, you know, feeding
everybody, getting the clothes clean, all that."

"And keeping your grades up," Fay guessed, as she turned over the eight of coins for the more recent past.

"I did O.K.," Colleen said.

Fay picked up the Sun card, and patted the girl's hand. "Well, there's one thing we don't have to worry about. All that study is going to pay off for you one day. Look at this Sun. That's just about the happiest ending you could ask for."

"You're doing the wrong thing," Colleen said. "You're reading for me. I asked you to read for the baby."

"I can't read for the baby," Fay said, covering quickly, "because the baby can't shuffle the cards. It's a very old rule."

"Then I want my money back," the girl said, straightening up in the chair.

Fay thought a minute. The one thing she did not want to do was turn this girl out into the street. "That's fair," Fay said. "I should have told you about the shuffling business in advance. So I won't charge you. But I'd like to finish the reading, if you don't mind."

"It's free?" the girl asked.

"Absolutely," Fay said.

"O.K., then," the girl said. "But I have to be home at three-thirty." It was just then one o'clock.

Fay studied the last four cards. The King of Cups,

probably the abortionist; the Moon, so his place was
filthy after all; the Empress, so this girl was more
worried about her mother than she was about herself; and
finally, The Star, so at least there was hope. Well,
what good was that? Hope was cheap.

"What should I do?" the girl asked.

"I don't know," Fay said. "Can you make tunafish?"

"You mean right now?" Colleen asked.

"You haven't eaten yet, have you?"

"No," the girl said.

Fay stood up. "I always eat. It makes me feel
better. Do you like tunafish?"

"I like it," Colleen said, following Fay into the
kitchen. "But I don't like eggs in it."

"Me either," Fay said. "If we wanted eggs, we'd
make egg salad, right?"

"Right," the girl said. She opened the refrigerator
reached for the mayonnaise, and an embarassed grin
flickered across her face. "I'm starving," she said.

"Another good reason to eat," Fay said.

"I know," the girl said. "But I don't want to. .
show, you know."

"What will you do if you don't have the abortion?"
Fay asked. "If this man says he won't do it, or your
mother finds out and locks you up somewhere."

"I don't know," she said. "Run away, I guess. Get
a room. Get a job."

"Do you have family you can go to?"

"Not without mother finding out."

"Can you marry this boy?"

"It wasn't his fault."

"He was _there_ though."

Colleen was silent a moment. "I don't want to," she said. "That really would be the end of me."

Fay couldn't help noticing, as the girl put the slices of bread into the toaster, that her fine blond hair needed washing. And the limp gray T-shirt probably looked better on the older brother who had worn it out.

"I know I have to have the abortion," the girl said. "I'm just scared, that's all."

"I'd be scared too," Fay said.

"What I thought," Colleen said, as she washed the lettuce, "was maybe you could tell me who the baby was. And then, if it was going to be the President someday, or Beethoven, then I'd think about it some more."

"What do you want to drink?" Fay asked. "I have cokes and milk and water."

"A coke," the girl said, as the toast popped up.

"You fix the glasses, then, and I'll make the sandwiches," Fay said.

They worked now in silent comfort. Fay was not thinking about what to say. She just wanted the tuna not to squeeze out of the other end of the sandwich when Colleen took her first bite. There was a trick to that, and Fay was proud to know it.

Colleen carried the plates out the back door to the
tiny garden behind the apartment. Then she came back
for the glasses and picked two paper napkins out of the
plastic pumpkin Fay kept them in.

"This is nice out here," Colleen said, as Fay
followed her out and they sat down in the rusty iron
chairs.

Fay knew the rust wouldn't ruin anything either of
them had on, and, while the air was heavy and still,
there was at least more of it outside. She took a bite
of her sandwich.

"Somebody special," Fay said, more to herself than
Colleen. "What if the baby is somebody special."

"Yeah," Colleen said. "Somebody there's only one
of in the world. Somebody born to do something."

Fay reached for her glass. "Colleen," she said,
"there are a lot more people born to do something than
ever grow up to do it."

Fay wished she'd made iced tea. Or lemonade.
Lemonade would be perfect.

"It's not enough to be born Beethoven," Fay
continued. "For all you know, you might have been a
Beethoven yourself."

"No," Colleen said, shaking her head with absolute
certainty. "We couldn't have afforded the lessons."

"That's what I mean," Fay said. "A lot of special
people are born. People who could straighten out this

mess we've made in the world. Healers. Singers. Horn
players. Good people. Real gems. Magicians.
Inventors. Storytellers. People who know about money,
people who could fix anything, people who could make
things that wouldn't break."

"So where are they?" Colleen asked.

"We just can't raise them," Fay said, "or don't
know how to, or don't recognize them soon enough, so
they get away from us. We lose them. You see them
later on the streets, though, hundreds of them, all the
time. And you wonder why they look so empty. It's no
wonder, really."

"I'd try to raise it right," Colleen said.

"I know you would," Fay said. "And if you have the
baby, I'll help you. You can bring him over here every
week and play every phonograph record I've got."

Colleen took the last bite of her sandwich and
stared at the paving stones. She wished Fay wouldn't
watch her chew. Her mother had told her she chewed her
food like nobody she ever saw.

"I'll help you in any way I can," Fay said. "But I
won't tell you you've got a Beethoven in there because,
with you so young, and things so tough, I just don't
think he'd make it."

Colleen nodded.

Fay went on. "And, I don't want you to have the
baby and then blame him later if he cost you so much and

didn't turn out to be Beethoven after all."

"But I want him to be special."

"When you're ready to have a baby," Fay said,
"you'll take any kind you can get. You won't care about
special. In fact, you'll get down on your knees every
night for nine months and pray to God he's normal. That
would be blessing enough."

Colleen drank the last sip of her coke. "I'm not
ready, then."

"No," Fay said. "You're too young."

Colleen brushed something away from her face, like
a mosquito she wished were there. "It makes me feel
bad," she said.

"I know," Fay said.

"Is it a sin?" the girl asked, her voice breaking.
"Is abortion a sin?"

Fay took a deep breath. "Maybe," she said, as the
first drop of rain plinked on the table between them.
"But it's not the only one."

There was no more talk. They carried the dishes
inside. Fay's mind was racing, flipping through the
rest of what might be said. What comfort could she give
the girl? And what else was worth giving? Nothing.
She had done all she could do.

She gave the girl an umbrella, handed her a banana
to eat on the way home, kissed her good-bye, closed the
door and wept.

But the next time Fay took Lizzie to the dentist,

there was a new receptionist. The dentist told her Mrs.
Masters had resigned due to a death in her family.

"It wasn't Colleen, was it?" Fay asked, terrified
to hear the answer.

"I don't know," the dentist said. "She didn't say,
and I didn't ask."

Fay was furious. "You mean there was a death in
that lady's family and you didn't even ask who it was?"

"No," the dentist said. "Sorry," and he turned to
Lizzie, certain that the novocaine had taken effect by
now.

Fay got up from her chair at the end of the room,
pushed back the tray in front of Lizzie, pulled her up
out of the big gray dental chair, and never saw the man
again. She didn't try to explain it to Lizzie, but she
did apologize to Lizzie all afternoon. She held her,
rocked her, and didn't let go of her hand until they
both fell asleep that night on the rug in the living
room, with every last one of Lizzie's stuffed rabbits
tucked in tight around them.

* * *

Standing by the pay phones, the Chief and Arnie had
worked out a pretty fair plan for controlling the scene
at the truck. The mothers would meet at the Burger King
lot across the street. Policewomen would escort them to
the truck. The shopping center would remain open, but
the chief would tape a personal message for TV and radio
asking the public to stay away. That way, they hoped
they could limit the crowd to hoodlums, of course, and
bookish types who didn't watch TV during the day, and a
few hundred normal people whose car radios had been
stolen by the hoodlums.

"I'll be downtown," the Chief said, as he left.
"If you get anything new from the spirit world," and he
nodded in Fay's direction, "let me know."

"Will do," Arnie said, and placed one more call,
arranging for a detective to watch Fay's apartment and
alert him the minute Lizzie showed up. Then he went
back into the coffee shop and sat down with Fay.

"They never put enough ice cream in these things,"
he said, picking up his coke float. "You're supposed to
fill up a glass with ice cream, then pour the coke in a
little at a time."

"That's the way you do it," she laughed.

"Sure it is," he said. "That's the way I like it."

She smiled. "They do it this way because the ice

cream is supposed to float, Arnie. Coke float."

He took a big sip through the straw and caught her up on everything they'd learned. Little Timmy Willis had no idea where he'd been. It sounded like he'd been asleep the whole time.

The kidnappers had called all the mothers from pay phones in supermarkets. But nobody in any of the supermarkets remembered seeing anyone use the phones. Anyone special, that is. People used the phones all day, they said. That's what they were there for.

The mayor's wife had gotten a call too, so there wasn't any point in keeping their boys a secret any more. She'd be at the truck with everybody else.

Arnie looked up from his float and noticed the woman in the beige pantsuit. "There's that lady again."

"Yes, I know," Fay said. "She came back in just after you left. Her name is Edith Masters. She used to be the receptionist at Lizzie's dentist. I'd like to go say hello to her before we leave."

"Fine with me," Arnie said, standing up. "I'll meet you outside."

He took the check to the cashier while Fay made her way over to the table by the window.

"Hello, Mrs. Masters, it's. ."

"Of course I remember you, Fay," Mrs. Masters said, blotting her mouth with a napkin. "How are you?"

"I'm fine," Fay said. She was shocked to see how old Mrs. Masters looked up close. The lines in her face were so deep, they looked like scars.

"How's Lizzie?" Mrs. Masters asked.

"She's fine. She's all grown up," Fay said.
"How's Colleen?"

"She's in California," Mrs. Masters said.

Fay tried not to show her relief. "What's she
doing there?"

Mrs. Masters retied the bow at the neck of her
blouse. "She's working."

Fay was not good at casual conversation, but she
had to keep trying. "I hear it's pretty in California.
What does she do there?"

Mrs. Masters nodded in the young man's direction.
"Fay, I'd like you to meet a new member of our church."

Fay shook his hand. "Pleased to meet you," she
said, noticing his hammer thumb. "What church is that?"

"He's just moved to town," Mrs. Masters said.

Fay tried not to stare at his hands. She'd never
seen a thumb hug a forefinger so close. It wasn't a
good sign. But she saw it in his face too. This was a
vengeful, spiteful man.

"Where are you from?" Fay said to him. "Someplace
south, I guess, with that tan you have."

"Fay is a fortune teller," Mrs. Masters said.
"She even helps the police from time to time."

The young man swept his hands off the table quickly
and clasped them together in his lap. But he didn't say

a word. That was peculiar, Fay thought. Almost
everybody says something when they hear you're a fortune
teller.

"I didn't get your name," Fay said to him.

"It was nice seeing you again, Fay," Mrs. Masters
said quickly.

"Yes," Fay said, backing away, "you too. Tell
Colleen hello for me the next time you talk to her."

"I'll do that," Mrs. Masters said. "Good-bye,
Fay."

Fay walked quickly up to meet Arnie. Were they or
weren't they? Should she tell Arnie? Tell him what?
That Colleen was working in California?

"How is she?" Arnie asked.

"She's fine," Fay said.

Arnie held the door open for her and they walked
down the steps into the parking lot. When they passed
the window of the coffee shop, he looked up and caught
Mrs. Masters staring at him.

"Is she screwing that boy?" he asked.

"If she is," Fay said, "she's not paying him
enough."

"I have to go to the radio truck," Arnie said.
"Want to come?"

"No," she said. "I want to talk to Lizzie."

"There's a man in front of your house waiting for
her," he said. "As soon as she shows up, I'll take you
there."

"No matter what else is happening?" she asked.

"Scout's honor," he said.

"All right, then," she said. "I'll come." Then
she thought minute. "Can you find out if somebody's
dead?"

"If they died in the state, we can know it in two
minutes."

"Her name is Colleen Masters," Fay said.

"No problem," he said, writing it down. "Colleen
Masters."

11:00 A.M.

The parking lot was beginning to look like the
staging ground for police training maneuvers. The truck
sat, roped off and guarded at the far end like a time
bomb. Shoppers who stopped to look at it, were waved
away by the officers, but the police themselves gathered
in small groups to stare at it, to study it as though it
were a tactical assault problem at the police academy.

"So," Arnie said, as they approached the police
command center, "What do you think about Wyoming?"

Fay had said she would tell him tomorrow. Was this
tomorrow? "Wyoming?" she asked.

"We can do whatever you want about furniture," he
said. "Take it all or leave it all. Makes no
difference to me."

"I don't know," she said. "I like your bed."

"I like that big arm chair at your house," he said.
"And your porch things, you know, that wrought iron
table and chairs. They'd be good in Wyoming." Then he
pointed to the benches set up by the First Aid station.
"Are you going to be O.K. out here?" he asked.

"You go on," she said, wiping her forehead on her
sleeve. "I'm happy to sit for a while." Then she
walked to the First Aid station and asked for a glass of
Ginger Ale. Where was Lizzie? Dance class? Shopping for
deck shoes?

Fay knew she couldn't get the answer by demanding
it like this. She should just relax, think about
something else. Like what? Like where were the other
twenty-four children? No.

What if Lizzie didn't want Fay to find her?
Could she disappear? No. Lizzie wouldn't do that. She
never minded Fay knowing where she was. Or did she?
Fay tried to remember another time Lizzie had
disappeared, tried to remember what she actually knew
about her daughter, tried to know how much of it was
true.

Oh sure, Lizzie disappeared all the time as a
little girl, but all kids did that. Lizzie would ask if
she could go get a popsicle, and an hour later, between
clients, Fay would charge up the street and find her in
the girlie show ticket booth where old Charlie would
have her counting out quarters and putting them in
little paper rolls. That didn't mean anything, did it?

Well, that particular time it did, but they worked
it out, they talked about it. Lizzie liked the girlie
show girls. She said they smiled at her when they came
to work, even the one with the pink hair. She asked if
she could see them dance sometime.

"Absolutely not," Fay said, taking the girl's hand.
"It's dirty."

"What's dirty?" Lizzie asked, waving good-bye to
Charlie.

"They dance around naked," Fay said. "Don't make

me drag you down the street, O.K.?"

"Why is that dirty?" Lizzie asked.

"Because men come to see the girls dance," Fay
said, unlocking the door, "and men shouldn't see women
naked unless they're married to them."

"Why not?" Lizzie asked, leaning up against the
front of their building now, pretending that the door
wasn't open and her mother wasn't standing there holding
it for her.

"Because your body is just for you and your
husband," Fay said. "Now come into this house, please."

"It's not a house," Lizzie said defiantly.

"We call it a house."

"I don't," Lizzie said, more determined than ever,
digging into the sidewalk with her heels.

"All right," Fay said, closing the door. "What do
you call it?"

"It's a rat trap," Lizzie said.

"Who said that?" Fay asked, trying to keep her
voice low, so people walking past them on the sidewalk
wouldn't hear. "Did one of those girls say we lived in
a rat trap?"

Lizzie tugged on her hair and didn't answer,
concentrating instead on the stoplight turning from
green to red at the corner.

"Elizabeth. . " Fay grabbed her arm.

"Arnie sees you naked," Lizzie said, "and he's not

your husband. Your husband is my daddy."

"Your daddy's not my husband any more, Lizzie, you know that," Fay said. "We got a divorce. And I'm sorry he doesn't come to see you, but that's just who he is, and that's why we got the divorce in the first place."

Lizzie looked down at her feet. "That's not what you told me before," she said. "You said. . "

"I know what I said before," Fay sighed. "I said he didn't want to help take care of Granny, but it's the same reason."

Lizzie kicked at the patch of grass trying to take root between the concrete squares under her feet. "I bet Daddy doesn't live in a rat trap now," she said proudly.

Fay knelt down beside her. "Lizzie," she said, "I know you miss your Daddy, but we do not live in a rat trap. Our house is the cleanest house on the block."

Lizzie started to object. "It's not a. . ."

"I know it's not a house," Fay said. "But I wish it were a house, so I pretend, all right?"

Fay's knees were shaking from trying to hold this position, from trying not to touch the sidewalk, but trying to stay on the little girl's level.

"All right?" Fay asked again.

"O.K.," Lizzie mumbled. "It's a house."

"Good," Fay said. Then she grasped Lizzie's chin and turned her face around so she could see her eyes. "Now, I want to know how many times you've been in that

girlie show. If I can't trust you to go where you say
you're going, I can't let you go, Lizzie."

"You're hurting me," Lizzie cried, jerking her head
away.

Fay knew she'd said the wrong thing. She ran back
over the conversation. Girls. Dirty. Naked. Arnie.
Daddy. There it was. Arnie saw Fay naked and Lizzie
had seen it. Oh boy.

"Lizzie?" Fay asked, "are you mad that Arnie comes
to see me?"

"It's dirty," Lizzie said.

"It's not dirty," Fay said, as calmly as she could.

"He's not my Daddy," the girl said simply.

Fay took a deep breath. "What did you see,
Lizzie? Did you see us in the bed together?"

But Lizzie couldn't answer that. Her head hung
limp now. She was ashamed, she had done something bad,
but she didn't know what it was, or what was bad about
it. Fay pulled Lizzie to her and hugged her tight.

"Oh Lizzie," Fay said, stroking her hair, and
patting her back as she would a baby, "Arnie loves me, and
I love him, and we sometimes sleep in the bed together
because it makes us have good dreams. The reason we're
not married is I love you more, and I never want anybody
to come between us."

She picked up the little girl's hand and kissed it.
"Lizzie," she said, "When I tell you a place is dirty, I

mean that it's not safe."

Lizzie's knees gave way and she slipped down the door and sat on the sidewalk.

Fay stretched her legs out beside the girl, but kept talking. "But Arnie spends the night with us to make sure we're safe. He loves us. Both of us." She paused. "O.K.?"

Please God, Fay thought, let it be O.K.

Lizzie was crying. "I'm sorry," she whispered.

"I know you are," Fay said. "I'm sorry too."

Fay stood up, clasped Lizzie's hand tightly in hers and opened the door.

"Miss Morgan?" a voice behind them said.

"Yes?" Fay turned.

"I'm Brenda Cross," the dull-eyed matron said. "I have an appointment at 5 o'clock."

Fay felt Lizzie's hand squeeze even tighter. "We've had a little problem this afternoon," Fay said to the woman, nodding down at Lizzie. "Would you mind if we made it another time? I know I have Monday at 5 free."

"Please," the woman begged, "I'm getting married tomorrow. I have to know now."

Fay looked at the woman's rounded shoulders and puffy gray cheeks, and sensed immediately that the marriage was being made out of nothing but fear.

Fay shook her head. "If you really loved him," she said, "you wouldn't have been able to wait, what is it, eleven years, to marry him?"

"Yes," the woman nodded, startled by the accuracy
of Fay's count. "Eleven years tomorrow."

"Go spend a week with your mother," Fay said,
reaching for the door knob.

"She's sick," the woman said.

"I know that," Fay said. "Make your peace with her
before she dies." Fay opened her door. "And then," she
said. "there's somebody else at home who's eager to see
you. Stewart, somebody."

The woman brightened instantly. "Stewart Day?"

"Go," Fay said. "Your boyfriend knows it's not
right either. You've both just given up on the world,
that's why you've been together. But that's no reason
to get married."

The woman leaned over suddenly and kissed Fay on
the cheek. "Thank you," she said. "How much do I owe
you?"

"Nothing," Fay said. "Not a thing."

The woman wanted to say good-bye, but was
embarassed to, so she made a peculiar waving gesture
with one hand, and simply backed away.

Fay smiled, turned, walked in the door, drew the
drapes, and flipped over the sign that said CLOSED.
Lizzie scampered off to see what was in the
refrigerator, and Fay sank down deep in her old rust
velvet arm chair and missed Arnie desperately. She

wanted nothing more than for him to walk back in from
the kitchen with Lizzie, the two of them holding hands
and eating cold fried chicken.

Maybe she should have married Arnie years ago.
Given Lizzie a real Daddy. Given Arnie a real place in
her life. Made a real home. Was that what Lizzie had
been asking for that day? For more than just a mother?
And how would Fay ever know?

"Good news or bad?" Arnie asked.

Fay jumped. She had no idea how long he'd been
standing behind the bench where she was sitting. "Bad,"
she said.

He walked around to sit beside her. "That girl you
asked me to check on, that Colleen Masters? She's dead.
Fifteen years ago. She was seventeen. The death
certificate said massive internal bleeding, cause
unknown."

Fay nodded. "Did you ask them what. . ."

"Abortion," Arnie said. "The coroner said the guy
before him didn't like the word, so he always put 'cause
unknown'."

Fay looked away.

"Is Colleen her daughter?" Arnie asked. "The woman
in the coffee shop?"

"Yes," Fay said. "What's the good news?"

"Lizzie's on her way out here to have lunch with
us!" he grinned. "Our man picked her up at your house
ten minutes ago."

"Here?" she asked.

"Why not?" he asked. "We have to stay here anyway.
I thought you'd be happy to see her."

"I am," Fay said. "It's just that I know I'm going
to say the wrong thing."

"Are you sure?" he asked.

"Absolutely," she said, smoothing out her skirt.

"Well," he put his arm around her, gave her a
comforting squeeze, "whatever you think's best," he
said.

She had to laugh.

"They say the food at the bowling alley is pretty
good," he said.

"Fine," she said.

"We can go on over there if you want," he patted
her arm. "Unless you have something I should tell the
team in there."

"You mean like where the other kids are?" she
asked.

"Yeah," he said.

"No," she said.

"O.K., then," he pulled her up. "Let's go."

* * *

The mayor sat at his desk. His fears that the
kidnappers would use his children against him
politically, were turning out to be unfounded. His new
fear was that his wife was going to use his children
against him politically.

In the ten o'clock staff meeting, Vi had said she
wasn't going to the truck, wasn't going to give in to
the kidnappers' demands. She said if nobody else was
brave enough, she was. She would go on national
television, stand up to the kidnappers, and defend
abortion to the whole country.

He knew it was exactly the opportunity she had been
waiting for. The real reason she'd go on national
television was to become a star. He wondered how long
he had felt this way. He was afraid it was a long time.
He tried to think of somebody else he might love.
Secretaries, salesgirls, old girlfriends, neighbors,
anybody. But no names came immediately to mind.

When the mayor heard her knock on his door, he was
studying the photograph of his two boys, his wife, and
his big Irish Setter who had died in March.

"Yes?" he called, and slipped his personal address
book back into the drawer.

"See that we're not disturbed," Vi said to his
secretary as she opened the door.

"Good morning, sweetheart," he said, standing up as she entered.

"Sit, sit," she smiled.

And he wished for an instant that he was that dead red dog in the picture.

"I guess it's time for us to have a little chat," she said, taking the chair the secretary used for dictation.

"How are you feeling?" he asked. "Did you get any breakfast?"

"Juice is all I need in the morning, Peter," she said.

He wondered if that was something new, a diet, maybe, or if she'd stopped eating breakfast some time ago and he just hadn't noticed. He was sure he remembered her eating breakfast sometime. When was that?

"I think there's something you ought to know," she said, crossing her legs at the ankles, then tucking them neatly behind the leg of the chair.

"All right," he said. He knew he had to convince her to go to the shopping center. But he could let her talk first.

She cleared her throat. "I had an abortion when I was in high school."

"I see," he said, and put the top back on his pen.

"And then I helped some other girls get them from

the same man. I imagine he's dead now, but they're
not."

"I don't understand what you're getting at, Vi."

"They could be part of this, dear," she said.

"Vi," he said wearily, "if you helped those girls
then, why should they want to hurt you now?"

"I don't know. Maybe they wish they had those
babies back."

"Do you?" he asked.

"No, I don't," she said. "But I'm not like a lot
of other people."

The mayor stood up, walked to the window, opened
the blinds, and looked down to the street. He envied
the shoppers with their packages, the lawyers with their
briefcases, and the mailmen with their heavy pouches.
He wished he had something to carry down the street. He
wished he could say where he was going.

"I just wanted you to know," she said, "that if the
press ask me about it, I won't deny it. I'm not ashamed
of it."

"The press won't know to ask about it unless you
tell them," he said. "I think you're safe."

She sighed. "I am not interested in being safe,"
she said.

"No, I can see that," he said. "You're proud of
it, aren't you."

"I was right to help them."

"It was against the law."

"The law was wrong. Everybody can see that now,"
she said.

"Who was the father?" he asked.

"Just a boy."

"Did he have a name?" he asked, turning back to the
window.

"Yes, darling, he had a name," she said, "but that
isn't really the point, is it?"

"Do you not remember his name, or do you just not
want to tell me?" he asked, surprised by his own anger.

"What are you asking, Peter?"

"Did you tell the boy about it, or did you just
have the abortion and then tell him later?"

"Peter, darling, I fail to see what this has to do
with. ."

"You didn't tell him at all, did you," he said.

"No," she said, "I didn't, but. . ."

He didn't let her finish. "It wasn't his business,
was it. Like my boys aren't my business now, are they."

She grabbed the arms of the chair. "And just what
does that mean?" she hissed.

"The other mothers. . " he began.

"You want me to be like the other mothers."

"The other mothers want their children back. The
other mothers are scared."

"You want me to be scared."

"I want you to go to the truck."

"This is no time to be scared," she said. "What do you think they're going to do? Kill the children? No. They'd be crazy to kill the children. Look what they did already. They turned one in, right?"

"Right."

"And that's exactly what they'll do with the rest of them as soon as they've made their point."

"What point?"

"That abortion is wrong. But we can't let them say that. We have to stop them right now."

He lashed out at her. "Can't you think about anything else!" He was nearly choking on his rage. "Not once, not once have you talked about Kevin and Kerry! Do you remember _their_ names?"

She took a deep breath. "You think I don't care about the boys, is that it?"

"Yes. That's exactly it."

"You're wrong."

"All right, then. Prove it."

"I have to prove to you that I love my boys?"

"You have to pick up your package and go to the truck because your package may have some important piece of this puzzle in it, and my boys are missing and I want them back."

Her voice was clear, but as cold as he'd ever heard it. "I am their mother," she said. "But that is not all I am. I refuse to stand here and grieve for your entertainment."

And now he realized the difference between them.
"All I am," he said, "_all_ I am is their father."

She shook her head. She hoped he wasn't going into
one of his 'worthless me' moods.

He walked back to his desk and sat down. He took
the top back off his pen and straightened a pile of
papers. "You will go to the truck?" he asked, as
officially as he could.

"I will go to the truck," she said, "because that's
where the press is expecting me," she said.

"Then I will see you there," he said, and buzzed
his secretary. "Mrs. Foley, I have some letters for
you, please."

Vi reached across the desk, snatched up the photo of
the two boys, turned and prepared to smile at Mrs. Foley
who was just opening the door.

"Don't you look lovely this morning," Vi said to
the secretary.

* * *

Fay and Arnie found a table near the front of the
bowling alley snack bar, and waited there for Lizzie and
the other detective to arrive.

"Are you hungry?" she asked, putting on fresh
lipstick.

"No," he said. "But who knows when we'll eat
again."

She looked better. The lipstick actually made
a difference.

"So. . ." he started, genuinely sorry he'd had to
leave her sitting on that bench outside. "How are _you_?"

"Arnie," she blurted, "did you ever want to have
children?"

He drained his water glass. "With you, sure," he
said.

"Why didn't you say so?" she asked.

"I don't know." He set the glass down on the table
and motioned for a refill. "I figured you were happy
with Lizzie."

"I was."

"I don't mind it," he said, picking up the menu.

"Not having children?" she asked.

"Yeah," he said. "I wouldn't have seen them very
much," he said.

"You could still have them," she said. "With
somebody younger than me, of course, but. .

"No thanks," he said.

"Arnie," she said, annoyed at his seeming
indifference to his own needs, "if you wanted to have
children, you should have said something. And if you
want them now, you should go do it."

He dipped his handkerchief in her water glass and
mopped his forehead with it. "I don't think about it,
Fay," he said. "There are plenty of kids in the world,
and I'm happy, O.K.?"

He turned and checked the front door for Lizzie and
the detective. "It's all right that I don't have kids,"
he said. "I'll do that next time."

"What next time?" she asked.

"Next time around," he said, "next life. You know.
Don't you think there's a next time?"

"I don't know," she said, quite surprised but
trying not to show it. "I didn't know you ever thought
about it."

He smiled. "There has to be, don't you think? How
can people feel as strongly as they do about certain
other people here, unless they knew them before? I
mean, one life is barely long enough to learn people's
names, much less love them, or hate them."

Fay didn't didn't quite know how to respond. "So
you think there's another life, huh?" she said.

He shrugged. "I'm not sure I believe it, exactly.
But it's a real good explanation for something I'd be

real confused about otherwise."

"Like what?" she asked, marveling at how one new piece of information could rearrange everything else she knew about him.

"Well, look," he said. "Detectives don't fall in love with psychics. Detectives don't believe in all that shit."

She flinched.

He continued. "But I'm a detective, and I love you. So I must have known you before."

"Arnie Campbell!" she laughed. She couldn't hold it back any longer. "I don't believe this is coming out of your mouth!"

"Well it is," he grinned. "You ought to be real grateful too. Think how many lives you've had to live to hear me say it. The first time around, I was probably some sheriff's henchman. I probably burned you at the stake."

And now they both laughed, and Fay was about to ask him what he thought happened the next time, when the front door opened and Lizzie walked in.

* * *

Arnie felt Fay freeze. He grabbed her hand. "Just remember," he said to her, "Lizzie is proud of you. She's probably been listening to the radio. All they can talk about is you."

He stood up to wave to Lizzie, but she had already seen them and was on the run.

"It's fabulous," Lizzie said, hugging Fay, then kissing her on the cheek. "You found three kids!"

Fay steadied herself using the back of the chair. "Thanks, love," she said.

"No," Lizzie said, sitting down. "Everybody's talking about you. The radio, the TV, everybody!"

Fay looked at Arnie. This was sounding a bit rehearsed. "It was both of us," Fay said. "It wasn't just me."

"Hi, doll, " Arnie said to Lizzie, genuinely glad to see somebody smiling today.

Lizzie patted his stomach affectionately. "Hi, Arnie," she cooed.

The other detective sat down now, and Lizzie introduced him. "This is the famous Fay," she said gaily.

"Proud to meet you, Mam," he said, extending his hand to Fay. "Jake Hawley."

"Thanks for finding my girl," Fay said.

Jake spoke with a dry Western accent, and had the
lean muscular build of a ranch hand. His hair was too
long for the regular force, but then, so was Arnie's.

"Texas?" Fay asked.

"Yes Mam," he said. "Abilene."

"It's just great, Mom," Lizzie said.

"It's not so great if the rest of them are dead,"
Fay said.

"Mom," Lizzie paled. "They can't be dead."

"Well," Fay opened the menu, "let's hope not."

Lizzie had expected Fay and Arnie to be more
excited. She looked at Arnie, then back to her Mother
who'd put on her glasses to read the menu, then decided
Arnie was a better bet for an answer.

"So," she said, "you guys been up all night?"

Arnie winked at her. "You're not supposed to tell
us old people we look bad," he whispered. "It hurts
our feelings."

"No!" she said. "You look terrific! I didn't mean
that!" She tried to calm down.

"Well, for people who've been up all night, I guess
we do," Arnie said. He patted Fay on the arm. "What are
you going to have?" he asked her, looking around for the
waitress.

"I'm not hungry," Fay said, taking off her glasses.
"I'll just have cottage cheese."

"Have an omelet," Lizzie said. "Eggs are good for
stress."

"I don't want an omelet," Fay said. "I want to know where you were all night."

Lizzie shook her head. "I was on a boat," she said, with a sly look to Arnie. "On the biggest boat you ever saw!"

"All night?" Fay asked.

"I'm having the tuna melt," Arnie said. "Jake?"

"I always order chicken out," he said, but I'm going to my Dad's house for dinner, and he always has chicken, so sure. Tuna's good."

"Whose boat was it?" Fay asked.

Lizzie reached for a menu. "Mother," she said, "you don't even <u>know</u> these people. You can't hate them already."

"I don't hate them," Fay lied. "I just want to know who they are."

"You already know who they are," Lizzie said. "You're the one who told me he had a boat, remember?" Lizzie leaned over to Jake. "Mother knows all this stuff already, see. She just asks so we can fight. The guy is gorgeous."

"He's lazy," Fay said.

Lizzie opened the menu. "What difference does it make if he's lazy? He's rich."

"It makes a big difference," Fay said. "Everything is too easy for him. Including you."

Lizzie looked at Jake again. "Is my mother calling

me a whore?"

Jake laughed. "I don't think so," he said. "Not
yet, anyway."

Something about Jake's quiet eyes and easy self-
assurance made Lizzie feel better. "Will you let me
know when she does?" Lizzie said.

"You bet," he said.

"So tell me what you did with him then," Fay
demanded.

Arnie interrupted again. "Is there any trick to
getting waited on here?" he asked.

"Mother," Lizzie said, trying to speak calmly, "we
just went to a party on a boat, O.K.?"

"What kind of a party?" Fay asked.

That did it. "A party," Lizzie grumped. "You
know. Fun? You remember fun, don't you?"

"So all he does is go to parties, is that right?"

Lizzie made no effort to cover her exasperation
now. "It was a party, Mother. You don't ask that at a
party."

"He would've lied about it anyway," Fay said.

Lizzie didn't answer, as the sudden appearance of
the waitress startled them all.

"What do you want?" the waitress said, as if they
had knocked on her door for a handout.

Lizzie pointed to Fay. "We'll both have cottage
cheese and a Tab and she likes lots of crackers, so
bring the whole basket, and they'll have the tuna melt."

"And a coke," Arnie finished.

"Beer for me," Jake said. "I'm done for the day."

The waitress wrote down the orders and a bus boy
brought four glasses of water.

"I'll let you drink your beer," Arnie said to Jake,
"but you're not off duty."

"Oh I know," he drawled. "I just don't like to
alarm the subject."

Lizzie caught on. "Am I the subject?"

"Yes, Mam," he said. "As far as I know, I'm on
your tail til midnight."

She laughed. "Are those your official orders? On
my tail?"

He winked at Arnie and lit a cigarette.

But Lizzie wouldn't quit. "I thought you had to go
to your Dad's for dinner," she said. "Do I have to
go to your Dad's for dinner?"

He looked at her, shrugged his shoulders as if her
long legs and loose blouse didn't matter at all. "I
made that up," he said.

"Lizzie," Fay asked, "Did Paul want to know what
you do?"

"I don't do anything," Lizzie said. "I take dance
class."

"You're studying," Fay said.

"Not very hard," Lizzie said.

"Well how can you be studying if you spend the

whole night on boats?"

"Boat, Mother," Lizzie said. "Boat."

"I don't pay all that tuition for you to go to a
party on a boat."

"You need some sleep, Mother," Lizzie said.
"You're making a scene."

"I'm worried about you," Fay said.

"So what else is new?" Lizzie grumbled.

Arnie was relieved when the manager appeared with
their lunch. He'd seen this fight before. But then,
when he looked down at his food, he felt like he'd seen
that before too. Maybe it was Fay, being with her all
day like this. It changed the way you looked at things.

"I just want to know," Fay said, "what you're doing
with this boy."

With her free hand, Lizzie pinched Jake's arm.
"With _this_ boy?"

"Let's eat, huh?" Arnie begged.

"With Paul," Fay said.

"We're going to the boat again tonight, if that's
what you mean," Lizzie said, digging into her cottage
cheese.

"You are not," Fay said. "I absolutely forbid it."

"Mother," Lizzie said, "it's just another party.
Except it's a better band, Paul says. I survived last
night, didn't I?"

"It's not like last night," Fay said. "This time
the boat is sailing, and once it goes, you're on it for

good."

Lizzie tried to understand. "It's not me that's lost, Mother, it's all those little kids. I'm just fine."

Fay started to interrupt, but Arnie wouldn't let her. "Eat your lunch, Fay," he said.

Lizzie tried again. "We're going to a party, Mother, that's all. A party. The boat's not going anywhere. I'm not going anywhere. Except to the party." Lizzie looked at her watch, wadded up her napkin and reached for her purse. "I've got to go," she said, nudging Jake to let her out of the booth. "I've got class in twenty minutes."

Fay stretched across the table and grabbed Lizzie's arm. "I said No," she said.

Lizzie looked at Arnie, Arnie looked at Jake.

"You're with her every minute, right?" he asked. "She takes a shower, you take a shower?"

Jake said that was right and Arnie gently pried Fay's fingers away from Lizzie's arm.

"Let her go, Fay," Arnie said quietly.

"I'm all right, Mom," Lizzie said. "I've got my class, I've got my cop. . ." She turned to Jake. "You can even take the class if you want to," Lizzie said. "Anybody can take a class."

"Now that's something I'd like to see," Arnie laughed.

"Lizzie. . . " Fay said, trying to stop her.

"It's all right, Fay," Arnie said. "She's just going to class." He looked at Lizzie. "Right, kid?"

"Right, Dad," Lizzie said, leaning over to kiss the top of his head. She stroked his face. "You got a good shave this morning."

"Thanks," he said. "I try."

"O.K.," Lizzie said carefully. "See you later."

"When, later?" Fay asked.

"I don't know, Mother. Just later, O.K.?"

"I want to know when," Fay said.

"Please, Mother," Lizzie said. "I just want to have a good time."

Fay took a deep breath. "And I just want you to be there when I wake up."

"I'll be there," Lizzie said. "I'll be there," and she blew Fay a kiss. "Bye."

Arnie watched them go, looked around for the waitress for a cup of coffee, then wondered why, if the waitress didn't feel like doing anything today, she didn't just stay home where nobody would bother her.

"I said the wrong thing," Fay said.

"It wasn't so bad," Arnie said. "You just acted like her mother. She's used to that."

"What would you have done?" Fay asked.

"All she wanted to do was trade stories," he said. "She's not going anywhere, Fay. She wouldn't leave while this case is going on. No way."

Fay knew better, but she didn't say anything. She
was mad and hurt, and she wouldn't admit to being
jealous, but she was. "Who is this Jake person?" she
demanded.

Arnie sighed. "Oh, you know," he said, "he's just
another one of those convicted rapists we hire from time
to time."

"That's not funny."

"It is to me," Arnie said.

She gestured angrily toward the other customers in
the snack bar. "Stand up and tell everybody, then," she
snapped. "See if they think it's funny."

"Fay, Fay," he said.

"What?"

"Eat your cottage cheese."

Fay knew she was behaving badly, but she didn't
know how to stop it. "I don't like cottage cheese," she
said. "I never liked cottage cheese."

"Eat some crackers, then," Arnie said. "You like
crackers, I know. You have to eat, Fay. So you'll feel
better. So you'll act better," he paused, "so I don't
strangle you before we find those kids."

He reached for the basket of crackers, pulled it
toward her, unwrapped a packet of butter and picked up
his knife. "Want me to fix one for you?"

Fay looked at him and shook her head. "I'm sorry,"
she said.

"It's all right," he said.

She coated a cracker in butter and took a bite.

Arnie knew not to talk about Lizzie, but he wasn't
sure if he could talk about the missing kids either. He
wondered if he could bring up Wyoming again. The longer
this day got, the better Wyoming looked to him. Maybe
they could rent a little farm out there and buy a horse.
Lizzie would come visit if they had a horse. Fay would
like riding, too, he knew it. He was sure he'd remember
how. It had a lot to do with how you talked to the
horse, he remembered that much anyway.

Fay was into her fourth packet of crackers now.

"If Lizzie makes one move toward that boat," she
said, "packing, buying a bathing suit, anything, I want
her stopped."

"Will do," Arnie said, standing up. "Are you
ready?"

The waitress saw Fay stuffing the rest of the
crackers into her purse and came over with the check.

"Don't go away," Arnie said to her, "I think I have
it right here." He counted out sixteen dollars and
twenty-eight cents, the exact amount of the bill, and
put it in her hand.

"What about a tip?" the waitress snarled.

"O.K.," Arnie mused. "I'd say you probably ought
to quit before they fire you."

The waitress turned abruptly and left.

"What do you want to do now?" Arnie asked Fay.

"See Gail," she said. "Find Beth."

"Good," Arnie said. "Good."

12:00 P.M.

* * *

For the last hour, Gail had fought off her fear and
anger by writing sick sympathy cards, cards she already
knew she couldn't sell. Who wants to buy a card that
says

I'M SO SORRY,

turn the page,

BUT WHAT DID YOU EXPECT?

Or

FATE,

turn the page,

DOESN'T GIVE A SHIT

She did like

JUST WHEN YOU THINK IT CAN'T GET ANY WORSE,

turn the page,

YOU DISCOVER IT WAS ALL YOUR FAULT.

But her favorite was

THE DARKEST HOUR,

turn the page,

IS JUST BEFORE THE END.

Then, her fear winning out after all, she wrote
what she knew would happen if her daughter died. She
wrote the reason people would send cards instead of
visiting. It said. .

> I WOULD HAVE CALLED OR COME BY TO SEE YOU,
>
> turn the page,
>
> BUT I DIDN'T WANT TO.

Her career was finished. She threw the notebook
into the trash and poured herself a glass of water.

Marvin was still in the bedroom sitting on the side
of the bed reading Sports Illustrated. It was an old
issue, Frank Shorter was on the cover. Marvin didn't
know why he'd saved it. It had been years since Shorter
was winning marathons. But every week, despite the
arrival of a new issue, Frank had stayed on the top of
the pile. Somehow, just sitting there with the elegant,
articulate, Ivy-league runner made Marvin feel in
control.

Marvin did not have, that he was aware of, any
special skills, or even any particular personal traits.
His childhood had not been especially tortured, and his
high school career was largely undistinguished. He had
graduated from State College with a degree in Sociology
and married an average height brown-haired woman. For
twelve years, they'd slept in a regular double bed and
lived within their means.

Marvin had lived some forty years following his
Dad's advice to "show up and be friendly." Today was no
exception. He couldn't imagine anyone wanting his
daughter, Beth, an plain-looking child whose parents
didn't have much money, so, he thought, this kidnapping
business was simply a mistake. When the kidnappers

realized they had the wrong girl, they would give her

back. All he had to do until then, was encourage the

police, and cheer up his wife.

He checked his watch. It was time to go pick up

the package the kidnappers had left for Gail at the

bowling alley. Then they had to meet the other parents

at the Burger King across from the Indian Point Shopping

Center.

"Are you ready?" he said to Gail as she appeared at

the door of their bedroom.

Gail had been ready for the last three hours, but

she didn't tell him that. She didn't say what a stupid

question she thought that was, or how angry she was that

her husband was so cheery. All that could wait. Maybe

it wouldn't have to be said at all. Gail's mother was

meeting them at the Shopping Center. Maybe Gail could

just grab Beth's hand as she came down out of that truck,

take her to her mother's car and never see Marvin again.

"I'm ready," Gail said finally, and turned around

and walked back down the hall.

"Let's go then," Marvin said to the empty doorway.

They drove to the bowling alley in silence. Gail

picked up the package - a small white envelope - and

they started for the shopping center.

"What is it?" Marvin asked.

"Just a slip of paper," Gail said, holding the

envelope up to the light.

"Could be the combination to a lock," he said, pulling the car out into the traffic.

"You haven't even looked at it!" she snapped.

"I know," he said. "But that's how they lock those big trucks. With chains and a combination lock on the back door."

Gail bit her lip. Marvin didn't know anything about big trucks. He'd just followed them down the highway, followed them for a hundred miles because he didn't have the guts to pass them.

As they neared the Center, traffic slowed to a crawl. Gail cursed and turned on the radio. They heard the Chief of Police tell people to stay away from the Shopping Center, and they heard the Traffic Control helicopter say that cars were backed up bumper to bumper for three miles on all routes leading there.

"How far away are we?" Gail asked, as Marvin pulled onto the shoulder and passed ten other cars. Then he came to a bridge over the expressway and had to flag the car behind him to be let back onto the road.

"About a mile, I think," he said, shifting into neutral as the traffic came to a dead stop.

"I'll have to walk," she said, opening the door. "It's the only way I'll make it on time. We should have left earlier."

She put the envelope into her purse and stepped out of the car.

"Gail?" he called after her.

"What?" she said, closing the door.

"I love you."

Gail bent down to look in the window. "Goodbye,
Marvin," she said.

* * *

As Gail walked along the highway, people stuck in
the traffic jam rolled down their windows and asked if she
could see anything up ahead, asked her if she wanted a
lift, asked her if she was, by any any chance, one of those
poor mothers.

She said the road looked like a parking lot, that's
why she was walking. She said she just got out of her
own car so why should she get in theirs, and she said
no, she wasn't one of those poor mothers, she was just
trying to get to the Burger King for lunch.

The scene was worse than she could have ever
imagined. The Burger King looked like a fort under
siege. The parking lot was jammed. Gail could see two
remote camera crews, at least eight police cars, a
couple of ambulances, and a whole flock of motorcycle
cops.

Finally, she saw Fay and Arnie across the lot and
screamed at them. Fay waved, and Gail ran toward them
dodging policemen who told her to slow down, and cars
who honked at her to get out of the way.

Fay and Gail got in the back seat of Arnie's car.

"Did you get your package?" Fay asked.

Gail showed her the envelope. "Marvin thinks it's
the combination to the lock on the back door of the
truck."

"Could be," Fay said, feeling the slip of paper

inside it. "How's Marvin holding up?"

"Please," Gail said. "Let's not talk about Marvin."

Fay patted her on the knee. If there was some state just before shock, Gail was in it.

"I'm sorry I asked you about Lizzie this morning," Fay said, "but all night long I'd been seeing her going away on this big boat. I just didn't think about how it would sound to you."

"It's O.K.," Gail said. "I didn't mean to scream at you. I was just so upset. Marvin was. . .I don't know, I guess he was trying to make me feel better, telling little jokes and straightening up the living room, but why isn't he mad at them, or something?"

Fay reached over for her hand. "Honey, Marvin is every bit as scared as you are. I promise. Men are just funny about things like this."

Gail put the envelope back in her purse. "Lizzie and I had a nice visit," she said. She zipped her purse closed, then open again. It was hard for her just to sit here like this, but she knew it wouldn't be any better outside.

"Is Beth in the truck?" Gail asked.

"No," Fay said.

"Did somebody look?" Gail asked.

"No," Fay said. "The police are doing exactly what the kidnappers said to do, leaving the truck alone til the mothers got here."

"Then how do you know the kids aren't in there?"
Gail asked, her eyes watering suddenly.

"We would have heard them," Fay said.

"Not if they were tied up and gagged," Gail said.

"They're not there, Gail," Fay said. "The most we
can hope for in the truck, is the instructions for
finding them."

"That's not enough," Gail said. "I want Beth back
right now."

The mayor knocked on Fay's window.

"Who's that?" Gail asked.

"The mayor," Fay said. "Let's get out and see if
they need you."

Gail followed Fay, numb and blind.

"This is Gail Wilkins," Fay said to the Mayor as
they stood together, with the car between them and the
crowd. "Her daughter Beth is one of the children."

Fay turned to Gail. "And this is Peter Ewing. His
boys, Kevin and Kerry, are missing too."

"The newspaper didn't say anything about your
boys," Gail said.

"I know," he said, extending his hand to shake
hers. "I thought if the kidnappers. . .never mind. It
was stupid what I thought."

"How old are they?" she asked, noticing his palms
were clammy and cold.

"Three and five," he said. "Yours?"

"Four," Gail said.

"Are you a hiker?" he asked, referring to her shorts, but basically just trying to stay sane.

"Yes," Gail said, looking back at the crowd. "You?"

"I'm sorry," he said. "What a dumb thing to say. I'm going fucking crazy with this."

"I'm hating everybody I know," she said. She shook her head and tried to laugh.

Fay saw her chance and took it. "I have to find Arnie," she said. "Can you two keep each other together here?"

They said sure, and when Fay left, they walked around to sit on the back bumper of the car.

"Shouldn't you be . . somewhere?" Gail asked.

"I'd just be in the way," he said. "My wife is talking to the press, and my staff is handling the rest of it. Where I should be . . ." He couldn't finish.

"Go on," she said, knowing that as long as he kept talking, she wouldn't have to.

"I'd like to be at my desk making kidnapping punishable by death in this city," he said. "Or making everybody stand outside their houses while I went door to door and found our kids. Or appointing somebody else mayor so if I ever get my boys back we can go hiking or something until they're grown up."

Gail was quiet a minute. "You're absolutely right," she said. "Who ought to be kidnapping our kids

is us. Take them away where the world can't mess us all
up."

"What do you do?" he asked.

"I write greeting cards," she said, "and think
about where I'd rather be."

"Is it any place in particular?" he asked.

"Someplace cool and high," she said, staring at the
hideous commercial landscape and the clogged highway
that ran through it.

"Sounds like the mountains," he said, then looked
at her and added impulsively, "or drugs, I guess."

"Or both," she said.

"God are we depressed."

"Are we going to get them back?" she asked.

"I don't know," he said. "They keep telling us we
are."

"Right," she said. "Do you believe it?"

He loosened his tie. "I have to," he said. "I
have to."

"Yeah," she said. "We can do that, I guess."

"I have to have another chance with them," he said.
"I've. . missed too much of their lives already."

She nodded, knowing exactly what he meant. "Beth
is the only thing in my life that makes any sense," she
said. "I'd do it all different except for her."

"So," he said, grasping her hand, "we've got to
find them. If we don't. . ."

She squeezed his hand. "We'll find them," she

said quietly. "We will."

They stood up, and she shielded her eyes with her hand so she could look directly up at him.

"Thanks," she said.

"Yeah," he put his arm around her and patted her shoulder. "You too."

"O.K.," she said.

"I'll be here all day," he said, looking behind him at the women beginning to gather under the MOTHERS sign.

"Yeah," she said. "Me too."

"So I'll see you later," he said.

"O.K.," she said. "What do we do now?"

"Whatever they say," he said, and he walked off toward his press aide, who had promised the TODAY show woman an interview with him.

Gail scanned the crowd briefly for Marvin, didn't see him, smoothed her shorts and walked over to join the other mothers in front of the cameras.

                              * * *

          "What's that all about?" Arnie said. He had been
    watching the Mayor talk to Gail.
          "They have to talk to somebody," she said.
    "They're doing what we're doing. Trying to get through
    this."
          "Did they know each other before?" he asked,
    thinking the conversation looked more than polite.
          Fay saw what he meant. They looked better together
    than she'd seen either one of them look all day. Of
    course, she also had the knowledge that both marriages
    were in trouble, but that wasn't so unusual any more.
          Fay's favorite thought about marriage came from a
    Russian psychic she heard speak at a dusty old library
    in an Italian neighborhood. The woman had said that
    when married people went to sleep, their souls, free of
    the captivity of their bodies, flew off to spend the
    night with their spiritual mates. They never had to
    decide what to do next, they just did it. And they
    didn't relate the events of their days, they just
    played. They'd take long walks and whistle, they'd tilt
    their heads back and drink the dew as it fell, or
    sometimes just dance til daybreak to the blue strains of
    the moon.
          Occasionally, the woman said, people did recognize
    these soul-mates in their waking life, and if that

happened, then sooner or later, not usually in this life, but sometimes, they would find a way to be together, though that was often quite costly. But, she said, even if soul-mates married, the life they'd spend together in the kitchen would bear very little resemblance to the deep satisfaction their spirits would enjoy without them at night.

Fay remembered the looks exchanged by some of the couples in the room. One person would squeeze the other's hand as if to say, "We're one of the lucky ones, we've found each other." And the other person would return the squeeze, but turn back quickly to face the podium and sigh, wondering how long it would be until the next life got here.

In the Tarot pack, on the card called The Lovers, there is a picture of a young man standing between two women, trying to make a choice. Depending on the pack you are using, and the interpretation you've been taught, the choice is either between virtue and vice, between celibacy and the carnal life, or between the beautiful maiden and the loyal mother. The odd thing is, that in nearly every deck, there is a little Cupid over the boy's head, about to let fly with an arrow and, presumably, make the boy's choice for him.

When this card appeared in a prominent position, Fay usually told people they were torn between two loves, work and life, for example, and that the choice had to be made. That wasn't so much an interpretation of the cards as it was a common old fact of everyday life. It was so common that Fay could, if she felt like it, call people at random from the phone book and tell them that. In a reading, however, her clients generally responded quickly to this insight, and told her their version of this ancient dilemma.

Fay liked it when someone recognized that one of their loves was, in a sense, sacred, and the other, profane. Profane loves weren't so bad. They were certainly distracting, moderately entertaining, and relatively inexpensive to maintain. For most people, profane loves were just fine, and whole industries had developed to help people find them. But the choice to honor a sacred love was always a costly one, and Fay could help a client determine if they were willing to pay the price. A sacred love, she insisted, could cost your whole life and then leave you anyway in the end.

Occasionally, Fay talked to artists, or people who wanted to be artists, who felt, for their talent, something they called a sacred love. All too often, it turned out that they simply adored the idea of being famous, which, of course, had very little to do with art, and was just about the most profane kind of love going.

Real artists, Fay knew, had no choice. Real lovers had no choice. That's what the Cupid was doing in the picture, making the choice for these people. Fay

figured if you could make the choice yourself, you
should. But if there didn't seem to be a choice, well
then, that was your answer, but you'd still have to pay
for it.

The thing about love was, that feeling it _for_ someone,
for something, feeling it in the first place, was the
gift. It filled you with energy and purpose, and the
more of it you gave away, the more of it there seemed to
be. To love one person was to like everybody a little
better, and to love some one thing was to begin to
understand the rest. Usually, love made you generous
and brave, but even if it made you obsessive and
grasping, it at least pumped you up, pointed you toward
the path, and sent you charging into the world believing
that you and the world were somehow related for a
change.

Receiving love, however, either in return, or from
someone you merely knew, was a totally separate matter.
To _be_ loved was to know you didn't really deserve it, to
worry about losing it, to try to keep doing whatever it
was that made them love you in the first place, and to
feel somehow responsible for it although you knew it
really wasn't yours. Yes, receiving love was quite
complicated, and very difficult to do with much grace.
Better to feel it. Better to be the one who loves.
Better to love something that can't love you back.
Better to serve.

As far as Fay knew, God was the only one big-
hearted and gracious enough to allow himself to be loved
completely. And how did He do it? Well, like a good
soldier, by staying in the fields of Heaven, sending the
occasional homesick telegram, but never actually
applying for leave.

The people who loved Him had it made, Fay thought.
The martyrs, the saints, even just ordinary believers
had it pretty good. They got to love as much as they
wanted to, and God never said stop, that's enough, I
can't take it any more, love the dog why don't you, I
need a break.

"Why don't the police just open the packages?" Fay
asked Arnie.

"They checked for bombs," he said. "But the Chief
is still taking your advice, going along with the
kidnappers."

Fay nodded, and wished she'd brought a hat. The
sun was really brutal now.

Arnie wanted something to happen. He wouldn't have
minded if, say, a bomb went off. Then at least he could
tell somebody what to do. He'd already told the Chief
he should clear all these extra people out of here, but
when the Chief pointed out that, with the highway
blocked, it would take an airlift to get rid of them,
Arnie gave up. This wasn't his show and he knew it.
The Chief had told him his job was to protect Fay, and
that even if he saw somebody breaking the law, he wasn't

to interfere unless Fay was threatened.

"Are they in the crowd somewhere?" he asked her.
"The kidnappers?"

"I don't know," she said. "It feels bad here, but
I don't know how it could feel good. It's just all this
fear."

"I want to know where all these tacky people came
from," he said. "I've never seen so many fat. . "

She had to stop him. "Arnie," she said, "Arnie,
just calm down. It's O.K. These people are worried for
the mothers. That's why they came. They thought there
might be something they could do."

"There's not a damn thing anybody can do," he said.
"All I wanted to know was why they're all so fat."

"They're not fat," she said. "They're just hot and
their clothes are wrinkled, that's all, they just look
fat."

"You could never love a fat man, could you Fay?"

"No, Arnie," she smiled, "I don't think I could."

He was silent a moment. He seemed to be a little
better. "How many minutes now?" he asked.

"Four, Arnie. Four," she said.

* * *

Vi had enjoyed her interview with the woman from
the Today show, although she was disappointed to find
the woman was so short. Once she thought about it,
though, Vi realized that height, like depth, just didn't
matter on TV.

Vi had begun by stating that this incident was a direct
attempt to destroy the women's movement. Then she went
on to say that the women's movement was the obvious
target for all kinds of hostilities now, remarking that
it wouldn't be long before the growing epidemic of AIDS
was blamed on the women's movement. The reasoning would
go something like, if women were who they used to be,
then men wouldn't be turning gay in droves and heading
for the bath houses instead of taking a shower at home,
where somebody who loved them disinfected the stall once
a week.

The Today show woman asked Vi if she wasn't putting
words into the mouth of the enemy. Vi said gays weren't
the enemy, the world was just in a mess now. And, since
there were only two new things in the last twenty years,
Moslem fundamentalism and the women's movement, one of
them had to have caused all this trouble. The Ayatollah
was too far away. Blaming women was easy.

"Everything is our fault," Vi said. "Restaurant
prices are higher because women don't cook like they
used to. Clothing prices are higher because women have

to have clothes to work in. More men are unemployed
because women are taking their jobs. City services are
less dependable because there aren't enough housewives
left to call up and bitch about things. Products are
shoddier because women aren't mechanical, divorce rates
are going up because women aren't making happy homes,
and kids don't read any more because their mothers don't
teach them how to."

"Are you going to lead the mothers' group?" the
woman asked.

"Yes I am," Vi said, and excused herself. She had
done quite well, she thought. And she knew she looked
good. She had dressed for the cameras, a high necked
blue silk blouse, and a flower print slim skirt.

Most of the other mothers had worn whatever they
had on when the call came, work clothes, jeans or khaki
pants, and old shirts. Dolores Garcia came straight
from the studio, so she still had on her leotards, but
she had borrowed somebody's dance skirt and put it on as
she drove out here. Betsy Griffith had an arbitration
that morning so she was wearing her legal gray suit and
red paisley bow tie.

As they waited for someone to take charge, the
women talked uncomfortably with each other, exchanging
accounts of how their children had disappeared, and what
the kidnappers had said to them on the phone. They were
scared and angry. They wanted to storm the truck. They

wanted to sue the fairgrounds. They wanted to kill the
kidnappers for putting them through this. None of them
wanted to be here, and none of them had any choice.

Fay was standing just behind the mothers with
Arnie. The Today woman came up, introduced herself and
asked if, by any chance, they knew who the local psychic
was who was working on the case. Arnie lit a cigarette,
and Fay said she'd heard about it, but she, herself, was
only here because one of the mothers was a good friend.

When the reporter left, he took her hand. "You
can't dodge the reporters forever, you know."

"It's not that I mind talking," she said, glad to
have his hand in hers. "It's just that I don't have
anything to say right now."

"What do you think of the group?" he asked, looking
at the mothers.

"They're scared," she said. "That's going to be a
problem."

"Scared they won't be able to do what the
kidnappers want?" he asked.

"No," she said. "Scared of each other. Each one
of them thinks she'd do better by herself." She paused.
"It's . . a problem women have."

"Do you have this problem?" he asked.

"Oh yes," she said. "I know it's wrong, but it's
another one of those real old things."

Vi began to address the group. "We have," she
said, "one minute to cross the street. The police will

clear the path, and protect us as we go. All we have to
do is ignore the crowd and walk calmly. When we arrive
at the truck, a policeman will ask each of you for the
names of people you want admitted to a kind of family
circle over there. We will work inside the barricades
next to the truck, but your husbands or mothers or
friends will at least be a little closer than the rest
of the city."

Vi stretched out her hand, and the police path
opened up. Several of the women gasped. Nobody had
quite believed they could rearrange such a large crowd
so quickly.

"And now," Vi concluded, "God bless us. And
everybody else . . .get out of our way."

Vi walked to the path the police had made and the
mothers formed a line behind her. Fay and Arnie
followed at the end of the line, in a group that
included the Chief of Police, the Mayor, two emergency
medical men, and the owner of the Shopping Center.

Their passage was a silent one. Once they reached
the other side of the street, however, once Vi stepped
into the shopping center parking lot and the newly
positioned cameras switched their lights back on,
everybody started to talk again. What will they make us
do? Who are they? How long will it take? What do they
want? Where are our children? And who the hell are all
these other people?

* * *

"Lizzie thinks I spied on her," Fay said to Arnie
as they made their way to the truck.

He wasn't listening. He was surveying the security
set up along the route. "What?" he asked.

"All Lizzie wants is to get away where I can't know
what she's doing."

"You can't help it if you know things," he managed,
wondering what the big hook and ladder was doing here.

"I'm not prying," Fay said. "I want her to have
her own life. I always have."

He saw the four officers on the roof of the
shopping center, saw their rifles and telescopic sights.
"You just want her to tell you things," he said.

"She doesn't have to tell me everything," Fay said.
"It's just that it was so nice to share it."

"When she was little, you mean."

"Remember how she'd run in the door all full of
what the teacher said, or what her girlfriend said, or
how she saw a Daddy long legs crawling up a stop sign?"

"I remember," he said. The coroner was here too,
he noticed. "But she doesn't have the same kind of
things to tell you now, Fay."

"Yes she does," Fay said. "I don't know anything
about her dance classes, I don't know where she buys
her shoes. Or she has a new dance bag, only it doesn't

look new, so she must have found it or traded it with
somebody, but who was it?"

"Here," he pointed to a row of bleachers set up for
the police. "We'll sit here."

"Why won't she tell me?" she asked.

"Want anything?" he asked. "Coffee, soda,
anything?"

"I want to know why she won't tell me things," she
said.

"It's not that she won't, Fay," he said. "It's
just that she doesn't."

"All right," she said. "Why doesn't she tell me
things?"

"She's busy," he said. "She's doing them. She
doesn't have time to tell you about them."

"How much time would it take?" she protested.

"To know everything you want to know?" he asked.

She wound her watch and tried not to wonder where
Lizzie was.

"To know everything you want to know," he said,
"you'd have to be _her_. That's why she won't tell you.
She doesn't want _you_ to be her. _She's_ her. She's just
trying to keep it that way."

Fay scooted across the bleacher seat and forced
herself to look at the mothers standing around the table
in front of the truck. Where were these children?
Where was Lizzie?

1:00 P.M.

* * *

The mothers stood around the long table set up in
front of the truck. Vi had asked the Chief for folding
chairs, but nobody felt like sitting. This wasn't a
committee meeting.

Behind the mothers, three bleacher sections held
the police, the press, and the fathers and families of
the kidnapped children. Camera crews were positioned to
the right of the bleachers, and emergency vehicles to
the left. Behind the bleachers there were portable
toilets, a first aid station, and a barricade of police
cars and fire trucks. The whole encampment was then
ringed by firemen standing shoulder to shoulder.

The firemen were the Chief's idea. Something about
firemen made people feel better. Even the Chief.
Actually, when he was a little boy, he'd wanted to be a
fireman, but when he grew up, somehow he knew he wasn't
nice enough.

Fay looked more closely at the mothers.
"Something's wrong," she said to Arnie. "I mean,
somebody's wrong. One of these mothers is not a
mother."

"The one in the pink sweatshirt," Arnie said.
"Undercover. The real mother's in France."

Fay saw immediately that the policewoman was trying
too hard to be calm, to seem normal. The other mothers

were agitated, eager to get started.

Arnie wiped the sweat from his forehead. "The
father's here, though." He pointed to the man.
"Merriweather."

Vi set her package down on the table in front of
her, and the other mothers followed. "I think we should
open them one at a time," Vi said.

The mothers grumbled among themselves. What did Vi
think this was, a baby shower? The point was to get it
done, wasn't it?

Gail held up her envelope. "Mine has the
combination to the lock on the truck," she said.

The mothers cried almost in unison, "Open it!"

And Gail tore the end off the envelope and fished
out the tiny strip of paper. "9 Right," she said, "21
Left, 3 Right."

Nobody moved. What if the truck blew up when they
opened it?

"It won't blow up," Fay said to Arnie.

"I know," he said. "The bomb squad checked it."

"But the kids aren't there either," she said.
"There's a letter in one of their packages. That's what
we have to find."

But at the table, the mothers were ripping their
packages open with no regard to what might be in them,
or what order might make the contents understandable.

"There's the key to a padlock," Arnie said.

"And a slide projector," Fay said, standing up for
a better view of the table. "And slides," she added, as
the mother who got the projector opened one box of
slides and held one of them up to the light, then sank
back into the chair behind her, clearly sickened by what
she saw.

"It's an abortion," the mother said to the woman
next to her.

But before she could get the slide back in the box,
a woman at the far end of the table screamed. "It's our
babies!" she cried, and flipped through the stack of
photos to find her own boy asleep on a kitchen table,
his head leaning up against a toaster.

The mothers left their places and swarmed around
the photos, desperate to see their children. Were they
really sleeping? How could they know they weren't dead?

"They're not dead," Fay said to Arnie.

"Til we find them, they might as well be," he said.
And now he could see some of the other things the
mothers had unwrapped. Megaphones, felt-tip markers,
poster board and wooden stakes, a ream of white paper,
two dozen ballpoint pens, flashlights, a cassette tape
player, twenty-seven pairs of white baby shoes, and nine
jars like you'd see in a laboratory, containing little
white things floating in liquid.

Gail looked up to find Fay in the bleachers and
held up the photo of Beth.

Arnie grabbed Fay's arm to keep her from running to

her friend. "It won't help," he said. "They have to
finish."

But Fay knew what Gail was thinking. It was time
for Beth's nap. Had they fed her any lunch? Any
breakfast? Was she tied to the bed? Did they let her
go to the bathroom? Give her any water? Were they
watching her at all?

The woman next to Gail held her photo in her teeth
while she finished unwrapping her package. A clock.
Gail sat down, took the clock from the woman and shook
her head. A harmless wind-up kitchen clock with a
bright yellow face and a sunflower in the middle of the
dial. The kind of clock you hear ticking when you don't
know what to say to the person across the table.

Arnie was mad. "This is the most cruel, goddamn
mean thing I've ever seen. How can these women..."

"Oh my God," Fay interrupted.

At the far end of the table, the woman in the wheel
chair had just lifted the top off a black plastic
garbage can, pulled out a sack of little arms and legs.

Fay's hands flew to her mouth. "Oh no," she
whispered. "Please, God, no."

But the woman next to her pulled one of the little
arms up to the edge of the bag so she could see it
better. "It's dolls," she said, checking another one
just to make sure. "It's not babies."

But the woman in the wheel chair was crying anyway.

"They can't go on like this," Fay said.   "Whoever
did this was . . ."

"Anti-abortion," a mother called to the group,
pulling the pamphlets out of her envelope.

"Class photos," said the woman who had checked on
the doll arms.   "Only every fourth head is cut out."

The woman in the wheel chair had stopped crying.
"What does that mean, one out of four," she asked,
looking numbly at the class photos.

"It's abortion," the other woman said.   "I read it
somewhere.   That's the number now.   One in four
conceptions end in abortion."

"One out of four?" the woman in the wheel chair
said blankly.

"That's what the number's _always_ been," the nurse
on the other side said.   "These people are sick."

Most of the mothers were sitting down now.   There
were only two packages left to open.

"That one's going to take all of them to unwrap
it," Fay said, pointing to the box that was easily the
size of a coffin.

But the Chinese woman started pulling white sheets out
of the duffel bag she had been given, and a letter fell
out on the ground.

"There it is," Fay said.

Three mothers dived for it.

"Wait!" Vi called.   "Don't. . ."

But nobody was about to damage this letter.   They

weren't sure they wanted to hear what it said, but they
weren't going to fight over it either.

The Chinese woman walked it around the table and
handed it to Vi.

"Good," Fay said. "They should wait til they know
what's in that big one."

The outside of the big box was secured with metal
tape, and the box itself was double wrapped in heavy
brown paper. The edges of the box were taped all the
way around, and each item inside was enclosed in bubble-
pack,. reinforced with masking tape, then surrounded by
those styrofoam amoebas that fly all over everywhere and
three months later you're still finding them down
between the sofa cushions.

It took three of them ten minutes to get it all
undone. They spread the items on the table. One life-
size inflatable woman, and a full set of the surgical
equipment necessary for performing an abortion. The
stirrups, the dilators, the curettes, the works.

Nobody said a thing. They were finished. A bitter
depression settled around them. This was not what
they'd expected. Maybe they'd thought they would each
receive directions for finding their children. Or maybe
they thought they would simply break into the truck and
their kids would come running out, hungry and tired, but
alive. But no. They saw now that this was not the end
of the anguish. This was just barely the beginning.

They had been mad before, but now they felt the ragged anger of outrage, the hostile anger of despair. And none of them could move.

Vi was still standing. "I'll read the letter now," she said, looking around the table.

"Kill them," somebody whispered. "Kill them all."

The Mayor came up to sit with Fay and Arnie.

"I don't understand," he said. "I just don't..."

"Just sit," Fay said, patting the bleachers. "Just sit. It's O.K. It's not much longer now."

"Good afternoon," Vi read from the letter. "Your children are safe. But you will not see them again until you have collected 40,000 signatures and addresses, on a petition demanding that abortion once again be outlawed in the United States."

"Can't do that," Arnie whispered. "It's blackmail."

"Abortion," the Mayor said. "What's abortion got to do with my boys?"

Vi continued. "You will set up an exhibit in the truck. When people have toured the exhibit, they can then sign the petition."

"It's ridiculous," Arnie said. "They could get that many signatures just passing the thing around the parking lot."

"Would you sign it?" Fay asked.

"Sure," he said. "If I thought that's all it took to get those kids back, I'd be first on the list."

Vi was still reading from the letter. "You will keep a vigil around the clock, carrying signs you will make, until you have the required number of signatures. Do not be tempted to cheat. We are watching from very close range, even, perhaps, from inside your group. You will turn the signatures over to the mayor's wife, who will take them to Washington and put them in the hands of the Chief Justice of the Supreme Court of the United States. Then, and only then, will your children be returned."

"Would she do that?" Fay asked the Mayor. "Take the petition to Washington?"

"I don't know what she'd do," he said. "Maybe."

Vi cleared her throat, grasping the letter firmly in her hand. "There is only one right position on this issue," she read. "Abortion is murder, murder is wrong. If you are energetic and passionate as you talk to people about it, that will weigh heavily in our decision as to the fate of your children."

Vi had spoken very distinctly. No planes had flown over while she was reading. Fay and Arnie, and everyone else in the bleachers had heard every word of the letter.

"Goddamn them," Arnie said to Fay, as Vi folded up the piece of paper.

"What do we do?" the Mayor asked.

"It's up to the mothers," Fay said. "They have to

decide whether. . ."

"What choice do they have?" the Mayor asked.

But the fight had already started at the mothers'
table. Vi, determined to stay in charge, asked the
Chief if he didn't need to go over the contents of the
packages for clues. What she meant was, the mothers
would listen to him if he said to take a break. And
maybe during the break, she could decide what they
should do.

"If I could have your attention," the Chief said to
the mothers.

They kept talking.

"We have no intention of letting you go through
with this preposterous plan," he said.

They heard him, but they didn't believe him. They
weren't even sure it was any of his business.

"We need to search this material," he gestured
toward the table, "for clues."

They went back to talking.

"If you will eat your lunch now," he said, a little
louder, "that will make it easier for us."

"I brought mine," one mother said. "Let's go on."

"What is there to talk about?" another mother said.
"We have to do what they say or we won't get our
children back."

Four mothers stood up and headed for the lunch
table. There was going to be an argument, that was
clear. And the argument was going to take more energy

than the work the kidnappers were demanding.

They didn't need the Chief to tell them to eat.
They were all mothers. Mothers know when to eat.

The Mayor stood up. He'd been watching Gail for
the last ten minutes. He had to go to her. He stepped
down out of the bleachers and headed over to her. She
needed him.

* * *

"Would you really sign the kidnapper's petition?"
Fay asked Arnie, as the police garrison around them
broke up to go to work.

Arnie threw his cigarette down on the ground,
stubbed it out with his shoe, shook his head slowly from
side to side, then took out his handkerchief and wiped
the sweat off the back of his neck. It might have
looked, to someone who didn't know him, as if he was
thinking about it. Fay knew better.

She asked again. She had to know. But she tried
to ask in her normal tone of voice. "What _do_ you think
about abortion, Arnie?"

He looked up and watched the mothers walking away
from the table. For some reason, he couldn't look
directly at Fay.

"It doesn't matter what I think about abortion," he
said. "It doesn't matter what any man thinks about
abortion. It doesn't happen to us."

"Of course it happens to _you,_" she said.

"No," he shook his head again. "It happens real
close to us, but not directly to us, like it does to
women."

He went on. "If somebody aborts our child," he
said, "we might be mad it's gone or glad it's gone, but
we didn't feel it go. But if she _had_ the baby, we

wouldn't know what that was like either, because we
wouldn't be there all day with it. So we shouldn't be
making this decision. This is for women to decide."

He stopped for breath. "I think it's wrong. But I
don't want to be asked what I think. It doesn't matter
what I think."

"Do you think the fetus has a soul?" she asked.

"It has something," he said. "Maybe not a soul,
exactly. But maybe the threat of a soul."

"And that's what you want to save?" Fay asked.

He thought for a moment. "No," Arnie said.
"That's what makes me sad to kill it. I'm a Catholic.
Remember?"

"I remember," she said.

"I like being a Catholic," he explained. "I mean,
I like being something besides a cop, so I'm a Catholic.
But I don't believe much of it any more. Maybe abortion
is the only way I can still call myself a Catholic.
It's something to hold onto anyway."

"Do you believe in contraception?" she asked.

"Sure I do," he said. "Same way I believe in
locking the front door at night."

"So it's all right to stop babies from coming into
the womb, but not all right to stop them from coming
into the world."

"I guess so," he said. "I don't know."

She looked up at him. "Don't I have the right to
defend myself if somebody breaks into my house?"

"You don't have the right to kill him except in
self-defense," he said. "And babies aren't trying to
hurt you." He stood up. "Let's go see the Chief."

"No," Fay said, pulling him back down beside her.
"Please. One more minute."

"All right," he said, almost angrily. "Yes, if
somebody breaks into your house, I'd say shoot him.
You don't have the right to do it, but you do it just
the same. But I don't like it. And I don't like
abortion either. And you can talk at me all day if you
want to. I still won't like it."

"I'm not trying to convert you," she said. "I'm
just trying to understand what you feel."

"I don't want people to hurt each other," he said.
"That's why I became a policeman in the first place.
But the first thing you learn being a cop is you can't
stop them."

"Arnie," she began.

But Arnie wasn't through. "I don't want the women
hurt, you understand. I just don't want the babies
hurt."

"The only way to keep women safe is keep abortion
legal," she said.

"You're right," he said. "I know that. All right,
then. I just want them to be sorry."

"I think they're sorry," Fay said.

He shook his head. "They just want it over with,"

he said.

Fay was beginning to suspect Arnie was talking from experience here. She spoke softly. "Maybe they do," she said. "But they're still sorry."

He turned away.

Did she dare ask him about it? Why had he kept it a secret all these years? Was he still ashamed of it? Still sad about it?

She asked as carefully as she could. "Weren't you sorry?" she said. "Wasn't she sorry?"

"Yes," he nodded. "We were the sorriest two people I ever knew."

"Well," she said, "that's how sorry they all are."

Arnie wound his watch distractedly, looked up and saw that the mothers had all left the table, and the Chief was motioning for him. "All right, then," he said. "I guess I can't sign the petition, can I."

"We can sign it to get the children back," she said.

"No," he said. "That wouldn't be right. We can find those children, you and me."

Fay wondered if she would ever hear this story, this abortion story of Arnie's, wondered how many other people had one to tell, people she thought she knew.

Arnie couldn't ignore the Chief any longer. "Let's go," he said, standing up. "Here," he helped her down from the bleachers. "Give me your hand."

Fay saw through the crowd that Gail was talking to

the Mayor at the lunch table, while Vi gave yet another
interview. She hoped Gail would be careful with the
Mayor, hoped she wouldn't get confused about what was
happening, hoped she could forgive herself if she did.

When Fay and Arnie arrived at the mothers' table,
the Chief was ready for Arnie, wished he'd been with him
the whole time, in fact. "Well," he snapped. "Got any
good ideas?"

"I think you should send the mothers home," Arnie
said, leafing through one of the anti-abortion
pamphlets.

"They wouldn't go," the Chief said.

"Yeah," Arnie said, picking up a set of dilators
and trying to suppress his revulsion. "I guess you
should've picked up the packages yourself and never let
this thing get started in the first place."

"How could I do that?" the Chief asked.

"I'd like to see the pictures of the children," Fay
said. "Where they're sleeping, I mean."

The Chief glanced over at the mothers at the lunch
table, noticed that they were no longer chatting among
themselves, but instead were now totally absorbed in the
sandwiches he knew to be completely tasteless.

"Let's let the gals finish their lunches, huh.
When they come back to the table, I'll gather the
pictures up for you."

Fay nodded.

"It's going to be a goddamn circus out here," the
Chief said, irritated at Arnie's seeming lack of
interest. "This thing could go on for weeks."

"I think you'll be through before dark," Arnie
said.

"I don't see how," the Chief said, biting off the
end of his cigar. "The people have to walk through the
truck before they can sign the petition, right? Now how
many people can walk through a truck in an hour? Maybe
a hundred, and that's with nobody stopping to read
anything. Forty thousand people at one hundred an hour
is four hundred hours. That's..." he paused to do the
math, "sixteen days, Arnie."

"If you want to get names," Arnie said, "just set
up twenty tables and let the people who are already
against it, go ahead and sign. I mean, nobody's going
change their mind about this just because they get a few
new facts. Abortion isn't about facts."

"But the letter said. . ." the Chief began.

"Yeah, I know what the letter said." Arnie slid
the full color abortion close-ups out of the envelope.
"What are they going to do, send a team of kidnappers
over here to validate the signatures?"

Arnie threw the pictures down in disgust. "It's all
just a show, Chief," he said, "just a damn show for the
damn TV. Just get it over with so the rest of us can go
to work."

"Doing what?" the Chief said.

Arnie didn't answer. He was examining one of the pickled embryos floating in its jelly jar.

"What is it you want to do?" the Chief repeated, as calmly as he could.

Arnie shoved the jar back down in the box. "I have to stay with Fay. But somebody needs to talk to the pro-life groups around here," Arnie said. "See if they know who could have done this, see what they have to say about it."

"Good," the Chief said, relieved that Arnie had started thinking again. "Good idea."

"I want to talk to Gail," Fay said to Arnie, "before they start up again."

But the Chief wasn't finished with her. "Do you think there's a kidnapper in the group?" he asked. "One of the mothers?"

"Has to be," Arnie said. "Probably the lady who got the slide projector."

Fay gasped. Of course. That's exactly who it was.

"What makes you think that?" the Chief grumped. Then he looked over at the lunch table and saw that Lynn Waldo, who had gotten the slide projector, was also the only one who'd brought her lunch.

"They don't want it broken, that's why," Arnie said. "So they gave it to somebody they knew could run it."

"Anybody can run a slide projector," the Chief

said.

"No," Fay said. "I can't. A lot of people can't.
I think Arnie's right."

"So what good does that do us?" the Chief asked.
"We can't arrest her for anything."

"No," Arnie said, checking his watch. "But you can
go to her house and see if her kid's there."

Fay saw it instantly. "She's at her
grandmother's," she said.

"Right," Arnie said, taking Fay's arm. "Send
somebody to see the grandmother."

Grandmother, Fay thought. Grandmother. She turned
around to look back at the coffee shop.

"What is it?" the Chief asked, sensing her alarm.

"I don't know," she said. "It might be nothing."

"What?" he demanded.

"Do you remember that woman in the coffee shop this
morning, the one I said could be one of them?"

"Beige pantsuit?" the Chief said. "Gray hair?"

Fay nodded. "Her name is Edith Masters. And if
she's still in there watching all this, then I think you
should keep an eye on her."

"We can take her in is what we can do," the Chief
said, his spirits lifting at the thought of it.

"No," Fay said. She didn't know what to tell him.
"Just don't let her get away."

Arnie pointed toward the mothers. "Gail is looking
for you," he said to Fay.

"I'm ready," she said.

The Chief watched them go, envied their hold on
each other, wished he weren't married, and wondered why
the hell he hadn't gone on vacation last week.

Fay took Arnie's hand as they walked. "Maybe we
should have gone to the Grandmother's," she said.

"No," he said. "I know you want to get out of
here, but I want you to be the first one inside that
truck when we open it. And we can't do that til the
mothers leave."

"Are you sure they'll go?" she asked.

"If they've got any guts they will," he said.

Fay looked up at Arnie. Whatever his story was,
the pain had never gone away. However long ago it was,
he felt as bad today as he did the day it happened. She
had never seen this look on his face before. There was
no other word for it. He looked lonely.

* * *

One of the firemen had pulled Gail away from the
other mothers, and was giving her what looked like bad
news.

"I hope it's not Marvin," Fay said to Arnie.

But it was.

Gail turned to Fay, her eyes crazed, her hands out
of control. "Marvin climbed the goddamn Indian," she
blurted, pointing high off in the distance, clear at the
other end of the shopping center. "My daughter is gone
and my husband is sitting on the goddamn Indian."

Fay looked where Gail pointed. It couldn't be.
That little speck on the giant redman's bicep was
Marvin?

"But how did he get there?" Fay asked, her arm
wrapped tight around Gail's shoulder.

"He was halfway up before anybody spotted him," the
fireman said. "Latched onto the loincloth and scooted
up easy after that. Then the crowd closed in, I guess."
The fireman chewed on a toothpick. "If it was a kid
we'd go after him right now. But the Chief said wait.
He's safe enough. Somebody's likely to get hurt if we
try to move the ladder truck through this crowd." He
paused and looked at Gail. "Unless you want us to, Mam.
We'll go get him right now if you say so."

"No," Gail said weakly. "Whenever you think's

best." She looked up at Arnie. "Why did he do this?"

"Got the best seat in the house," Arnie said.

The fireman shook his head. "We don't think so," he said to Arnie. "We figure, the way that big arm is crooked at the elbow, him sitting on the arm where he is, we don't think he can see a thing."

Arnie swallowed his laugh, not altogether successfully.

Gail blew her nose. "It's all right," she said. "Go ahead. Laugh." She sniffed. "At least I know where he is."

"I'm afraid there's more, Mam," the fireman said.

Gail looked at Fay. "Do I want to know this?"

"It's your car," the fireman said.

"It's his car," Gail said.

"Well, the fireman said, "it's our car now, Mam."

Gail nodded.

The fireman explained. "It seems he paid this lady ten dollars to park it in her yard. Only he didn't want to park too far up in the yard, so he eased it right up against the hydrant. We had to impound it." He took the toothpick out of his mouth. "You understand."

"Can I go now?" Gail asked.

"How did you find out it was his car?" Arnie asked.

As the fireman turned around to look at the Indian, he eased his hat back on his head. "Just a guess," he said.

Fay took Gail's arm and walked her back toward the

lunch table. "I'm so sorry," Fay said.

"I just don't understand how I got to here," Gail said. "All my life, I did just what I was supposed to do. I went to church, I was sweet to my mother..."

"You didn't do anything," Fay said. "This is not your fault."

"I married Marvin," Gail said. "Was that it? I mean I knew he wasn't the right man, but the wedding was all planned and everything by the time I knew..."

"Marvin didn't do anything either," Fay said. "He climbed the Indian because it's real hard to think straight when there's something this awful going on."

They stopped a moment. Fay couldn't go any further with Gail. Most of the other mothers were back at the table now. The mood over there looked pretty grim.

Gail grasped Fay's hand for courage. "Peter says we shouldn't do it," she said. "Make the signs and all. Get the signatures."

"Yes," Fay said. "I saw you talking to him."

"But I'll do anything to get Beth back," Gail said. "I don't care how crazy it is."

"The problem is," another mother came up beside them, "even if we do exactly what they say, we still don't know if they'll give our children back."

"What does Arnie think?" Gail asked Fay. "What do you think?"

"I don't know," Fay said. "I wish I did." She

looked around for Arnie. "And it might work, they might
give them back if you do what they said." She squeezed
Gail's hand. "But what I really think is. . ."

"I have to go," Gail faltered, pointing to the
table. "They want me."

"I'll be right here," Fay said.

"It's O.K.," Gail said. "If you have to go. If
it's Lizzie or something. . .I'm all right."

"I'm going to try to find Beth," Fay said. "But I
can't promise I'll be able to. I just don't know where
to start."

"I'm O.K.," Gail said again. They embraced and
Gail walked blindly toward the table.

Fay did not want to sit back down and listen to the
discussion. She wanted to know where Lizzie was. If
she left on the boat with Paul tonight, what happened?
Did the boat sink? Did Lizzie become addicted to some
terrible drug? Did she die in childbirth or get bitten
by a scorpion and be paralyzed for life? Did he sell
her into white slavery in Brazil? Did an anaconda drop
down out of the trees and squeeze the breath out of her?
What?

* * *

"What's up?" Arnie asked, coming up behind Fay.

"I can't stay out in this sun any more," she said.
"Is there some other place where we can. . ."

"Listen to the mothers?" he asked.

She nodded.

"Sure," he said, looking around. "The radio truck,
the Chief's car, the undercover van, the coroner's
wagon. . ."

"And when are we going to hear from Lizzie?" she
asked. "Isn't that Jake person supposed to call you?"

He led her toward the undercover van. "She's
fine, Fay," he said. "He'll be with her all day."

"I've been with her all her life," Fay said, "and
she's gotten away from _me_."

"Not yet, Fay," he said, opening the back door of
the brown UPS delivery truck. "Not yet."

"Is this yours?" she asked, grasping the handrail
and stepping up into it.

But one look inside the truck answered her
question. The walls were lined with television
monitors. Arnie nodded to two detectives who were
wearing earphones and sitting in front of sophisticated-
looking consoles.

"Lizzie's at dance class," Arnie said. "Jake called
in about ten minutes ago. He's sitting on a bench

outside the door, watching. Got her in plain sight.
He'll call us when it's over."

But Fay didn't hear him. She was startled by the
sudden darkness of the truck, the slight moist chill in
the air, the eery green computer glow, the steady hum of
the machinery, the total tomblike silence. She sat down
on the folding chair Arnie opened for her, and saw
Lizzie for herself.

Wearing champagne lace and long spun-honey strands
of antique pearls. Walking up the aisle. Alone.

A mission. A big one. An old one. San Diego maybe.

Carrying a single orchid. Someone whispered as she
passed. The orchid was flown in this morning. Blessed
by the Archbishop of Portugal, they said.

A single stream of sunlight came through the big
window, lighting her way. A blessing.

Her hair was loose, but brushed back from the rare
topaz drops which fell from her ears. Villa- Lobos from
somewhere behind her. Ahead, a sandalwood altar with
its alabaster votaries and burnished gold tapers.

Paul extended his hand and they knelt close
together as an angel child sang. A love song.
Brazilian.

Fay turned back to find herself in the crowd, but
her pew was empty. Her whole side of the church was
empty, in fact.

Fay blinked back the tears, and Lizzie was dancing

with Paul's father at the reception. Laughing about the
half empty church.

"I liked it," Lizzie smiled. "I had so much room
over there."

She was as light as Fay had ever seen her.

Paul's father was all silver, black and white,
elegant and at ease at the center of things. "You will
at least allow me to send pictures to your mother," he
said.

They swept across the sparkling floor. "She
doesn't look at pictures," Lizzie said. "It's something
about," she whispered, amused, "the spirits, I think."

"But it's her own daughter's wedding," he protested
gently.

Lizzie laughed again. "She has a thing about
weddings, too," she said.

"She doesn't believe in them?" he asked.

"Something about the church," she whispered, a
glint in her eye for him. "An old gypsy thing."

"What a wicked girl you are," he teased. "What a
dream." And they spun off the floor together and the
guests applauded.

"What did I do?" Fay asked. "Did I say something?
Why didn't she. . ."

"Shh," Arnie said, patting her arm. "We can't talk
in here. They're almost ready to go out there."

"Lizzie doesn't invite me to her wedding," she
whispered.

He handed her a pair of earphones. "It's just
another five minutes now," he said. "Vi is collecting
the pictures for you."

She knew what he was asking. When are you going to
start seeing something other than Lizzie? Don't you
care what happens to these children? Aren't you even
going to try?

2:00 P.M.

* * *

The Chief had decided to take the coffee shop
assignment himself. He wanted to arrest somebody,
anybody, and Edith Masters was the only name he had.
He was actually thrilled to see that she was still
there, sitting in the booth next to the window.

He sat down at the table directly across from her
and asked if he could borrow her ashtray. She said
certainly, and even seemed relieved that the disgusting
thing was out of her sight. When he said thank you, she
smiled to reveal a mouthful of perfect little teeth,
like rows of young white corn.

"What's going on out there?" he asked her, hoping
to pass as a businessman.

Her smile vanished instantly. "I should think
you'd know that by now," she said crisply. "You've been
in charge all morning, haven't you?"

"Just because I'm there doesn't mean I'm in
charge," he laughed, and ordered the fried chicken
platter and coffee. "You probably know more than I do."

"One of the mothers is a friend of mine," she
explained, not looking at him. "I just wanted to be
nearby in case she needed me."

"Well how about that," he said. "Which one?" and
dumped two packets of artificial sweetener in his
coffee.

"Lynn Waldo," she said.

"She got a slide projector," the Chief said.

"Did she?" Mrs. Masters said. "I couldn't see that from here."

"In her package, I mean," the Chief said.

"Yes, I know about the packages," Mrs. Masters said steadily. "Lynn called me right after the kidnappers called her."

She was nervous. He liked that. "Do you always come here for breakfast?" he asked.

"No," she said, adjusting her watchband. "I don't."

"But you were here this morning," he said.

"Yes, I was," she said, looking up at him now. "A young man at our church, a new member, needed someone to talk to."

She was a pretty cool customer, this lady. It was possible that she was telling the truth, but the Chief didn't think so.

The waitress brought his food and he asked for a glass of iced tea, then turned back to Mrs. Masters. "So what church is it?" he asked. "Does Mrs. Waldo go to the same church?" He took a bite of cole slaw. "What do you believe at this church?"

"We believe in God," she said.

"Yes, I thought you might," he laughed. "What else?"

"Are you a religious man?" she asked.

"I don't know," he said. "Maybe."

"Do you believe in the life hereafter?"

"Well I'd sure like to," he said, motioning to the waitress. "But how can I believe in it til I know what it is?" He asked the waitress for some vinegar.

She reminded the waitress about her check and then asked him, "Are you lonely?"

"Sure," he said. "Isn't everybody?"

"No," she said. "There's your answer."

"What answer?" he asked.

"Whether you're religious or not."

"You mean if I'm lonely, then I must not be religious?" He tore the chicken leg away from the thigh.

"Jesus came so we wouldn't be lonely," she said.

"But then he left again," the Chief said. "Doesn't that make us more lonely?"

"He didn't go so far away," she said. "Where two or three are gathered in my name, there am I in the midst of them."

The Chief hadn't done battle with a real Christian for a long time. Looking across the table at the brittle matron, he remembered now that it wasn't worth it.

"What's it all about?" she asked, as he buttered his roll. "Do they know that yet?"

"Abortion," he said.

"I see," she said.

"The kidnappers want the mothers to conduct a
vote," he lied, "like a referendum, I guess. Set up
tables and let people sign their names, pro or con."

She coughed and covered her mouth. "A referendum?"
she asked.

"Yeah," he said. "Crazy, huh?" He splashed the
vinegar on the fried chicken.

"But didn't they. . ." she stopped herself and
looked out the window.

Good, the Chief thought. She went for it. I've
got her.

She cleared her throat. "How did they know about
this. . referendum?" she asked.

"There was a letter," he said. "One of the girls
got a letter of instructions. It said the government
needed to know what the people thought, all the people,
give everybody a chance to have their say. As soon as
the mothers finish the voting, they get their kids
back."

"I see," said Mrs. Masters, and reached for her
purse.

He saw the waitress coming with the check and knew
it was time to push. "But we're not going to let them
do it. We're sending them all home."

"But what about the children?" she asked.

He lowered his voice. "We have to assume the
children are dead," he said. "We found two of them dead

already."

She reached for her water glass.

"The news people don't know it yet, though," he said. "We didn't want to scare the rest of the mothers."

"No," she said, turning slightly more gray. "That wouldn't be right."

He watched as she took her wallet out of her purse. She was scared all right.

The Chief wondered now what might be in that purse. A list of phone numbers, maybe? There had to be some paper somewhere in this scheme. You didn't plan a thing this big without writing something down. The waitress put Mrs. Masters' check on the table.

"I guess they're lucky there's no more death penalty," the Chief said.

"Who's lucky?" she asked.

"The kidnappers," he said. "Just life in prison."

"What makes you think you'll find the kidnappers?" she asked.

"Even planning a kidnapping is a life sentence in this state you know. You might not have touched a single one of those children, just planned it, it doesn't matter, off you go, bye-bye."

"Excuse me," she said. "I have to make a phone call."

"There's a pay phone in the hall," he said.

"Yes, I know," she said.

The Chief took a swig of tea and congratulated himself for keeping the tap on the line out there.

"I'll watch your purse," he said cheerily.

"Thank you," she said, reaching for her jacket and looping her purse over her shoulder, "but I won't be coming back. I've enjoyed talking with you."

"Yeah, same here," he said. "If you think of anything, anything at all that might be helpful, just come right up to the front over there. I'll leave your name with the officer. Tell them I said to let you in. It's Masters, right? Edith Masters? Where do you live Edith?"

"Excuse me," she said, and marched off.

The Chief waited until she rounded the corner and then pulled out his radio, identified her for the officer he'd left standing outside the coffee shop, and told him to follow Mrs. Masters wherever she went.

"Watch her purse," he said. "I want that purse. And I want to know where she goes if she leaves the parking lot, and who she talks to if she doesn't."

Then he realized he better get back to the mothers, took one last bite of his mashed potatoes, put a ten dollar bill down for the waitress and left.

* * *

Inside the UPS truck, Fay had trouble hearing over
the earphones, but from what she could gather, there
were three groups around the table; mothers who wanted
to do what the kidnappers said, mothers who thought it
was blackmail and wouldn't give in, and mothers who
couldn't decide.

The lawyer mother had just suggested a compromise.
Turn it into a vote, she said. Ask people to come up
and sign for or against, like a referendum. Someone
else objected instantly, saying the kidnappers wouldn't
be very happy if the vote turned out for abortion to
stay legal.

But the very mention of the word abortion produced
a new argument, or rather, the old argument about
abortion. It was murder, some said. And somebody had
to stop it. But if you take away our right to an
abortion, others said, what's next? Our right to own
property? Our right to work?

Then somebody said abortion was a sin. And very
quickly, somebody else said she didn't believe in sin,
she only believed in bad luck, but she didn't believe
you should have to send your bad luck to college.

When the hubbub over that died down, a weary voice
spoke with conviction. "It doesn't matter how we feel
about abortion. This is an act of terrorism, pure and
simple," she said, "and we can't give in. The President

himself wouldn't give in to this kind of threat and he
hates abortion."

"He doesn't just hate abortion," someone else said,
"he hates women. And he's doing everything he can to
keep women poor. First he's going to force them to have
all these babies, then he's going to cut their welfare
so they can't feed them."

So then they fought about the president. "He's
cutting the welfare," one said, "because he wants people
to get jobs, instead of mooching off the rest of us."

But two other mothers had tried to get jobs lately
and they wondered what jobs the first woman was talking
about.

Vi tried to stop them, saying they weren't here to
talk about the president.

But they wouldn't listen. "One old man cannot
dictate to all the women in the country what they should
do with their lives," somebody said.

"Yes he can," another mother said. "That's why we
elected him."

And then there was a chorus of "I didn't elect
him," from around the table.

So Vi was firmer this time. "The President is not
the subject here," she said. "We are. Our children are
gone. Now, please, these people have told us what we
must do to get our children back."

And there was silence.

Inside the UPS truck, Fay looked over at Arnie and shook her head. "This could go on all day," she said.

But then from the table, one of the undecided mothers offered a new solution. "It seems to me," she said, "that the people who want to make signs should make them, and the people who don't want to, can just sit."

And that made somebody else lose control completely. "They'll kill our children!" she screamed.

Then Fay recognized Gail's voice. "Nobody would kill twenty-seven children," she said. "I don't care how crazy they are."

Arnie reached over and squeezed Fay's hand. "That's our girl," he said. "Good for her."

Gail went on. "I mean, O.K. What do we know about these people? One thing. They're against abortion."

The mothers seemed to be listening to her.

"They think abortion is killing children and they want to stop it."

Fay nodded in agreement.

"Now if they're really against killing children," Gail said, "do you really think they'd kill our children to stop people from killing children? No. They wouldn't. Our children are safe."

And the silence was with them again. Gail had offered them the opportunity to feel better, but could they really accept it?

The Chinese doctor mother interrupted their thinking. "What would happen," she asked quietly, "if we all just walked away from the table and went home?"

Arnie nodded his approval.

"Kidnapping is a crime," she said. "The police should solve this crime and we should all just go home."

"Right," Arnie whispered. "Right."

But it would look like we didn't care about our children, somebody said.

Gail spoke up again. She liked the Chinese woman's idea. "Yes," she said. "When they see that it hasn't worked, they'll have to give the kids back. These aren't rich people who did this. They can't afford to feed another kid forever. And they can't actually want another child in their house, can they. A child that isn't theirs? A child who's crying and saying she wants to go home all the time? No," she said, "they can't."

"God, that's brave," Fay said quietly.

But then a strident voice announced that she was staying, was doing exactly what the kidnappers told them to do, and some number of others, Fay couldn't count them, said they were too.

"That's seven," Vi said, apparently counting the hands held up around the table. "And how many refuse to go along with the kidnappers?"

There was quiet while she counted.

"Seven," she said. "A tie."

"How many didn't vote?" Fay asked Arnie.

"Six," he said, adjusting his earphones.

"And the rest of you?" Vi asked.

There was a different kind of tension now. Opinions were no longer the issue. Issues were no longer the issue. Their children's lives might be on the line here, and they all felt it.

The undercover policewoman spoke first, saying she wasn't really one of them, so she didn't feel entitled to a vote. Then Barbara Chambers said that since Fay had found her two girls, she didn't feel she should vote either.

"All right," Vi said, going on to the next woman. "Diane?"

It was a voice Fay hadn't heard before. A hesitating, frightened one. Thin and weak. "I want Robert back," she said, "and I'll do anything to get him back. But I just had an abortion last month, and if I hadn't gotten it, well, we just couldn't afford . ." she faltered. "I'm sorry. I just don't know what to say. We have four children as it is."

Silence.

"Oh boy," Fay said to Arnie. "Here we go."

"I had one too," another voice said softly. "But that's what turned me against it. They told me it would be sick, that's why I did it. And then they checked the," she paused, "they checked the scrapings, and they were right, she was sick. But then it didn't make sense any more. She was my baby, sick or not. A lot of people have sick children and they do just fine."

Something was happening at the table.

Fay knew exactly what it was, and so did Gail, who spoke next.

"Maybe we better find out how many of us have had abortions," she said.

Fay could feel the women looking across the table at each other, then glancing back to their husbands and families behind them.

"I have," someone said, finally, "in college."

"I have," Vi said, "in high school."

"And me," said another. "When my husband left me. And I can vote now. I don't want to make the signs for these people. I want to go home."

And around the table they went, accounting for, among the twenty mothers, some sixteen abortions. Some of them had had more than one. And there were as many reasons as there were abortions. These weren't teenagers who resorted to abortion because they didn't think about contraception. These were devoted mothers who had all felt, at some moment, that they had no choice, that their other children, or their marriages, or even just their futures came first.

As Fay listened, she felt them becoming a whole group again, a sadder, older group. A random group of women telling the sad, old truth.

A return to the days of illegal abortions would affect every woman at this table.

Vi sighed. "So what do we do?" she asked.

"Can we please just go home," the tiny-voiced Diane said.

Vi asked for another show of hands. And this time, all but two of the mothers voted to go home, to leave their packages on the table for somebody else to clean up, and go home.

The group agreed that if those two women wanted to make signs with the materials the kidnappers had sent, that was all right, but the official answer of the group would be "No."

Vi said she would go on television and explain their position, and explain that the two remaining mothers were just two individuals who were doing what any two individuals are free to do in this country, speak their minds.

"Good," Arnie said, taking off his earphones, "good."

"I guess so," Fay said, exhausted from listening. "I guess they didn't really have a choice."

But she felt their loss, knew their confusion, and wondered what they would do all afternoon, alone in their houses.

By the time Fay and Arnie got back outside near the table, the Chief had collected the pictures of the missing children, and assured the mothers that every lead was being followed. Then he gave them a special number to call, and asked that no one leave the city without telling him where they could be reached.

Then, just as everyone thought they were finished, the Chief made another announcement. "And now, Mrs. Waldo," he said, smiling at the woman who had gotten the slide projector, "I have the great joy of telling you we have just found little Karen."

Lynn Waldo practically jumped out of her chair and into the arms of the detective who was standing behind her to make sure she didn't get away.

"If you'll go with Officer Corbin, he'll take you to her," the Chief said.

The group applauded and Lynn started to cry as she was escorted to a squad car.

Fay grabbed Arnie's arm. "Where was the little girl?" she asked.

"Just where you said she would be," he said. "At her grandmother's." They stepped back a little so he could explain the rest of what he knew. "But it's real strange. Everybody says the kid just got there, the grandmother, the neighbors. They say she was dropped off in the grandmother's front yard, ten minutes before the police got there."

"How old was she?" Fay asked. "Was she old enough to know her grandmother's address? To tell the kidnappers, I mean?"

"I don't remember," he said.

She thought a moment. "Could anybody else have
been listening to what went on around the table?"

"What do you mean?" he asked.

"Well if they heard it," she said, starting toward
Gail, "then they could be about to return the kids of
the anti-abortion mothers."

Arnie rushed over to the Chief to tell him what Fay
thought. If she was right, then those mothers who had
originally voted to go along with the demands, should be
told to get home fast and stay there.

* * *

Vi was giving another interview, so the Mayor found Gail as she walked away from the table.

"You did the right thing," he said, wanting to put his arm around her, but well aware that everyone would see it if he did.

"I guess," she said. "I feel so weak. I feel like I need to sit down. But I've been sitting for the last forty-five minutes."

"You need for this to be over," he said. "Maybe..." he paused, "maybe your husband should take you home so you could rest."

She sat down on the hard bleacher seat behind her. "Do you see the man sitting on the big Indian?" she asked, staring down at her feet.

He shaded his eyes with his hand and looked off across the parking lot. "Is that a man?" he asked.

"It's Marvin," she said.

He sat down beside her.

"You're supposed to be laughing," she said.

"No," he said, and took a deep breath. "My wife is telling the press that if the kidnappers give the children back, she'll travel all around the country speaking out against abortion."

Gail looked up. She wasn't sure she'd heard him correctly.

"Against abortion?" she asked. "I thought she was for it."

"She was," he said. He rubbed his knee. "She says she changed her mind." He loosened his tie. "But I think it has something to do with the size of this crowd out here."

Gail wanted to respond, but had no idea how to.

"I tried to tell her they wouldn't do that," Peter said, "that it wouldn't work. But she didn't agree."

Gail heard what he was saying, but appreciated his not saying it. Clearly, Vi would do and say whatever would get the most attention.

"Maybe," Gail offered, "she's just so worried about your boys, that she doesn't know what she's doing." She stopped. "Like Marvin."

"Maybe," he said, and thought a moment. "And if I asked you to have a drink with me later, or take a walk, or offered to take you home when you're ready, would that be because I didn't know what I was doing either?"

"No," she said quietly. "You'd just be trying to help me feel better."

"I'd like to do that," he said, "if I could."

Gail looked up and caught Fay watching them.

"If it would help you," Gail said, "if it would make you feel better," she patted his knee and stood up, "then yes. The answer is yes. I'll have a drink with you, or take a walk, or let you take me home when I'm ready, or whatever you say."

He stood up too, but tried not to seem too eager.
"So what should we do?" he asked.

"I'll be here," she said, squinting up into the sun
at him. "You come get me when you're ready."

But when Gail looked back into the crowd to find
Fay, to ask her if this was a mistake, if she was already
in enough pain today and shouldn't make it worse, Fay
was gone.

Gone on purpose. Fay had seen Arnie looking for
her too. She just wasn't ready to be found yet.

* * *

Fay wandered up to the sidewalk, and paused in
front of the poster in a tea and sandwich shop window,
a poster of an apron-frocked English woman holding a cup
of tea in each hand.

Anybody else would have seen a two-for-the-price-
of-one offer. Fay saw the Temperance card.

The Tarot's vision of Temperance is a willowy blond
angel in flowing white robes mixing the liquids in two
vases by pouring back and forth between them.

In general, Tarot readers took this card to be a
warning. Let your passion cool, they said, dilute your
rage with reason, control your desires. Remember that
the past is all mixed up in the present, they said.
Wait and see.

But Fay had trouble with that interpretation.
Sure, she appreciated the virtues the card represented -
patience, tolerance and humility - but she also thought
the modern world was too cool already. People didn't
need Fay to tell them to take it easy. Everybody told
them that.

Relax, the world said, don't let it get you, don't
say anything you'll be sorry for later. Calm down,
people said, think before you speak. Think before you act,
too. Be fair. Play it safe, don't dwell on it. Don't
blame them and don't blame yourself. These things are
nobody's fault. Breathe deeply. Sit down. Good. None

of this is going to matter in a thousand years, anyway,
so don't worry about it.

Yes, that's what the world said to people these
days, with the result that nobody ever bothered to do
anything any more. Nobody stopped you from talking, so
nobody said anything. And nothing was forbidden, so
nothing ever really happened.

It was all just O.K. now, whoever you were,
whatever you did. Even if you chopped up your neighbors
and put them out in the alley in plastic garbage bags,
it would only mean you were crazy, and we certainly
wouldn't punish you for that.

When the Temperance card came up in a reading, Fay
ignored it. Why should she tell people to be careful?
She already knew they would be. That was what was the
matter with them.

Fay thought there were too few fires, for us to go
around stamping them out. There was precious little
passion today, or rather, what passed for passion today,
was too precious and too little. No, Fay wasn't about
to go tell Gail she was making a mistake talking to
Peter. But she couldn't tell her to have an affair with
him, could she. What she had to do, was stay out of it
for a while.

Maybe if she got busy and found their children,
they would have a chance to cling to each other out of
something other than terror.

* * *

"O.K.," Arnie said, coming up behind Fay on the sidewalk. "All done. Now what?"

He had startled her. She turned around, her eyes open once again to the scene in front of her, the table, the mothers, the police, the truck. "I'll look at the pictures of the kids, I guess," she said.

"He's ready when you are," Arnie said, pointing to the Chief.

But as soon as Arnie took her hand, Fay realized the other reason she had avoided talking to the Mayor and Gail.

"Arnie," she gasped. "The mayor's boys are in trouble."

He whirled around, convinced she was seeing them behind him. "Where?" he asked.

"It's a quarry," she shook her head. "Some big rocky place."

Arnie's mind raced. There was a gravel company down by the river. And Rock Creek Swimming Club was in an old quarry. And how about Cliffside Park?

"They're climbing on these rocks?" he asked, hurrying her back inside the police barricade.

"These are little boys, Arnie." She was almost running to keep up with him. "They don't know _what_ they're doing."

He grabbed a remote radio from the first officer he

saw, and rattled off the details.

"Red shorts," Fay said, "white shirts. Both blond, both thin. By themselves."

"Goddamn," Arnie said, as they neared the table, and quickly told the Chief about it.

"It's not their fault," Fay said, walking carefully toward the stack of pictures on the table.

"Whose fault?" the Chief snapped. "What does fault have to do with it?"

"The kidnappers," she said, sitting down at the now empty table. "It could happen to anybody." She spread the pictures out in front of her. "Kids go off and get in trouble, that's all."

Arnie and the Chief backed away. Fay had forgotten the Mayor's boys as quickly as she had remembered them. All she could see now were these pictures. She planted her elbows on the table and clasped her hands in front of her.

Arnie had never seen her do this before. Was she praying? They were both worried. What if she failed? What if the pictures didn't help? What if all of the children were in trouble like the Mayor's boys? How could they possibly find them in time?

Fay grabbed the edges of her chair and scooted closer to the table. She closed her eyes again, and wiped the shopping center from her mind. Then, in the blackness, she let her eyes fall on the pictures.

Gently, naturally then, they were drawn to one picture
in particular. In the middle row, a little to the left
of center. A little girl, she thought. She opened her
eyes and picked up the photograph. Yes, a little girl.
Kimberly Chen, lying on a yellow flowered sofa, covered
with a khaki army surplus blanket.

Get up, Kimberly, Fay thought, take me through
the house. I'll follow you wherever you go.

The child's eyes opened slowly and she brought one
tiny fist up to her mouth and chewed on her knuckles.
Fay smiled. That's good, baby, but let's take a walk,
why don't we. Like over to the telephone maybe, or past
some piece of mail so I can see the address?

The little girl raised her head and saw a truck on
the floor, a carved wooden one with a long string, and a
stuffed toy right beside it. Daffy Duck? Is that Daffy
Duck? Fay didn't know they still made Daffy Duck.

Kimberly pulled her knees up under her, like an
inchworm, then pulled herself up to sitting, using the
arm of the sofa for balance. Now, Fay thought, hop
down, go see the duck.

The child scooted off the edge of the sofa and down
onto the blanket, then crawled across a brown braided
rug past the duck to the truck. And not the truck
itself, but the string. Smart girl, Fay thought. Now
pull the truck to you. Or how about racing the truck
out the front door so I can read the number on the
house.

Kimberly held the truck in her lap and looked up.
Directly in front of her there was a rocking chair with
orange foam rubber cushions on the seat and the back.
Fay looked around, and saw what she needed, a basket of
magazines on the floor between the end table and the
chair. But Kimberly didn't care about magazines.

Well, then, Kimberly, Fay thought, let's roll the
truck the other way. Good. Now Fay could see the other
side of the sofa, where there was a round orange
ottoman, vinyl, another chair, brown, like a recliner,
and a small bag, like a flight bag or a gym bag maybe,
on the floor beside the ottoman.

Kimberly jumped. Somebody was coming. She
scrambled across the rug toward the recliner, looking
for a place to hide. Get behind the bag, Fay coached.

The door opened, and in walked a very tall woman
with straight brown hair. She scooped Kimberly up in
her arms and walked out of the room.

But Fay was still down behind the gym bag. Could
she get into it without Kimberly to help her? She could
try, she guessed. No, wait. There was a plastic thing
on the front, like a see through thing for an address.
Fay moved her eyes carefully, up to the zipper, around
over the top of the bag, now down the front. There.
There it was. A name. An address. O.K., Fay thought,
calm down. Real easy now. Just. . read it.

She got the numbers first. "Two, two, eight," she

said outloud, then called out the letters one at a time.
"H..U..M..M..I, Hummingbird Drive."

"Arnie!" Fay screamed, jumping up out of her chair
and into Gail's arms.

"I've got it," Gail said, waving a piece of paper.
"I wrote it all down. But what on earth were you. . "

Fay collapsed back into her chair, the sweat
popping out on her forehead and temples, then pouring
down her face.

Arnie was there by now too. "Are you all right?"
he asked.

Fay was shaking.

Gail held her tight, stunned by what she had just
witnessed. "I've never seen anything like that in my
life," she said to Arnie. "I mean, I came over here and
said hello to her and she didn't even hear me. She was
just staring at that picture and talking to herself like
she actually went right into the picture."

"Please," Fay whispered, pointing to Gail's piece
of paper, "That's where Kimberly is."

Arnie grabbed the piece of paper and headed for the
radio truck.

Gail still couldn't believe it. "228 Hummingbird
Drive? How did you do that?"

But Fay couldn't answer.

Gail felt for Fay's pulse, but it was very faint,
her hands cold and clammy. Gail rubbed Fay's right hand
between her palms, trying to get the circulation back.

"I'm O.K.," Fay nodded, her arms falling limp into her lap.

"Let's not do any more of that, huh?" Gail said gently.

"Any more of what?" Fay asked, still not completely conscious.

"Whatever you call it," Gail said. "That trance stuff. There has to be some other way." She felt Fay's forehead, which was now blazing hot, and motioned for one of the officers to bring her some water.

But as Gail continued to hold her hand, the tears began streaming down Fay's face.

"Fay," Gail said, "come on. You're scaring the shit out of me."

"Is she all right?" Arnie asked, coming back up behind them.

"I'm all right," Fay said, drinking the water the officer had brought her. She looked at the two of them staring at her so intensely, and laughed, and choked on her water.

And then Arnie couldn't wait any longer to tell her. "There's more news, Fay," he said carefully.

Fay sat up straighter and Gail tensed behind her.

Then he realized he'd scared them. "No," he said. "Good news!" He crooked his elbow and tightened his fist in the traditional gesture of victory. "We got two more kids!"

"Where were they?" Fay asked.

Gail tightened her grip on Fay's shoulders.

The Chief came over to congratulate Fay. "Jennifer Bell and Alice Hart," he crowed. "And you were right on the money. The kids were dropped off in their own front yards. And both of their mothers had voted to go along with the kidnappers."

Behind Fay, Gail was failing fast. "But how did the kidnappers know how we voted?" she cried.

"We don't know," the Chief said. "Unless one of these reporters is a lip reader. Or somebody could be patched into our radio truck somehow."

Gail sank into the chair beside Fay, burying her head in her hands.

"Gail," Fay said quickly, turning around to comfort her, "you did the right thing. You can't feel bad about it, you just have to. . ."

"I can feel as bad as I want," Gail said, and stood up, her anger rising with her.

And now it seemed to Gail that this was all Fay's fault. "I believed you!" she screamed at her friend. "You said I could do whatever I wanted. You said she would be all right!"

She stopped for a breath, and realized it was her own fault. "What was I thinking about? I don't care what they do about abortion! How could I have sat there and. . ."

"Gail, Gail," Arnie said firmly. "Fay is right.

It won't help to get mad now. We need you to stay real cool here." He grabbed her arm, forcing her to listen. "And it doesn't matter if we find Beth first, or we find her last. We're going to find her."

Gail tried to pull away from Arnie but he held her firmly. She couldn't listen. She couldn't. How could she have risked her child's life for some . . . She couldn't finish the sentence, even in her thoughts.

"Gail," Arnie said. "I promise you. . . "

Gail looked away. All there was to look at, though, were the walls of humans surrounding her. So she looked up. And no, that's not all there was to look at. There was also Marvin.

3:00 P.M.

* * *

All in all, Marvin had enjoyed himself on the
Indian. He had studied the air conditioning system on
the roof of the shopping center, and figured out the
synchronization of the traffic lights for a mile in
every direction.

He couldn't see Gail in the crowd gathered below
him, but he had seen things break up over at the truck,
so he assumed it was all over. Maybe Gail was even home
with Beth by now, in which case, he wanted to get down
and be with them. But getting down by himself was not
really possible, a fact he had known for some two hours
now.

On their way across the parking lot, the Chief put
his arm around Gail. "Poor Marvin," he said, with as
much compassion as he could muster. "Has he ever done
anything like this before?"

"Not this exact thing," Gail answered, letting his
arm rest where it was.

The Chief wondered why she was so calm. "Are you
mad at him?"

"Not any more," Gail said. "What would be the
point?"

"We'll have to take him downtown, you know," the
Chief said, "procedures and everything, after we get him
off the Indian, I mean."

"What will you do with him?" she asked.

"Have him talk to the psychaitrist, I guess."

"And then he can go home?"

"No. Then we charge him with something and let him out on bail." He felt sorry for her. "What else can we do?" he said. "We can't have people climbing the fucking Indian all the time."

"It's just so ugly," she said. "I wouldn't even want to touch it, much less climb it."

"We ought to put a fence around it," he said.

"Electrified," she said. "Barbed wire on the top. Like a reservation."

The Chief laughed. He liked this woman. She didn't think much of her husband, but at least she wasn't bitching about him. He wondered if she'd like to come to work at the department.

"I'll go get him myself if you want," he said. "Some of these firemen could be pretty hard on him, pulling a stunt like this."

"I thought firemen were sweet," she said.

"That's what everybody thinks," he said. "Makes it tough being a cop."

"I'll stay here," she said, as they approached the ladder truck.

"You do that," he said. He winked at her. "You stay cool, now."

"Thanks," she said.

"Come on up!" Marvin yelled, as the Chief grabbed
hold of the ladder. "Plenty of room!" he called.
Marvin was feeling better all the time. As the Chief
took his first step, Marvin sang out gaily, "Don't
fall!"

"Thanks, Marvin," the Chief mumbled to himself,
his hands beginning to sweat.

Marvin saw that the Chief was not used to climbing
ladders. He was looking down, for one thing,
concentrating on his feet instead of his hands. And
every time he took a step, he stopped and waited for the
ladder to stop swaying before he took another step.
Marvin knew that wasn't the way to do it.

"Don't fight it," Marvin coached. "Just let the
momentum carry you. Don't think about where you've
been, think about where you're going. Look up! Look
up!"

The Chief's shirt was soaked through now, and his
street shoes were slipping badly on the treads. But
people were watching him. He couldn't stop or go back
without embarassing the whole department. He was,
however, beginning to remember the other reasons why he
hadn't become a fireman.

The top of the ladder was resting on the Indian's
clavicle. Marvin decided it was time to turn around so
he could face the Chief. He grabbed the Indian's mouth
and pulled one foot up under him. "Here I go!" he
shouted.

"No!" the Chief screamed. And there were shrieks
of terror from the ground below. "Sit down," the Chief
shouted. "I'm coming, I'm coming."

"I know," Marvin said pleasantly, now that the
Chief was in talking distance. "I'm just turning around
so I can see you."

The Chief didn't believe him. "I said sit down,
Marvin."

When Marvin sat down, the crowd cheered.

"Well," the Chief said casually, as if they had
just met on the sidewalk, "how are you doing, Marvin?"

"Pretty good," Marvin said. "Thanks."

"Your wife is down there, you know," the Chief
said.

"She's the best wife in the world," Marvin said,
spotting Gail and waving.

The Chief looked down and a wave of nausea came
over him. "How do you think this makes her feel,
Marvin?" he asked.

"Wait til she sees the parking place I found!"
Marvin said.

The Chief shook his head. "You know we set up a
place over there at the truck for all you fathers," the
Chief said.

"No," Marvin said. "I didn't. I never got that
far, I guess."

The Chief grinned. "You just saw the Indian and

knew he was for you, right?"

"There were just so many people everywhere else,"
Marvin began. "But I'm ready to come down now. I'm
thirsty, for one thing."

"In a minute, Marvin, in a minute," the Chief said,
pulling his handkerchief out of his pocket and drying
his palms.

Marvin thought he should keep the conversation
going. "You can see pretty good up here, don't you
think? Kind of like a fire tower."

"I can't see a goddamn thing, Marvin," the Chief
said, "except your feet and his neck."

"Don't lean back!" Marvin said, as the Chief leaned
back to put his handkerchief back in his pocket.

"Listen, Marvin," the Chief said, clutching the
ladder and waiting for it to stop shaking, "I want to
know why you did this. I mean, your wife says you're
not crazy."

"She's sweet," Marvin said. "I told you she was
sweet."

"Yes she is, Marvin. And you're not a kid either,
so you didn't do this just for fun, and you're not
malicious are you, Marvin?"

"No sir," Marvin declared.

"So you didn't do it to cause trouble. So why did
you do it? I mean, I'm a policeman, Marvin."

"Yeah, I figured you were."

"And policemen need to know why people do things.

People do all kinds of things, Marvin. You wouldn't
believe the things people do."

"Oh yes I would too," Marvin said. "I read the
paper every day."

"Well if we're ever going to get people to quit
doing these things," the Chief said, "we have to know
why they did them."

"Right," Marvin said. "I'll go along with that."

"So?"

"So what?"

The Chief sighed. "So why did you do this?"

Marvin thought he saw something in the Indian's
mouth.

"Don't play with the Indian, Marvin."

"There's something in his mouth."

"I asked you a question."

"I'm sorry," Marvin said, feeling around the
Indian's molars. "Ask me again."

The Chief tried a confidential whisper. "I asked
you why you did this."

"I've got it!" Marvin said, finding the object and
wrenching his wrist back out through the Indian's rough
lips.

"I'm happy for you, Marvin," the Chief said.
"Answer my question, please."

"I don't know," Marvin said. "If it wasn't for the
view, then it doesn't make much sense."

"No, it doesn't," the Chief said, sorry that he ever started this discussion. "I'm going down now, Marvin."

"Wait a minute!" Marvin said. "Don't you want to know what this is?"

"No, Marvin," the Chief said his knee shaking wildly. "I don't."

"Didn't you come up here to get me?" Marvin asked.

"No, Marvin, I didn't," the Chief said.

"I could get down by myself now that the ladder's here."

"Yes, Marvin, I know," the Chief said. "Why don't you do that."

"Hey look!" Marvin shouted at him, holding the hard little ball out so the Chief could see it. "It's bubble gum!"

"That's great," the Chief said wearily. "That's just great, Marvin. So you're not even the first one up there."

"The sculptor put it here," Marvin explained. "It's a joke, see?"

"No, Marvin," the Chief said, stopping his descent for the last time. "It's not a joke. My coming up here was a joke. This whole day is a joke. But I tried, O.K.? I wanted to try. I wanted to give you a chance. I wanted to prove to myself that I still cared. But you know what? I don't."

He paused. Marvin was listening.

"I'll tell you why you climbed up here, Marvin, in case you're interested," the Chief grumped. "And I knew it from the ground."

"O.K.," Marvin said.

The Chief couldn't help saying it. "It's because you're one stupid fuck, Marvin." And with that he went down the ladder.

Marvin just didn't understand a man like this. Where was his spirit of adventure, his sense of fun, his joy in doing something just for the sake of doing it? And what about the wad of gum? Wasn't he the slightest bit intrigued by that? It made Marvin sad to think about a man giving up on his life that way.

Marvin put the gum in his pants pocket and reached for the top of the ladder. When he was three steps from the bottom, the crowd began to applaud. He saw the photographers waiting on the ground, smiled and waved as the flashbulbs popped. He hadn't prepared anything to say to the reporters, but he guessed he'd just show them the gum and the conversation would just go from there.

As his foot hit the bottom step, someone grabbed his jacket roughly and snapped a pair of handcuffs around his wrists.

"What do you think you're doing?" Marvin asked.

The officer had to laugh. "You're going to jail, Tonto."

"What for?" Marvin asked, incredulous.

"Let's go," the man said, and grinned at one of the firemen. "We'll let the nice doctor tell you later."

Another officer pushed Marvin off from behind, and when he landed, he recognized Gail's shoes four inches from his face on the ground in front of him. He didn't want to stand up, but he did.

"Are you all right, Marvin?" she asked.

"I'm sorry, sweetheart," he said, leaning over to kiss her. "I was just trying to see everything."

"I know you were, Marvin," she said.

"I just didn't think about all of this," he said. "I just knew we were in trouble and I had to do something."

"I know, Marvin," she said, as the policeman pulled him away. "I'll see you later." She backed away.

"Yeah," he said, hoping to reassure her. "This shouldn't take too long. Can you get home all right?"

Gail gestured toward the truck. "I'll be fine," she said. "The Mayor offered me a ride."

"O.K., then," he said, as the officer pushed him into the car. Then he stuck his head back out the window. "How's Beth?" he asked.

Gail took the Chief's arm. "She's gone, Marvin," she said.

"Still?" he asked, as the policeman reached across him and rolled up the windows.

Gail didn't answer, but she did manage to wave.

Marvin couldn't wave back because his hands were

cuffed behind him. So, he just nodded.

He looked nervous, Gail thought. And hungry. She
was glad they were keeping him overnight. Maybe they
could help him.

* * *

Down at Police Headquarters, Lynn Waldo, the mother
who got the slide projector in her package, the mother
whose daughter was the first one returned by the
kidnappers, was being questioned by Bud Heller and
Benjie Davis, the two men detectives who had gone
through the church with Arnie earlier in the morning.

Benjie Davis had begun by asking Mrs. Waldo what
kind of bloody Nazi crusade this was anyway.

Then Heller tried to comfort Mrs. Waldo. "You have
to understand," he said. "Davis is Jewish."

Mrs. Waldo didn't understand.

"Jews never forget," he said.

Mrs. Waldo asked when she could see her little
girl.

"Not til you tell us where you've got the rest of
the kids," Davis snarled.

"I don't know what you're talking about," Lynn
Waldo said.

"We're talking about those other mothers'
children," Davis barked. "Yours was at your mother's
the whole time."

"No she wasn't," Lynn pleaded. "She was gone."

"Tell us who's in this with you," Davis said, "and
we'll let you see your girl."

"Please," Lynn said. "Is she all right?"

Heller patted her hand. "She's all right," he

said. "All we want to do is find the rest of the
children before anything happens to them."

Davis jumped back in. "If you go to prison for
this, you'll lose your little girl for good, you know."

"You can't send me to prison," Lynn said, reaching
for a Kleenex. "I haven't done anything. I don't know
anything."

"Oh you know all right," Davis said. "We saw that
church this monring. Is that were the group meets?"

"What group?" Lynn asked, near tears. "What
church?"

"The group who planned this kidnapping," Davis
said. "The one that meets at your church."

"I go to church," Lynn said, "but the only group
that meets there is the Ladies Bible Class."

"Is the Ladies Bible Class against abortion?"

"We've talked about abortion," she said. "It's the
sixth commandment. Thou shalt not kill."

Davis spat his gum into the wastebasket. "If one
of these children dies, that will be killing, Mrs.
Waldo."

"Please," she said, "I don't know why you're asking
me these questions."

Heller thought it was time for his approach. "Mrs.
Waldo," he said softly, "we're just as confused as you
are about this. Why would the kidnappers return your
child and keep all the rest of them?"

"You didn't say they returned her," she said. "I
thought that fortune teller found her!"

"No," Heller said. "The kidnappers brought her
back. Or that's what your little girl says, anyway.
Now the only reason we can think of, why the kidnappers
would bring her back, is that you're one of them."

Suddenly Mrs. Waldo was scared. "Is she sick?" she
asked. "Is that why they brought her back?"

Heller continued in his helpful tone. "Maybe this
group thinks you're on their side because you belong to
some other group. Have you ever gone to an anti-
abortion meeting?"

Mrs. Waldo was silent.

"Answer him," Davis snapped.

"Please," Heller said to Davis. "Shut up."

Lynn Waldo did have something to say, but she began
quietly, looking down at her Kleenex. "When I had my
abortion, there was a lady outside the clinic handing
out pamphlets. It was the same pamphlet that was in one
of the packages this morning, the red one with the big
knife on the cover."

"That's good," Heller said. "Go on."

"That's all there is," she said.

"The hell it is," Davis said.

She turned back to Heller. "I felt real bad about
the abortion," she said.

"Of course you did," Heller said, handing her
another Kleenex.

"And I couldn't tell anybody about it. I didn't
even tell my husband about it."

"So," Heller said calmly, "you called the phone
number on the pamphlet and somebody talked to you and
they made you feel better."

The tears ran from her eyes. "Yes," she said.
"They told me that everybody feels bad."

"So," Heller said, "when you got to feeling better,
you called them back, is that right? To thank them?"

"Please," she said, "I didn't have anything to do
with this kidnapping."

"Come on, honey," Davis said. "We don't have all
day."

Mrs. Waldo looked at Davis. She didn't want to
tell him anything. Heller told Davis he could handle it
from here and Davis stormed out of the room.

"I'm sorry he's so rough," Heller said. "I don't
think he likes women much."

Mrs. Waldo blew her nose.

"I don't think he likes anybody much," Heller said.
"His family left him a coupla months back." He smiled.

Mrs. Waldo knew she had to tell the rest of the
story, but she appreciated the detective's patience.

"When I called back," she said, "I asked the lady
what I could do to help."

"What was this lady's name?" he asked.

"Edith Masters," Lynn said.

He wrote it down. He'd heard the name on the
police radio. Edith Masters was the woman Arnie's
fortune teller had seen in the coffee shop.

"And what did Mrs. Masters say?" he asked.

"She said they had this special phone system. That
the phone number on the pamphlet rang at her house
during the day, and at this other lady's phone at night.
Then she said if they could send the calls to my phone
one morning a week, then she wouldn't always have to go
to the grocery store at night."

"How long ago was this?" Heller asked.

"Three years," she said.

"Are you still doing it?" he asked.

"Yes," she said. "Every Tuesday morning. But all
I do is talk to the people who call up crying."

"And how often do you talk to Mrs. Masters?" he
asked.

"She calls once a month to see how I'm doing."

"And how often do you call her?"

"I don't," Mrs. Waldo said. "She's told me about
some meetings but I can't go to them because Karen isn't
in school yet."

"So your only contact with this Mrs. Masters is
when she calls you?" Heller asked.

"Yes. But I know there are other women answering
the phone now. But I don't know any of them."

"And you just listen when people call?"

"Yes. Or sometimes, if they want more information,

I take their names and when Mrs. Masters calls me, I
give the names to her and she sends them things, but I
don't know what things."

Heller stood up. He believed her. And he believed
that this was everything she knew. "All right, Mrs.
Waldo," he said, "you can go. Your mother is waiting
with Karen just down the hall."

"You're not going to put me in jail?" she asked.

"Can you think of any reason why I should?" he
asked.

"No," she said, managing a smile.

"All right, then," he said. "But I might be
calling you again if I can't find this Mrs. Masters."

"That's fine," she said. "I'll help all I can."

"I know you will," he said. "Oh, what's the
number, the anti-abortion phone number you answer on
Tuesday mornings?"

"It's 456-LIFE," she said. "456-5433."

Heller wrote down the number, opened the door and
escorted Mrs. Waldo down the hall to meet her mother and
little girl.

* * *

Fay sat at the table in the parking lot, poring over the other pictures. But she knew it was no use. The only reason she'd been able to find Kimberly was that there was, apparently, some very old spiritual bond between them. Fay did believe in that. But the other kids, no, she had never known them.

She looked up from the pictures to the truck. It was a closed, forbidding mass. A time bomb. A tomb. A road-worn brute, a silent, stolid, scheming crate. The answer, she knew, was inside it. But that was the one place she didn't want to go.

Maybe the kidnappers would return all the rest of the children. Maybe the police would find them. Maybe she wouldn't have to see what was inside that truck. Or see it in person, anyway. She'd already seen a good bit of it, just sitting out here trying to ignore it.

On the back wall, there was a sign written in blood. But she couldn't read what it said yet. And a gray T-shirt. Why, she wondered, of all the things in the truck, would she be so certain there was a limp gray T-shirt in a cardboard box? And what did it mean?

Nobody had asked her to go into the truck yet, but Arnie was coming toward her now. That could be exactly what he was going to say. She wasn't ready. She hadn't even been able to stand up since she found Kimberly.

How could she do it? This truck scared her. Whatever
was in there, was awful.

"More good news!" Arnie said, sitting down beside
her. "Six more kids!" He read from the list. "Juan
Garcia, Robert Vick, Matthew and Michael Wilson, Vicki
Layne, and Scott Lewis."

"So how many do we have now, altogether?" she
asked, blinking hard to bring her eyes into focus.

"Twelve," he said. "Timmy from the hospital this
morning, then Shelley and Susan from the house by the
church, and nine from the mothers who voted to
cooperate."

Fay cleared her throat. "Where's Gail?" she asked,
looking around. "Does she know this yet?"

"No," he said. "But there's something I want you
to hear." He pulled out a tiny tape recorder and set it
down in front of her.

"What is it?" she asked.

"From the radio," he said. "They called in."

"The kidnappers?" she asked.

"Play it," he said. "I thought you might want to
listen more than once, so I had them make a tape for
you."

"I don't think I even want to listen the first
time," she said.

But he'd already punched the play button. He hated
to push her like this, but it was almost four o'clock

already.

". . .fear for their safety," the voice said. A
male voice. Gruff. Commanding. "They are safer where
they are than in homes where their mothers do not
understand the value of human life. We will not be
mocked. The other fifteen children will not be
returned. They will remain, like all the victims of
abortion in this country, missing for all time. There
will be no further communication."

Then there was a click, and silence.

Fay shifted in her chair and stared back up at the
truck.

"Well, look," Arnie said. "I just thought it might
help. You know, trigger something."

Fay shook her head.

"O.K.," he said. "Now the other thing," he paused,
"is that Lynn Waldo, that woman who got the slide
projector?"

"I remember," Fay said, gathering the pictures of
the children up into a pile.

"Lynn Waldo named Edith Masters."

"Named her as what?" Fay asked, squaring the edges
of the pictures against the table.

"Said Edith hands out pamphlets at an abortion
clinic, and runs a counseling service on the phone."

"That doesn't necessarily mean she's involved in
this, Arnie," Fay said.

"O.K.," he said, "but the Chief had her tailed when

she left the coffee shop, and she made a phone call."

"To whom?"

"To another phone booth. Somebody she called `Dear one.'"

"And what did she say?" Fay asked, putting the photographs into her purse.

"Dear one, don't forget to feed the chickens," he said.

"What does that mean?" Fay asked.

"Beats me," Arnie said. "But it was about two-thirty when she made the call."

"So?"

"Well," he hesitated, "everybody I know, feeds their chickens in the morning."

Fay nodded.

"But she never left the shopping center. Been here all day. They're bringing her over here right now."

Fay jumped. "I can't see her, Arnie. I can't."

"You don't have to," he said. "I'm going to talk to her."

"Have we heard from Lizzie?" she asked.

"They went shopping," he said. "Jake took her shopping."

"For what?" Fay asked.

"Jesus Christ, Fay!" Arnie snapped, and stood up. "What do I have to do to get you to work on this? I put a man on Lizzie all day. Do you want me to put her in jail? Is that what it takes? We've got fifteen kids to find, and no sign of them, anywhere!"

She swallowed hard. Swallowed the hard words she had ready. She stroked her throat. "I need a glass of something," she said. "Tea, or something." She pushed her chair back from the table. "And I have to get out of this. . ."

"I'm sorry," he said, reaching for her arm. "I'm really sorry. It's just. . ."

"No," she said. "You're right. You talk to Edith, and I'll go have a glass of tea." She pointed to the tea shop where he had found her before. "I'll be right over there. And when I've had my tea, I'll go inside the truck." She paused. "O.K.?"

"I won't be long," he said.

"And I won't run out on you," she said.

"Good," he said. "The further we get with this, the more I know we can't do it without you."

"Yeah, yeah," she smiled. "That's what they all say."

* * *

"Eyewash," Fay said to herself as she made her way
to the tea shop. "It's not me that's not working, it's
my eyes. It's being out in this sun all day."

She thought about going back to the first aid
station the police had set up, but decided not to. She
wanted to sit someplace cool and try to forget about
Lizzie.

The tiny bells on the door tinkled shyly as she
opened it. "One," she said to the hostess.

"We have a lovely garden, if you'd care to sit
there," the hostess soothed.

"No thank you," Fay said. "Just a quiet table will
be fine."

The woman led Fay to her most quiet table, and
smoothed the lace tea cloth as she left, and Fay sighed
deeply. Her mother would have loved this little place.

Fay wrapped her arms around herself and remembered.
She had asked her mother one night, "Was there a day
when you first felt old? Were you standing there in the
kitchen eating a dinner you wouldn't force on your own
worst enemy, and did you realize that's exactly who you
were, exactly what you were doing?"

But her mother didn't remember.

Fay had followed her into the bedroom, sorry she'd
asked. "It's easier to forget, I guess."

"Oh, no, child," her mother said. "It's damned

hard to forget, but you'd better learn how. Unless you
want to feel old for the rest of your life."

"You don't really mean forget, do you?" Fay asked.
"Don't you mean find some other way to think about it?"

"No," her mother said, stepping out of her house
slippers, "there isn't any other way to think about it.
You just forget."

"Forget what?" Fay asked.

"I don't know, dear," her mother said, getting into
bed. "What are we talking about?"

Fay pulled the quilt up over her. "Does it matter?"

"No," her mother said, "I don't think it does. But
then," she turned out the light, "I forget."

Now, reading the tea shop menu, Fay couldn't
remember what had made her feel so old that day. So at
least she __was__ forgetting. But she still felt old.
Maybe she wasn't forgetting the right things.

She ordered a scone and a glass of iced camomile,
then closed her eyes. Lizzie was in the shower,
a big shower, marble walls, gold fixtures, soap that
smelled like apples. The day was hot, the air a heavy
yellow out the bathroom window, a canyon in the
distance, brown and blistered from a searing summer sun.
California. It had to be California.

Lizzie tilted her head back and let the stream of
water soak her hair. She grabbed the sponge and soaped
it foamy then ran it down her low huge belly.

Fay was ecstatic. Lizzie was having a baby! And
pretty soon, too. Maybe a little Leo. Oh yes, if
anybody could handle a Leo it was Lizzie. What fun that
would be. Let her blow and fume, let her get her way,
let her run the show. Oh a little Leo.

Lizzie lifted her hands high above her head and
stretched. Bless her heart, Fay thought, seeing the
untanned bikini line under the baby, Lizzie's gone
swimming the whole time, happy to be pregnant, happy to
have everybody know.

Lizzie stopped. Water running down her legs.
She'd heard about her water breaking, read about her
water breaking, but would she know what it was when it
happened? Yes. This was it. The baby was coming.

Lizzie whirled around to turn off the water, then
stood holding the handles. "Mother!" she screamed.

"I'm here, I'm here," Fay said. "Call me. I'll
come get you. I'll stay with you. I'll talk with you,
you'll grab my hand, I'll. . ."

Lizzie wiped her eyes, stepped out of the shower,
and reached for the towel. She checked between her
legs. It is water. Good. It's just water. It's not
blood.

Not yet, Fay thought. "Call me."

Lizzie stepped into her house slippers, wrapped
herself in the oversize terrycloth robe, then steadied
herself a moment grasping the sink.

"Call me," Fay said. "Call your mother."

Lizzie walked into the bedroom, picked up the phone
and dialed, Fay counted, seven numbers.

"O.K.," Fay thought. "Call the doctor first. Then
call _me._"

The doctor told her he would meet her at the
hospital. He asked her if Paul was still out of town,
then told her to call a cab.

"I'll be all right," she said, "I'm not a baby."
She laughed and patted her stomach. "The baby is the
baby." She told the doctor good-bye.

"Now," Fay said, "one more call."

Lizzie dialed again and told someone named Lucy to
see if she could find Paul and tell him the baby was
coming.

"Sure," Fay thought, "that's all right too. But now
Mother, O.K.?"

Lizzie held the receiver in her hand. "Mother,
Mother, Mother," she whispered.

Fay smiled.

But Lizzie didn't dial again. She held the
receiver, held it with both hands, pressed it between
her breasts, then slid it down to rest on the mound made
by the soon to be born child.

"Lizzie, what are you doing?" Fay asked.

But she knew what Lizzie was doing. Lizzie was not
calling her. But why wasn't she calling her? Fay would
be there as fast as she could. Would stay as long as

Lizzie needed her. Why didn't she call?

Lizzie pulled on a pair of sweat pants and a big
shirt, Paul's probably, slipped on her sandals, grabbed
her purse, then stopped to pick up the already packed
leather satchel waiting beside the door.

Outside, Lizzie put the top down on her
convertible, turned on the radio and backed out the
drive.

Fay reached out and held the glass of iced tea
between her hands to steady herself. The baby was a
girl. Her name was Katie. And she was coming fast.

Lizzie drove through the canyon and down onto the
flats, speeding, Fay thought, but who wouldn't. Then
she made a sharp turn onto a tree-lined residential
street.

A huge red moving van was sitting out in front of a
house. The movers, eating lunch on tail gate of the
truck, waved. One man whistled. Lizzie waved back,
patted her huge stomach and sailed past them, honking
her horn.

As Fay reached for her butter knife, the baby was
born, taking her first bite, the name was given. Taking
a sip of tea, Lizzie's room was filled with orchids and
Paul was on his way.

Lizzie would have to call sometime, wouldn't she?
Or would she have someone else call for her? And
someone else take care of her. And someone else bathe
the baby while Lizzie napped.

Lizzie would have to let Fay see Katie, wouldn't she? Send a present? See Katie wear the present? Wouldn't she?

Fay covered her pounding heart with her hand, then looked up quickly, as the little bells rang again, and the tea shop door opened. No one could have known she was here. But Fay had a visitor, just the same.

4:00 P.M.

* * *

Inside the police barricade, Edith Masters was
sitting with the woman officer assigned to guard her.
Arnie was ready to talk to her, but he wanted her to
wait a minute, wanted her to worry a little.

"Don't you want to sit in on this?" he asked the
Chief.

"I want the prune in jail," the Chief said.

"Do my best," Arnie said, lighting a cigarette,
studying Mrs. Masters from the back.

Edith was making no effort to talk to the officer.
And she wasn't watching the traffic police clear the
parking lot, or the TV people pack up their cameras.
She wasn't smoking, of course, or rummaging through her
purse, or fiddling with her hair. She was simply
sitting perfectly still. She didn't seem worried at
all.

"Does Fay think they're serious?" the Chief asked
Arnie. "They won't give the other kids back? They
won't make any other demands?"

"She said that's what women do," Arnie said. "She
said the way they win is to quit."

"They can't just quit," the Chief said. "They're
terrorists. How are they going to win if they don't
keep playing?"

"Fay says it's not a game." Arnie stood up.

"O.K." he said. "Let's see what old Edith has to say for herself."

"I just don't get it," the Chief said, turning to walk away. "I don't know what we're doing here."

"Go back downtown then," Arnie said.

"Can't," the Chief said. "I want to know what's in the truck."

"You and me, pal," Arnie said, dropping his cigarette on the ground and stubbing it out with his shoe. "There's a bowling alley down at the end, there," Arnie said. "Maybe that would straighten it out for you."

The Chief shook his head. "I can't bowl for shit," he said.

"That's too bad," Arnie said. "Be just the thing."

Arnie signalled to the officer that he would talk to Mrs. Masters now. The officer nodded, stood up, picked her cigarettes up off the table and walked away. But Mrs. Masters took no notice of the officer's departure.

As he started toward her, Arnie was annoyed by the lone gray curl lying limp along her neck. He didn't want to do this. He had no idea how he would begin the interview. He wished he weren't a policeman so he could honor his first impulse which was to grab her purse and run.

"Good afternoon, Mrs. Masters," he said, laughing

at himself, "I'm Detective Campbell."

"Something has amused you?" Mrs. Masters said,
drawing herself up in the chair.

"Don't know what it is," he said, still chuckling.
"I almost stole your purse."

"Actually," she said, lifting the purse into her
lap and folding her arms around it, "my purse has been
stolen a number of times."

That made him laugh outloud. Quickly, he reached
in his pocket for his pen and notebook, hoping that
would restore his concentration. "And you always find
it, or somebody turns it in?"

He wet the point of the pen in his mouth. "I mean,
if they keep stealing this same little purse of yours,
that means you keep getting it back so it's there for
them to steal again. Right?"

He looked up, composed and detached, saw her
squinting eyes, and burst out laughing all over again.

"I'm very sorry," he said, desperate to get control of
himself. "But I've been up all night, and all this
confusion today and everything, I guess I'm cracking up."

"That's quite all right," she said primly, "you take
your time."

She placed the poor purse square in front of her on
the table, and studied it. She held it at the top, with
both hands as if it were trying to get away. She turned
it to the side, tried the clasp, then snapped it shut.
She examined the seams, moistened one finger and rubbed

off a spot of something yellow on the lizard vinyl trim.
Finally, she looked up at Arnie. "I just can't imagine
what it is about this purse."

"Well," he said, reaching for it, "let's have a
look."

"Am I under arrest?" she asked, pulling the purse
toward her.

"We can do it that way if you want," he said. "But
I think you'll find it much more pleasant to let me look
at the purse here rather than at headquarters."

"I haven't done anything you could arrest me for,"
she said.

"Suspicion," he said. "That's all we need."

"Suspicion of what?"

"Planning this whole thing," he said. "Getting your
group organized, finding the driver who stole the truck,
kidnapping the children, contacting the mothers by phone,
buying the stuff for the packages, then delivering the
packages so the mothers could pick them up."

"That's absurd," she said.

"You did a helluva job," he said, smiling.
"With planning like that, you could've pulled a pretty
nice robbery, Mrs. Masters. Why didn't you do that? A
Brinks truck, maybe? The Federal Reserve Bank? That
kind of money would have bought a lot of TV time for
your cause. Done a helluva lot more good than this
stunt."

"Yes," she said, smiling. "I see what you mean.
But you have the wrong person."

"No, I don't think so," he said.

"I wish I could help you," she said, "but I don't
know anything about this. I'm only here because one of
the mothers is a friend of mine."

"Lynn Waldo," Arnie said.

"Yes," she said.

"From your church."

"Yes."

"What church?" he asked. "Where is it located?"
But she didn't answer.

He looked up. "Mrs. Masters?"

"My religious persuasion is my personal affair,"
she said.

Arnie was getting annoyed. "I can look up the damn
address in the phone book," he said. "Who's your
preacher at this church?"

She looked away.

"All right," he said. "Tell me about this
telephone tree, your group of anti-abortion mothers who
answer the phone."

She opened her purse and took out a roll of Necco
wafers. Arnie couldn't remember the last time he saw
that candy, but he did remember he liked the brown ones
the best. He was never sure what the brown flavor was
exactly, chocolate maybe, or rootbeer, he just knew he
liked it. If she offered him one, he'd take it, he

knew. But she didn't.

He resumed his questions. "Mrs. Waldo told us all about this telephone tree, Mrs. Masters. We know that you recruit these women, that this phone number is listed in your name, and the bill is paid from your checking account."

She unwrapped the wafers, picked through the stack to find a pink one. "Counseling is not against the law," she said, slipping the candy into her mouth.

"Who is Dear one?" he asked.

She bit the wafer in two.

"You called someone named Dear one, Mrs. Masters. Is Dear one your husband?" he asked.

She chewed the wafer properly and swallowed it.

"What does 'feed the chickens' mean?" he asked.

She rolled the tube of candy back and forth in her hands like cookie dough.

"Who is Mitchell Masters?" he asked.

"My husband," she said, opening the Necco package again.

"And what does he do?"

"He's disabled," she said. "He's retired." She selected three more pink ones and put them all in her mouth at once.

"What did he do when he worked?" Arnie asked. "Did he sell surgical supplies, maybe?"

She crossed her legs.

"You have a daughter named Colleen, is that right?"

"Colleen is no longer with us."

"Did she die having an abortion?"

"Colleen is in California."

"No," Arnie said. "I'm afraid not. Of course, we're not absolutely positive it's your Colleen who died, but somebody named Colleen Masters with a mother and father named Edith and Mitchell, who live at your address, died of internal bleeding at General Hospital fifteen years ago this week."

Mrs. Masters closed her eyes.

"We checked the property tax rolls, Mrs. Masters. The house has not changed ownership in twenty years. So if I could see your driver's license to verify your address, please. . ."

She opened her eyes. "Absolutely not," she said.

"You refuse to let me see your driver's license?"

"I do," she said.

He closed his notebook. "Mrs. Masters, you are under arrest," he said. "You have the right to remain silent. Anything you say can and will be used against you in a court of law." He motioned for the officer standing to one side of the table. "You have the right to be represented by counsel. If you cannot afford a lawyer, the court will appoint one for you."

"You are wasting your time," she said.

"If I am wasting my time," he said, standing up, "at least I have the comfort of knowing I am also wasting yours."

The officer came up behind her and took her arm.

"Put the cuffs on," Arnie told him. "And get me a
warrant to search the house."

She offered him the purse. "You can search my
purse, my house, my car, everything I have, Detective.
But you will not find one shred of evidence that links
me to this crime." She flinched as the officer snapped
the handcuffs around her wrists.

"Help me, Mrs. Masters," Arnie said. "If Colleen
died from an illegal abortion, shouldn't you want to
protect other girls by keeping abortion legal and safe?"

She didn't answer.

"Is it your husband who planned this thing?"

She didn't answer.

Arnie nodded to the officer. "Take her downtown.
And when you get her prints, check them against the ones
we found in the church this morning."

Arnie watched her go. He knew he could be making a
mistake, taking her in. If she stayed loose, she might
do something that would lead to the others. But he was
beginning to think there weren't any others. He was
beginning to think this whole thing could be the work of
two little people. It was, he thought, the American way.

* * *

The Mayor and Vi didn't know yet that Fay thought their boys were in trouble. The Chief had decided not to frighten them until there was something real to be afraid of.

They stood together on the sidewalk, at Vi's request, having what felt to Peter like a meeting.

"Are you listening to me?" she asked, smiling at the people passing by.

"I don't think so," he said, also smiling at the people passing by. "Are you saying anything?"

She signed an autograph. "I said I want to borrow one of your speech writers to help me prepare a statement against abortion."

"I can't do that," he said, shaking someone's hand. "They're on the city payroll."

"I have to do this," she said. "It's the only way I know to get our boys back."

"I don't think that's why you're doing it at all," he said.

"I've helped <u>you</u>," she said, "I've campaigned for you, posed for pictures with you, given little dinners for you. . ."

"I heard what you told that reporter, Vi. And I <u>don't</u> think women's real work is recreating the lost world of the American family. I <u>don't</u> think the women's

movement sold American women to industry as cheap labor.
And I <u>don't</u> think legal abortion is why mothers don't
have time for the PTA."

She shook her head. "The PTA was just an example,
Peter. What I meant was that women are too tired from
working to take care of their children."

"You've reversed yourself completely!" he said.
"You've betrayed everything you ever stood for."

"Who was that woman you were talking to?" she
asked. "During my interview."

"You know very well who she was," he said. "It's
Gail Wilkins, one of the mothers."

"And what were you talking about?" she asked.

He smiled. "Why her husband climbed the Indian."

"And what else?" Vi asked.

"What else is none of your business, Vi," he said.

"So you admit it?"

"Admit what?"

"That you were talking to her about something
else."

"Yes," he said. "Terrible, isn't it."

She tugged at the tail of his jacket. "All I was
doing in that interview was admitting I'd been wrong
about abortion."

"No," he said. "You just looked at the crowd and
said what they wanted to hear."

"Peter," she said. "Think how many people there
are who have no one to speak for them on this."

"Oh yes," he said, "and a lot of people secretly thought lynching was a good idea, too. How do you feel about that?"

She turned away. "It's not the same thing and you know it."

He ran his hand through his hair. "The real reason I'm not giving you one of my speech writers," he said, "is that none of them is really good enough to handle your problem."

"Your attitude right now is the only problem I can see," she sighed.

"Oh no," he said. "It's slightly bigger than that." He scratched his head. "If you're going to become the chief defender of the American family, how are you going to explain our divorce?"

"We're not getting a divorce," she said.

"Oh yes we are," he said. "And it can be messy and public or quick and quiet. Whatever you want."

"A divorce will destroy your career," she said.

"Yes," he said, "if people like you get in power, I imagine it will. You're not very forgiving, as a group. Anybody that fucks up, pays."

"Don't use that language with me," she snorted.

"Vi," he said, "it is my fondest desire not to use any language at all with you. But I have to say just one more thing. The boys are mine. As soon as I get back to my office, I'm suing you for divorce and custody of the boys."

"On what grounds?" she demanded.

"You forget," he said. "This is a no-fault state.
But maybe you can get rid of that too when you get
elected."

She pulled a small mirror from her purse and
checked her lipstick. "Peter," she said, in her most
soothing voice, "a more active life for me does not mean
there will be less of our life together. The more
involved I am, the better I'll understand the pressures
you've been under all these years."

He motioned for one of his aides to come get him.
"I'm not happy, Vi," he said. "It's as simple as that."

"Of course you're not," she said. "But now that
I'm in politics myself, you'll have a real ally, instead
of just a wife."

"No, Vi," he said, as the aide approached. "To be
allies, you have to be on the same side."

Vi extended her hand to the aide. "Hello, Rudy,"
she cooed. "I want to send a letter to all the mothers.
Can you get their addresses for me?"

"Sure," Rudy said, assuming Vi had the mayor's
approval here.

"I need Rudy myself," the mayor said, clapping his
arm around the aide's shoulder and standing his ground.

Vi took a step backward. "I'll just go downtown,
then," she said.

"Fine," he said.

"I have my car," she said.

"Good," he said. "If I hear anything about our
boys, I'll call you."

And the Mayor stood with Rudy and watched as Vi
strode off toward the black and white police cruiser
that was waiting for her.

As she drove away, he sent Rudy for some coffee and
spotted Gail, sitting by herself at the mothers' table.

* * *

The sign on the door of the tea shop said CLOSED,
but Arnie knocked anyway. Maybe they knew where Fay had
gone.

But there was no answer.

Then he tried the door and found it open. "Fay?"
he called, seeing the pleasant-looking hostess reading a
mystery novel at a table by the wall.

"Would you be Detective Campbell?" the hostess
inquired.

"I'm looking for Fay Morgan," he said. "Sexy
black-haired lady about this tall?"

The hostess blushed at his description. "She's in
the garden," she fluttered. "She said if you came, I
should ask if you'd be so kind as to wait in here."

As Arnie walked toward the back window, the hostess
stood up. "Could I bring you a cup of tea?"

"No thanks," Arnie said. "Unless you've got a
beer."

Arnie took her silence to mean "No" and pulled the
curtains away from the window.

And sure enough, there was Fay, sitting quietly,
studying two acorns she held in the palm of her hand.
But she was not alone. Perched on the edge of a
wrought-iron table like a snowy egret, was an old lady
Arnie had never seen before.

He couldn't believe it. Who was this woman? Fay
seemed to know her all right, so why hadn't he ever met
this bird? And where did she come from, a tree? Yes,
he thought, as he watched her move with no visible
effort, this lady might very well have come from a tree.
The only tree in this acre of concrete, the knotty oak
planted in the middle of the tea shop patio.

Arnie had never seen Fay sit so still, or listen
so intently. But what in God's name were they talking
about?

He couldn't interrupt them, he knew that, but could
he stand here and spy on them? He wasn't spying, he was
waiting for them to finish. He did have to go to the
bathroom, though. But what if he missed something?
What if this old girl left while he was gone and Fay
never mentioned it again?

What if it had something to do with the case? He
had informers, didn't he? So why couldn't Fay? But who
knew more than Fay?

He really did have to go to the bathroom. But now
something was really happening out there. Fay was
shaking her head. "No, No," she was saying. But the
old woman was insisting, "Yes, Yes" and tapping a bony
finger on the table, pressing her point.

Fay looked away. She didn't even want to discuss
it any more. The old woman pulled herself fully
erect, grabbed Fay's shoulder and demanded her
attention. This was the whole shooting match right here.

Fay looked up at her, mad and hurt, and started to
bolt from the chair. But the old bat blocked her. Fay
sat back and crossed her arms over her chest. Then the
woman backed up, propped her hands up on her h   Arnie
couldn't believe they were fighting over two
acorns? But then, he wondered, where had they even
gotten the acorns? It wasn't time for acorns yet.

The old woman reached carefully into the center of
Fay's palm and picked up one of the acorns. She rolled
it between her thumb and forefinger. Then, with Fay
watching, the old woman brought the acorn to her lips,
kissed it sweetly, then put it in   Arnie couldn't be
lieve they were fighting over two
acorns? But then, he wondered, where had they even
gotten the acorns? It wasn't time for acorns yet.

The old woman reached carefully into the center of
Fay's palm and picked up one of the acorns. She rolled
it between her thumb and forefinger. Then, with Fay
watching, the old woman brought the acorn to her lips,
kissed it sweetly, then put it in her pocket and patted
it. Nice and safe, she seemed to be saying. See how
easy that is?

And that made Fay start crying! Made her look at
her lonely little acorn and cry. What the hell was this?

And then, the old lady lost her balance, and
grasped the edge of the table to steady herself.

Fay was still crying, but could see that the woman
was failing, and sprang up to help her into the chair on
the other side of the table.

Then Fay laughed, apparently at something the old woman said, bent down and kissed the crest of her head and the woman laughed too, a little.

Good, he thought, straightening up. Now I can go to the bathroom. And when he returned, the door to the garden was open.

"Arnie," Fay said to him as he came out, "I'd like you to meet my godmother Katherine. Katherine Swift."

"It's a pleasure," Arnie said, extending his hand and trying not to crush hers as he pressed it. "Where's Fay been keeping you all this time?"

"Oh no," she said in her silvery voice, "I don't like to bother her."

"Katherine," Fay protested, "I can never find you! I call your house all the time but you're never there."

"I'm always there," the old woman said calmly, "but if you're just calling me to make me feel better," she smiled, "I don't answer it. I go rest." She paused. "That always makes me feel better."

Fay shook her head.

"How do you know it's Fay?" Arnie asked.

Godmother Katherine squinted. "How do _you_ know it's Fay?" she asked. "She looks like Fay, doesn't she? She sounds like Fay." She folded her hands in her lap. "So it must be Fay!"

As a triumphant grin frisked across her face, Arnie knew he was way out of his league. He looked at his watch. "Fay," he said, "if you want to go in the truck, you have to do it soon because. . ."

"Yes," Fay said. "I'm ready." She pushed her chair under the table. "Godmother Katherine, can we get someone to take you home?"

"No," the old woman said. "I'll just rest here a while, I think."

Fay rubbed her hands down her skirt. "Well, then..." she said.

As Godmother Katherine rose from her chair, her arms swept open and Fay rushed, released, into the infinite compassion of the embrace. "Please, Fay," the old woman whispered, "please, please be careful."

Arnie didn't know how long they held each other. Maybe it was only a minute, but he knew he had no business watching. He backed up toward the door.

This was a love he knew nothing about. This was an ancient unbreakable bond. But not just between Fay and her godmother. This went all the way back to the edge of time, he thought, to the first two women who stood up, walked out of their caves, saw each other and hugged.

Somehow, he thought, that same embrace had been passed down to these two. And while it was fully theirs to hold for the moment of their lives, he knew they wouldn't keep it, couldn't keep it, but had to pass it on.

Then he realized what they had been talking about,

and he felt a little dim for not knowing it sooner, and
then a little blessed for getting it at all. Of course.
Fay and Godmother Katherine had been talking about
Lizzie.

* * *

"An amazing woman," Arnie said, once they were back
inside the tea shop.

"Who, me?" Fay chirped.

"Yes, you," he laughed. He knew she didn't want to
talk about it, but he couldn't just pretend it didn't
happen.

"How long were you standing there watching us?" Fay
asked.

"I don't know. Ten minutes," he said, nodding to
the hostess, who was setting out trays of tea
sandwiches. "You don't have to tell me what you were
talking about," he said. "Just tell me how she found
you."

"She always knows where I am," Fay said.

Arnie nodded. "Does Godmother Katherine read
cards?"

"No," Fay said. "She just came today because she
knew I needed her."

"She looks like one of your cards," he said. "The
lady, what's her name?"

"The High Priestess," Fay said. "Yes. She does."

"Will she be all right by herself?" he asked,
opening the tea shop door.

But Fay wasn't quite ready to face the scene out
there. "She's been by herself her whole life." She
looked back toward the garden. "She told me to tell you

I had a gun in the house."

"What house?" Arnie asked. "What gun?"

"My house," Fay said, stepping out onto the
sidewalk. "It was Mother's."

He followed her quickly, taking her arm as they
neared the curb. "What did your mother need a gun for?"

She looked across at the truck. "Snakes," she
said.

"Snakes?" Arnie hooted, holding his arm up to stop
a car crossing in front of them.

Fay nodded. "Yes, snakes. You know, for winter in
the country, when they crawl into the house to get warm."

Arnie had to laugh. "It's damn tough to hit a
snake with a gun," he said. "You're better off with an
axe."

"Yes, I know," Fay said. "I think Dad used an
axe."

"Where is this gun of yours, Fay?" Arnie asked, as
he waved to the Chief.

"In the record cabinet."

"Are there any bullets for it?"

"I don't have any extras," she said. "But it's
loaded, if that's what you mean."

"Jesus, Fay," he said. "You've got a loaded gun in
your house?"

"What's the matter with that?" she asked. "I'm the
only one who knows about it."

Arnie moved a piece of the barricade so they could slip through. "Did Godmother Katherine have any ideas about the kids?" he asked.

"No," Fay said. "She thinks it's awful."

* * *

The High Priestess, the card Arnie thought looked
like Godmother Katherine, is the most powerful card in
the Tarot deck. The High Priestess does not, however,
derive her power from religion or law or earthly force
or womanly charm. She doesn't, in fact, do anything.
She simply knows the names of the mysteries and
understands how they work.

The High Priestess represents what so many people
are afraid of - that there might be uncontrollable
currents which influence their lives, secrets which sway
their decisions.

One reason people go to psychics is to cozy up to
these mysteries, to hear about them so they can feel in
control again. Control, however, is simply not to be
had where mystery is concerned. You cannot know a
mystery, you can only know it's there.

Did Fay know what the secret system was? Did Fay
know how things worked? Yes and no. She did know some
of the patterns, but she had no idea why they were
necessary. She did see some of the connections, but
didn't know why they were so inevitable. She knew that
separation was one of the evils, but she didn't
understand why closeness was so difficult.

When Fay was a girl, and first learning the cards,
she thought the High Priestess looked like Carole
Lombard, and slinked around Heaven wearing a silver

slip, listening to old Sinatra tunes. But as Fay got
older, she realized that if there were a Heaven, and if
the High Priestess were there, she would probably just
wear a pink chenille bathrobe and make tea and toast
when folks were feeling blue.

To Fay, the High Priestess was the sense it would
all make when she finally understood. In the darkness,
this wise old woman grasped Fay's hand and found her a
safe place to sit.

The High Priestess kept things from getting lost.
The loose ends that people left dangling, she gathered
up and held until they were ready to pick them up again.
When things fell apart, she kept the pieces in one place
until you were ready to put them back together. If you
swore never to speak to your brother again, she'd stay
in touch with him, keep him thinking about you, until
you realized you needed him back.

And as for power, Fay's High Priestess didn't make
things happen to you, she simply moved you toward things
that were going to happen, then stood by to see if you
got it. Most of the time, of course, you wouldn't get
it. What she did then was calmly arrange another
opportunity.

Fay knew The High Priestess was at work on her
today, she could feel it. And she knew it had something
to do with Lizzie, but what was it? These visions Fay
was having, Lizzie getting married, Lizzie having a

baby, Lizzie not talking to Fay, what did they mean?

Maybe the High Priestess was warning Fay that this was her last chance to hold onto her daughter. Maybe Fay was supposed to do something different this time. But how could she? All she'd ever done was try to keep the girl from getting hurt.

This was exactly the same thing. Paul was <u>not</u> the right man for Lizzie. His family just barely tolerated her. They probably laughed at her behind her back. They didn't appreciate who she was. They weren't there when she needed them.

Lizzie would starve there, would turn into someone as materialistic and shallow as they were. She would forget everything Fay had taught her, might even forget Fay altogether. If Lizzie went away with Paul, she would turn into someone else, someone Fay didn't know. She had to be stopped.

Godmother Katherine meant well, but she was wrong.

5:00 P.M.

Gail and the Mayor were waiting for Fay at the
Mothers' table with the Chief. They were all glad to
see her coming now. The Chief wanted her to make this
whole thing disappear. Gail and Peter simply wanted to
be there when she found their children.

That's all they'd been talking about til the Chief
came up. The Mayor said he didn't think either of his
boys would go into politics, that Kevin liked science
and Kerry wanted to be a baseball player. Gail said
her little Beth liked applesauce and wanted to be a cat.
Peter said he had always wanted a big family. Gail said
she came from a big family, and it was nice except in
the morning.

When the Chief came over, Gail asked if the city
would send them a bill for rescuing Marvin.

"You already paid," the Chief said. "Taxes."

Gail forced herself to laugh. "I think Marvin
cheats on our taxes," she said.

Now the Mayor laughed. "Well, we'll just have to
keep him in jail, then."

"Marvin would like jail," Gail said. "He doesn't
care what he eats, and he always wanted to learn to fix
radios."

They were real uncomfortable here. Gail stood up
and walked over to meet Fay. Another detective rushed
up to the Chief with a message, and Arnie came over to

the Mayor who had been left sitting by himself.

"Is she going to go in the truck now?" the Mayor
asked.

"That's what she says," Arnie said.

"What does she think is in there?" the Mayor
asked, as he watched Gail talking to Fay.

But before Arnie could answer, the Chief came back
with the news.

Fay saw the look on his face and grabbed Gail's
arm. "It's Peter's boys," she said. And they rushed up
to the table in time to hear the end of it.

"Shit," the Chief said, "I didn't even think about
the weather. An electrical storm with the two of them
on that cliff..."

Arnie was mad. "Why can't somebody just climb out
and. . ."

"It's like a natural bridge," the Chief said, as
the Mayor waved for his driver. "And the only way to
get to it, is the same way the boys did, crawling
through this tiny passage."

"Why can't the boys crawl back out?" the Mayor
asked.

"From where they are," the Chief said, "they can't
see the opening any more. What we need is somebody
small, real small, to go after them. Somebody small
enough to sit on the ledge with them and convince them
they can crawl back."

"And what's on the other side of the ledge?" Gail

asked.

"Air," the Chief said. "Almost a straight drop,
hundreds of feet, and pretty serious rocks at the
bottom."

Fay knew what Gail was thinking.

"Am I small enough?" Gail asked.

"No, Gail," the Mayor said. "There has to be
something they haven't thought of yet. I don't want you
to..."

"At least let me come with you," Gail said, as the
Mayor's car pulled up in front of them.

"No," he said. "You should be at your house in
case the kidnappers drop Beth off there."

Gail grabbed his arm. "Mother's there," she said.
"Mother's waiting for Beth. Please," she lowered her
voice. "I can't just sit at home and . . ."

"Go on," Fay said to Peter. "Take her with you."

And that was all the encouragement Peter needed to
sweep her into the car.

"Be careful," Fay waved to Gail through the window,
and then they were gone.

As they walked to the truck, the Chief had some
other news for Fay. They had found Kimberly Chen sound
asleep at 228 Hummingbird Drive. But by the time the
detectives arrived, the woman Fay had seen was gone.

"Somebody is listening to everything we do," Arnie
said.

"Who owns that house?" Fay asked.

"Vernon Lockhart," the Chief said. "Out of town. Nice people, the neighbors say. Haven't caused a minute's worth of trouble in the five years they've been living there."

"Maybe the neighbors are lying," Arnie said.

"Maybe," the Chief said. "We're checking on the car."

"Was Kimberly all right?" Fay asked.

"Looks all right," the Chief said. "They're doing a blood test on her now, for tranquilizers, that kind of thing. I mean, if I had to deliver twenty-seven kids in the middle of the night, I'd sure put them to sleep first."

Fay was glad they'd had something to talk about on the way to the truck, but she froze as another detective handed the Chief the keys.

"You ready?" the Chief asked.

She didn't trust herself to answer, so she simply nodded. She hadn't been this close to it all day. Beads of perspiration popped out on her forehead.

"Want me to come with you?" Arnie asked.

"Yes," she whispered, and squeezed his hand. "Thank you."

The Chief climbed up to the step tread and put the key in the padlock. It worked easily and he pitched the padlock to the leader of the lab team, then spun the cylinder on the combination lock.

Fay was trying to remember the contents of the packages now. "Did anybody play that cassette tape?"

"Yeah," Arnie said. "It's real cute. One voice says 'Can I see my baby?' Then another voice says `No.'"

"That's all?" she asked, trying to keep her knees from shaking.

"That's all," Arnie said. "For 45 minutes, over and over."

The Chief unwrapped the chains and dropped them to the ground. "Everybody ready?" He jumped down. "Fay?" he asked.

She shook her head. "Arnie's going in first."

Arnie stepped up to the truck, grabbed hold and pulled himself up to the step tread. Then he grasped the door handles. "Stand back," he said. Then with one massive effort, he jerked the doors toward him, then pulled them apart. A wave of darkness washed over him.

He stood there stunned by the chill inside the truck. He'd expected it to be hot, an oven. "Somebody got a flashlight?" he asked.

"What about prints?" a lab man asked the Chief.

"I'm not touching anything," Arnie said, as another lab man handed the flaghlight up to him. "Come on, Fay," he said, "get up here."

She backed up quickly. "No, Arnie," she said, "I'll go through it once you've . . ."

"It's O.K.," he said, catching the Chief's eye. "Help the little lady up, huh?"

And before she could resist, the Chief put both hands around Fay's waist and hoisted her up into the bed of the truck.

"Just relax," the Chief said. "It's just an ordinary truck. Nothing's going to hurt you."

But Fay knew better.

Arnie flashed the light around the inside of the truck and found, just as Fay had feared, a sign taped to the back wall. The letters, easily four feet high, were red. Blood, the lab would say later, type O positive.

Arnie read it aloud. "MISSING CHILDREN."

She shook her head. "There's more," she whispered. "Little words." She couldn't move.

He walked forward and saw them himself. "Oh boy," he shook his head. "Oh boy oh boy." Then he read the whole message to Fay, pointing out the words with his flashlight. "WE... ARE ...MISSING ..OUR ..CHILDREN."

She nodded and swallowed.

"What does it mean?" he asked.

"It means what it says, Arnie," she said, and closed her eyes.

The Chief yelled up to them. "What have you got?"

"A sign," she said. "Come see." She wanted more company in here.

Once the Chief was inside, Arnie lit up the words more time. "WE..ARE..MISSING..OUR..CHILDREN."

The Chief nodded, just as Fay had, then stood there sad for a moment, unable to speak.

Behind him, someone called that they had some portable lights if they needed them. Grateful for something to do, the Chief turned and reached down for them.

"Some sign, huh?" he muttered to Fay.

It was clearly a plea for comfort.

"Yes," she said. "Me too. I miss mine too."

"I wasn't home enough," he said.

She smiled wearily. "Terrific," she said. "I was home all the time."

Arnie walked forward and took the lights from the Chief.

"See anything else back there?" the Chief asked him.

"Pictures," Arnie said.

"What pictures?" Fay asked.

"Girls," Arnie said. "Under the sign." And he placed the lights down the middle of the truck.
"There." He flipped the switches and looked around.

The lamps did not fully illuminate the inside of the truck, but rather created pools of light separated by dim, and then dark places.

"Let's each take a side," Arnie said, "and call out what we find, just to get a sense of it, and then we'll call in the team. Fay, you take the pictures."

The Chief began. "Folding chairs, a lecturn, a
portable microphone system, and three electric fans."

Arnie continued with the inventory. There were
posters rolled up in cardboard tubes, and a folding cork
screen.

"This box is all books," the Chief said, holding
one of them up to the light. "This one's some kind of
source-book for people wanting to adopt children. And a
camera."

And Fay spoke for the first time. "How fast can we
get the film developed?"

"Twenty minues," the Chief said, walked to the
door and handed the camera to the lab team.

"What have you got, Fay?" Arnie asked.

"Boxes," she said, stooping down under the row of
pictures. "Is it O.K. if I open one?"

"Just one," the Chief said.

Carefully, she lifted the lid of the small
cardboard box, reached inside and picked up a ragged
scrap of faded pink fabric. As she rubbed it between
her fingers, her eyes welled with tears.

"What's that?" he asked.

Fay cleared her throat. "It's all that's left of
her favorite blanket," she said, "you know, the one she
wouldn't go to sleep without, the one she dragged around
the house all the time, the one she'd put up to her face
and smell when she was scared."

"Whose blanket?" he said. "Colleen's?"

"I don't know," Fay said. "Her." And she pointed to the picture above the box.

Fay counted the pictures. "Arnie," she asked, "how many tables were there in that church this morning?"

"I don't know," he said.

"One for each of these girls?"

"Maybe," he said. "The report would have it. Want me to find out?"

"I have to get out of here," she said, turning around to face the open back door of the truck.

"Oh no you don't," he said.

"I have to find Lizzie," she said.

"She's with Jake at a place called Sound Effects," he said. "Having a drink."

"It's a tomb in here, Arnie. I have to go!" she cried.

He grabbed her arm and held her fast. "No, Fay."

She turned around angrily, twisting her arm to get free of him. "Arnie, I've got to make sure Lizzie doesn't. . ."

"No," he said firmly. "No. You've got to do what only you can do. You've got to tell us who these people are and where they're keeping the rest of the children."

She was really mad now. She looked away from him. "While my own child disappears."

"We'll shut the doors," he said, "and turn out the lights and leave you in here for a while."

"No," she said.

"It's what you came here to do," he said. "You
can't just walk out of here as though you were any other
woman on earth and not. . ."

"Arnie," she begged, "you <u>know</u> what I'll see."

He had never seen her this afraid. "No, love, I
don't. That's just the point."

He let go of her arm and she turned to face the
side wall.

"Fay," he said, speaking more softly this time, "as
soon as we find these children, we can spend the rest of
the night with Lizzie. We can kidnap her ourselves if
that will make you feel better, put her in the car and
drive all night, all the way to Wyoming if you want to."

She stared at the wall. "They were all here," she
said finally. "The children were all in this truck."

"That's good," he said. "That's a good start."

She turned back to face him, her face drawn and
pale. "But we already knew that, Arnie."

He reached for her hand. "Just try," he said.
"That's all I'm asking you to do."

"And where will you be?" she asked.

"Right outside the door," he said. "I'll sit on
that little step and knock every now and then if you
want me to."

"No," she said. "Don't knock. Just stay there."

He rubbed her shoulder.

Tears filled her eyes again. "And what if I can't

do it?" she asked.

"Then you can't, that's all. Then I'll take you to
Lizzie while I go to the Masters' house."

"No," she said. "I want to go to the Masters house
with you."

"How long do you need?" he asked.

"Ten minutes," she whispered. "Open the door in
ten minutes."

"And if you want to come out before then, just
knock and I'll open the door."

Her hand started to tremble.

He wanted to help her somehow. "I wish there
were something I could. . ."

"Just go," she said, squeezing herself as though
she were cold. "Just. . go on. Let's get it over with."

Arnie took a step backward and gave her a thumbs-up
sign.

When she turned away, he walked quickly to the big
doors, stepped out, and closed them behind him.

* * *

As the heavy doors clanged shut, the sound
ricocheted around the walls of the truck. Fay flipped
the switch on the light next to her, then walked to the
other one, took a deep breath and turned it off. Then
she simply stood there quietly and waited, as the
history of this truck, pressed back against the walls by
the light, sensed its freedom and crept toward her in
the darkness.

First there came the whispers, the soft sobbing,
the furtive shuffling of the little sneakers. Then
the sound of sandals and a pair of flip-flops.

A baseball cap fell to the floor. A hand reached
down to get it, brushing past knees, shorts, and
shirttails. Little overalls and spotted t-shirts sagged
in the shadows. Two hands clasped tight. Somebody sat
down. Kerry leaned back against the wall. Kevin curled
up beside him. Beth sucked her thumb. All the children
breathing at once, but slower now, softer now, as sleep
settled over them like a down comforter.

"Before this," Fay whispered, "before you were
here, you were outside, at the fair." Beth listened.
"Tell me who brought you here. Tell me why you came with
them."

A clown, she saw floppy clown shoes, green like
pickles. Pickles. Of course they would follow a clown.

They might even ask. Can I go see the clown? And the
clown had brought them here for the magic show.

"But we can't start the magic show til everybody
gets here," the clown said, "so why don't you have some
lemonade. Cowboy Bob will give you some lemonade, and
after the lemonade and the magic show, he'll let you
ride his pony."

But after the lemonade they were all asleep.
Cowboy Bob and Pickles the Clown drove the truck out the
main gate to a farmhouse in the country, a dirt road, a
big black dog.

They unloaded the kids, all asleep. Put them in
the barn. Kevin. Kerry. She didn't see Beth, but she
had to be there. Dark. Mirrors. Bathtubs. Beth?
Where's Beth?

Look closely, Fay.

It's Edith Masters.

And the young man in the coffee shop this morning.

The other one's in a wheelchair. An older man in a
wheelchair. Small legs, big chest, sleeves rolled up,
arms like a boxer. Stubble on his face, wire glasses
and a hearing aid. Gray stubble on his head, an army
blanket over his legs.

Where is this barn, she asked. And Beth? Where
did you take Beth?

But all she saw was the church. The church with
the Tarot's Hanging Man in the yard. Inside the church,

husbands and wives were standing in back of the tables,
their boxes in front of them. A picture in their hands.
Pieces of blankets. Baby clothes and rattles in the
boxes.

Were those the pictures on the wall of the truck?
Yes. Were those the boxes on the floor below? Yes.

"Lay it down," the man in the wheelchair was
telling them. "Lay it down and let her go."

Let who go? The girl in the picture?

Fay struggled to put it together. The Tarot card.
Edith. The pictures. The boxes. The man in the
wheelchair.

Had Colleen Masters bought a deck of Tarot cards
after she had come to see Fay? Did Edith find them?
Did Edith say they were evil? And then did Colleen die?
Yes.

Fay whirled around, opened her eyes and raced
toward the sliver of light between the massive metal
doors.

"Arnie!" she screamed.   "Arnie, are you out
there?"

She heard him jump up, felt his hands grab the
handles.

"I'm here," he shouted back. "Are you all right?"

"I'm all right," she managed, "I just wanted to
make sure you were there." His voice steadied her.

"Are you ready to come out?"

She knew she couldn't. Colleen had to be there,

had to be one of those children on the back wall. Her
toys had to be in one of those boxes. If Colleen were
there, that would be real proof. They could force Edith
to tell them where she took the children.

"No," she said to Arnie. "I need another two
minutes."

"All you have to do is knock, love," he said.

"Thanks," she said, and stood up straight and took
a step, then a second.

"Find Colleen," she said to herself. "Find
Colleen."

Fay stopped at the back of the truck and stared
into the wall of pictures, but it was too dark to see
any more than the outlines of their white frames. She
turned around to go get a flashlight, and then stopped.
Suddenly, she understood.

Edith wouldn't put anything in this truck that
could lead to her. If a group like that had met at the
church, she'd just used the idea of it, not the actual
pictures and boxes. These pictures, she'd cut out of
magazines. These boxes, she'd collected at the
Goodwill. These girls did exist, all right, and these
girls all died having abortions, but these weren't their
real pictures. Fay was finished. Edith had won.

She sighed and sat down in the darkness. What was
she going to tell Arnie? That Edith was mad? That a
cowboy and a man in a wheelchair helped her? What good

would that do?

She nudged one of the boxes with her foot. She
knew exactly which box it was, the one with the little
scrap of blanket in it. She knelt down in the darkness,
lifted the lid, reached for the piece of blanket, raised
it to her face and inhaled, deep and long.

A new smell. Sharper, younger. This little girl
had dark curls and long thin legs. Like a colt she was,
with bright black eyes. And she never could hold still,
but now her mother was trying to brush her hair.
"Katie!" her mother said, and the little girl squealed
in laughter, and Fay shivered in recognition. It was
Lizzie's laugh. It was Lizzie's little girl.

"Hold still!" Lizzie said. "I have to brush your
hair before Grandma comes. You <u>know</u> how Grandma likes
your hair to look nice."

"I like it like it is," the girl said.

Fay liked it the way it was too. Her hand, still
clutching the blanket, dropped now to her side as she
watched them play this ancient squirming game.

"It has to hurt," Lizzie said, "or it won't do any
good."

Fay smiled. She didn't believe that any more, but
she remembered saying it often enough.

"But it won't stay combed," the little girl
protested.

"It would if you would behave yourself," Lizzie
nagged.

Fay shook her head.

The little one tried again. "Grandma says the next time I go over there by myself she's going to cut it all off anyway."

Fay stood up. She wasn't the Grandma they were talking about, was she. No. But they were saying Grandma like there was only one. Didn't they have some way to tell the Grandmothers apart? How could there be only one Grandma? Fay didn't know. But she did know the little girl had Paul's blazing devil black eyes.

Fay wrapped the little piece of blanket between her fingers and turned around slowly. Once again, she was alone in the truck. The odor of spoiling oranges engulfed her. She gagged.

"Arnie!" she screamed, as the metal walls seemed to close in on her.

"Arnie!" she screamed again, racing for the doors and pounding to be let out.

He jumped up from his seat on the tread. "O.K., O.K.," he said.

"Arnie! Hurry!"

"I'm right here, hon," he said through the door, "but back up a little, O.K.? I don't want you falling out when I open the doors."

Fay stepped back, shaking with terror, and stuffed the scrap of blanket into her pocket.

Arnie jerked the doors open and she fell into his

arms.

"It's all right, love," he said. "Everything's all
right now."

"It's Edith and a man in a wheelchair," she
whispered into his shoulder. "They did it to get back
at me, to punish me for what I did, for what I told
Colleen that day."

"Fay, Fay," he said. He didn't hear most of this,
and didn't understand what little he heard. He carried
her down the steps and walked her toward an empty chair.
"You need some air, love," he comforted. "You're all
right."

"Do we need the medics?" the Chief asked, then
turned around and barked at one of his aides for some
water.

Arnie smoothed her hair, talking quietly. "Now
then," he said. "Isn't that better. Isn't that better
to have some air?"

She nodded and reached for his hand.

The lab team stormed the truck now, with their
gloves and bags and labels. Fay knew the Chief was
eager to hear her report, but she didn't know if she
could talk at all, much less remember what she had seen.

Arnie motioned to the Chief to back off a little,
then waved him back in when Fay cleared her throat and
sat up a little straighter in the chair.

"Just tell us if there's something we should do,
Fay."

She looked up at the Chief. "It's Edith," she
said, "and a man in a wheelchair."

"Her husband, Mitch, is in a wheelchair," Arnie
said. "She just told me."

"Mitch Masters," the Chief said, drawing a piece of
paper from his pocket. "Purple Heart, Korea."

"I thought we sent somebody to their house," Arnie
said.

"He's not home," the Chief said. "Our guy just
left there. The nurse said he went to the fair."

"He has wire-rimmed glasses and and gray stubble on
his head," Fay said. "Sixty maybe."

The Chief headed for the radio truck.

Arnie didn't like the wildness in Fay's eyes.

"This does have to do with me," Fay said, when the
Chief was out of range. "Edith and Mitch think I'm
responsible for what happened to Colleen. That's why
they put the Tarot card in front of the church."

"But Colleen has been dead a long time now," he
said. "Surely they don't think you could bring her
back."

"No," she said, "but. . ."

"They did all this to get back at you?" he asked.

"I know," she said. "I know how it sounds, but
that's what I saw."

"Did Edith drive the truck away from the
fairgrounds?" Arnie asked.

"No," she said. "That man we saw her with this
morning in the coffee shop, that Cowboy Bob, he did. He
drove it to a farmhouse. A farmhouse with mirrors and
bathtubs in the barn."

Arnie shook his head. "Was there any proof in the
truck," he paused, "any proof that it was Edith?"

"No," she said. "Just that I saw her there."

"It's O.K.," he said. "We'll get her."

She didn't answer.

"Don't be scared of them," he said. "They can't
hurt you. We'll find Mitch at the fairgrounds, get him
to tell us where the Cowboy is, and lock them all away."

"Beth wasn't there," Fay said. "They took Beth
someplace else."

"We'll find her," Arnie said.

The Chief returned from the truck. "O.K.," he
said. "They're looking for him. There's a wheelchair
race at six, some Veterans thing. He's signed up for
it." The Chief was looking better. "I think we've got
these bastards."

"Well," Arnie said, "we still don't have anything
to prove it."

"We'll get it," the Chief said. "We've got a
million people on this thing. Do you want to be there
when they find him?" the Chief asked.

"I want to go somewhere," Fay said, beginning to
recover. "This is longer than I ever spent in a
shopping center in my life."

"Yeah," the Chief nodded. "I don't know how my
wife does it."

"She has things to carry," Fay said. "That helps."

Arnie offered his arm and she stood up.

"I'll be downtown if you need me," the Chief said,
checking his watch. "And sooner or later, I guess I'll
have to go home."

"Yes," Fay said, looking at the Chief, "I think you
should."

Her tone of voice alarmed him. "Is something the
matter?"

"No," she said, realizing she scared him. "They
like you, that's all. More than you think."

He decided not to ask her how she knew that. He
was afraid she was right.

* * *

"I need a cup of coffee," Arnie said, as they
started for his car.

"Not that coffee shop again, please," Fay said.

"I know," he said. "I'll get it at the fair." He
took her arm. "Do you want anything?"

She stopped. "I want you to believe what I said.
About this whole thing happening because of me."

He lit a cigarette. "If they wanted to get back at
you, hon," he said, "they could just hire somebody to
kill you."

She nodded, oddly undisturbed by the idea.

He went on. "To dream up this drill, all these
mothers, twenty-seven children and a tractor trailer
truck would be positively demented."

She didn't answer.

Arnie got in his side of the car and started the
engine.

"Does it hurt to get shot?" she asked.

"It's no fun," he laughed. "Why?"

"Because maybe when this doesn't work, they'll just
give up and kill me," she said.

"I won't let him kill you, Fay."

Somehow, they both knew they were talking about
the man in the wheel chair.

"Don't even think about it," he said.

"Wouldn't you think about it," she asked, "if somebody were planning to kill you?"

"Nobody's planning to kill you," he said. "We're just talking about all of this."

He pulled out of the shopping center, picked up his radio and told the operator to find Jake and Lizzie and have them come to the information booth in the West Wing of the Fairgrounds.

"Because if he did," Fay said, as though they were still talking, "then that would explain why Lizzie doesn't call me."

"Lizzie calls you all the time," he said.

She started slowly, fearing that he wasn't going to believe this either. "No," she said, "when I was in the truck I saw Lizzie, years and years from now. She has a little girl."

A proud smile spread over Arnie's face. "Did she get the family hair?" he asked.

Fay nodded, but couldn't manage a smile yet. "Yes. She did. But she has Paul's features."

He sighed. "Come on, Fay, don't you think you're being a little . . ."

"Lizzie was brushing her hair. For Grandma," she said. "But this Grandma wasn't me. This little girl only has one Grandma, otherwise they'd use some other name to say which Grandma they were talking about."

"O.K." he said, trying not to comment.

"So," Fay asked, "if he kills me, maybe that's why Lizzie doesn't call me any more."

"Maybe it wasn't a good time to call," he said.

"No," she said. "She doesn't call me."

"Fay, for Christ's sake," he said.

"It's what I saw, Arnie," she said.

"Fay," he said, "can you just let the future take care of itself? Can you stop trying to. . ."

"You said you didn't want me to think about Mitchell Masters killing me, so this is what I'm thinking about instead."

He threw the cigarette out the window. "Isn't there anything, anything else you can think about, Fay?"

"You want my full attention," she said. "Is that right, officer?"

"Yes," he said. "I do."

She thought a minute. "And would you give me your full attention in return?" she asked.

"Sure," he said. "I always do."

"You do not," she said.

"O.K." he said. "I don't."

"So what would we do with our full attention?" she asked.

"For how long?" he asked.

"For forever," she said. "Isn't that what we're talking about? You quit the force and I give up the future?"

"I don't know what we'd do, Fay," he said. "Maybe

we could rent boats."

She had to laugh. "I'm sorry?"

"Rent boats," he explained. "Have a little boat
rental shop. Live on the lake and rent boats."

"For what?" she asked.

He was no longer able to conceal his frustration.
"For fun, Fay," he said.

"That's what Lizzie says," she said. "That I don't
know what fun is."

"I didn't say that, Fay."

"You're both right," she said. "I don't."

"You could," he said.

"I'd like to learn it," she said. "Really I would.
I don't know how I missed it."

"Tell you what," he said, reaching over for her
hand. "As soon as Mitchell Masters doesn't kill you and
Lizzie doesn't run off with Paul, we'll work on it.
We'll have some fun."

Neither one of them knew what to say next, so they
didn't mind when the radio operator broke in with a
report from the fairgrounds. Mitch Masters hadn't shown
up for the wheelchair race.

The information hit Arnie like a jolt of
electricity. He turned on the flashing red lights,
pulled up on the median of the six-lane expressway, made
a terrifying U-turn and floored it.

"Where are we going?" she screamed over the siren,

bracing herself against the door.

"We're goddamn fools, all of us," he shouted back.
He got on the radio again and commanded the operator to
find Jake and Lizzie and redirect them to the Masters'
house. But Jake was to call Arnie before he went in.

"Arnie! What are you doing?" Fay screamed, as he
sped down the exit ramp with his left tires on the
shoulder.

"We've done this all wrong," he said. "We've just
been following you around waiting for you to do our work
for us. This is a crime. And that's exactly how we're
going to proceed from now on. If it gets too bad for
you," he swerved around three cars and sailed through
the red light, "close your eyes."

There wasn't anything for her to do now but hold
on. However jarring the ride was, it was good to have
him back in control again.

And she was glad they weren't going to the
fairgrounds. If Mitch Masters were planning to kill
her, that had seemed like an ideal spot for it.

* * *

Let the future take care of itself, Arnie had said.
Rather like mind your own business, Fay thought. Like
the future wasn't your business. But then, people said
all kinds of strange things about the future.

They'd meet your new boyfriend and say, "That's got
no future, honey." But what they'd mean was, you'd
spend a lot of years, or it would seem like a lot of
years, and after all that screaming and screwing and
watching TV and going over to his mother's for dinner,
you'd find yourself alone, right back where you started.

But you weren't really back where you started. You
were older, and you <u>knew</u> you were older. No, the more
life seemed to go in circles, the more inexorable was
its forward march.

Some people thought about it another way. They
stood still while the future came to them, like weather.
"Someday," that was like one of those weird storms off
the coast of Peru. "In the not too distant future,"
that was like a hailstorm over in the next county.
"The immediate future," that was put on your boots.

Fay thought the future was never too distant, but
as close as your next breath. You exhale the past, she
thought, and inhale the future. And the present? Well,
Fay wasn't sure there <u>was</u> a present.

No present? Of course there's a present, people

said to her. My old job is the past, the job I have now
is the present, and the job I'll have next is the
future. Simple.

Yes, she'd say, but the first time you were passed
over for a promotion, or the first day you didn't want
to come back after lunch, that was when the future
started. A long time ago. And the end of the past,
well, as far as Fay knew, nobody ever outlived it.

They were, the past and the future, two powerful
parallel rivers, Fay thought, flowing side by side in
opposite directions, each carving out its own side of
the same great valley. If you had to have a present,
maybe you could draw a line across the two rivers and
say, "There. Where the past and the future meet, that's
the present." But you wouldn't want to try to walk that
line. You couldn't even see it for more than a second.
How could you think you could live there?

Fay's advice was to let the past carry you, let the
future come, and try to keep your head up. But the
currents are tricky, she'd caution. They can trap you
against the shore, send you back downstream, pitch you
over the falls, or dump you into the white water with no
warning at all. The only real comfort, she'd say, is
that we're all in the water. It's not just you.

Sometimes, people would ask if they could influence
the future. Could they change what would happen later
by what they did now?

"Can you survive the white water if you choose the route?" she'd ask.

They wouldn't answer.

"Right," she'd say. "It depends." She'd smile. "Which route are we talking about?" She'd take their hand. "And who else is in this boat?"

Fay wasn't sure that made people feel any better about the future. But it was all she knew to say.

6:00 P.M.

* * *

By the time the Mayor and Gail arrived at the
quarry, ominous yellow gray clouds had choked off the
entire sky, and funnel swirls of loose gravel spun out
wildly from the mouth of the ravine and swept across the
road. They parked behind the last ambulance, and headed
up the hill.

A paramedic jumped out of the ambulance and pointed
the boys out to them, huddled together on the distant
ledge. "Kerry's baseball cap just blew off," he said.

Gail strained to see the blue dot that was Kevin in
the distance, and hoped Kerry didn't look over the edge
to see where his cap went.

One of the firemen called to the boys over a
megaphone. "Don't move," the voice said. "Stay right
where you are."

The boys called back, but the wind carried their
words off in the wrong direction, bounced them around
the walls of the quarry, then dumped them in the pile of
boulders below.

"I can't stand it," the Mayor said. "I can't stand
it," and grabbed Gail's hand.

"We'll figure it out," she said. "It's going to be
all right."

They were close enough now to see that a rock

climbing team had descended into the quarry and was
trying to approach the boys from below. Then they both
heard the shot and ran toward the edge of the path in
horror.

"Jesus Christ!" Peter said, as he saw the net drop
down over the boys and flatten them on the rock, "I
thought it was the kidnappers."

"But what do they do now?" Gail asked.

"I guess they pull the ends together," he said,
"and use it like a slide or something."

But then they both realized that the net hadn't
gone far enough over the boys, there wasn't enough
hanging down on the other side to gather up.

"Goddammit to hell," Peter said, his eyes filling
with tears.

"It's O.K.," she said. "At least the net will hold
them there for a while."

And they both turned and ran the rest of the way up
the hill.

"That was our last good idea," the firemen
said. "The only thing to do now is call the chopper."

The Mayor shook his head, handed Gail the binoculars
and turned away from the sight of his frightened boys
bagged on the ledge like mad mountain lions.

She lifted the glasses to her eyes, found the boys
lying face down now, and watched as Kevin scooted
closer to Kerry and put his arm around him. To get
back, they'd have to go up over the ledge, then back

across an eight inch natural bridge, then drop down
about two feet into an open chamber in a section of
honeycombed limestone. That tunnel, she guessed, opened
again somewhere on the top of the cliff.

"Peter," she said, "If I can get through that
channel, would that help?"

"No, Gail," he answered, taking her hand, "I don't
want you to. . ."

The fireman interrupted him, speaking to Gail.
"It could be real slippery in there, Miss," he said.
"Are you afraid of snakes?"

She smiled. "Do you have a snake-bite kit?"

"No," the Mayor said. "Call the chopper."

"Peter," Gail said, "I can't do a damn thing for
my Beth. Let me do something. Please."

"It's worth a try, sir," the fireman said. "The
smallest man we've got weighs twice as much as she
does."

Gail trusted this fireman. "Let's get going," she
said, not looking back for fear of losing her nerve.

"If you bring my boys back. . ." the Mayor said,
understanding at last.

Gail rubbed her palms together, building up her
courage. "You'll do whatever I want, right?"

The fireman motioned to one of his men, then turned
back to her. "I'll do whatever you want, too, " he
said. "The entrance is up there."

As they started up the hill, Gail grabbed small trees to pull herself forward. "I want to eat dinner at the firehouse," she said. "With all the men sitting around polishing their boots and the cook feeding the leftovers to the dog."

The fireman reached back to help her up over a moss-covered boulder. "I'm sorry, Mam," he said. "But the dog doesn't get the leftovers. He gets his dinner right after the blessing, right out of the pot like everybody else."

At the entrance to the cave, the fireman strapped her into a harness and handed her two additional harnesses for the boys. He explained that the rigging to the harnesses would be anchored to one of the trucks, but that didn't mean you couldn't get hurt if you fell. He gave her a flashlight and a miner's hat with a light on the top. He said he figured she would lose the hat in the tunnel, but it still seemed like a good idea to have it along.

The Mayor reminded her that Kevin was the big one, Kerry the little one, and hugged her. "Please be careful," he said. "I don't want anything to. . ."

"Me neither," she said, kissing him on the cheek. "We'll be fine."

"We found their jackets right here," the fireman said, pointing out the hole, which was roughly two feet in diameter. "We shined a light in as far as we could," he said. "We think it opens up a little once you get past this first part."

"Let's hope so," Gail said, stooping down to look,
then stretching out on the ground.

"The man at the geologic survey says he doesn't
think there's a big drop off or anything," the fireman
said, "but he couldn't be absolutely sure the cave on
his map was this exact cave."

"Thanks," she said.

The fireman knelt beside her now and attached
something else to her harness. "This is a light cord,"
he said. "Before you leave the cave, just unhook it.
Then when you get back, the little lights will point you
right back here."

"Like bread crumbs," she said.

"Better," he said.

Finally, there wasn't anything else to do. "O.K.,"
Gail said, grabbing the inside of the opening. "Here we
go."

* * *

Gail pulled herself into the opening on her side,
then found it was easier to slither on her stomach,
snake-like, using her hands to pull herself along. The
ground was getting wetter, the smell danker, the air
blacker, and she was sure she heard some other scurrying
sounds ahead of her. Little claws scratching the walls.
Maybe the Mayor's boys didn't want to crawl back because
of something they had found in here, something she
hadn't come across yet.

"Go on," she barked at the whatever it was. "Get
out of here. You don't want to see me, and I don't want
to see you, so beat it!"

It occurred to her that babies must feel something
like this as they are on their way to being born. But
if there were some fascinating insight to be gained from
this comparison, she didn't know what it was. Maybe she
was just desperate to find something to think about
other than how bad she was going to look if she ever got
out of here.

The passage opened up a little, and there was a
sharp new smell that made her nose tingle, a cold green
smell, like the inside of an old tin can. Gail stopped
to readjust the miner's cap, allowed herself to look
ahead, and was immediately sorry.

He wasn't a big snake. Or she. Not fat anyway,

and not a constrictor. But a snake is a snake. If the
snake knew Gail had arrived, though, he wasn't letting
on. Was there, she wondered, the slightest chance that
he was dead? Or was he simply playing dead? And would
she be able to tell the difference in time?

Well, she couldn't turn back because of a snake. The
only way she could turn back would be if she couldn't
get through some curve in this passage. Even then, she
couldn't actually turn around, but would have to back
out feet first. That alone was reason enough to
continue.

So why was the snake just lying there in the path
with his head around the corner? Her eyes burned from
the smell. She wanted to hold her nose, but realized
the smell was on her hands now too, under her
fingernails, beginning to penetrate her skin.

It would be so much easier if the snake were dead,
if he had done what every good snake should do. Crawled
into a hole and died.

She batted the snake's tail with the flashlight.
Nothing. Then she smacked him again just because nobody
was watching. Good. Dead. She nudged him over into the
ooze and slipped by him to the corner, which was such a
sharp bend that she had to turn over on her side to get
through.

She could see some light from the outside now, and
could see that the snake's head wasn't on this end of

him at all. Where the hell was the snake's head? And
why did she care?

If the boys came through here without a light, they
probably missed the snake, she thought. Good thing.
Maybe they crawled right over it. And now, for the
first time, Gail wondered what had made the boys come
this far into the dark in the first place. She could
understand two kids starting into a tunnel like this
just out of curiosity, but what kept them going in the
pitch black of the middle section? Something about who
was waiting for them if they went back, she guessed.

She could make it the rest of the way on her knees.
The fresh air felt good and she even indulged herself in
a cough, now that she wouldn't risk bumping the miner's
helmet and losing her light.

She crawled out of the tunnel and brushed off her
hair, hoping to dislodge any loose spiders she'd picked
up. Then she stared, still on her knees, at the narrow
rock bridge that led to the ledge.

"Shit, shit, shit," she said outloud, her stomach
knotting at the prospect of crossing four feet of air on
eight inches of rock. She leaned back against the mouth
of the tunnel and decided to scoot across sitting down.
"Kevin!" she yelled, "can you hear me?"

A terrified scream came back immediately. "Mom!"

This wasn't the time to explain who she was. "I'm
right here!" she screamed, moving onto the bridge. "I'm
coming to get you!" She inched forward, holding the

bridge with both hands in front of her. "Just stay
where you are!"

She leaned over to hug the bridge. That felt
better. She moved another inch and heard a burst of
applause from somewhere in back and to the left.

"Shit," she said again. "They're watching. The
firemen, Peter, everybody. They've got their goddamn
binoculars too, don't they." She reminded herself to
watch her language when she got to the boys, scrambled
up onto the ledge, tripped and fell flat on her face.

As she rested there, she knew exactly why the boys
didn't want to go back the way they came. She didn't
want to go back either. Except that was the only way to
collect from the Mayor for this mission. And see Beth
again, if Beth was there, if she got to see Beth again.
She stopped herself. She couldn't think about Beth.
Not now. Beth would be all right. Somebody would save
her little Beth the way she was saving Kevin and Kerry.

"Mom?" Kevin called to her.

She pulled up to her knees again and crawled over
the curve of the ledge to them.

"My name is Gail," she said, patting Kerry's head
through the net. "I was the only one little enough to
get through that tunnel."

"Did you see a snake?" Kevin asked her.

"I sure did," she said. "I didn't see his head
though."

"Show her," Kevin said, nudging Kerry.

"Be careful," Gail said, judging the ledge to be
around the size of a pool table. "We don't have a lot
of room up here."

Kerry reached into his pocket and pulled out the
beady little beginning of the long black tail. "It's
mine," he whined.

"It's yours, it's yours," Kevin said wearily, then
turned to Gail. "He thinks it's a big deal."

"What are you going to do with it?" Gail asked the
smaller boy, wondering why the snake's eyes didn't pop
out onto the ledge.

"Put it in my room," Kerry said.

"The thing to do," Gail said, unhooking the extra
harnesses, "is pick up his tail on our way back, and
then get a taxidermist to stuff him."

"No!" Kerry cried. "I want to keep him!"

Gail strapped him into the harness. "He'll keep
better if a taxidermist puts him back together," she
said. She reached past Kerry and slipped the other
harness over the older boy's head.

"I want to keep him under the bed," Kerry said.

"I know what you mean," Gail said. "When I was a
girl, there were snakes under my bed all the time."

"Big snakes?" Kerry asked. He wanted to hear all
about it.

"Now, look," Gail said, "what we've got to do is go
right back the way we came."

Kerry's voice dropped to a whisper. "We can't go back. The rat will get us."

"If we go back right now and get the snake," she said, "then the rat can't eat it."

"But then the rat will starve to death," Kevin said, remembering what his teacher had said about nature's way.

Gail shook her head. "The rat is gone," she said. "I just came through there, and he was gone."

That was exactly what they wanted to hear. She smiled to see them relax, then checked the harnesses and retied Kerry's shoes. "O.K.," she said. "Who wants to go first?"

"Me," Kevin said, suddenly sounding very brave. "But you better hold onto Kerry because he forgets things."

"If anybody falls, the harnesses will catch us," Gail said, hoping it was true.

"I want to wear your hat," Kerry said.

"All right," Gail said, "but I can't put it on you out here. As soon as we get in the cave. . ."

Kevin was tired of Kerry getting all the attention. "Well, what are we waiting for?" he asked.

"I'm ready when you are," Gail said, grateful for his help.

Kevin crawled over Kerry and past Gail, lifted the edge of the net and crept over the ledge to the bridge.

"Wait for us, Kevin," she called, but she was too late, he was already across, knowing, instinctively, that the trick was to keep going.

She wrapped one arm around Kerry and they crawled up the ledge together.

"I have to pee," he said.

"A cave is a great place to pee," she said. "Everybody pees in caves."

"They do?" he grinned.

"Sure they do," she said. "That's what the smell is in there."

"It didn't smell like pee to me," he said.

"New pee doesn't smell the same as old pee," she explained. "Old pee smells like caves."

When that satisfied him, she asked about the snake. They didn't see the big rat kill it, he said, but they heard this grindy sound and a flip-floppy thing, and then a scratchy sound and then something ran away. And then he put his hand down right on the snake's head, only he didn't know it was a snake's head until they got out of the tunnel. Gail said she thought it all worked out just about perfect, and blew Kevin a kiss across the bridge.

She sat Kerry down in front of her, their legs on either side of the bridge, then decided it was too dangerous to push him across like that. She turned him around to face her, and wrapped his arms around her neck, his legs around her waist.

"What you have to do now," she whispered in his ear,
is pretend you're asleep. You're the Baby Bear and I'm
the Mama Bear, and I'm taking you back to the cave so you
can sleep for the winter."

He liked that idea a lot, went completely limp, and
started making sleepy bear cub sounds into her shoulder.
Beth liked bears too. They played bears all winter.
Sometimes in the morning, they ate their oatmeal out of
great big bowls and said they were the three bears.

She had to stop worrying about Beth. Think about
this little boy, she said to herself. You're not out of
this yet. Please, she asked, please let me think about
what I have to do here.

And suddenly, the sweetness of his tiny embrace
took her breath away. His skin smelled so new, his
round little belly nestled just under her breasts, his
bottom in her lap. This was different from Beth, this
was what it was like to have a little boy, this hot
little hug, this little penis nuzzling her navel.

She inched across the bridge. Half way. Boys and
their mothers, she thought. Two more feet. Men and
their mothers. She grinned. Boy oh boy. With six
inches left to go, she pushed him into the opening to
the tunnel and leapt in behind him.

"Can I pee now?" he asked.

"Be my guest," she said, wiping her hands on her
shorts and pulling the harness ropes in after her.

Instantly, a fierce stabbing pain shot through her head.
They could have died out there. All of them.

She told the boys to go on ahead now, sneezed
violently four times and tried to push her hair out of
her eyes with her forearm. By the time she got to the
corner where the snake had been, Kevin was already
outside waving it around for his father and telling him
about the taxi driver who was going to stuff it.

Gail was close to the opening of the cave, close
enough to crawl on out. But, for some reason, she
wasn't quite ready to leave yet. She reached behind her
and reeled in the light cord, gathering it into a neat
little bundle the way she would a string of Christmas
tree lights.

The Mayor's head appeared at the opening now.
"Gail?" he called. "Are you all right?"

"I'm fine," she said. "Here's the flashlight."
She handed it out to him. "Now the lights."

He took the lights, then stretched out on the
ground so he could see her face. "I wish I could get in
there with you," he said quietly.

"Yeah, I know," she said, looking back the way
she'd come. "It's nice in here."

"Can I see you tonight?" he asked. "Can I meet you
some place or come over and thank you?"

"I'll be at home," she said softly, wiping her eyes
on her shirt.

"Where's home?"

"248 6th. Third floor."

"Good," he said, reaching in for her. "Give me your hand."

"I'm a mess," she said, grasping his wrist and pulling herself toward the opening.

"You're fine," he said.

"I don't think I'll ever get clean," she said. "I smell like snakes. Don't touch me, you'll ruin your shirt."

"Gail, please. . ." he said, hauling her up into the light.

He lifted her up off the ground and held her tight, while the firemen clapped and cheered. His skin smelled just like Kerry's, she thought. Cleaner, yes, and more tired, but it was the same, dear, male smell.

"Please," she said, her nose buried in his neck, "don't let me fall in love with you."

"It's not a problem," he said, setting her down gently. "It's fine with me."

Then the boys ran over to hug her. She kneeled down, folded them up in her arms, squeezed them as tight as she could, and wished with all her heart, that Beth were here too.

* * *

In their car, Arnie and Fay heard the report. And
if they hadn't had any proof before that Fay was right,
they had it now.

At the fair, Kevin saw the clown with the green
shoes give Kerry something to smell, then pick him
up. So Kevin followed them to the truck where the clown
said they were going to see a magic show with the other
kids. But once they got inside, Cowboy Bob wouldn't let
them out. Then they had some lemonade and some cookies
and the next thing they knew, they woke up in this old
farm house.

Kevin knew he should call home, but there wasn't
any telephone. There was just this growly dog chained
to the fence. So they took off looking for another
house with a phone, but Cowboy Bob came after them in
the pickup truck. He chased them up to the quarry and
they hid in that little cave. Once they were in there,
they kept crawling because he said he was coming back to
get them with that growly dog.

The truck was blue and rusty. Cowboy Bob was
skinny with a blue shirt and tight black jeans. The
farm house was white and there were a lot of bathtubs
out back in the barn, toilets and doors and things, like
the insides of a lot of houses all taken apart. Kevin

thought there was a swing on the porch, and Kerry said there was a redbird on the mailbox, but Kevin said Kerry was just making that up so he'd have something to remember.

"Good," Arnie said. "That's just what I was waiting for."

Fay didn't ask Arnie what he meant. But she did wonder where they were going that took so long to get there.

She tried to relax.

"Close your eyes if you want to," Arnie said. "We're still about fifteen minutes away."

Fay knew if she closed her eyes, she'd see Lizzie again, and she didn't want to keep seeing Lizzie in the future. She wanted to see Lizzie in their house, now, asleep, safe for the night, with Paul gone from their lives.

She wanted to ask Arnie where Lizzie was, but she already knew what the answer would be. With Jake, he'd say. On their way to the Masters' house.

"This wind is really whipping up," Arnie said. "Can you feel it?"

She looked out the window and saw the edge of a huge gray thunderhead rolling in from the west. The air had been heavy all day. A good storm might break this heat.

She smiled. Lizzie would like a storm too. Lizzie had liked storms even as a little girl. Awakened by a

deafening thunderclap in the night, Fay would rush
around the apartment closing windows, only to find
Lizzie standing at her bedroom window, clutching the
sill with her tiny hands, squealing happily and hopping
up and down as the rain pelted her face and the curtains
whipped her ears.

"Did they say it was going to rain?" Fay asked
Arnie, trying not to think about Lizzie.

"Not that I heard," he said. "But what do they
know?"

"Right," she said, and looked out the side window
again. "I read a thing in the newspaper last month,"
she said, "about a queen in Africa who really could tell
when it was going to rain."

"Yeah?" he asked.

I might as well tell it, she thought, it's better
than talking about Lizzie.

"Apparently she really could do it," she said.
"A reporter brought a doctor to the cave one day . . ."

"She lived in a cave?" he asked.

"She lived in the sacred cave, even, and this
doctor said she had something special about her eyes,
something that allowed her to see moisture in the air or
electricity before a storm, only she could see it a long
way off, days and days."

"O.K.," he said.

"And if you wanted to come see her, you had to

bring either whiskey or money."

"I love it," he said. "So what happened?"

"Well," Fay said, "the tradition in the tribe was
that at a certain point in her reign, when she was still
strong enough to do it, the Queen was supposed to retire
to the sacred cave and kill herself."

"Jesus," Arnie said.

"Right," Fay said, beginning to wonder why she
remembered this story today. "But this queen didn't
feel like killing herself, so she refused."

"Sounds right to me," he said.

"It didn't go over very well," Fay said. "What the
people in the tribe did was pile up all these rocks
across the the mouth of the cave, close her in, and go
away for a year."

"Nice folks," he said.

"Yes, well, the guy was writing the article
because the women of the tribe were gathered in front of
the cave again. Whichever one of them could roll the
rocks away and discover the dead queen, would become the
new queen."

"Which country was this in?" he asked.

"I don't know," she said. "I forget. I remember
the headline though. Tradition Requires New Queen."

"Yeah," he said. "So the old girl might as well
have killed herself," he said.

"I guess," she said.

"If you have to lose anyway, it's better to give

up," he said. "Don't you think?"

"Go into the cave and kill herself?" she asked.

"That's what I'd do," he said.

"That's crazy," she said.

"Not to me," he said. "I'd a whole lot rather do it myself than have them do it to me."

I don't know," she said. "I don't know."

"You'd do it to," he said. "You know you would."

"No," she said, "I don't think so. I think I'd convince them we had to have a new tradition."

"No such thing as a new tradition," he said. "If you can't be the Queen forever, then you can't be the Queen forever and that's all there is to it."

"Does that go for mothers too?" she asked, angry at herself for telling the story.

"I think it does, hon," he said.

Fay closed her eyes and wished desperately she'd closed them when he'd first told her to.

* * *

At headquarters, the Chief called the Mayor and congratulated him.

"I'm so relieved," the Mayor said. "So grateful. I don't know what I'd have done if. . ."

"That Gail seemed like a good little woman to me," the Chief said. "Just the kind of thing she'd do, save your boys."

"Yes," the Mayor said. "She insisted. I was afraid for her, but she just. . ."

"You ought to take her out to dinner," the Chief said. "Some place with dancing. Good oysters, you know."

"I'll find some way to thank her," the Mayor said, "but until her Beth is back, I don't think. . ."

"Harbor Lights is nice," the Chief said. "There's a table by the window with the best view you ever saw."

The Mayor was eager to get off the phone. "I'll remember that," he said.

"Look," the Chief said. "If you want to go, use my name." He paused a moment. "Hell," he said, "use my account. I'd like to do something for the two of you."

"Thanks, Chief," the Mayor said, then called out to his aides who had just arrived at the house.

"O.K., then, I'll let you go," the Chief said. "Tell Gail I said congratulations."

"Right."

"Tell her anytime she wants a job, all she has to do is call."

"I'll do that Chief. Good-bye."

The Chief didn't want to hang up. "Right, right," he said, hearing the click of the Mayor's phone.

He said good-bye to the dead air, then sat there a moment. He didn't want to go to the jail to see Edith Masters, but he didn't want to go home either. And if he kept sitting at his desk, people would just keep asking what he was doing there. So there wasn't any choice, really.

"Mrs. Masters?" he said, approaching her cell. "I'd like to speak with you a moment."

"Not without my lawyer," she said.

"It isn't about the case," he said, and motioned to the guard to unlock the door. "There's a little conference room just down the hall."

"I'd rather stay here," she said.

He sighed. "Mrs. Masters, I've been on my feet all day. I have to sit down."

"Come in, then," she said. "There's a seat right over there." She pointed to the toilet.

"Lock it," he said to the guard as he walked in.

She rubbed her palms together as if she were trying to warm them up. Or, he thought, as if she were getting ready to eat him.

"What is it you want to talk to me about?" she

asked.

But he didn't know, of course. "I grew up in the
church," he said, hoping that would make her more
comfortable.

"So did I," she said, leaning back against the
bars.

"I don't go to church now though," he said.

"No," she said. "You think you don't need it. You
think you can do it by yourself."

"Do what by myself?"

"Direct your own life," she said. "Comfort
yourself, forgive yourself. . ."

"And I can't?" he asked.

"For a while you can," she said. "But then
something happens and. . ."

He got up, walked to the bars, and banged on them.
"Let's have some coffee," he called.

"None for me, thank you," she said.

"You were drinking it this morning," he said. "I
saw you."

"Decaf," she said.

"So you like the taste anyway," he said, wondering
why he said that.

"Actually," she said, "I can't taste anything any
more. It's a medicine I take. It kills my taste buds.
I can't even tell hot or cold."

"Can you tell if it's a liquid?" he asked, reaching

through the bars as the guard handed him a mug.

"I can _see_ that it's a liquid," she said.

The Chief was beginning to wonder if this was better than going home. Maybe, he thought, if I stay here long enough, I'll actually want to go home.

"Now," he said, "you said I couldn't forgive myself. Forgive myself for what?"

"For your bad thoughts," she said.

"I don't have bad thoughts," he said. "I just don't know what I'm doing here."

"You're protecting society," she said.

He took a sip of coffee. "Can't be done," he said. "Society is just people. To protect society we'd have to give everybody a bodyguard."

"No," she said. "That wouldn't help. It's their thoughts that are the problem."

"Oh, yes," he remembered. "Bad thoughts."

"All of us," she paused, "have bad thoughts. Without the love of God, we are all criminals."

"I don't have bad thoughts," he said. "What bad thoughts do I have?"

She clasped her hands together, then pointed her two index fingers at him and smiled. "You wish your wife would die," she said.

He turned around quickly to face the bars. That was exactly what he wished.

"That's a fairly common one," she said. "Lots of people wish that."

"I've thought about a divorce," he said, "but I'm just too old to go through it all, then make a fool of myself over some young.."

"But if your wife were to die," she said, "if the Lord were to take her. . ."

"Yes," he said. "That would be different. Then I'd have to do something, you know, to go on living."

She nodded. "And the children would understand, of course."

"Everybody would understand," he said.

"And instead of laughing at you over this young woman, they'd be happy you'd found somebody."

The Chief looked into his cup. This might be the most peculiar conversation he'd ever had.

"So, Edith," he asked, "what do I do? May I call you Edith?

"Ask the Lord how you're supposed to carry this load," she said. "He never gives us a burden but what he gives us the strength to carry it."

"Has he helped you that way?" the Chief asked.

"Not just me," she said. "Anybody who asks."

"So why don't we all feel better?" he asked. "Why isn't the world a happier place."

She thought for a moment. "What is your name?" she asked finally.

"Chester," he said.

"Chester, the world is a happier place than you

think."

"Sitting in jail you can say that?"

"Only my body is here."

"And the rest of you is. . ." He stopped. "What _is_ the rest of you, Edith?"

"My spirit."

"Where is your spirit, Edith?"

"With my husband, of course."

"Has he been down to see you?"

"Oh no."

"Why not?" the Chief asked.

Edith rubbed her palms again. "It's hard for him to get around," she said. "I know he misses me."

He finished his coffee and set the mug on the floor. "I think you're just a swell woman, Edith." He smiled. "What the hell are you doing in jail?"

"You put me here," she said.

"All you have to do is give us some reason for letting you out and you can go."

She folded her hands in her lap. "I can wait," she said.

"Edith," he said, "nobody likes to spend the night in the jail."

"It's comfortable enough," she said.

"Do you have a picture of your husband?" he asked.

"You have my purse, Chester."

"Oh that's right," he said.

"What did you really want, coming to see me?" she

asked. "Did you want to talk about my husband?"

"No," he said. "I just didn't want to go home."

"There seem to be plenty of empty beds here," she said pleasantly.

He leaned toward her. "You know what, Edith," he said confidentially, "I think you got yourself arrested on purpose."

"Why would I do that?" she asked.

"Because you didn't want to go home," he said.

"Why wouldn't I want to go home?" she asked.

"I don't know," he said. "But you must want to be here, or else you'd have called your lawyer. And I know you didn't call your lawyer because if you did, you'd be out of here."

"Is that so?" she asked.

"Yes it is," he said. "We don't have anything on you."

"No?" she asked.

"But I know you made a phone call, Edith. Who did you call?"

"Isn't the line bugged?"

"No," he said. "Can't do it. Freedom of speech, or something. Freedom of something."

"They didn't tell me I could call my lawyer," she said.

"I see," he said.

"I called the Weather."

"Right," he said. "Who's the Weather?"

She sighed. "The Weather number, you know, they tell you what the weather's going to be tomorrow."

He banged on the bars for the guard. "And what did they say?"

"Hot," she said. "Hot and humid."

"Like today," he said.

"Like today exactly," she said, as the guard appeared. "I appreciate you coming."

"My pleasure," he said.

"Do you feel any better?" she asked.

The guard unlocked the door. "I do," he said. "I actually do."

"Good," she said. "I'll see you tomorrow."

The Chief walked straight down the hall, up the stairs, through the lobby and out the front door before he allowed himself to think about anything. Then, standing on the inlaid marble seal of the city, he knew exactly what to do. There was a bar right across the street with a big screen TV. If he hurried, he could catch the beginning of the local news. He had to be on it, right? With all those reporters, and all the film they'd shot today at the shopping center, he had to be there somewhere.

It was a great idea. He didn't have to think about his life, he could just go watch it on TV.

7:00 P.M.

* * *

"I thought we were going to Edith's house," Fay
said, as Arnie turned off the main highway and onto a
narrow country road.

"He wouldn't go home," Arnie said. "He knows we're
looking for him."

"Mitch?" Fay asked.

"Cowboy Bob," Arnie said. "We just passed the
quarry," Arnie said, "so the farmhouse has to be..."

He slammed on the brakes, pulled a hard left turn
and bumped off the road onto a gravel path.

"Right here," he said. "See the redbird on the
mailbox?"

"No I didn't," Fay said.

"Right back there," he said, as his front left tire
sunk in a crater in the road.

She turned back to look as Arnie gunned the engine
and the car shot up out of the hole, slamming them back,
then forward as the rear tire chunked into the same
depression.

"Arnie," she pleaded, bracing herself against the
dashboard, "he's dangerous, this young guy. If he's out
here, you know he's. . ."

"He's trying to get rid of the rest of the kids,"

Arnie said. "Taking them to other hiding places."

"Does anybody know where you are?" she asked.

He grinned. "I'm with you," he said.

The Mayor's boys had not mentioned the low
overhanging trees, or the bullet-ridden No Trespassing
Sign, or the barbed wire fence that ran along Arnie's
side of the road.

She reached for the radio. "Call headquarters,
Arnie. Tell them what you're doing. Where we are."

He didn't move.

She picked up the handset. "If you don't, I will."

They rounded the last bend and the house came into
view. He stopped and looked at the radio in her hand.

"I'm just trying to speed things up a little," he
said, taking it from her.

"You don't have a warrant," she said.

"I'm counting on an invitation," he said. "There's
the barn."

She forced herself to look at the house. The roof
was a wreck and one gutter hung down across the front
door. There was a washing machine on the porch, and a
hay wagon full of trash half-buried in the front yard.

They heard the back door slam and a fierce-
looking Doberman tore around the side of the house.

"Roll up your window," he said to her as he
unlocked his door, then smacked it open into the dog's
chest.

"Arnie, no!" she cried, reaching for him, but she

was too late. The dog rebounded quickly from the blow

and charged into Arnie at full speed.

She watched in horror as he tore the dog's mouth

away from his shoulder. Arnie's yells and the dog's

barks rose together in a vicious crescendo. Fay tried

to understand what Arnie was saying to the dog, but it

sounded more like cheerleading than combat.

Then suddenly, Arnie bolted up from the ground,

cuffed the dog sharply on the head and the foaming beast

backed off. "There now," Arnie said, daring him to

move, "all you needed was a little exercise, huh, boy?"

Arnie knocked on the window, and the dog came around

to his side as if on command. "You stay here, Fay,"

Arnie said, winded, but flushed with victory, "I'm going

in."

She cracked the window. "Arnie, please, don't..."

The dog bit down on Arnie's hand, eager for more.

"I think he's in there," he said. "You just stay put."

She was frozen with fear for him.

He wiped his mouth on his shirt. "Look, Fay," he

said, "if I got by the dog, the man's a snap."

There was a bright red stain on the back of Arnie's

shirt and his right sleeve was ripped to the shoulder.

She tried to remember if Arnie had had a tetanus shot

lately.

Fay reached for the radio, lifted the handset out

of its cradle and pushed the button. "This is Fay

Morgan," she said. "Is anybody there?"

"Go ahead, Fay," the operator responded.

"I'm with Arnie Campbell." She stopped. "He's
gone into this farmhouse." She looked out the window.
"Can you send somebody out here?"

"What is your location please," the operator asked.

"It's that road where the quarry is," Fay said.

"What quarry, please."

"The one where they found the Mayor's boys."

Arnie disappeared around the side of the house.

"Which direction from the quarry?" the operator
asked.

"Further out," Fay said. "There's a mailbox at the
road with a redbird painted on it."

"How far out, please."

"I don't know," Fay said. "But the driveway turns
off to the left."

"Just a moment please," the operator said.

"No! Wait!" Fay said. "I just got you!"

Now the operator sounded like a recording. "Keep
the channel open please."

Fay let the handset fall into her lap and stared up
at the farmhouse.

"Mother?" Lizzie's voice came over the radio.

Fay grabbed it. "Lizzie! Where are you?"

"Where do you _think_ I am?" Lizzie said. "I'm
outside this dumb little house you sent us to. Locked
up in Jake's car!"

"At Edith Masters' house?" Fay asked, staring
into the handset, wondering how this happened.

"I guess," Lizzie said. "Where are you?"

"I'm nowhere, Lizzie," Fay said. "I'm staring at a
farmhouse waiting for Arnie to get blown up."

"What _is_ all this anyway?" Lizzie asked.

The operator interrupted them. "Mrs. Morgan,
officers are on the way. Stay with your vehicle,
please."

"O.K., O.K.," Fay answered.

"What's going on?" Lizzie's asked again.

"There were three people who kidnapped the kids,
Lizzie. One of them is in jail. One of them lives at
the house where you are, and one of them lives out
here."

"Terrific," Lizzie said, and Fay could hear her
lean back against the seat and sigh.

And then Fay heard the shot.

* * *

Fay jumped out of the car and ran halfway up to the
house before it occurred to her that that might not be
the best thing to do. The front window shattered and a
second shot stung the ground just to her left, causing
her to trip and fall against a rusted wheelbarrow.

Two more shots blasted the old pickup truck beside
the house, and as she watched, the back left tire began
to deflate.

When the next barrage of gunfire sent the front door
flying into the yard, she tucked her purse under her arm
and sprinted for better cover under the old hay wagon,
about five feet ahead.

Then Cowboy Bob, the young man who had been with
Edith Masters in the coffee shop, backed out of the hole
where the door used to be, shooting up the front of the
house with a sub-machine gun.

He stopped suddenly, listened for a moment, then
broke into a run toward Arnie's car, got in, revved the
engine and backed out of the driveway.

She waited as long as she could then started for
the house. Where was that dog, she wondered. After the
smoke cleared, wasn't a dog supposed to start barking?
Should she go around to the back? Peek in the windows?
She tried to remember what people did in the movies.
When the shooting was all over, could you just walk in
the front door?

"Arnie!" she screamed.

"In here!" he called back, somewhat muffled, from somewhere on the left side of the house.

She ran toward the sound of his voice, into what, owing to the presence of a squatty old refrigerator, would have to be called a kitchen.

"Jesus Christ," she gasped.

"I'm all right," he said.

But he was covered with debris, and pinned to the floor by a massive oak table and a dead dog.

"What happened in here?" she said.

"The dog got the worse of it," he said from the floor.

"I like him better this way," she said, studying the placement of the table.

"I don't think there's anybody else here," Arnie said, "but all the same, let's get me out of this, huh?"

She stooped down to peer at him. "Are you hit?"

"Winged," he said. "Can you lift the table?"

"The dog's the problem," she said, standing back up.

"Oh for God's sake, Fay. . ."

"O.K., O.K.," she said.

She held her breath, grabbed the dog's leg and slung the beast across the room where he thwacked up against the refrigerator, then slid to the floor.

Arnie winced at the sound. "I liked that old dog,"
he said.

She wedged her knee under the end of the table, got
hold of one corner and lifted it up to standing.

"That dog saved my life," Arnie said.

"And me?" Fay wheezed from the effort.

"Thanks," Arnie said, scooting up to sitting.

She saw his arm clearly now. "How bad is it?" she
asked.

"It's nothing," he lied. "Come here."

As she helped him up, Arnie looked over her head
and out the back window. Someone was in the barn.

Fay slipped out of his arms. "I talked to Lizzie,"
she said. "They're at the Masters' house."

"Is Masters there?" Arnie asked.

"She didn't say. Jake was still inside the house."

"Must not be, then." He tucked his gun into his
belt. "Somebody ought to bury that dog," he said.

"I called headquarters," she said. "They're sending
some cars."

"Good," Arnie said. "They can do it." He stepped
over the rest of the trash and started for the hallway.

Fay wanted to tell him how scared she'd been, how
scared she still was, how the sight of his blood on his
shirt bothered her in a way she couldn't quite explain.
But he was still on duty.

They made their way through the rest of the
Cowboy's heap of a house, through the living room,

furnished only with orange crates and beer bottles, and
into the bedroom, which was completely empty except for
a sleeping bag laid out against the far wall.

"Travels light, this guy," Arnie said. And then he
opened the closet. "Holy shit."

"What?" Fay asked, from across the room.

"Two flannel shirts and a pair of black jeans," he
said.

"So?" Fay asked.

"And four shotguns and a case of ammunition, two
deer rifles, a telescopic sight, a hatchet, a skinning
knife, a machete, a chain saw, a pair of binoculars..."

"I told you he was dangerous," Fay said.

Arnie stooped down to check. "And an empty box of
Milkbones," he said.

"Does this prove he's in on it?" Fay asked.

Arnie walked to the bedroom window and looked at
the barn. Something just moved past the open half-door
at the far end.

"I don't know," he said, walking into the bathroom.

She started to follow him.

"Stay away from the window, Fay," he said.
"There's somebody in the barn."

She froze.

"It's O.K.," he said, motioning for her to crawl
under the window. "I just wanted you to know. If he
were coming after us, he'd be here by now."

But Fay couldn't move.

He had never seen her so scared. "I think we're all right," he said, then smiled. "All we have to do is stay inside and wait for the police."

Fay didn't know what they should do, but just waiting didn't sound right, didn't sound like Arnie.

"We have to wait," he said, "because I'm out of bullets." He turned back to examine a small photograph taped to the mirror of the medicine cabinet.

"Right," she said, and forced herself to sneak under the window on her knees.

"So who do you think this is?" Arnie asked. "His girlfriend? His wife?"

Fay joined him at the mirror and stared at the standard wallet-sized high school yearbook photo. "It's Colleen," she said. "It's Edith's daughter, Colleen."

"It looks like Beth," he said. "Like Beth will look in ten years." He studied the photograph. "Same pale skin, same watery blue eyes. . ." He held it up to the light. "Is this a pink barrette in her hair?"

Fay walked out of the bathroom and leaned against the bedroom wall. She was shaking. Was that why Beth wasn't with the other children? Had Mitch seen Beth, seen the resemblance to Colleen and. . .

She couldn't finish the thought.

She walked on into the living room and stared at the orange crates. "Where did the Cowboy sit?" she asked. "How can you live without chairs?"

Arnie looked around the room. "Chairs," he said. Then it hit him like an electric shock. "Chairs!" he shouted, and ran for the front door. "Come on!"

"Arnie!" she screamed. "What are you doing?"

But he was gone. If she wanted to hear the answer, she'd have to follow him.

When she caught up, he was at the back corner of the house, watching that half-open barn door.

"You're right," he whispered. "You have to have chairs. I don't care how weird you are, you can't live without chairs. So he did something with all his chairs."

"Maybe he burned them," she said.

"Or maybe he tied somebody up in them." He leaned over to kiss her. "Like kids, Fay. That's who's in the barn!"

Fay wasn't so sure. "But Arnie, Mitch might be in there with them. I thought we were waiting for the police."

"You wait if you want to," he said, dropped her hand and bolted across the scrubby yard dodging the tin cans and broken tools that lay in his path as he ran.

Angry and afraid, Fay fell back against the house and waited for the shooting to begin again.

"Fay!" Arnie called to her from the barn.

"Oh thank God," she breathed, and ran toward the open door.

But she didn't get four steps forward before a tiny
terrified face peeked around the side of the barn door.
She stopped again. The child waved. She recognized him
instantly. He was the only black child in the group.

"You must be Mondo," she said, trying not to scare
him by running or screaming.

He grinned.

"Your Mama is sure going to be glad to see you,"
she said, kneeling down in front of him.

"I was tie to a chair," Mondo said, squeezing
her tight. "And then a man come."

"He's a policeman," Fay said, standing up. There
was blood on Mondo's shirt, but she decided it was
Arnie's.

Inside the barn, she saw the rows and stacks of
bathtubs and sinks that the Mayor's boys had seen.

"Here they come," Mondo said, pointing to another
doorway on the right wall of the main room. Fay turned
quickly and recognized two more of the missing children,
Tinker and Sandy Talbott, fair-haired five-year-old
twins. They still looked scared.

She pointed to their feet. "Somebody needs their
shoes tied," she said, still holding Mondo's hand.

"Mommy ties them," Tinker said, "but she isn't
here."

"How about if I do it now," she said, moving toward
them carefully, "and then when you get home, Mommy can
do it again."

The twins nodded, and met her half way, starting to tell the same story about being tied up.

"Arnie," she called, "are you all right?"

"Doing fine," he said. "Just keep them all together."

As Fay finished tying the fourth shoe, a truly stately six-year-old came up behind the twins.

"And who are you?" Fay grinned.

"John Merriweather," the boy reported. "I'm the oldest. Are we on TV?"

"You're all over the place," she said. "You're big stars."

"My mother is in Spain," he said. "Are we on TV in Spain?"

Fay stood up. "John, can you watch these little ones while I go help Arnie?"

But the twins clutched at her skirt and held on tight. "O.K.," she said, smoothing their hair. "I'll just stay right here then."

"There's more," John Merriweather informed her. "There's nine of us."

"Nine!" Fay said, and tried to remember if that was all the rest of the missing children.

"There used to be more, but the Cowboy took them away," John said.

"How did you get here?" Fay asked.

"We woke up here," John said.

"Was it the Cowboy who tied you up?"

They all nodded.

"Did you see anybody else?"

They all shook their heads.

"What's your name?" John asked her.

"I'm Fay," she said. "Let's go help Arnie." But none of them would move. Not even the cerebral John Merriweather wanted to go back into that room.

"Who's Arnie?" the twins asked.

John sighed. "He's the man who untied us. He killed the Cowboy and then he came to get us."

"No," Fay said, "he didn't kill the Cowboy, he just chased him. . " but she couldn't finish, because Noah and Seth Clark bounded through the door like little linebackers. "Two more!" she said, beginning to believe this now.

"Where is this?" Seth asked her, little hands on little hips, ready to go. But before she could answer, he ran to one of the bathrubs and jumped in. "Full steam ahead," he shouted, as Mandy Jones appeared in the doorway.

"Be careful," Fay called to him, reaching out to Mandy.

"I don't think you should let him play over there," John said. "There could be bombs."

"Enemy approaching!" Seth shouted, grabbing the side of the bathtub. "Fire torpedoes!"

"Oh, I don't think there would be any bombs," Fay

said to John.

"I saw a rat," Mandy said.

"A mouse," John said, not moving an inch.

Noah was sitting in a sink now, high above his
brother's bathtub. "Turret gunner ready," he shouted.

"If those people didn't want us to get out," John
said to Fay, "they should've buried us."

"Noah," Fay said, "please don't. . ."

John went on. "Buried us in little coffins with
little breathing holes so we didn't die right away."

And then Arnie walked through the doorway with a
child in each hand. "This is Todd Griffith," he said,
"and this is Bonnie Boyter."

They looked up at him, waiting.

"And I told them I would tell you," he smiled,
"that the reason they don't have the same last name is
because they don't have the same daddy."

Fay counted the children. "Nine," she said. "Nine
of you."

John Merriweather nodded. "I told you that while
ago," he said.

Then they all heard the sirens come screaming up
the drive.

"Don't run!" Fay shouted after Seth as he took off
for the door.

"Let him run," Arnie said. "The kid's been tied up
all morning."

And with that, all the children except John Merriweather flew across the barn floor, whooping and screeching as they decided that the last one to reach the police cars would be a rotten egg.

Arnie laughed and put his arm around John. "It was a rotten egg when _I_ was in school," he said to Fay. "You'd think there'd be some new rotten thing by now."

"They don't even know what a rotten egg looks like," John said, relieved to be with the adults where he belonged.

"John," Arnie said carefully, "was there a little blond girl tied up with you? A little girl that looked like this?" And Arnie pulled Colleen's photo, the one he'd found in the bathroom, out of his back pocket.

The boy took the picture and looked carefully at it. "No," he said.

"Was she with you in the truck?" Arnie asked. "At the fairgrounds? Before you had the lemonade and went to sleep?"

"I don't know," John said, handing the picture back to Arnie. "There were too many of us then."

Arnie put the photo back in his pocket. "O.K.," he said. "Thanks."

"Haven't you found her yet?" John asked.

"No," Arnie said, glancing at Fay. "We don't know where to look."

* * *

The police arrived at the farmhouse prepared for a
hostage action. And while they weren't exactly
disappointed to find the captives already free, the lack
of a real situation did leave a lot of them standing
around with nothing to do.

While the medics tended to Arnie's injuries, Fay
walked back to the barn. Since they couldn't disturb
the evidence, it was the only place to sit down.

She stepped around the bathtubs, counted the
mantels, found a box of doorknobs, and looked at herself
in maybe fifty mirrors stacked against the wall. It was
oddly disturbing to see so many useful things lying
around useless on the floor. But then, Fay was feeling
that way herself, like a sink that had been disconnected
from the pipes that filled it.

Arnie had known to come here, known this was where
the Cowboy would be. Arnie had known there was somebody
in the barn. Arnie had found these children, she
hadn't.

But nine wasn't enough and Fay knew it. Two boys
and Beth were still missing. Gail's little girl Beth.
Why couldn't Fay see where they had taken her?

But Fay knew the answer to that. She didn't see
where they took Beth because all she could think about
inside that truck was Lizzie.

She walked into the room where the children had
been tied up. Seeing the chairs, the ropes, the

blindfolds, she understood. The Cowboy had not planned
to take care of them, feed them, make sure they were
safe. No. His plan was to leave. His plan was to let
them die.

Fay sat down. Beth was in trouble. Those other
two boys were in trouble. The kidnappers were no longer
worried about keeping them alive. All they could think
of now was getting away.

She heard a baby crying.

Not in the barn. Where? She closed her eyes.
Where are you Beth? Beth in the yellow overalls. Beth
with the pink barrettes.

But the voice Fay heard was too old for Beth.
Katie. It was Lizzie's little girl Katie.

And Lizzie, deep in a sleep of exhaustion, was
trying to wake up, pushing herself out of the chair
beside the hospital bed. Katie is so hot, fiery hot and
wet all over.

Lizzie runs across the room, pushes the door open
and steps out into the bluish light in the corridor.
She staggers down the hall and collapses on the nurses'
station. "Please come," she says, "my little girl..."

The nurses respond quickly, leaving Lizzie slumped on
the counter, and rush silently down the hallway. Lizzie
can't move. Her eyes close, her knees give way, her
hands lose their grip on the counter and she faints to
the floor.

Orderlies rush by her on the way to the child's room. Why doesn't somebody pick her up?

Slowly she regains consciousness. A cool cloth on her forehead. She's lying in a bed now. "Katie," she whispers.

"She's all right," a voice says. A pleasant voice, a practiced calm. "You're the one who needs some. . ."

Lizzie reaches up weakly, slides the cloth back on her forehead and opens her eyes. A young doctor.

"Where is your husband?" the doctor asks.

Lizzie tries to sit up. "Colombia," she says.

The doctor continues. "His parents, then? A friend?"

Lizzie shakes her head.

"Don't you have somebody who can come help you? What about your mother?"

"No," Lizzie says. Her head falls back on the pillow. Asleep. The doctor checks her pulse, takes off her shoes, pulls a blanket up over her and walks out of the room.

Fay didn't hear Arnie come into the barn.

"There you are," he said, walking over to her. "What are you doing in here?"

But Fay couldn't answer.

"Fay?" he said. "We can go now if you want," he said.

But still, there was no response.

"The kids are all taken care of," he said.

She bent over double in the chair. "Arnie, Arnie," she whispered finally, reaching up for his hand. "Something's happening to me."

"Something's happening to me too," he said, straightening up. "I'm getting hungry. I want a real dinner, with like salad and drinks. How's that sound?"

"I don't understand," she said. "I keep seeing these. . . I don't know what they are. I don't know what I'm seeing. They're not the right thing. They're not what I want to see."

Arnie didn't know what to say to that, so he put his arm around her and helped her stand up. "How about seeing me home?" he asked.

She nodded. He was right, this wasn't the time. "Are the kids all right?" she managed.

"They're fine," he said. "The Chief is going to present them to their parents on TV. They asked me if you could be there, but I said you had a date."

"Good," she said. "Thank you."

"Now," he said, "I'm serious about this nice dinner. We'll go to my house and I'll change, and then we'll go to your house and you'll change. . ."

He waved to the group of officers smoking on the farmhouse steps, then pointed her toward the black and white he'd have to drive til the highway patrol found his car.

As he opened the door, she seemed so frail, so

small, he began, for the first time today, to worry that
she might not pull out of this, whatever it was.

He started the engine. "What are you seeing, Fay?"
he asked. "Lizzie again, or something about the kids."

She sighed, as if it were an old story, one she'd
heard before. "Katie was in the hospital," she said.
"The doctor asked Lizzie if her Mother could come help
her, and Lizzie said, 'No.'

Arnie wished he were better at this. But the best
he could tell, Fay was trying to determine what could
explain a series of events that hadn't happened yet.

"Maybe," he said, as he pulled the car up into the
yard and turned around toward the driveway, "maybe
Lizzie just lives too far away for you to come on such
short notice."

"Arnie," she turned to him in desperation. "I'm
seeing a world where I don't exist!"

"Fay," he said, "I promise you. Mitch Masters
isn't thinking about killing you. Not any more he
isn't." He looked over at her. "We're after him now
and he knows it." He hoped this was working. "All he's
thinking about is getting away with this, throwing us
off the trail. You're all right. You're safe."

But he wasn't sure she wasn't listening.

"O.K.?" he asked, raising his voice.

"O.K.," she said quietly.

"That's better," he said, hoping it was. "Now,
what kind of food would you like?"

"Tell me what else is going on," she said, "with
the police, I mean."

Arnie was encouraged. At least she remembered what
was at stake here. "Masters is still loose," he said.
"But Jake found a picture of him with the Cowboy at the
house. And two people who took packages for the mothers
recognized the Cowboy as the one who left them. And it
looks like Edith bought the stuff from the stationery
store, you know, the pens and paper they gave the
mothers."

He paused for breath. "And we found the lab where
they got the jars of fetuses and the dead frogs. Edith
worked there couple of months ago, some Kelly Girl,
temporary thing." He grinned. "And there's a whole
passle of fingerprints inside the truck."

"His or hers?" Fay asked.

"Hers," he said.

"I'd like to talk to Edith, I think," Fay said.

"Sure," he said, "but we better do it tonight," he
said. "Masters has to be thinking of leaving town. And
I have a hunch he has the last three kids with him."

"Tonight, then," she said.

Fay was sounding better, he thought, but he knew
she needed a break, so he lit a cigarette and turned on
the AM radio. Maybe if she heard what a hero she was,
she'd feel better. He needed her to feel better. He
needed her help here.

* * *

As they pulled out onto the highway and headed back
toward town, a single star was rising in the mauve
streaked sky. Yes, Fay thought, The Star. Think about
The Star, The Tarot card The Star. The quacks all said
it meant hope. Maybe it did.

Hope the other kids could be found, hope Edith
started to talk, hope Mitch made a mistake, hope the
highway patrol caught the Cowboy in Arnie's car, hope
Lizzie wouldn't leave, and yes, hope that the world
where Fay didn't exist would wait til she was ready to
go.

But since Fay didn't tell her clients the Star
meant hope, how could she say it to herself?

The picture on the card was a naked woman kneeling
by a stream emptying one jar onto the land, and the
other jar into the stream.

When the card came up in a reading, Fay would
counsel a period of quietness. She would tell the
client it was time to return the books he had borrowed.
She would remind him that all the gifts we receive must
ultimately be given away again, and anything we have
learned here, must be taught to someone else, lest the
lesson leave the earth with us.

But right this minute, as Fay thought about the
picture, she wondered if it didn't just mean that sooner
or later, everything would be empty.

Then she remembered Mrs. Peace.

"Are those our dreams?" the fourth-grade teacher
had asked her. "Is that an angel pouring our dreams
into our heads at night?"

Fay smiled, knowing that if she just kept quiet,
the teacher would keep talking.

"How can I know what my dreams mean if I don't
remember them?" Mrs. Peace asked.

Fay remained still.

"What are dreams, anyway?" the teacher asked. "Are
they the same as hopes?"

"No," Fay said. "Hopes are what your waking mind
can imagine. Like prayers. Like bridges you can cross
to a better place. And however wild these hopes may be,
they are still basically thinkable things."

"But dreams," Fay went on, "dreams are the
unthinkable, the unsayable. Dreams are. . . I don't
know, illustrations from the book your soul is writing
about you."

Mrs. Peace flinched at the word "soul."

"I'm sorry," Fay said, "but you do have a soul. If
you didn't, it wouldn't make you so uneasy to hear about
it."

Mrs. Peace tried to relax. "So my soul is only
active when I'm asleep?"

"No," Fay said. "During the day, our souls gather
their...impressions of us, how our lives feel. And

sometimes, we even sense these impressions ourselves.
Sometimes in the middle of a sentence," she laughed,
"I'll suddenly realize I'm saying it to the wrong
person."

"Yes," Mrs. Peace said. "That happens to me, too."

Fay took a deep breath. "Our spirits collect these
impressions, keep them together, like wisps of smoke in
a bag. Then, when we're asleep, our brains open up
these bags of smoke," Fay smiled, "and take a look."

Mrs. Peace was quiet now.

"So dreams," Fay said, "are our poor old brains
trying to say, sometimes in words, but mainly in
pictures, what the smoke is. Or was. And sometimes
dreams don't make any sense because the brain can't or
won't understand. But other times, they're so real that
you wake up screaming. Or smiling, or turning to the
person in bed with you and. . ."

Mrs. Peace stood up now, angry now. "What good is
gathering up this smoke if I can't understand it?"

Fay spoke as gently as she could. "Your dreams
can't tell you what to do," Fay said. "That's not their
purpose."

Mrs. Peace looked away. "Then what good are they?
What is the point of trying to remember them?"

Fay was weary now, and well aware that she was
talking to the wrong person.

"There is no point in trying to remember your
dreams," Fay said. "There is only the unspeakable joy

of eavesdropping on your spirit, catching tiny glimpses
of its independent life, resting for a moment in its
wisdom, puzzling, laughing sometimes, over what it's up
to, what it makes of you."

"Forty dollars?" Mrs. Peace asked, opening her
wallet.

"That's right," Fay said. "Cash if you have it."

After Mrs. Peace left, Fay considered taking The
Star out of the deck altogether. She couldn't do that,
of course, but she did vow never to discuss the card
like this again. People wanted control of their dreams
like they wanted control of their lives. And what they
didn't want was anybody knowing more about their life
than they did, even if it was their own spirit who knew.

Fay hadn't understood Mrs. Peace's anger that day.
But she understood it now. Fay wanted control of her
dreams today, wanted her spirit to think better of her,
wanted to know what she was so guilty of that her
daughter didn't want her around. Wanted her dreams to
turn out differently. Wanted different dreams.

Arnie had seen the star now too, and thought maybe
Fay was ready to talk again. "Did you ever meet Mitch
Masters?" he asked.

"No," she said. "I thought he was dead. Or they
were divorced, or something. Edith never talked about
him. Neither did Colleen."

"Could you tell anything about him, when you saw

him in the truck?"

"Just what he looked like," Fay said. "Why?"

"We checked on his Purple Heart," he said. "The
guy's a fucking hero, a real one. Decorated to death.
If we charge him with something, and we're wrong, it'll
look real bad."

"Am I sure it's him?" she asked. "Is that what you
want to know?"

"Yes," he said. "I don't want to get fired over
this." He laughed. "Take all the fun out of quitting."

"I'm sure," she said.

He didn't respond.

"It's the one thing I know for sure," she said.

"O.K., then," he said. "Here we go."

And he turned off the expressway and headed for
Fay's house.

8:00 P.M.

Seven people had called Gail to tell her the
children from the farmhouse were going to be given back
to their parents on TV. She had just turned on the
television when she heard the Mayor buzz downstairs.

She checked her hair in the mirror, then walked to
the intercom and buzzed him in without answering. She
wondered if he was wearing a suit, or rather, if her
peach blouse and silk balloon pants looked all right.

"They found some more kids," Gail said, as Peter
arrived at her door.

"Yes," he said, noticing the television. "Are you
sure you want to watch?"

"No," she said. "But I can't just. . ." She
turned and walked back to the sofa, sat down and clasped
her knees to her chest. "I'm not talking very well any
more," she said, patting the cushion next to her.

On the screen, the Chief of Police looked wrinkled
but proud. In the audience, the reporters and
photographers outnumbered the mothers and fathers three
to one. But it was easy to spot the mothers and
fathers. They were the ones who didn't seem to be doing
anything.

"It is my great pleasure," the Chief said, "to
announce to the city and to these worried parents, that
nine more missing children have been found."

Peter wanted to hold her hand. "You're real brave
to be . . ."

"Where were they?" she said.

"In a farmhouse near the quarry," he said. "Fay
and Arnie found them."

"And they didn't see anything of Beth?" she asked.
"A shoe or a sock or. . " She couldn't finish. "Come
on, come on," she said to the TV. "We want to see the
kids."

The Chief turned to the officer guarding the door
and nodded. "As I call the children's names," he said,
"would the parents please come forward to receive them."

The Mayor had told them not to make such an event
of this, but he didn't want to tell her how cruel he
thought it was.

The Chief looked at his piece of paper, then leaned
over the microphone. "Mandy Jones," he said proudly.

The cameras had some difficulty locating Mandy's
mother, and missed the actual moment when she heard the
name. When they did catch up with her, the announcer
said this was Linda Graves, Mandy's mother, but the man
leading her through the crowd was unidentified.

Gail stared hard at the screen as Mandy ran into
her mother's arms. "They should've had the parents up
front," she said. "It's mean to make them wade through
all those people."

"Mondo Washington," the Chief announced, and
Mondo's mother, Monica, squealed and ran forward. Her
mother, standing beside Monica, said 'Praise Jesus,' and

followed her daughter to the front of the room.

"We've found the kids all right," Peter said, "but now the Dads are missing."

"Todd Griffith and Bonnie Boyter," the Chief called out. And the Mayor was pleased at first, and then puzzled to see not just one, but two daddies escorting Betsy Griffith toward the front.

Gail stared at the reunited parents and children standing inside a circle of police officers. "Can't they just go home now?" she asked.

"Not til they're all together," he said.

"It's a show," she said. "It's all a damn show, isn't it." She stood up and walked to the window.

As Anne Clark walked toward her boys, the announcer informed the audience that Dr. Rowland Clark had been called to the hospital to perform emergency surgery, but the hospital had installed a television in the operating room so he wouldn't have to miss the occasion.

"I liked her," Gail said, pulling back the curtains and looking down at the street.

"I've met her before too," Peter said. "I think she's in Historic Homes or something." He wished the Chief would hurry up with the last two.

"And finally," the Chief said, "last but not least, Miss Tinker and Master Sandy Talbott."

An enormous cheer rose up from the crowd, and Gail turned around to look. Sissy and David Talbott, husband and wife, mother and father, walked up to their twins, knelt down, and embraced one child each.

The Mayor knew instantly why the Chief had saved them for last. There on the floor, in a circle of light, was the All-American family that all of America wanted desperately to believe still existed.

The tears poured quietly down Gail's face.

The Mayor stood up, walked over to her. "She's all right," he said, pulling her into his arms, his shoulder absorbing her sobs. "I know Beth is safe. All the rest of them have been all right, haven't they?"

Gail was shaking badly.

He stroked her hair. "Every single one," he said.

"But why wasn't she with the others?" Gail sobbed. "What have they done with her?"

"They just hid her somewhere else." Peter tried to sound convinced.

Gail pulled away from him and walked across the room for a Kleenex. "I want to believe that, Peter, I really do." She blew her nose.

He came up behind her, put his hands on her shoulders and spoke as quietly as he could and still be heard over the commercial on the television.

"You have to believe it," he said. "You have to."

She reached for another Kleenex.

He knew he had to keep talking. "We're real good at thinking up all the terrible things that could happen," he said.

"They do happen," she said.

"Yes," he said, "They do. But the truth is,
terrible things don't happen very often." He paused.
"Think how long you've been driving a car, right? And
in all that time, have you ever had a real front-page
accident?"

She shook her head.

"I didn't think so. Or sick. Sure people get
sick, but we only need one hospital bed for every ten
thousand people or something, so not _that_ many people
get sick."

"Everybody dies," Gail said, staring at the corner
and hoping he had an answer.

"Not every day," he said. "Not every day."

Gail turned around quickly and clung to him.

"Beth is just fine," he said. "She's hungry and
tired and scared, but she's just fine. Everybody in the
city is looking as hard as they can. . ."

"I'm not!" she cried. "I'm not doing anything. My
baby is gone and I'm watching television! Tell me what
_I_ can do. Can I walk the streets? Can I knock on
doors? I'll do anything!"

"You can believe she's all right," he said. "And
you can hold yourself together for just a little
longer. Can you do that?"

"Can you stay with me?" she asked.

"I'll stay with you as long as you like," he said.
"And if you're hungry. . ."

"Peter, we can't go have <u>dinner!</u>" she·said.

"We'll have it delivered if you want," he said,
"but you have to eat. I've told the Police Chief that
you're with me, so he knows how to find you. And
believe me," he smiled, "they find me real fast."

"What if they call me to come get Marvin?" she
asked.

"I checked on Marvin, too," he said. "He can't go
beore the judge til ten o'clock tomorrow morning."

"Did you talk to him?"

"No," Peter said. "They said he was asleep." He
shook his head. "Hard to believe, I know, jails are
usually pretty noisy at eight o'clock, but. . ."

"No," Gail said soberly. "Marvin is a good
sleeper."

He was pleased to see her standing a little
straighter. "So let's have some supper," he said.

"O.K.," she said.

"Out or in. Up to you."

"Out," she said. "I sent Mother home." She
paused. "And now I don't want to be here either." She
wiped her eyes. "Are these pants too silly?" she asked,
her voice still shaky.

He thought she had more guts than anybody he ever
saw. "They're not silly at all," he said. "They look
good."

As he walked over to turn off the television, he

hoped Gail hadn't heard the announcer say what was
coming on next.

"Ladies and Gentlemen," the announced said, "Mrs.
Vi Ewing."

Peter turned off the TV.

"Don't you want to hear what she says?" Gail asked.

"No," he said, "I don't."

Gail turned the television back on.

"All right," he said. "We'll watch her. But let's
not sit back down."

Gail smiled for the first time since he had arrived
and they stood in front of the television and listened.

Vi was wearing a white suit with a lavender flower
at the neck of her blouse.

"I have come here tonight," she said, "to plead for
the return of the three children who are still missing.
Their names are Beth Wilkins, Joshua Beckstein and
Richard Isaac."

"She ought to show their pictures," Gail said.

Vi looked directly into the camera and addressed
herself to the kidnappers. "I know what you were doing,"
she said. "You were trying to warn us."

"Oh boy," Peter said. "Here she goes."

Vi seemed quite composed. "You were trying to warn
us that thousands of American children are being taken
from us every day, legally murdered by abortionists in
every state of the union."

"Show us Beth's picture," Gail said.

"I see now," Vi said, "that you are right! And I will lead your fight all the way to Washington."

Peter shook his head.

Vi raised her right hand. "We will replace the addled graybeards on the Supreme Court with men of spirit, spiritual leaders, leading citizens who live by Our Heavenly Father's holy commandment, Thou Shalt Not Kill."

She turned now to face the other camera. "In return for the lives of these three children, I pledge my self, my energy, my money, my very life itself, to the elimination of legal abortion in this country."

Vi folded her hands on the desk in front of her. "Abortion is a sin against God, a sin against the future of this country, and a sin against ourselves. Only when we reclaim our proud religious heritage can we believe in ourselves again. Only when we stop this massacre of innocents, can we stand and say One Nation Under God. Only then can we return to the prosperous and blessed America of our childhoods."

Vi put her hand down on a Bible. "I, Vi Ewing, give you my solemn oath. The Age of Abortion is over."

Peter and Gail stood frozen in place as Vi's face was replaced by the station's logo, and the announcer said that the preceeding message had been paid for by People Against Murder.

Then Beth's picture flashed on the screen, and Gail

dropped to her knees.

Peter knelt with her and held her tight as the
announcer said Beth was five years old, had dark blond
straight hair which, when she was last seen, was held
back with a pink barrette.

Then after Beth came a picture of Joshua Beckstein
who wore thick brown glasses and cowboy boots, and
finally, Richard Isaac who had braces on his teeth and
Superman on his T-shirt.

As the hotline phone number flashed on the screen,
Gail stood up. "Let's go," she said.

Her fear sent chills through him. "Right now," he
said, "right now."

She noticed the drops of moisture on his forehead,
and wiped them away with her hand.

He looked away. "I feel as bad as I have ever felt
in my life," he said. "Absolutely powerless."

She took his hand and they walked to the door.
Suddenly she looked up at him. "I haven't had a date in
a long time," she forced a smile. "Is this how they go
now?"

He had to laugh. "It's just this first part that's
hard," he said. "After this, all we have to do is eat."

"Are you hungry?" she asked.

He laughed again. "No," he said. "You?"

"No," she smiled, heading down the stairs. "I
think we're in for a rough time, you and me."

* * *

As Arnie stopped for the light, a block from
Fay's house, they both saw the glossy old Rolls-Royce
parked directly in front of Fay's building.

"It's Paul!" Fay shrieked. "Run the light!" And
she beat on the dashboard as if she were honking the horn.

"Lizzie's getting out of the car," Arnie said.
"What's the problem?"

"Go, Arnie," Fay screamed.

But a wrecker was coming through the intersection
in front of them, and by the time it passed, the Rolls
was pulling away from the curb.

"Arnie!" Fay shouted, as though he couldn't hear
her. "You have to catch him! You have to tell him he
can't take her!"

"He didn't take her," he said. "Lizzie's standing
right there on the sidewalk."

The light turned green, and Arnie proceeded through
the intersection even more slowly than normal.

Fay was furious. "You're letting him get away!"

Arnie answered firmly. "I can't go after him, Fay.
All the guy did was leave me a parking space."

"Do you want Lizzie to go off with him?" she
demanded.

"I want you to settle down before you talk to her."

Lizzie had seen them now, and was walking up the

sidewalk to meet them.

"Here she comes," Arnie pointed. "Now straighten
up."

She bristled at his tone.

"If you looked at me the way you're looking at
her," he said, "I'd run away from you too."

Lizzie waved now, then laughed while Arnie
intentionally parked badly, then pulled the car up to
try it again.

Fay was still fuming.

"I'm buying you some time here," Arnie said to her.
"Are you using it?"

Lizzie could see the blood on Arnie's shirt and
pointed to it, asking her mother, in gestures, what
happened.

Fay made a gun shape with her hand, at which point,
Lizzie's hands flew to her mouth in fear.

"See?" Arnie said. "She's worried about you."

"She's worried about you," Fay said.

He stopped the car abruptly. "She's worried about
us," he said. "Look at me."

Fay turned to him in a rage.

"Did you see Jake leaning up against the building?"
he asked.

She started to turn around.

He pulled her head back to face him. "No, you
didn't. Well he's been there all the time. But if
Lizzie wanted to escape, she could have, easily enough.

She could've driven right off with Paul. But she
didn't. Did she."

"You're treating me like a child," she said.

"Yes," he said.

She dropped her head, then shook it, finally
getting the message. "You're right," she said. "You're
absolutely right. I'm sorry."

"It's O.K.," he said, settled the car perfectly
into the space and unlocked her door.

"Mother!" Lizzie squealed, as Fay got out. "You
found nine more!"

"Yes," Fay said. "But not Beth. We still didn't
find Beth."

"And what happened to Arnie?" Lizzie could see the
bandaged arm clearly now.

"Somebody shot him," Fay answered and waved to
Jake.

Lizzie met Arnie as he came around the car. "Are
you all right?" she asked, wanting to touch the wound.

"It's O.K.," he said, amused by her concern.
"Happens all the time."

"It does not," she said.

"No?" he asked, and kissed the top of her head.

"What's the matter with mother?" Lizzie asked.

"She saved my life," he said. "It's hard work."

Now Jake came up to join them. "You folks have a
nice afternoon?"

Lizzie put her arm around her Mother. "Did you really save Arnie's life?"

"No, no," Fay said. "Somebody would have found him sooner or later."

"But what if they didn't?"

"Well," Fay said, getting out her keys, "if they didn't, then I saved his life. How was dance class?"

And as Lizzie told her it was too crowded today, but the new teacher was terrific, Fay fished her keys out of her purse, opened the door and they walked in.

Arnie turned back to Jake. "What's the story on the Cowboy?"

"He ditched your car real fast," Jake said, lighting a cigarette.

"He's the one we won't find," Arnie said, as they followed the women into the apartment. "This guy could live under a rock the rest of his life. A real goon." Arnie's arm was beginning to throb.

Fay put her purse on the table and turned back to Arnie. "Do I have time for a shower?" she asked.

"A quick one," he answered. "And see if you've got an old shirt of mine anywhere around here. Save us a whole lot of time if we don't have to go to my house."

"Have you had dinner?" Lizzie asked.

"No," Arnie said, "and we're starved. Want to come with us?"

"Sure," she said, not knowing whether to follow her mother into the bedroom or stay out here with the boys.

Fay squeezed Lizzie's hand. "Stay out here," she said. "We'll talk later."

Lizzie smiled. "Thanks, Mom."

"You're welcome, Lizzie," Fay said and left the room.

"So nobody saw Masters at the Fairgrounds?" Arnie asked.

"Not yet," Jake said. "But I thought you'd want to see this," and he handed Arnie a promotional flier he found on Masters' desk, and a receipt from a trophy shop.

Fay walked back in the room wearing her bathrobe and holding up a shapeless old Shetland sweater. "Is this yours?" she asked Arnie.

Lizzie jumped up in protest. "It's _mine_!" she said. "Arnie gave that to _me_, Mother!"

"Do you mind, Lizzie?" Arnie asked, stuffing the flier in his pocket and taking the sweater from Fay. "I'll give it back, I promise."

"Give me ten minutes," Fay said to Arnie.

"Great hon," he said, then turned to Jake. "Help me put this sweater on, huh? My arm's getting a little lazy from this hole in it."

"We've got an APB on his van," Jake said, "and every toll booth leading out of the state's got a picture of him on the wall."

"He wouldn't drive his own van," Arnie said, as he

undid the buttons and slipped his shirt down over the
bandage on his left arm.

Lizzie hadn't seen Arnie without his shirt for a
long time. She stared shamelessly, admiring the muscled
chest with its various scrapes and scars and scattered
gray hairs.

"Let's take the bad arm first," Jake said,
gathering up the sweater and slipping it over Arnie's
head.

Arnie gave a slight gasp as the it passed over the
bandage. "Does anybody else know about that flier?" he
asked Jake.

"The guys at the Fairgrounds have to know," he
said. "It's on the marquee."

"Yeah," Arnie said, pulling the flier out of his
pocket. "But Masters Invitational Handicapped
Basketball. . ."

"Yeah," Jake said. "Could just mean skill level.
Doesn't have to mean the guy it's named for."

Arnie lowered his voice. "But this is his
signature on the trophy receipt?"

"I'm no expert," Jake said. "But it sure looks
like the rest of his signatures to me."

"Good work," Arnie said. "So how's he getting
around til it's time to present this trophy?"

"You don't think he'll really show up there, do
you?" Jake asked.

"He's a hero," Arnie said. "And the one thing

heroes always do is show up. But how's he getting
around in the meantime, and where did he stash Beth?"

"He wouldn't have her with him, would he?"

"Depends on why he took her," Arnie said.

"Well," Jake said. "He can't drive anything other
than a handicapped vehicle, so. . he borrowed one?"

"Something with a sign on it," Arnie said.

"A hospital, maybe, Disabled Vets," Jake said.

"Jesus Christ!" Arnie said. "We've got to stop
every van on the road," Arnie said, and flew out the
door to his car.

Fay stepped to the door of the living room.
"Lizzie?" she called.

Lizzie stood up, putting her magazine down on the
table. "Arnie and Jake went outside," she said. "They
didn't feel right, talking with me listening. Want me to
go get them?"

"No," Fay said quietly. "I need you to help me."
She motioned for Lizzie follow her.

"Sure," Lizzie said, happy to have something to do.

Fay picked a light jacket from her closet.

"You look better," Lizzie said.

"Thanks," Fay said, putting on the jacket. "I feel
better."

Lizzie walked over to Fay's dresser and opened one
of the drawers. "You need a scarf or something," she
said, selecting a green one with coral stripes. "I mean

if you're having a big deal dinner, the least you can do is deck out a little."

"I don't want to have dinner with Arnie," Fay said, tying the scarf around her neck. "I want to go down to the jail and talk to Edith Masters before she goes to sleep."

"Edith Masters at the dentist?"

Fay was startled. "Do you remember her?"

"Sure I do. She was mean," Lizzie said, sitting on the bed. "What do you want me to do? Have supper with Arnie?"

"I want you to come with me to see Edith. I think if you're there. . ."

"She won't remember me, Mother."

"Her daughter died, Lizzie, having an abortion."

"I'm sorry," Lizzie said. "Did I ever meet her?"

"No," Fay said, "it's just that Colleen's death is connected to this kidnapping thing somehow. Edith is in on it, that much we know."

"Sure," Lizzie said.

But Fay wanted her to understand. "I guess I thought if I took you. . ."

Lizzie stood up. "Sure, Mom."

Fay didn't believe it was this easy. "What?"

"Do I look all right?" Lizzie tucked in her shirt.

Fay smiled. "You look fine."

Lizzie grinned. "So how do we ditch the boys?"

"We'll just tell them," Fay said, and turned out

the bedroom light behind her.

"Fay!" Arnie called, coming in the front door.
"It's time to go."

"I'm not hungry, Arnie. I want to. . ."

"Of course you're hungry," he said. "What are you
talking about?"

"O.K., I'm hungry, but I want to go eat with Edith.
They have food at the jail, don't they?"

"I'll take you to the jail after dinner. I thought
we decided this already."

She looked at Jake, whose smile told her all she
needed to know. "Arnie," she said, "I know there's
something you want to do without me, so why don't you
just go do it?"

"Because I don't want you running around loose,
that's why," Arnie said.

She shook her head. "Lizzie will come with me.
As soon as we're finished, we'll come back here and wait
for you. Now how do I get in the jail?"

"Front door," he said. "I'll call ahead to the
desk." He paused. "Are you sure about this?"

Lizzie thought this was pretty funny. These two
were dying to get away from each other.

"I'm sure," Fay said, as Arnie stepped onto the
sidewalk.

Arnie gave her a light kiss, told her to be careful
and practically ran to his car.

Fay waited until they drove away, then, as Lizzie
waited for her on the sidewalk, Fay went back in the
living room and picked up her deck of Tarot cards. She
remembered the spread she had dealt for Colleen that
day. Maybe she could show it to Edith, prove she was
innocent. Or maybe Edith would convince her she was
indeed guilty and Fay could simply destroy the cards and
quit.

* * *

"Why didn't you ever marry Arnie?" Lizzie asked, as they walked down the dark street to the parking lot where Fay kept her old Buick.

"Because I didn't have to," Fay said. "It never came up."

"Are you kidding?" Lizzie asked. "In all this time?"

"Believe it or not," Fay said.

"Not," Lizzie said, then turned to her mother and grinned. "Do I get married?"

Quickly, Fay unzipped her purse and started what she hoped was a convincing search for her keys. "I don't know," she managed. "What do you think?"

"I think you <u>know</u>," Lizzie teased.

"Well," Fay said, as casually as she could, "you probably do get married. Most people get married some time or other."

But Lizzie was serious. "Why don't you want to tell me?" she asked.

"Because I don't know," Fay lied.

But Lizzie knew she was lying. "What else haven't you told me, Mother?"

"What do you mean, hon?" Fay asked, unlocking her door and flipping the switch to unlock Lizzie's side of the car.

"I mean," Lizzie said as she got in, "what else do you know. . . that I need to know. . . that you haven't told me?"

Fay started the engine. "That you <u>need</u> to know? Like what?"

"Mother," Lizzie said, exasperated with Fay's evasion, "I can't tell you what it is I don't know," she buckled her seat belt, "because I don't know it."

"Like what it is to be a mother?" Fay asked, driving out of the lot. "Like how you think they'll feel about you? Like what you'll get back for all that work?"

"Is it work?"

"It wears you out like work," Fay said. "And it takes all your time like work. So you can't help but feel you ought to get paid for it like work, or get something to show for it anyway."

"And you don't?"

"No, you don't. Not like you think anyway."

"I haven't thought about it," Lizzie said.

But Fay knew better. "You feel a little foolish doing all that work," she said, "so you say to yourself, 'Well, look, I'm doing all this because they're mine.' My children. My husband. Whatever. And that keeps you working. But after a while, you begin to believe it."

"Is that so bad?"

"Well," Fay said. "Just about the time you believe they're yours, they leave you." Fay paused. "And you feel betrayed, you feel lied to. Like they made you a promise and they didn't keep it."

Lizzie was silent.

"But the truth is, they never made you any such promise. You only dreamed up this promise business so you wouldn't feel foolish. But, in the end, you feel foolish anyway, so it didn't work. It only. . . got the job done."

Lizzie had understood. "Are you sorry you did all that for me?" she asked quietly.

"No," Fay said, staring straight ahead. "No."

"But if I stayed with you forever," Lizzie questioned, "wouldn't you feel like I was a little weird, like I never grew up?"

Fay couldn't look at her. "No," she said, "I wouldn't. I'd think. . . I'd just think you loved me, that's all."

"But I do love you," Lizzie protested.

"All right," Fay confessed. "I'd think you loved me best."

Lizzie turned away and stared out the window, twisting a lock of hair between her fingers.

"Are you sorry you asked?" Fay asked after a while.

"Oh no," Lizzie answered softly.

Fay laughed. "Are you sorry I answered you?"

"No, Mother," Lizzie said, trying to reassure her.

"Then what? Are you sorry it's the truth?"

"No," Lizzie said, "I'm not sorry about anything. I don't think it _is_ the truth." She paused. "I don't believe you."

Fay thought about that for a minute. "No," she said finally, "I wouldn't have believed it either."

And in the silence that settled around them, Fay understood that Lizzie was the one irreplaceable love of her life. That it was a love affair, only there wouldn't be, couldn't be other lovers to comfort her when Lizzie left. Lizzie loved her as a daughter loves a mother. But, Fay realized, that was never going to be enough.

Lizzie picked up the deck of Tarot cards lying on the seat between them. "Edith isn't a client of yours, is she?"

"No," Fay said. "But her daughter came to see me when she was pregnant."

"And you told her to have an abortion?"

Fay shook her head. "She wanted to know if the baby was going to be Beethoven."

Lizzie laughed. "Because she'd have it if it were Beethoven?"

"Something like that," Fay said. "I told her it probably wasn't Beethoven. Or that she wasn't old enough to raise it to be Beethoven." Fay felt uneasy, suddenly. "She was just a kid, Lizzie. Younger than you."

"So you told her to have the abortion."

"No. I didn't say that."

"You might as well have, Mother."

Fay hesitated. "Yes, I guess so. I'm sure that's
what Edith thinks anyway."

Lizzie fiddled with the old blue scarf wrapped
around the cards. "You did the right thing, Mom," she
said. "Can I look at these?"

"Lizzie," Fay said, thinking the girl didn't
understand. "Colleen died."

"I know," Lizzie said, thinking her mother didn't
remember telling her. "But you couldn't help that,
could you? Can I look at your cards?"

Fay was having trouble keeping up. "Sure," she
said. But she had to know more. "Lizzie, is this
really all that simple for you?"

"Huh?"

Fay spoke slowly. "Is abortion all that simple for
you?"

"Yeah," Lizzie said brightly, flipping through the
deck. "It's like anything else. Either you get
pregnant on purpose, or it's an accident. If it's on
purpose, you break out the champagne. If it's an
accident, you try to fix it."

Fay was quiet a moment. "Is that what your friends
think too? Is it only us old people who have trouble
with this?"

"I guess so," Lizzie said. "You make everything a
lot harder than it has to be."

"You don't think life is sacred?" Fay was testing.

"No, I don't." Lizzie said. "I mean, it's nice,
but it's not sacred. What is this card?" She held it
up.

But Fay didn't want to talk about cards. "Lizzie,
she asked, "what _is_ sacred to you?"

Lizzie didn't have to think very long. "Time," she
said.

Fay turned down the street where the church was,
just to see if the Tarot card was still standing in the
front yard.

"Is this the way to the jail?" Lizzie asked,
convinced that her mother was lost.

"I just wanted to see this church again," Fay said,
slowing down in front of it. "We think this is
where..."

"I know this church," Lizzie said, rolling down her
window. "This is where that women's health thing is."

Fay stopped the car. "What women's health thing?"

"I've never been to it," Lizzie said, getting her
hairbrush out of her purse, "but I've heard people talk
about it. I thought it was closed though." She ran the
brush through her hair. "Yeah, I remember, they had
some trouble or something, some weirdo kept putting acid
in their water, stealing things, you know."

"What did they do at this place? Was it a clinic?
Did they do abortions here?"

"Mom," Lizzie groaned, "it's just an information
thing, feel good about your body, don't be ashamed of

it, you know, do pelvics on each other, look at your vagina in a mirror, that kind of thing. It's no big deal."

"Well," Fay said, pulling out onto the street again, "you may not think it's a big deal, but a lot of people would."

"They're just scared of it," Lizzie said.

"They think it's bad," Fay said. "Wrong."

"O.K.," Lizzie said. "It makes them sick, women touching themselves, women knowing that stuff. But that's their problem."

Fay was astounded at Lizzie's ease with all of this. "Lizzie," she said, "if these people are in the Congress making the laws you have to live by, it's not just their problem. They will make it your problem."

"What are they going to do?" Lizzie asked. "Tell me I can't have an abortion if I want one?"

"Maybe," Fay said.

"If I want an abortion," Lizzie said, trying to end this conversation, "if I want to have an abortion, I'm going to have an abortion whether it's against the law or not."

Fay was dumbfounded. "And that's all there is to it?"

"Yes." Lizzie turned on the radio. "That's all there is to it."

9:00 P.M.

* * *

The way Arnie had it figured, Mitch Masters really thought he was going to get away with this. Edith would get nailed for the kidnapping, and the Cowboy, if anybody ever found him, would go to jail as an accomplice. What Mitch would do then was walk off with Beth and start over somewhere, take his new little girl and disappear.

As he and Jake approached the main entrance to to the Fairgrounds, Arnie waved to the guard, drove through the Pass Gate, then circled the horse barns and parked behind the West Wing, where a huge HANDICAPPED OLYMPICS sign hung over the ramp leading to the back door.

"Once we're inside," Arnie said, "you don't know me." He looked out across the acres of vans and handicapped vehicles. Beth could be in any one of them. But they couldn't search them all. Their only hope was getting Masters to lead them to the girl.

"Masters could be monitoring the band," Arnie said. "So don't report in, huh?"

"Got it," Jake said.

As they approached the entrance to the exhibition wing, two clowns passed them headed for the portable toilet, sharing a joint.

"What's security do out here anyway?" Jake asked, inhaling the second-hand marijuana cloud.

"They deal the stuff," Arnie said. "They
confiscate it from the farmers, and sell it on the
midway."

Arnie was unprepared for the size of the crowd
inside. He waited while a teacher passed in front of
him leading a covey of children on crutches toward the
candy stand, then made his way toward the bleachers that
surrounded the basketball court.

He stepped aside to make room for the orderlies
transporting an overwrought paraplegic out of the arena
for some air, then caught sight of the scoreboard.
Eight minutes left in the last quarter, fifty-two to
fifty in the finals of wheel-chair basketball.

He scanned the courtside officials, then the
players, then the benches and coaches, but Masters
wasn't there. Just his name on the banner hanging over
the court. MASTERS INVITATIONAL TOURNAMENT.

There was time to make a quick tour of the huge
hall. He stopped for a moment to watch six blind
children race a hundred yards holding onto ribbons
dividing the lanes, then passed a seated tug-of-war,
noted the pile of discarded crutches, braces and other
therapeutic devices beside the contestants, and then he
spotted the real heavyweights, the real brutes, grunting
and swearing at each other in the arm-wrestling
competition.

Yeah, these were the big guys, Viet-nam vets,
motorcycle accidents, fullbacks off the field for good.

Their wheelchairs were rolled up to sturdy tables which had a center line marked on in them in masking tape.

Arnie noticed a sign over a registration table. HANDICAPPED CHAMPIONS TAKE ON THE CROWD, it read, and he saw several normal guys signing up on pieces of paper below. He got in line, just to get a look at the list of champions, and when it was his turn, there it was. Just the name he was looking for.

MITCH MASTERS. He had a sheet of paper all to himself. And there was a special condition typed in under his name. $100 FEE, it said, DOUBLE OR NOTHING. Then in smaller type, PROCEEDS TO GO TO THE MASTERS INVITATIONAL TOURNAMENT. So far, nobody had signed up to wrestle him.

Arnie reached for the cheap ballpoint chained to the table, and signed his name. "Will you take a check?" he asked the young, one-armed, black man sitting behind the table.

"You got your I.D.?" the man said.

"Sure do," Arnie said. "Do you want the check now or after the contest?"

"Up to you," the man said, then laughed. "But you gonna have to write it, man. I been sittin' here for ten years, and he's never lost a one."

"I'll wait," Arnie said, realizing his driver's licence identified him as a policeman.

"Starts at ten o'clock sharp," the man said.

"I'll be here," Arnie said, and moved away to make
room for the next man.

"You got a light?" a familiar voice said from
behind him.

"Sure," Arnie said, turning around to face Jake.

"Catch the game?" Jake asked, in his best all-
purpose, male, conversation-with-a-stranger style.

"The real action's right here," Arnie said. "Guy
named Mitch Masters, supposed to be some kind of
undefeated hoo-doo, arm-wrestling Arnie Campbell at ten
o'clock."

"Thanks," Jake said, indicating the cigarette, and
disappeared into the crowd.

Arnie made his way back to the arena. He didn't
know what kind of man would present a trophy in
handicapped basketball, then drive a kidnapped girl
across the state lines, but he knew he was about to find
out.

* * *

Inside the reception area of the jail, Fay and
Lizzie surrendered their handbags and filled out the
visitors' forms. Fay hadn't said anything about Paul,
about the boat, about Lizzie leaving for good. She was
proud of that.

"What if Edith won't talk with me sitting there?"
Lizzie asked.

"If I think she's uncomfortable with you," Fay
said, "I'll just ask you to call Arnie and tell him
we'll be late."

"But we don't know where he is," Lizzie said,
confused.

"He's at the Fairgrounds," Fay said. "But I don't
really want you to call him. Just come back down to the
lobby and wait for me."

"How do you know Arnie's at the Fairgrounds?"
Lizzie asked, as the matron motioned for her to walk
through the metal detector. "Did he tell you?"

"No," Fay said, following her through the machine
and holding her hand out to be stamped by the guard.
"It's just radar."

Lizzie thought a moment. "If he were out with some
other woman, would you know that?"

"Not only would I know he was with her," Fay said,
"I'd know what she had on, _if_ anything."

The guard led them to the elevator.

"Is that how you know where I am?" Lizzie asked. "Radar?"

"Yes," Fay said.

She grasped Lizzie's hand as the gray elevator walls closed in around her. A terrible thought flew into her mind and lodged in a dark corner. When the doors opened again, would a psychotic killer be standing there with a machine gun?

"Can't you turn the radar off?" Lizzie asked.

"No," Fay said. "I can't."

Fay held her breath as the elevator stopped and the guard opened the door. But instead of a psychotic killer, she saw a dead white wall flooded with fluorescent light, and then, as she stepped out onto the floor, she saw more white walls and beneath them, organized groups of defiant blue furniture.

The guard ushered them to a carpeted lounge area, off of which, on either side, ran two long hallways of cells. There was a second tier of cells above each hallway, and ten, maybe twelve guards were stationed in a central vertical command post. Out of sight, above and to the left, Fay heard male inmates playing pool. And just across the way in the lounge, women inmates dressed in neon orange cotton jumpsuits were watching re-runs of All In The Family.

When she saw Edith come through the door, Fay stood up and started to walk toward her. But a shrill whistle pierced the air, and a harsh voice over the loud speaker ordered her not to move.

Lizzie reached out for Fay's hand and pulled her back to the built-in upholstered seat. Then the guard explained that they would have twenty minutes and that smoking was allowed so long as nobody dropped ashes on the carpet.

"Hello, Edith," Fay said, extending her hand. "This is my daughter, Lizzie."

"Yes," Edith said, her orange jumpsuit hanging on her, much as it had on the hanger. "I remember. How nice of you to come see me," as though she were in a convalescent home.

"Are they treating you all right?" Fay asked.

"I don't know what you mean," Edith said, dusting some invisible speck off the sofa before she sat down.

"Are they feeding you? Is anybody bothering you?" Fay asked.

"I'm fine," Edith said, folding her hands in her lap. "How old are you now, Lizzie?"

"I remember you from the dentist," Lizzie said sweetly. "I remember Colleen too. What is she doing now?"

Fay gave Lizzie a silencing look.

But Edith didn't flinch. "Colleen is in California teaching school."

Lizzie looked delighted. "Oh yeah?"

"American History," Edith said proudly. "Tenth

grade."

"Edith. . ." Fay tried to begin.

But Lizzie interrupted. "I thought Colleen died," Lizzie said. "I thought she had an abortion and died. That's what I heard anyway. I wanted to tell you I was sorry."

Fay was horror-stricken.

Edith was cool as could be. "Where did you hear that?" she asked.

"At school," Lizzie said.

Edith smiled. "You couldn't have heard that at school, dear," she said. "Colleen was much older than you are."

"Oh I know," Lizzie said calmly. "But the teachers still talk about it. In health class, they tell us about the clinics they have now. They say girls like Colleen Masters don't have to die any more."

Edith was a little more tentative this time. "I didn't know you went to the same school," she said, fiddling with one of the zippers on her jumpsuit.

"Well you never asked, did you," Lizzie said, her voice cold, her childlike hurt surfacing. "You never asked anything about me. You never even saw me, did you. I was just one more mouth, wasn't I." Lizzie stood up. "No, I wasn't even a mouth to you. Teeth. I was four-year-old teeth."

"Lizzie," Fay said, "please." Then she turned to

Edith. "I'm sorry, Edith, this is not what I. . ."

But Lizzie was mad now. "California?" she blurted.
"Who are you trying to kid?" She grabbed her purse.
"First you force your daughter to go to some butcher in
the middle of the night, and then you don't even have
the guts to admit it was your fault."

Edith didn't answer.

"I'll wait for you downstairs, Mother," Lizzie
said and walked off.

"Edith," Fay said quickly. "I had no idea she was
going to. . ."

Edith cleared her throat. "Why are you here, Fay?"

Fay realized that Lizzie had destroyed all
possibility of a gentle entry into this conversation.

"I'm here because of Beth," Fay said.

"Beth who?" Edith asked.

"Beth Wilkins," Fay said. "We've found all but
three of the missing children. Two boys, and my
neighbor's little girl, Beth."

Edith's face was a complete blank. "Yes," she
said, "I saw that on TV. But that doesn't tell me why
you're here."

"I'm here," Fay said, "because I think you know
where Mitch is keeping that little girl."

"My husband Mitch?" Edith asked.

Fay wished desperately that Lizzie were still here.
Her approach had worked a lot better than this one was.

"Oh my God!" Fay stood up.

"What's the matter?" Edith asked calmly.

But Fay couldn't tell her. Lizzie was gone again.
Escaped, just like that. Gotten Fay all settled in with
Edith and then vanished. She was probably calling Paul
right now from the phone in the lobby. Why hadn't Fay
seen what she was doing? How could she fall for a trick
like that?

O.K. Maybe it wasn't a trick. Maybe Lizzie was
sitting in the lobby right now, looking through a
magazine. But it sure felt like a trick. And from what
Fay could remember, there weren't any magazines in the
lobby. And Lizzie never could just sit. She was gone.

* * *

"Fay?" Edith asked, looking up at her. "Are you all right?"

Fay turned around, and started over. She couldn't afford to be patient now.

"I know that Colleen died," Fay said. "We found the death certificate."

Edith swallowed. "You're right," she said. "She did. She died."

Fay continued. "And I'm real sorry about that. I am. But that's no excuse for killing these last three children. Now I want to know where they are."

"I don't know anything about this," Edith said.

Fay sat down. "Edith. You have to help me."

Edith was quite stern. "You are the last person I would help, now or any time," she said. "It was you who told Colleen to have that abortion."

"I did not tell Colleen to have the abortion," Fay said. "I just told her that she was as important as the baby was."

"Exactly," Edith said coldly, standing up. "I have nothing more to say to you."

But Fay grabbed her hand and pulled her back down. "Edith," she said, "your fingerprints are all over the inside of that truck at the fairgrounds. That Cowboy, Bob, whatever his name is, we know he delivered the

packages for the mothers, and we found nine of the
children tied up at his house."

Edith blinked. She hadn't known they were tied up.

Fay noticed, and pressed harder. "We know you
bought the stationery, and. . ."

Suddenly Fay saw it clearly. "That clown suit you
wore when you kidnapped the kids, we found that in a box
marked HALLOWEEN in that closet under the stairs in your
basement."

Edith looked away. That's where it was, all right.

Fay tried to keep her voice down. "You're going to
spend twenty years in jail for this, Edith, and I <u>know</u>
it's not your fault! I know it was Mitch who was behind
it. But we have to stop him now before he leaves the
state with Beth and gets rid of you for good."

Edith looked down at her hands. "Get rid of me,
Fay? No, I don't think so."

"Well I do," Fay said, convinced she was right.
"Beth's hair is exactly the same color Colleen's was,
and her face, she has that same transparent skin, and
freckles. She even has freckles like Colleen."

"Is that so?" Edith asked.

But Fay went on. "Now whatever point there was at
the beginning of this, fighting abortion, whatever it
was, Mitch has forgotten all about that now. Your
husband has found himself a new little daughter and he's
planning to keep her!"

Edith closed her eyes.

"Edith!" Fay whispered. "It won't work! Even if you go to jail for him, even if they convict you and electrocute you, he still won't love you, Edith!"

"My husband does love me, thank you," Edith said, crossing her legs.

"No, Edith," Fay said, "he doesn't. Oh, maybe when he couldn't take care of himself, when he was first learning to do without his legs, maybe he appreciated you then. But he doesn't need a nurse any more. He doesn't want to be dependent now. And he hates you for reminding him he <u>ever</u> was."

Edith was quite pale. She rubbed her sweating palms against the cotton legs of her jumpsuit. "In the nursing literature," she said, "his anger would be interpreted as a healthy sign."

"O.K., then," Fay said. "You've done your duty. You've healed him. But your assignment is over, Edith."

Fay reached in her pocket, pulled out a Kleenex, and blew her nose.

"It's so dry in here," Edith said.

Fay was tired, and couldn't hide it any longer. "I don't want to guess about this, Edith," she said. "Why don't you just tell me."

"Tell you what?" Edith asked.

Then Fay gasped as the truth hit her. It was perfectly obvious. She would have gotten it sooner if she hadn't been so tired.

"It was you who gave Colleen the money!" Fay said. "That's why you're willing to go to jail. You think that's what you deserve for giving your daughter the money for the abortion, the money that killed her."

Edith's head snapped around, her jaw clenched, her eyes burning with hatred. Fay was right.

"Edith, Edith," Fay pleaded. "What else could you have done? She was a child."

Tears stung Edith's eyes now, but she made a valiant effort to bat them away.

"You didn't kill her," Fay insisted. "The abortionist, the hack she had to go to because it wasn't legal, he killed her."

Edith pressed her index fingers into the corners of her eyes, hoping to hold off the flood.

Fay spoke very softly. "What you did, Edith, was what mothers have done for all of history, or what they have had to do until now. You sacrificed your child because it was the law. A law that made her mistake a crime."

Edith's head bobbed sadly.

Fay couldn't say any more. If Edith didn't want to be forgiven, then there wasn't anything Fay could do.

A full minute passed in silence between them, and then Edith began very slowly.

"Colleen," she whispered, "was not my daughter."

Fay was dumbfounded. "Whose daughter was she?"

"Mitch and. . . I don't know her name," Edith said.
"I've called her Candy all these years," her eyes
watered, "just so I'd have something to say, but it
could have been a nicer name, I guess. When I met him,
in the Veterans' Hospital, he didn't say anything about
having a girlfriend. But a few years later, after we
were married, he came home one day with this baby."

"Did Colleen ever know?" Fay asked.

"No," Edith said. "I said I'd raise her as my own
as long as we never talked about it again, as long as
Colleen never saw her real mother."

Fay handed her another Kleenex and she took it.

"I have always imagined," Edith stared at the blank
wall behind Fay, "that her real mother was very," Edith
searched for the right word, "lively, I guess, a
different sort of woman from me."

"So when you found out Colleen was pregnant," Fay
said, "just like her mother before her. . ."

"I didn't know what to do," Edith said. "I don't,
as you know, believe in abortion. But I didn't want the
baby. We didn't have anything then. I was the only one
working. I thought I couldn't feed the baby."

"You can always feed a baby, Edith," Fay said.

Edith looked down. "All right." She clasped her hands
together. "Yes." She twisted her plain wedding band.
"I was ashamed of her."

"And. . ." Fay knew that wasn't all.

"And," Edith said, giving up, "I didn't want

another one of this Candy woman's children to raise,
another person Mitch would love more than me."

"Where did you get the money?"

"I took five hundred dollars from the dentist and
mailed it to her."

"And the dentist fired you."

"He could never prove it was me. He just fired
everybody who worked for him then."

"So where did Colleen think the money came from?"

"You," Edith paused. "I guess."

"And where did Mitch think the money came from?"

"You," Edith said. "I told him Colleen had been to
see you, and he drew the. . natural conclusion."

"So," Fay said. "I was right. He really <u>did</u> want
to kill me."

"Yes," Edith said. "For almost fifteen years now."

"And you have kept him from it?"

"You're sitting here, aren't you?" Edith said,
her face drained of all emotion now.

Fay spoke simply. "Thank you," she said.

"I'm not proud of it," Edith said.

"How did you. . ." Fay wasn't sure what to ask.

"Distract him?" Edith asked. "I convinced him
that abortion was the enemy, not you. I found the names
of doctors who performed abortions, and he turned them
in. Then, after it was legal, he robbed the centers,
stole their equipment, things like that."

"You could've reported him, Edith, any time."

"No," she said. "I couldn't. I didn't want that."
She dabbed at her eyes. "I needed him."

Fay understood that.

Edith stared at the wall. "But when the bombings
started, when people in Florida and New York started
bombing abortion clinics. . ."

Fay was catching on fast. "He knew he had to do
something more. . ."

"Manly," Edith said. "Yes." She cleared her
throat. "That's important to him."

"And suddenly, you were afraid he might. . ."

"Yes," Edith said. "I was afraid he would kill
somebody. So I told him to think of something else."

"So the kidnapping. . ." Fay said.

"Yes," Edith winced. "That's what Mitch thought
of."

"Who is the Cowboy?" Fay asked.

"He was one of Mitch's therapists. That's all I
know." She paused. "The children he tied up, are they
all right?"

Fay nodded. "Edith, who were the people at the
church? The parents of the other girls."

"What other girls?" Edith asked, genuinely
surprised.

"The group that met at the church," Fay said.

"They don't have anything to do with this," Edith
said.

"No?" Fay asked.

"How do you even know about them?" Edith asked.

"Just tell me," Fay said.

"That was actually a good thing he did," she said. "Counseling, I guess you'd call it. He just got those parents together to. . . tell their stories. He just let them grieve over their girls."

The guard came up at that moment to tell them their twenty minutes was up.

"I have five minutes I didn't use with my last visitor," Edith said. "Go check the report."

"This is the goddamn jail, lady," he said, reaching for her.

"Yes," she said, crossing her arms. "And unless you start checking things like reports, you will continue to be the lowest paid person in this jail."

"Five minutes," he growled and walked away.

Edith was calmer now. "I don't know where that little girl is," she said. "Or the boys. All I was supposed to do was watch what happened at the shopping center. Mitch and Bob were hiding the children."

"If we got you out of here," Fay asked, "could you find out where Beth and the two boys are?"

"I don't think so," Edith said. "I think Mitch was already . . . beginning not to trust me."

"Edith," she ventured. "This plan had to cost a couple of thousand dollars. Where did Mitch get the money?"

"I don't know his name," Edith said. "He's a
foreigner, a banker. Brazil, I think."

"All right," Fay said.

The guard returned and Edith stood up willingly
this time.

"I'll do what I can to help you," Fay said,
standing up too. "I'll tell them you talked to me."

"Just find that little girl," Edith said.

Edith extended her hand, and Fay shook it, then
stood there while Edith was escorted back to her cell.

Fay walked to the guard station and waited silently
for the elevator with the guard who had brought her up
here. Finally, as the door opened and he turned the key
to the control panel, she had to ask.

"Did you take my daughter downstairs?"

"I sure did," he grinned, "but I thought you were
sisters!"

"No," Fay said.

"Could've fooled me," he flirted. "She said she'd
see you at home."

When the door opened onto the empty lobby, she
turned to the guard. "Take it easy on my friend up
there," she said. "She doesn't really belong here."

"Yeah," he said. "That's what they all say."

And Fay pushed open the wide glass door and stepped
out into the night.

* * *

By the time Fay reached her car, it had started to
rain. She felt desperately alone. Edith was, she
realized, the Hermit. Number nine in the Tarot deck.
And whatever Fay may have thought about the card before,
she knew now it was a warning.

The picture is a bearded, robed, recluse who leans
on his shepherd's crook for support, and holds up a
lantern to light his solitary path. But he is not
searching for his sheep in the darkness. He is just
alone, sentenced to life in exile for some unpardonable
crime. But it is the Hermit himself who has pronounced
this sentence.

Edith had done exactly that, decided she was unfit
for life with other people, walked into the empty cell
and locked the door behind her.

And the more Fay thought about it, the more Hermits
she knew. Some of them even admitted it. They said
they'd rather be alone, or couldn't handle the demands
that other people made on them, or could only live or
work where it was quiet. And some of these people
actually did move to remote areas. But most of them
just went so far inside themselves that they weren't
reachable by ordinary human means, like physical contact
or conversation.

They were polite, as a rule, but they never talked
to you for very long about anything. Occasionally, they

did hold odd or unusually strong opinions, or exhibit
quirky behavior, but they didn't ever try to convince
you their opinion was right, or invite you to enjoy
their eccentricity.

In social situations, they would always expect to
pay the check, but would never expect to enjoy
themselves. They took their exercise like everything
else, as a punishment for getting older. And although
they did have sex, it was primarily because refusing to
might provoke a conversation about it.

The main way you could tell you were dealing with
one of these exiles, was you somehow felt you didn't
have much room to move around. The wrong word, the
wrong gesture, the suggestion of some silly
entertainment, or the sharing of a personal story would
elicit an only slightly disguised sneer from them. You
would be terribly embarassed and walk away. Unless, of
course, they pretended not to hear any of it and walked
away first.

It didn't bother these people if their children
didn't call them. In fact, as they saw it, the children
weren't really theirs. In having them, the Hermits had
merely acquiesced to the desires of their mates. They
didn't ignore their children though. Far from it. They
watched, hawk-eyed, for the first indication that the
child was as flawed as they were. When they spotted the
aberrant behavior, they punished it immediately. And

kept punishing it until it became an established part of
the child's personality.

These isolates were, finally, despite their skills
and intelligence, spectators. They watched the world
through the tiny window in their cell. They were, in
fact, comfortable in there. They knew the routine, they
recognized the guards' voices, and had found ways to
pass the time. Why should they venture out? They would
no doubt commit the same crime again, have to come back
inside again. What was the point? They might not even
get as nice a cell next time.

That was what Edith had done, all right, locked
herself up. And that's what The Hermit was about,
deadly self-seclusion. What was deadly about it, was
that people actually became proud of their solitude,
as though it meant they didn't need anybody else, as if
need were another crime they might commit if they were
free.

* * *

Lizzie was not home when Fay got there, and the
only message on the machine was from Gail, telling Fay
she was going out to dinner with the Mayor and would be
back by ten o'clock probably and to please call when Fay
saw the lights go on.

Fay knew that Arnie wouldn't be back for a while,
she didn't want to read or watch TV, but she was afraid
if she just sat in the dark, she'd fall asleep and she
couldn't do that. This night was not over yet.

She walked to the window and saw four angular young
men leaning against a car parked in the shadows. They
had seen her come in, she was sure of it. But who were
they? Were they just waiting while their friend went
inside to get his raincoat? Or was this the robbery she
had seen in the cards last night?

Or were these boys the ones who would kill her?
Was this why Lizzie wouldn't call?

She edged over to the side of the window and pulled
the drapes. She bolted the door and tried to remember
the last time she had actually been scared to be in the
house by herself. Then she called the police station at
the corner, told the man taking Arnie's place tonight
that she was here by herself and there were suspicious
characters on the street. Finally, she opened the hall
closet, fished her mother's pistol out of the sack of
knitted scarves where it had lain buried all these

years. She cleaned it, checked to see that it was
loaded and the safety was on, and then stuffed it behind
the needle point pillow in her big chair.

That done, she went to the kitchen, got one of
Lizzie's yogurts out of the refrigerator, turned on the
radio and heard the last part of an announcement that an
additional ten thousand dollar reward had been offered
by a South American philanthopist for anyone who located
the remaining three missing children.

10:00 P.M.

When Arnie got back to the basketball court, the
second overtime was just beginning. Those three
minutes were the most violent he'd ever seen in a
sporting event. And the victory celebration was even
more dangerous than the game had been. Coaches and
trainers who had useful legs were well-advised to keep
them off the court, away from the cracking wheels and
reeling chairs of the "helpless" cripples.

As the floor was being cleared for the presentation
of the trophy, the announcer informed the fans that the
Mayor, who had been scheduled to present the trophies,
was unable to attend, but that substituting for him
would be his wife, Vi Ewing.

When the crowd settled down, Vi appeared in her
fifth outfit of the day, this one a flouncy yellow suit
with a polka-dot blouse. She praised the spirit of the
youngsters she had seen competing in the hall, then
introduced the Chairman of the Fairgrounds Board, who
presented the trophy to the winning coach.

Then the lights dimmed and the band played the
Marine hymn. "The Most Valuable Player Award," Vi
said, "will be presented by the man whose heroic labors
on behalf of the disabled have earned him a citation
from the Surgeon General, as well as the love and the
gratitude of thousands of determined victims of
accidents and disease." She paused as the searchlight

found him. "Ladies and Gentlemen, a Four Star General
in the War Against Physical Limitations, . . . Mitchell
Masters!"

Arnie stretched to get a look. Entering the arena
wearing his Marine dress whites, and brandishing his
riding crop like a sword, Masters raised one arm high
over his head in a bold salute that brought the crowd to
its feet in deafening applause. With his taut muscular
neck, broad tanned forehead, his bulging shoulders and
massive chest, he was a startling, if not downright
stirring sight, wedged in a wheelchair.

As for his lower body, well, the chair _was_ his
lower body. This was not a man in a wheelchair. This
was a man on wheels, a man-machine, a satyr with steel
rims instead of hooves.

Arnie made his way to the floor, as Masters took
possession of the crowd. His voice was deep, his manner
deliberate and demanding, as he told the life story of
the young man he was about to name.

Arnie wondered if Vi, smiling down at Masters, her
hands clasped in classic rapture, had any idea who this
man was, or what else he had done today. It was almost
funny. Just two hours ago, she had made that desperate
public appeal to the kidnapper, and now here he was
right beside her.

Jake came up behind Arnie. "So that's the famous
Mitch Masters," he said casually, one bystander to

another.

"Yeah, he's quite a guy," Arnie said back.

"You hear about his partner?" Jake asked, picking
his teeth.

"What partner?" Arnie asked, his eyes straight
ahead.

"A cowboy," Jake said.

"No I didn't," Arnie said, determined not to react.
"What about him?"

"Blown to bits in a garage downtown," Jake said.

"He killed himself?" Arnie asked.

"No," Jake said, "a bomb. The parking attendant's
just sitting there and he hears this boom, you know?
Goes down to look and finds this Cowboy," Jake's arms
flew out, "all over the place."

"Jesus Christ," Arnie said.

"Yeah," Jake said. "Only whole piece left was his
hat." Jake threw his cigarette down on the floor. "See
you later," he said, and left.

At the center of the court, Masters gave the Most
Valuable Player his trophy, and sat by the boy's side as
the band played the national anthem. Then as the crowd
applauded, he invited the young man to be his coach at
the arm wrestling matches.

The kid, whose name was Dwight, said he better not,
because his mother had planned a party for the team at
home. Masters said he better go on then, because
mothers were worse than Marines. The boy laughed,

thanked him anyway, and followed as Masters led a great
crippled parade off the court.

Arnie arrived at the sign-up table just in time to
see Masters approach, chomping a cigar and entertaining
the troups as he rolled along.

"You my latest victim?" Masters boomed, as he saw
Arnie.

"It's a long list, I know," Arnie said.

The followers laughed and Masters' cold gray eyes
took stock of Arnie.

"You ever do this before, son?"

"Not lately," Arnie said.

"Too bad," Masters said, cracking his knuckles. "I
was hoping for some exercise."

"I'll do my best," Arnie said.

"I hope that's enough, soldier," Masters snorted.

The crowd was growing, around them. Arnie shifted
in his chair, and wiped his hands on his pants while
Rodney explained the rules.

Elbows here, shoulders like so, one foul and you're
out. Best two out of three, no disputing the umpire,
and the winner takes all and gives it to the tournament.

"Got that?" Rodney asked.

"Got it," Arnie said, massaging his shoulder.

"Left arm or right?" Masters asked. "Challenger's
choice."

"Right," Arnie said.

"What's the matter with your left?" Masters
smirked, taking off his watch.

"Hunting accident," Arnie said, scooting closer to
the table.

"Oh yeah?" Masters said, taking his cigar out of
his mouth and laying it on the white line directly under
where their hands would lock. "What do you hunt?"

"Somebody was hunting me," Arnie said.

Masters liked that idea. "What do you do, son?"

"I'm a cop," Arnie said, just to protect himself in
case Vi showed up.

"You're too old for a cop," Masters said, digging
his elbow into the table.

"You get old being a cop," Arnie said, stretching
his fingers wide apart. "If you're lucky, that is."

Masters snarled. "Come on, Dick, get your elbow up
here."

"The name's Arnie," he said, planted his elbow,
and grabbed Mitch's hand.

"All right!" Masters said, squeezing Arnie's hand
and nodding to Rodney to give the signal. "Let's find
out what we've got for cops these days."

"Go," Rodney shouted.

Standing at the back of the crowd, Jake heard the
cheering begin. But after a full minute, their hands
were still straight up, and both men were straining hard
to keep it that way. Arnie's forearm was a half-inch
longer than Mitch's, but the General's was at least two

inches broader. And Arnie had at least ten years on the
man, maybe fifteen. But Masters was mean.

"So what brings you out with the cripples, Arnie?"
Masters used his free hand to reach for his cigar and
take a puff.

"I tried to get in the tractor pull," Arnie
coughed, "but they were sold out."

Masters grinned and stuck the stogie back in his
mouth. "Just had the night off, huh?"

"Yeah," Arnie said, wiping away a drop of sweat
that had popped out on his temple. "I've been on that
kidnap drill all day. I had to do something."

Masters' elbow slipped slightly on the table.
Arnie took advantage of it, snapped his wrist and drove
Masters' arm down about two inches. But Masters gave a
fierce grunt and held.

Keeping the pressure up, Arnie went on talking.
"Yeah," he said, "been standing in the sun all day out
at that shopping center guarding a goddamn truck."

Masters looked up at Rodney, winked and whipped
Arnie's arm back to upright. The crowd cheered.

"So," Masters said, scratching his head calmly,
"You gonna catch those people?"

Arnie's bicep had begun to quiver. "Already got
one in jail," he managed. He took a breath and shoved
Masters' arm back to where it had been, and then down
another inch toward the table.

"The other one," Arnie paused, "just blew himself
up in a parking lot downtown."

"Oh, yeah?" Masters said, looking down at his
watch.

"Yeah," Arnie said. "They don't know his name yet,
though. Calling him the Cowboy on the radio."

Two vets in fatigues started chanting now in
support of Masters, but he nodded to them that there was
nothing to worry about.

"So that's who did it?" Masters asked, digging his
nails into Arnie's hand.

"They think there's one more," Arnie leaned forward
in his chair, hoping to get better leverage. He only
needed four more inches and he'd have him.

"Watch it," Rodney said, pointing to Arnie's
shoulder. "Any further and it's an automatic loss."

Mitch gritted his teeth. "Did the old lady talk
yet?"

"What old lady?" Arnie asked.

Masters started to sweat, finally. "The old lady
in the jail."

"I didn't say it was an old lady," Arnie said.

Masters gripped the edge of the table with his free
hand. "That's what they said on TV," Masters said,
gripping the edge of the table with his free hand.

Arnie looked up at him. "Yeah, I guess she's
talked some," Arnie said, wiping the sweat out of his
eyes. "Most people do."

"You ever talked to a really old lady?" Masters
asked, trying to keep his effort from showing on his
face.

Arnie closed his eyes. "Not lately."

"They don't say a goddamn thing," Masters grunted,
and reached for his cigar.

Arnie knew what that meant. The guy was about to
try something.

"Well," Arnie said, "she must have told them
something, because they're setting a roadblock for
midnight to catch the other one."

Masters leaned in. "Circle the whole city, you
mean?" He punched his shoulder forward.

"Calling up the national guard for it," Arnie lied.
"Any road he takes out of the city, they've got him."

"How do they know what he looks like?" Masters leered.

"They don't," Arnie said. "But they're gonna tear
up every car they see, looking for that little girl."

"What if he leaves before midnight?" Masters said.

"Well then, the bastard will get away, won't he,"
Arnie said.

Masters gave a hearty laugh, looked up at Arnie,
sucked in his breath, clenched the table, fought Arnie's
arm up to even, then whacked it down hard on the other
side, breaking something, a knuckle, probably.

"All right!" Mitch shouted, and the crowd exploded.

Arnie stood up quickly and backed away from the

table as Mitch's friends came up to congratulate him.

"You can take five minutes if you both agree to
it," Rodney said.

"I need something to eat," Arnie said, looking
around. "I need a hotdog."

"Take mine," Jake said from behind him.

"Thanks," Arnie said.

"Cost me two bucks," Jake said, for the benefit of
anyone listening.

Arnie reached into his pocket for the cash.
"Thanks," he said, and turned back to the table.

What kind of game was Arnie playing here, Jake
wondered. Why doesn't he just take the guy downtown?
But maybe Arnie thinks if he takes Masters in, the
little girl will just die wherever she is. Jake
conceded that that was a possibility, but he didn't know
how losing to the guy was going to get him to reveal
where he stashed the kid. And Jake was convinced Arnie
would lose here.

* * *

Fay picked up the phone on the first ring.

"Fay," the Chief said, "I think you better come see this."

She was so relieved to hear a familiar voice, she didn't even ask what it was she was supposed to see. "I'm ready," she said.

"It's a parking garage downtown," he said. "I'll have a patrol car pick you up. It's the Cowboy. Bomb blew up in his face. The car should be there for you in five minutes."

Fay started to ask about Arnie, but the Chief hung up. Had Arnie chased the Cowboy into the garage and been blown up with him? No. No, she thought. Arnie is at the Fairgrounds.

But somebody's there, somebody else. Why else would he want me to come? Those two little boys. That's who it is. Joshua and. . . what's his name? Richard? Yes. Wait a minute, are they blown up? No, she thought. Please God, no.

Fay knew Lizzie would come home to change before she went out, so she found a piece of paper and wrote her a note.

"Dear Lizzie," she began. "I have gone downtown to find the last two boys. If you need me, call the police and tell them I am with the Chief."

She started a new paragraph.

"Please don't leave with Paul before you see me."
She underlined please.

"I know you are going, but I also know some other
things about your trip, things I'd want to know if I
were you, like where you get married. You asked me
that, remember? So wait for me."

Fay thought a minute and then added. "Since I'm
never going to see you again after tonight, I won't
charge you a thing."

Then she skipped a few lines and signed it, "Love,
Mom."

She taped the note to the center of the table,
pulled the drapes apart, saw the patrol car approach,
grabbed her umbrella, unbolted the door, locked it
behind her, then ran out toward the waiting policeman.

Downtown, the Chief met Fay at the parking garage
and walked her past the barricades and over to the scene
of the explosion.

"It was a modified military device," he said.

"Somebody was trying to kill him?" she asked.

"That's what our guys think," he said. "The Cowboy
probably saw the bomb when he opened the car door. Then
when he tried to defuse it, it blew up on him."

Fay wasn't close enough to see any really sickening
details, but the acrid smoke still trapped in the garage
burned her eyes and nose. She coughed hard and asked if
there was any water.

"You don't have to go any further if you don't want to," the Chief said.

"Then why did you want me to come?" Fay asked, looking in her purse for a handkerchief.

"The attendant said the Cowboy was here earlier today, driving a pick-up truck. The truck sounds like the same one you saw at his house. And we know from the children you found, that he took those other two boys somewhere. . ."

"And you think they might be here," Fay said.

"Yeah," the Chief said, slightly ashamed of how obvious it sounded. "Maybe he brought them here, jimmied a trunk open and stuffed them in."

Fay shook her head sadly. "And you want me to tell you which car they're in."

"Be a damn sight easier than impounding every car that's here," he said.

"For you maybe," Fay said.

"There's an extra ten grand in the pot now, you know."

"Yes, I heard," Fay said, surprised that the Chief would think the money made any difference to her. "Whose money is it?"

"The name is Rafael Soares," the Chief said. "Ever heard of him?"

Fay reeled. No, she'd never heard the name before, but she knew who he was all right. The King of Coins. The financial wizard. Paul's father.

"No," she said, covering her mouth with the handkerchief.

"Big banker. From Brazil, originally," the Chief said. "Lives in California now, though. Big Catholic too, I guess."

"Why do you say that?" she asked.

"I don't know," he said. "Something about how he talked about the children."

"You don't have to be a Catholic to like children," Fay said.

"O.K.," he said, realizing he'd never tried to talk to Fay without Arnie around to translate. "Can you find the kids or not?"

"I don't know," Fay said. "Where should I start?"

"I'd start at the top," he said, pointing to the elevator. "I'll come with you if you want."

"That's all right," she said.

"It's pretty dark up there," he said, stuffing his hands in his pockets.

"All right, then," she said, knowing he was only trying to help. "Come with me. But you can't be right there, you know, I'll need a little. . ."

"I can do whatever you want," he said, putting his arm around her, as they started for the elevator. "You just tell me."

"And what if I can't find them?" she said, slipping out from under his arm.

"Then we'll seal the place," he frowned. "Bring in
a computer and a phone bank," he scratched his head,
"file for the search warrants and open all the trunks."

"How long will that take?"

"Start to finish, two days," he said.

She nodded. "And the kids will die. If they're
here. If they're not dead already."

"Well," he said, pressing the elevator button.
"You see why I called you."

* * *

Gail and the Mayor had been lingering over their
decaf for quite a while now, discussing, among other
things, whether the next cup should be real coffee. It
was hard to know, they said, whether the rest of the
evening held some event they'd need to be awake for, or
one they'd rather sleep through.

The dinner had been so-so. She'd had steamed mussels
and a salad, and he'd eaten the battered trout, which
was not what they'd called it on the menu, but rather
his description of the treatment it had received in the
kitchen.

The conversation had been lively, but was
punctuated by abrupt and seemingly unbridgeable
silences. He was relieved that no one had recognized
him, had come over to the table to say hello. She
suspected that several people had noticed him, but upon
seeing her, had decided that whatever they had to say to
him could wait til tomorrow.

What they had in common was a deep-seated fear of
leaving the restaurant. Gail realized they had become
terribly dependent on the structure it provided for
them. Once they left this table, the future would close
in around them like the dense foliage and treacherous
undergrowth of a tropical forest.

Once they hit the highway, somebody would have to
make a move, say whether to go home or not, together or

not. If anybody brought up the rules, what they
"should" do, there would be a discussion about it. And
a discussion would be the end of the evening, and
neither one wanted that. So they ordered more coffee.
Real for Gail, decaf and a brandy for the Mayor.

Just then, the Mayor spotted one of the policemen
assigned to guard him, talking to the maitre d'.

"If you have to go, please do," she said, reaching
for her purse. "I can call a cab or something."

"You can come with me," he said, as the Sergeant
approached.

"Sorry to disturb you, sir," the Sergeant said,
"but the Chief wanted you and Mrs. Wilkins to know."

"Know what, Sergeant?" the Mayor said, reaching for
his newly-arrived brandy.

Suddenly very afraid, Gail looked up at the young
officer. "I'm not ready for this," she said.

"Oh, no, Mam," he said, sensing her fear. "They
haven't found any more kids yet."

She was not relieved.

"I'm sorry, Mam," the Sergeant said.

"What is it, Bill?" the Mayor asked, hoping to get
back to Gail before she disappeared into the agony
again.

"It's that Cowboy where we found the other kids,"
he said. "He's dead. A bomb blew up on him in a
parking garage downdown."

"What was he doing there?" Gail asked.

"That's what I came to tell you," he said. "The Chief thinks he was hiding the other kids in trunks of cars. They're searching for them now. They've got that psychic down there and she's. . ."

Gail reached under the table for her purse. "Peter," she said, "we have to go down there."

"Thank you, Bill," the Mayor said, standing up.

The Sergeant thought he was being dismissed, but he wasn't sure. "If you need a ride, sir, I'll. . ."

"No thank you, Bill," the Mayor said, motioning for the waiter. "I have my car."

Gail put on fresh lipstick while the Mayor signed the check.

"Are you sure you want to go?" he asked Gail, as she closed her compact and dropped it back into her purse. "It could be. . ." he paused, wondering how to warn her, "it could be anything, I guess. It could be nothing."

"If Beth is dead in one of those cars, I want to see it," Gail said. "I don't want somebody calling me on the goddamn phone about it." She gulped down the last of her coffee.

"Well, then," he said, "let's go."

* * *

Arnie's hotdog had helped. He had won the second round of arm wrestling fairly easily. And except for some routine swearing and name-calling, they hadn't talked at all. Maybe Masters was thinking, maybe Arnie's lie about the roadblock was having an effect.

Arnie was tempted to have a beer. He hadn't had one all day. In fact, as he thought about it, he had missed all kinds of things today, like meals and chairs and the finals of the U.S. Open on TV. Arnie thought there ought to be certain things in a day or it didn't count. Like if you didn't have a decent cup of coffee, or see a pretty pair of legs, or get to work the crossword puzzle in peace, then you shouldn't have to be a day older at the end of it.

Arnie walked back to the table, quite aware that not one person slapped him on the back and said good luck.

"Want to double the stakes?" Masters asked, rolling up to the table.

"Can't do it," Arnie said, still standing, patting his wallet. "I can't afford to lose that much."

The crowd laughed.

But Mitch didn't like that attitude. "If you think you're going to lose," he pounced, "I'll save myself the trouble of beating you and just take your check right now."

"You're going to lose," Arnie needled, deciding he
would have a beer after all.

"I never have before," Mitch said casually, setting
the brake on his wheelchair.

"Why is that?" Arnie said, spotting the beer man
and waving to him.

Masters took a wet cloth from Rodney and wiped his
hands, then mopped his forehead. "I like to win," he
said, and handed the cloth back to Rodney.

"It's just a game," Arnie said, pleased to see that
his stall was making Masters nervous.

"Correction," Masters said. "Only boys play
games."

Arnie didn't agree. Masters was still playing his
games because he hadn't really won yet. From what
Arnie knew about military life, when you really knew
you'd won, you walked off the field and took a shower.
You didn't parade around in your bloody battle dress,
you wrapped a clean towel around your clean waist and
drank a beer.

Masters was a pretty fair actor, but he was only
playing the part. The real hero went home after the
game to the party his Mother had planned for him. The
real hero took his suffering in stride and refused to
feel special about it.

Masters asked the crowd to step back a little, give
them some air, he said, then nodded to Rodney. "Let's

with this, huh? I've got a date."

oin' to a dance?" Arnie quipped, as the man

im the beer.

none of your goddamn business where I'm

ters snapped, cranking his elbow into

llected his change and his beer, lifted up

nd undid his belt.

God's sake," Masters barked. "What are you

king you nervous?" Arnie asked, fixing it.

is right front pocket for something.

you," Masters said, tapping the table,

atch flop around like a freshly caught fish.

finally found what he was looking for, and

s badge down on the table.

ers scowled. "Get your ass in that chair,

mn badge was stickin' right in my leg," Arnie

He popped the top off the can of beer. "I'm

he said, and took a long deep drink, then set

n on the table and burped.

Masters planted his arm on the table again. "I'm

g you one minute or it's a default."

Arnie sat down, slid his elbow up to its place,

n clenched his fist repeatedly to pump up the blood

his arm.

Masters read the name off the badge, really
beginning, perhaps, to wonder if he might be in tr
here. His voice, when he spoke, was like the low
of a poisonous snake about to strike.

"Who are you, Campbell?" he rasped.

"I told you," Arnie said easily, stretching h
fingers wide. "I'm a cop."

They clasped hands.

"Go," Rodney said.

Masters gave it everything he had, clamped hi
shut, drew his whole face into tight focus, and tr
quick stab.

Arnie forced himself to laugh and rode it out
"What are you trying to do, old man? Beat m
lar

"You asshole," Masters swore under his b

"Hey, watch it," Arnie whispered back.   "Ther
people here."

"You fucking asshole," Masters mouthed. His
turned bright red, his cheeks puffed up then explo
showering Arnie with spit, but otherwise having no
effect on his defiant, upright arm.

Arnie reached for his beer. "Want a drink?"
asked, wondering how much longer he could pretend
be dying here. God, the man was strong.

Masters couldn't do it. He shook his head, r
his shoulders, resigned himself to another strateg
seige and asked Rodney to get him a beer.

Arnie inhaled and mashed Master's arm down an inch. "Is your wife's name Edith?" Arnie asked.

"Yeah," Masters hissed, his wrist stiffening into steel. "What of it?"

"A friend of mine knows her," Arnie said.

Masters yanked his arm back to upright. Rodney shouted his approval and set Masters' beer down on the table.

Arnie drove his arm down again. "She says your daughter is a real pretty blond. How old is she now?"

"She died," Masters said, jerking back to upright and holding there.

Arnie knew he could take this first inch anytime he wanted to, so he did it again, just for effect. "What happened to the baby?" he challenged.

Mitch batted away a wasp drawn by the smell of beer and sweat. "What baby?"

"My friend told me Colleen had a baby," Arnie said.

Masters' cheek twitched at the name. "Who is this friend of yours?" he asked, bouncing Arnie's arm back to upright.

Arnie lobbed the name across the table like a grenade, "It's Fay Morgan."

Mitch knew the name. "Fortune tellers ought to be against the law," he spat.

"People need somebody to talk to," Arnie said, a pain shooting up from his elbow like a lighted fuse.

Mitch returned a smile from somebody in the crowd

behind Arnie's head. "They can talk to their parents,"
he said flatly.

Arnie braced his left arm against his knee for
support. "Maybe they're afraid of what their parents
would say."

"Then they shouldn't do it," Masters said, taking
another drink of his beer.

"Do what?" Arnie asked, as their arms shook
together, dead even, over the center line.

Mitch looked him square in the face. "Do what they
go see the fortune teller about."

Arnie reached for his beer. He wanted to win here.
He knew it didn't matter, really. The Department would
pay him back the two hundred dollars if he had to write
the check. But it was personal now. He was not letting
Masters have the satisfaction of beating a cop. No way.

"Maybe she was raped," Arnie said, dropping the
tough-guy voice he'd been using. "Maybe it wasn't her
fault. Ever think of that?"

Masters noticed the change. "No such thing as
rape, Campbell," he said.

Arnie let him have an inch. "That's bullshit,
Masters."

"She was weak," Masters said, his knuckles white
from the pressure, the black hairs on the top of his
hands glistening with sweat.

Arnie leaned forward and lowered his voice. "She

was a kid, Masters."

Masters' back stiffened. The muscles in his neck
bulged. He wanted to kill this cop, he wanted to break
his arm, twist it right off like a chicken leg.

"She was no kid," Masters took a breath, then spat
out the words. "She was a slut like her mother."

Arnie closed his eyes, determined not to cave in.
He counted to eight.

Then, as Masters let out his last bit of air, Arnie
struck.

"Well," Arnie said, jabbing Masters' arm back to
upright, "I don't think so."

And before Masters could recover his will, Arnie
bashed his arm flat down on the table. And won.

"Yeah!" he shouted.

The crowd was silent. The hero had lost.

And only then, as she placed her icy fingers on his
sweaty shoulders and planted a prim kiss on his cheek
from behind, did Arnie realize that Vi Ewing had been
watching the whole time.

"Arnie! Arnie!" she said, pinching his left arm,
finding the exact center of his bandage.

"Ah-h!" he yelled, and sprang out of his chair.

"You were wonderful," she cooed, and slipped across
the end of the table to congratulate Masters.

"Well," she leaned down to Masters, "I'm just so
grateful I could see this."

Masters didn't look up.

But Vi Ewing wouldn't quit. "We have two heroes, here," she announced to the crowd. "This detective has found eleven of the kidnapped children all by himself!"

There was genuine applause from the crowd.

"Good match," Masters said to Arnie, releasing the brake on his chair and extending his hand.

And as Arnie shook it, somebody snapped a picture.

"Isn't that nice!" Vi said.

Masters rolled back a little. "All right," he called out. "Everybody who came in my van, we're leaving right now."

"What about the money?" Arnie called to him. "You owe the tournament two hundred bucks!"

"He's good for it," Rodney answered and wheeled Masters around.

"Don't I get a trophy or something?" Arnie yelled.

But he didn't get an answer to that. Four men in wheel chairs, one V.A. chaplain, and Rodney fell in behind Masters and proceeded through the hole that opened up for them in the crowd.

Arnie started off in the other direction, but Vi caught his hand. "It just makes me feel so good," she said, falling in step with him. "To know there are such dedicated policemen in this city, people who really care."

Arnie sped up to get away from her, but she just trotted along as gracefully as she could. When they

reached the exit, he pushed the door open, then held it
while two men on crutches slipped by him.

"Goodnight, Mrs. Ewing," he said, and strode off
down the sidewalk.

"Where are you going?" she asked, catching up to
him.

He stopped her. "I'm on duty, Mrs. Ewing. If you
need a ride home, there's an officer at the information
booth."

"I want to go with you," she said. "If you're
going to find those last three children, I want to be
there."

"I can't take you," he said. "It's against the
regulations."

She dropped her pleasant voice. "Maybe we'll just
call the Mayor and see about that," she said.

"Do it," he said. "But until I get a direct order
from the Chief of Police, you're not setting your little
fanny anywhere near me tonight."

"I could report you for that remark," she said.

"Please do," he said. "I hope it makes the front
page."

They rounded the corner of the building and Arnie
stopped. Mitch and his gang were loading into the van.

"I'm gone," Arnie said, ducking down behind a dark
Buick. "You do what you want."

* * *

When the elevator opened, Fay and the Chief saw
that the top floor of the parking garage was empty
except for a white Eldorado convertible and a dusty
brown Pinto hatchback stuffed to the gills with
somebody's whole life.

Fay stepped out onto the concrete. She didn't know
how to go about this exactly, but she'd seen enough of
these two cars already. The Eldorado, parked near the
elevator, didn't even have license plates.

"Somebody probably just drove it up here, ran out
of gas, and decided it was all for the best," the Chief
said.

Fay walked ahead of him down to the next tier of
cars. She ran her hand up the aerial of a black Lincoln
and wondered what a skillet was doing in the back window
of the tan Audi.

"It's not a new car," she said, and then she knew
what it was. "It's a car they don't make any more."
She was staring at a license plate that read TOM-86.

"Like a Rambler?" he asked. "Or a Viceroy or a
Valiant? Or do you mean really old like a Packard, or a
Studebaker, maybe, or an Alpine? Yeah! A Sunbeam?"

"What does a Dodge look like?" she asked.

"The old ones were real ugly little box cars, in
real dull colors like split pea, or mud. With big wide
strips of chrome along the side and. : ."

"That's not it, then," she said.

"Maybe we should just walk on a little further," he
said.

"There's no use walking if we don't know what we're
looking for," she said.

Sure, he thought. That makes sense. "Want me to
stand still or walk?" he asked.

"What's a Nash?" she asked, starting down the line
of cars.

"They made the Rambler," he said. "And all of them
were black and cheap like. . ."

"No," she said. "It's not black. What's a car
that smells like gasoline on the inside?"

"I had a Ford that did that," he said. "But almost
any old Volkswagon would too."

"It has rubber mats on the floor."

"Right," he said, admiring the wire wheels on a
slick silver Corvette.

"It has a broken lock on the glove compartment,
too," she said.

"What color is it?" he asked, thinking how much it
would help if she knew something about the outside of
this car.

"I don't know," she said. "It's dark."

He thumped the zippered cover of a little Fiat
convertible. "The car is dark? Or it's too dark in
here to tell?"

"Both," she said, hesitating behind a blue sedan.

"Is that it?" he jumped.

"No," she said. "I like the looks of it though."

"It's a '72 Volvo," he said, coming up beside her. "It's a helluva car. Drives like a tank. Rides like a dream. I took one out for a test drive once, used car, and the whole exhaust system fell out on the highway."

"What did you do?" she asked, moving on to the next tier of cars.

"Went real slow," the Chief said. "Cars won't hardly go at all without the exhaust. Limped up into a gas station, called the dealer, told him as soon as he fixed it, I'd buy it. Got a real good deal too."

She laughed. "I bet you did."

"Never had another lick of trouble with it."

"It's a bird," she said. "It's the name of a bird!"

"Falcon!" he said, starting to look for one.

"No," she said.

"Firebird?" he asked, trying to remember if they'd passed one.

"No."

"Lark," he said. "Skylark!"

"No," she said.

He walked on. "Hawk?"

"No."

"Phoenix?"

"No."

"Thunderbird!"

"Uh-uh," she said.

"Fiero?"

"Is that a bird?" she asked.

He was flat out of birds. "Are you sure it's not a horse?" he asked. "There's a whole lot more horses than birds. Colt, Mustang, Pinto, Pony, Charger, Bronco..."

"Stud," she said. "They ought to name one Stud."

He laughed. "Sell a million of 'em, I bet," he said, stopping to read the sign in the window of a red Mercedes turbo. RADIO ALREADY STOLEN, it read.

"The guy's lying," the Chief said.

"What do you mean?" she asked, walking over to the window on the passenger side.

He pointed. "See those wires coming out of that hole for the radio?"

She peered into the dark car.

"They're fake," he explained. "The guy's got one of those lift out radios, what-do-you-call-'ems, portables. Thing goes in the trunk at night. Then he just stuffs these wires in here to look like his radio was ripped out."

Fay straightened up. "Chester," she said, turning around slowly.

"Yes Mam?" he said.

"We found them," she said quietly.

She pointed in the back window of the car parked next to the Mercedes. "They're right there in the back seat of that. . ."

She grabbed the door handle and shook it hard.
"They're under that thing, that blanket, whatever it
is," she said.

But he was already at the other side of the car
yelling into his radio for help, and rocking the car
back and forth as hard as he could.

"Joshua!" she screamed. "Richard! Wake up!" But
if the boys were under the tarp in the rear seat, they
weren't moving.

The team arrived quickly from the street level,
broke the window, opened the door, released the parking
brake and rolled the car out. Then, when they had
enough room, they opened the back doors and lifted the
two boys out onto the waiting stretchers.

Fay backed up. She couldn't move. She hadn't
really thought they could find all twenty-seven children
alive, but the prospect of finding two of them dead
paralyzed her.

"Fay!" the Chief screamed. "They're alive!"

Her knees buckled. She turned quickly and clutched
the door of the Mercedes for support.

In another minute, as the boys were loaded into the
ambulance, the Chief came up beside her, but he could
see how shaky she was.

"It's all right," he said. "He must have given
them some kind of sleeping thing. They're going to make

it."

She wasn't responding.

"Fay," he soothed, "you found them!"

"No," she said, turning around carefully and
reaching for his hand. "You found them, Chester."

"No, no," he said. "I would've walked right by.
You did it." He thought she should be excited. "You
did it!"

"What kind of car is that?" she asked, still
dizzy, still empty.

"It's a Dart," he said.

"Is that a bird?" she asked, wiping her eyes.

"Yeah," he lied, taking her arm and easing her away
from the car. "I used to see those Dart birds all the
time as a kid. Little-bitty things. Fast though."

Fay smiled, shook her head, and held his hand as
they walked to the elevator. "You ought to be real
proud of yourself, Chester."

"Yeah," he said softly. "Thanks." He looked down
at his shoes. "I wanted to do something, you know?"

She squeezed his hand. "I know."

11:00 P.M.

As Gail and the Mayor drove up to the parking
garage, the ambulance carrying Richard Isaac and Joshua
Beckstein careened out the exit, its siren wailing.

Gail saw Fay standing on the sidewalk, and jumped
out of the car. "Who is it!" she screamed.

"We found the two boys!" Fay called, hurrying
toward her. "They're alive!"

Gail stopped cold.

Fay kept talking, pointing to the upper tiers of
the garage. "They were asleep in the back seat of
a car."

That was not what Gail wanted to hear. She wrapped
her arms around herself and held on tight. "But no
Beth," she said.

"Gail," Fay said, determined to reassure her, "if
these two are alive, then Beth is alive! All we have
to do is find her."

Gail looked away. "Did you check the rest of the
cars?" she asked.

Fay reached out to her. "She's not here, Gail."

"Did you look?" Gail demanded, backing up even
further.

"They're looking right now," Fay said.

"They should break into every car up there," Gail
cried. "Tear them apart!"

"Gail," Fay said more firmly, "Beth is not here.

She's with the other man. But Arnie knows who he is and
he's tracking him down right now."

"What other man?" the Mayor asked, coming up to
them now and putting his arm around Gail.

"There's another man involved, an older man in a
wheelchair. Beth is with him."

"Why?" Gail asked, grabbing the tail of the Mayor's
sport coat, wadding it up in her hand like an old
Kleenex.

"Why does he have her?" Fay asked, not wanting to
answer that question.

"Why Beth?" Gail asked. "Why did he take my little
girl, of all these children, of all the children in the
city. . . What did I do?"

"Gail," Fay said quickly, "Arnie has been after
this man for the last two hours, so any minute now,
we'll hear something. I know it."

"No," Gail said, reaching out for Fay's hand, "you
don't know it. You're just trying to make me feel
better."

"Nobody's ever gotten away from Arnie," Fay said.
"Ever."

Gail closed her eyes and took a deep breath, hoping
the air would hold her up. But it was no use. As Fay
watched helplessly, another of the thin threads of hope,
by which Gail had been suspended all day, snapped.

The Mayor slipped his arm around Gail's waist to
support her. "Do you want to go home?" he asked. "I'll

take you wherever you want."

"Just don't leave me."

"No," he said. "I promise."

"I'm going home too," Fay said. "If you want me to
come over, just call."

Gail nodded, her hands clasped even tighter to her
face now, and the Mayor led her around the car, placed
her in the seat, and buckled the seat belt around her.

"I have some Valium at my house," Fay said to him
when he came around to get in his side of the car. "If
she needs it."

The Mayor nodded. "What do you think we should do
about Marvin," he said. "He's still in jail."

"I don't think we should do anything until she
tells us to," Fay said. "If she wants him out, I'm sure
you can arrange that."

"All right," he said, "we'll see you at home then."

Fay waved as they drove off, then joined the young
officer who had arrived to take her home.

* * *

Card number twenty in the Tarot deck is called
Judgement. The picture is a rather routine Bible school
presentation of the Last Judgement. An angel blows a
trumpet and the souls rise from the ground and ascend
into heaven. But since souls are so hard to draw, most
decks make do with naked bodies, arms raised high,
standing in open coffins.

Most of Fay's clients felt comfortable with this
card, felt as if they'd seen it before, knew what it
was, and weren't all that worried about it. It was
just another one of the Bible's bribes. If you're good,
then after you're dead (we can't say when, but we'll
call you) we're going to have a great big dance, and
everybody comes nude and you'll be sick if you're not
invited, so behave yourself.

But even people who believed in the Last Judgement
on some spiritual level, even the folks who were looking
forward to it, didn't really think it would happen,
physically, that is, so you could see it, record it on
film, teach it in history class, that kind of real.

Some churches did hold, Fay remembered, that on the
Day of Judgement, the physical bodies would arise to be
reunited with their souls, but Fay couldn't see why
anybody would go to those churches. What's so good
about a Heaven where, one of these days, you're going to
get your embarassing old body back?

There were some people who liked to play with the

idea though. One client, a math teacher, actually
assigned the problem to his classes. There are this
many square feet of standable surface on the earth, and
at least this many people who have ever lived. Now, if
all those people were to rise up all at once, would
there be enough room for them? His answer was "Yes."

But generally, the Judgement card was not ever the
subject of much discussion around Fay's table. She was
glad for that. What she had to say about it might make
some people very uneasy.

For there really was, according to Fay, such a
thing as Judgement Day. But it wasn't the same day for
everybody, and some people might have more than one.
Then too, some people might miss theirs altogether, like
not hearing the alarm some morning. Exactly like not
hearing the alarm. Judgement Day was a sort of
celestial wake up call.

But it didn't have to come in the morning, of
course. You could be washing your hair or your car, or
eating lunch, or reading. It could feel like a breeze
or sound like a sigh. You might even think it was you
who sighed, but it wasn't. It was the angel's trump.
And the message was, if you want to rise, this is the
time. The ground is loose around your feet, the
currents are right. You're cleared for take-off. Go.

Go where, the angel didn't say. How to fly
exactly? No, the angel couldn't help with that either.

Nor could the angel speculate about whether you'd miss your old friends or your comfortable shoes, or if, aloft, you'd be a little airsick, and if so, for how long.

All the angel said was Come. It's time. Time for a change, generally, time to move on. Or maybe even time to quit. You could get a considerable lift out of that. Or time to push, or win, or play in the right league.

But you had to go the minute the angel called. Later on, after you'd thought about it, planned for it, installed an escape hatch in case it didn't work, strapped on your parachute and said your good-byes, the wind would have changed. Whatever altitude you'd gain then would be difficult to maintain.

Fay wasn't sure what made some people hear this call to rise above the rest. But she knew how to recognize them. They were lighter, they laughed more easily, their clothes moved with them when they walked, their talk was simple, straight and clear.

The judgement that was made on these Judgement Days of Fay's, was not whether you had been good, or obeyed the rules, or lived in peace with God and the world. The judgment was . . could you accept your rightful place in the company of the blessed. Could you, as they used to say in Bible days, rejoice and be glad.

As Fay drove home, however, she was afraid that Gail was feeling that hateful old vengeful style of

judgement. She had been judged and found wanting. For
her sins, her little girl had been taken away.

Fay knew that if Arnie were unsuccessful, if he
failed to find Beth, or found her too late, she would
have to be the one to tell Gail, to try to stand between
her and the abyss until the angel got there.

For yes, there were times, and this might very well
be one of them, when senseless earthly tragedy
interrupted the natural flow of things, threatened the
very life of someone the angels had been watching.

When that happened, the angels couldn't afford to
wait for the right time. They had to swoop down, chop
the ropes, lift them up and hold them safely aloft until
they woke up in a year or so, and realized where they
were.

* * *

Arnie and Jake had no trouble following Masters'
metallic gray van through the city.

Jake ran a check on the plates and when the operator
came back with the information, she said the Chief had
been looking for them for an hour and what the hell was
their location.

Jake told the operator they were tailing a possible
suspect who had a possible police radio in his car so
they couldn't say where they were, but they didn't need
any help right now.

"Find out what the Chief wants," Arnie said. "It
could be a message from Fay."

"Pick up passenger in car following you," the
operator said.

Jake whirled around in his seat to look.

"Who is it?" Arnie asked.

"Gold Oldsmobile," the operator answered. "Orders
from the Chief on request from the Governor."

"Goddamn fucking radio," Arnie said.

"Who is it?" Jake asked.

"The Mayor's wife," Arnie said.

"How do you know?" Jake asked.

"I ran into her at the fairgrounds," Arnie said.
"I told her to get lost."

"Forget it," Jake said, putting the radio back in
its cradle. "We just never found a convenient time,

that's what."

When Masters turned into the huge County Rehab
Center, Arnie pulled in the Doctors' entrance and turned
off his lights.

Three orderlies came down the front steps.

"I can't see a thing," Jake said, training his
binoculars on the van.

"Maybe I'll go watch," Arnie said.

"He knows you," Jake said, handing him the
binoculars, "I'll go." And before Arnie could object,
Jake opened the door and slipped across the grass to the
gravel driveway.

What was Jake going to do, Arnie wondered, pretend
he was the gardener? But as Arnie watched through the
binoculars, Jake developed an artificial leg just at the
edge of the driveway, and gimped his way right toward
the van. The guy's got a lot of nerve, Arnie thought.
Why doesn't he just get in the van while he's at it?

As Jake approached on the passenger side, Masters
saw him, assumed he was a recovering veteran, lowered
the passenger window and called out. "You're lookin'
good, boy!"

Jake gave him an appreciative thumbs up signal, and
continued on around the van.

Arnie watched as the first paraplegic went up the
ramp in his wheelchair followed by the orderly carrying
the man's thermos bottle, the giant stuffed panda he
must've won on the midway, and the banner he had waved

in the game.

The second one wore a baseball cap and had a lap full of popcorn boxes. The third one looked either asleep or sick, Arnie couldn't tell which.

The knock on the window made Arnie nearly jump out of his seat.

"What the. . ." He snapped his head around and reached for his gun.

"I told you I wanted to come," Vi said.

He rolled down the window. "What the hell are you doing?" he barked.

"I'm coming with you," she declared. "The Governor has made me a special deputy. There is a direct order from the Chief of Police."

"I didn't get it," he said.

"Call them on the radio," she said.

He looked in his rearview mirror and wondered how he thought he could catch Mitch Masters if he couldn't spot a gold Oldsmobile pulling up behind him and blocking his exit.

"Go move your car," he said.

"What are you following _him_ for?" she asked. "He's just that man from the Tournament."

"Right," Arnie said. "Go move your car."

She crossed her arms. "Not til you promise to. . "

"Lady!" he screamed. "If you really want to see what you're going to see by being with me tonight, then you deserve it! Go move your fucking car!"

He turned away from her to watch as a man in green
workclothes closed the back door of Masters' van, then
walked around and climbed into the passenger seat next
to Mitch.

Where was Jake? Inside the van maybe? Couldn't
be, Arnie thought.

Vi tapped on the passenger window. "Where do you
want me?" she asked.

"Get in the back," he said, putting the car in
gear. "And stay down."

"You think you can scare me, don't you?" she said,
closing the door behind her.

"I said you could get in," he muttered. "I didn't
say you could talk."

Masters' van pulled away from the ramp. Still no
sign of Jake.

"He's going around the back!" Vi pointed, as if
Arnie couldn't see that.

"Please sit back," Arnie said, feeling her breath
on his neck. "It makes me crazy when people. . ."

Masters had cleared the main building now, but
instead of turning back toward the highway, was
proceeding further into the grounds of the institution.
When Arnie reached the main building, he stopped, just
to give Jake one more chance to appear.

"Aren't you going to follow him?" she inquired.

"Please, Mrs. Ewing," he said as nicely as he

could, "shut up."

"Wouldn't it be easier if you called me Vi?" she asked, sitting back in the seat.

"No, Mrs. Ewing," he said. "It wouldn't," and he turned onto the road Masters had taken.

Was Jake unconscious in the back of the van?

"Do we think he's the kidnapper?" Vi asked, leaning forward again.

"Do we think I'm here for the scenery?" Arnie mimicked her coy tone.

"But he's a wonderful man!" she protested. "He's done all those things for all those brave people."

"Right," Arnie said. They drove past the Administration Building, then the old dormitories, then something that could be a greenhouse, then the low white modern structure Arnie knew to be the now unoccupied Children's Unit. Each building had safety lights installed on the roof, and each parking lot had one tungsten lamp posted in the center of it, but the roads were completely dark, and too narrow by modern standards.

"Didn't this used to be something else?" Vi asked.

"Mental hospital," Arnie said.

He followed the van past the playground, then the ball diamond, then the cafeteria, and the shop, and then stopped far back, as Masters turned off onto a smaller road marked by a little sign.

"Where is he going?" Vi asked.

"If I knew that," Arnie sighed, "I'd already be
there waiting for him."

"But how do you know it's him?" she asked.

"Look," he said, turning around to face her, "we
have to make some kind of deal here."

"Fine," she said, looking out the window.

"You don't ask me any more questions, and when we
get there, you don't get out of the car. You don't
interfere, in any way, with what happens."

"What does that mean?" she sniped.

Arnie exploded. "This guy is a killer! That's
what it means! A fucking killer! And I watched you
cozy up to him at that ballgame. . ."

"I didn't know he was the kidnapper!" she said.

"You don't know a goddamn thing," he snapped. "You
don't know how dumb you sound, and you don't know how
stupid you look. And maybe you just don't care, but you
should care. Like you should've cared when your boys
were missing, and you should've cared a lot that some
other lady took the time to find them. But no. All you
care about is your own damn self, and how much attention
you can get, and how much hypocritical bullshit you can
sling, and how many people will buy it. Well, I for
one, won't. I'm sick to death of you, and the last
thing I thought I'd have to tolerate is being locked up
in a car with you. But here we are, so I'm just warning
you to shut up or I'm going to kill you before he even

has a chance."

He took a breath.

She sat back in her seat. "What did I ever do to
you?" she pouted.

But Arnie didn't answer. He pulled onto the
smaller road, and followed it for about a quarter of a
mile, then stopped. Two hundred yards ahead of him, a
clearing opened up and he saw Masters pull up to the far
end of a building that could be, from the steam pouring
out of the stone chimneys, the laundry. An eery orange
glow came from a wall of casement windows on the right
side of the building.

Arnie pulled off the road and stopped under a clump
of low hanging trees.

"Who found my boys?" Vi asked, tentatively.

Arnie loaded his pistol. "It was another one of
the mothers around the table this morning."

Vi was genuinely surprised. "How did she do it?"

Arnie reached in the glove compartment for his
flashlight. "She crawled through a cave," he said.
"The whole fire department was out there trying, but
she did it, she saved them."

"I see," Vi said, nodding to herself. "Have they
found her children yet?"

"She only has one child," Arnie said, getting his
handcuffs out of the pocket on the door. "A little girl
named Beth. And no, we haven't found her yet. She's

the very last one."

Vi Ewing's voice cracked. "And you think this man
has her?"

"Yes," Arnie said. "I do."

She bit her lip. "I'm sorry," she said.

"Yeah," Arnie sighed, reaching for the door handle,
"so am I."

* * *

But before Arnie could get out of the car, the
front passenger door flew open and Jake slammed himself
into the seat.

Jake was panting hard. "Move it!" he gasped.
"He's coming this way!"

Arnie slammed the car into reverse, flung his arm
over the seat, looked out the back window, and mashed on
the gas. "Hold on," he said to Vi.

"What did he do?" Arnie asked, as the car slid onto
the road, and Arnie turned around and leaned his head
out the window to see where he was going.

"He just dropped off the other two guys," Jake
said, beginning to recover his breath.

"Didn't pick up anything?" Arnie asked, as the car
sped backward out the little road.

"Just a box of shirts," Jake said.

Arnie jerked the steering wheel hard and the car
bumped up onto the main road, then sprang forward with a
lurch.

"O.K.," Jake shouted. "Step on it! If we beat him
to the gate, we can. . ."

But Arnie's hands fell from the wheel.

"What are you doing?" Jake yelled.

"I'm thinking," Arnie said, sliding his foot onto
the accelerator and depressing it gently.

"If he sees us on this road. . ." Jake argued.

"I don't think he's _going_ anywhere," Arnie said,
and gave it a little more gas.

"The kid's not in the van, if that's what you
think," Jake said.

"I think Beth is right here," Arnie said, turning
into the Children's Unit and driving to the far side of
the lot.

"But why would he. . ." Jake started to object.

"He could've gotten anybody to bring those guys
home, couldn't he," Arnie said.

"Sure," Jake said, as he saw Masters' lights
turning onto the main road.

"So if he came here," Arnie finished, "then this is
where he wants to be." Arnie pointed to it. "And my
guess is this building right here."

He turned off the ignition. "It's wheel-chair
accessible, it has toilets and beds, it's perfect,"
Arnie said.

"But wouldn't somebody see him?" Vi asked.

"It's empty now," Arnie said. "Thank God. It was
a terrible place for kids. I used to bring them out
here from. . ."

But he stopped, as Masters' van came down the road,
turned into the Children's Unit parking lot and drove up
to a ramp on the west side of the building.

"That's the kitchen," Arnie said.

"O.K.," Jake said, checking his pistol. "How do

you want to do this?"

"I'll follow him in," Arnie said. "You wait for him on the outside."

"What do you want me to do?" Vi asked carefully.

"As soon as he leaves his van, call for a backup and an ambulance. But tell them no sirens."

"You mean talk into the radio?" she asked.

"Yes," he said, and looked over at Jake. "It's this black thing in the middle up here."

She sat up to look.

"And don't get out of the car," he said.

She nodded and whispered good luck, but they didn't hear her.

Arnie and Jake darted across the dark lot, then ducked down behind a concrete turtle and watched as Masters opened the door of the van and activated the ramp that would level his wheelchair onto the loading dock.

Arnie slipped through the low shrubbery and positioned himself just under the loading dock, then waited for Jake's signal that Masters was opening the door.

Then, when he heard Masters' wheels clack over the aluminum floor strip, he hauled himself up and raced for the door, and caught it before it slammed shut. Arnie remembered the layout of the first floor and knew it would take Masters about five seconds to get to the elevator in the lobby. Arnie counted to five, then drew his gun and eased the door open.

It still had that schoolroom smell, crayons and vomit. He stepped inside, pushed the button to unlock the door for Jake, then closed it behind him noiselessly.

He ran past the steam table, grateful for what little light was coming in through the windows, skirted the dining room, the chairs and tables stacked against the wall, then rushed along the hallway with its construction paper pumpkins, and cut-out witches still riding their brooms across the bulletin board.

He had always hated this building. Something about it made kids shit on the floor and slit their wrists in the bathroom. He'd always thought if he had to do some hard time, he'd rather do it in a real prison.

He stopped, just inside the door to the lobby, and listened as the elevator doors closed, then opened the door and watched as the indicator lights came on. Arnie's memories of this place were so clear. Second floor, Mike Evans fingerpainting. God Going To The Store, he called it. Third floor, adolescent Andrea with her thing for fluorescent tubes. Four, the infirmary. Masters was going to the infirmary!

Arnie bolted for the stairwell. As he reached the fourth floor landing, he heard Masters' wheels turn the corner. Arnie waited a moment, then opened the door a crack and saw Masters wheel into the last room on the left.

Sticking close to the wall, gun drawn, Arnie crept down the hall. Two doors away, he stopped cold.

A bed creaked.

Masters' voice. "Hey, lollipop," he crooned, as though it were a warm summer morning and just the two of them in the whole wide world.

Sheets turned back.

"Did you have a nice sleep?" he asked.

A chain hit the floor.

"I told you I'd come back," he whispered.

Then the bed creaked again, springing back louder this time, lighter. Like he picked her up.

Arnie made his move.

Six quick steps and he was in the doorway, feet spread wide apart, holding the gun with both hands, pointing right at Masters' head.

"Police!" he shouted.

But Masters didn't respond. He lifted the little girl's head up to his face. "Lollipop?" he faltered.

"Hold it Masters!" Arnie roared.

And this time, Masters looked up.

And the limp little head fell back into his chest.

Arnie couldn't see Masters' face, but only the outline of his seated body, backlit by the dim yellow safety lights outside the window. He was making no attempt to escape. But it was Beth all right. Lying across his lap, shoes off, her legs dangling over the

side of his chair, a loose arm falling into the single
stream of light not obscured by the wheelchair.

"Who is it?" Masters asked, his voice barely
audible, disembodied in the darkness.

"It's Detective Campbell," Arnie hissed, still
holding the gun on the man. "I want the little girl."

Masters stroked her fine silky hair.

If he had harmed her, Arnie couldn't see it. There
was no blood, her clothes seemed perfectly intact. Her
shoes were side by side on the little nightstand beside
the bed.

"This little girl?" Masters inquired, from what
seemed like miles away.

Arnie cocked his pistol. "Put her back on the bed,
please."

"It's not what you think," Masters remarked.

"How the fuck do you know what I think!" Arnie
bellowed, his fear for Beth mounting by the minute.
"Put the kid on the bed!"

"She's just resting," Mitch explained.

"She can rest on the fucking bed!" Arnie yelled.
"Or I'll blow your head off and don't tempt me!"

Slowly, almost mechanically, Masters turned his
chair to face the bed, laid her down and pulled up the
sheet.

"Now, back up," Arnie barked. "Over there!" He
pointed to the radiator across the room.

Arnie moved to the bed and bounced it with his hand. "Beth? He shook the little girl's shoulder. "Beth! Wake up!" Her neck was cold.

Arnie pulled his handcuffs out of his pocket.

"Goddamn you!" Arnie was hysterical. "You. . .

"I didn't kill her," Masters said, his hands folded in his lap.

"You brought her here, you chained her to this. ." Arnie slammed him back against the wall, then cuffed the chair to the radiator.

"I don't have a gun," Masters said as Arnie frisked him.

"If you did, I'd kill you," Arnie snapped, stepping back.

"Yes," Masters said. "So would I."

Arnie reached for his walkie-talkie. "Jake!" he screamed. "Get up here! Fourth floor. Hallway to the right, last door on the left."

He threw his gun on the bed, then bent over Beth, felt behind her ears, then her temples, but the signs were all there. Or not there. He checked her wrist.

He stepped back, still facing the wall, a tidal wave of rage swelling up in him. He had to get her out of here.

He picked up the weightless child, and turned to Masters. "I hope there's a God," he spat. "I hope you burn in hell."

Then he rushed out of the room, down the hall, and

stepped into the elevator.

The bright overhead light hurt his eyes. He folded
the cold child up to his chest and closed his eyes. But
the tears came anyway, bitter liquid pain running down
his face. He clutched her even tighter and sobbed
helplessly, her small heart so still, his massive one a
stabbing savage in a mean, dark cave.

He knew it. Beth was dead.

As the door opened, Jake was just running into the
lobby.

Arnie stepped out of the elevator, and Jake saw the
little girl, her yellow overalls wet from Arnie's tears.

"Oh, no," Jake said.

Arnie couldn't talk. "That goddamn. . . this
poor. . . . . .her shoes. . ."

And then they heard the shot.

Fourth floor, hallway to the right, last door on
the left.

* * *

Fay had made herself a grilled cheese sandwich and a cup of coffee, and for once, both of them actually tasted as good as they smelled. She was scrubbing the inside of the coffee pot when Arnie called. In her hurry to get to the phone, she carried the coffee pot with her, leaving a trail of suds across the floor.

"Fay," he said, "sit down."

"It's all right," she said, so glad to hear his voice. "Tell me."

"We found Beth."

She had been waiting for those words, but they didn't sound right. Her throat caught, her hand squeezed tight around the handle of the pot.

"Fay?" he asked. "Did you hear me?"

She dropped into the chair, soapy water sloshing out of the pot as it hit the arm.

He tried to say it gently. "She's dead, Fay."

"No, Arnie," Fay cried. "The other two boys looked dead too, but they weren't, they were just. . ."

"No, Fay," he said, forcing the words out of his mouth. "Whatever he gave her to sleep, he gave her too much."

"Oh my God," she whispered, holding her stomach.

"And Masters is dead too."

She doubled over, head on her knees.

"Fay?"

She coughed. "I'm here."

"The ambulance is taking Beth to the morgue right
now."

"Oh no. Sweet Beth," she cried.

"And as soon as I get home," he said, "we'll go
over to Gail's together."

She pulled herself out of the chair. "I think I
better go over there right now, Arnie," she said weakly.

She lifted her head and looked around the room,
trying to find something to hold on to. "Arnie," she
stuttered, "did he hurt her?"

"No," he said quickly. "He didn't touch her. She
just went to sleep, that's all."

She wiped her eyes. "And did you shoot him?"

"No," he said. "I chained his chair to the
radiator in the room where I found them. But when I
picked Beth up off the bed, I left my gun, and he. . ."
He paused, his chest heaving. "The guy threw his body
out of the wheelchair, dragged himself across the room,
pulled himself up on the bed, got the gun, and blew his
brains out."

Fay stared at her feet.

"Fay?"

"Yes, Arnie." Her head was so heavy.

"Vi followed us out here. I sent her home."

"All right," Fay said. "I'll tell Peter. What
about Marvin?"

"The Chief is taking care of it," Arnie said. He stopped. "So. . . I'll be home in twenty minutes. Unless you think I ought to call Gail right now."

"No," she said.

"O.K.," he said, "but can you tell her that I. . "

Tell her what. That I tried real hard but I didn't get there soon enough? That maybe if I had. . . what? That if things had been different, it wouldn't have worked out this way? What?

"That you're sorry," she said, "Yes, I will. Are you all right?" she asked him.

"No," he said. "I'm not. I'll see you in a little bit." Then he remembered. "They told me you found those two boys, Fay. That's real good." His voice cracked. "I'm real proud of you."

"Thanks," she whispered. And whatever else she might have said to him stuck in her throat. But she couldn't hang up. She pressed the phone into her shoulder.

"I'm so sorry, Fay."

"I know, hon," she managed. "It wasn't your fault. Please don't think it was your fault."

"I know," he said, "I just feel so. . ."

"Come home," she said. "Just come on home."

"I'll be right there," he said.

"Good," she said. "Bye-bye."

Slow motion, it all felt like slow motion. She lowered the receiver into the cradle. Water, it felt

as if she were wading through thick dark water. She
picked up the coffee pot and took it back to the
kitchen. Then she stood in the middle of the living
room and tried to think if there was anything she should
take with her, anything that would help. Then, finding
nothing, she got her raincoat out of the hall closet,
slipped it on, it took forever to get it on, and walked
out the door.

Her arm shook as she pressed the buzzer at Gail's
apartment. Peter answered the door.

"Beth's dead," Fay whispered, still standing in the
hallway.

But he had already seen it on her face. He stood
there, his arms stiff at his sides. He sniffed, his
head twitched involuntarily.

"How?" he mouthed.

Gail called from the kitchen. "Peter?" She was
talking to her father on the phone. "Who is it?"

"I'll tell her," Fay said, stepping into the room.

"Jesus God," he said.

Fay shook her head. She was glad Gail was in the
kitchen. She took his hand. "You stay out here, huh?"

"Sure," he said, closing the door. "Sure."

As Fay walked down the hall, she heard the end of
Gail's conversation. She called him Daddy, she told him
not to worry. She told him there wasn't anything he
could do but get a good night's sleep. Then she said

she loved him, and hung up the phone.

Fay stood in the doorway, Gail sat at the kitchen
table, facing the other way.

"Gail?" Fay said carefully, taking one step in.

"I'm all right," Gail said, wetting the dish towel
in her mouth and dabbing at a spot of raspberry jam
somebody had spilled on the table.

Fay walked up behind her, put her hands on Gail's
shoulders, then leaned down and kissed the top of her
head.

Gail wrapped the dish towel around her hand and
pulled it tight. She tried to laugh. "Daddy thinks the
Communists did it."

Fay kissed the side of Gail's face.

Gail unwound the dish towel, then quickly wrapped
it around the other hand.

"I told him I knew for a fact it was the
Republicans," Gail said. "He almost hung up on me."
She stared at the refrigerator.

Fay knew this was the worst sentence anybody ever
had to say. She pressed down gently on Gail's
shoulders, hoping to absorb some of the anguish when it
hit.

"Gail," Fay said quietly, "Beth didn't make it."

"What?" Gail turned around, as if she hadn't heard
it, her eyes begging for mercy.

Fay kept hold of Gail's shoulders. "Arnie found
her." She forced herself to go on. "But the man had

given her a sleeping medicine and . . ."

Gail grabbed the table.

". . it was too much," Fay finished.

"Beth is dead?" Gail asked, praying to have misunderstood.

"Arnie is so sorry," Fay started.

"Beth is dead?" Gail screamed.

"He got there as fast as he could, but. . "

"My Beth is dead?" Gail wrapped her arms around herself and dug her nails into her flesh.

Fay grabbed her as the convulsions began.

"BETH," she cried. "Beth!" And then the real scream tore through her, reached deep down into her chest, as the savage claws clenched shut around her heart and tore it out raw and whole.

"B--E--T--H----------------

Gail shook uncontrollably, knocking Fay into the table, knocking the table away from the wall. Fay held onto her as the tears poured down her face, but soon her hair was wet too, and her arms, her whole body was crying. And then suddenly, she began to shrink away, to disappear into the hole where her heart had been. Fay grasped the back of her neck, and they both fell back into the wall.

"B----E----T----H--------------"

"Peter!" Fay called for help.

He ran down the hall, grabbed Gail out of Fay's

arms, circled his arms around her like an army and
squeezed tight.

"You're all right," he said. "I've got you." He
held her head. "It's all right. You're going to be all
right."

He patted her back. "We're right here." He
massaged her neck. "I'm not going to let go." He
squeezed tighter. "You're all right. It's all right,"
he said, over and over and over again until something,
some ancient, blood-level survival instinct took over
and said to her to stop.

Gail lay limp against him, and Fay rose from the
floor. It is one thing to say that we are all connected
here. It is quite another thing to hear the sound it
makes when we are ripped apart.

Gail pushed away from Peter and stood up.

"Where is she?" Her voice cracked. She reached for
his hand.

"The ambulance is taking her to the morgue right
now," Fay said.

That word. Morgue.

"I have to change," Gail said.

"You look fine," Fay said.

"I want to change," Gail said, and she stumbled
numb toward the door.

Peter started after her, but Fay caught him. "I
think it's all right," she said. "We'll hear it if she
needs us."

        Fay opened the refrigerator and pulled out the
bottle of ice water, then went to the cabinet for two
glasses. She poured them each a glassful, and they sat
down at the table. She told him that Vi had been there
with Arnie, and that Marvin would be at the morgue. She
told him the name of Gail's minister, and the name of
the funeral home. She found Gail's address book, and
made a list of the relatives she knew Gail would want
someone to call.

        When he asked for more of the details, she told him
Mitch Masters had killed himself. Peter said he
thought, that in a while, Gail would want to know that.

        Then Fay went in to Beth's bedroom, where Gail was
standing in front of the little girl's closet. Fay took
her hand and said she didn't have to do this now. But
Gail said she wanted to undertaker to have everything he
needed when he picked her up.

        Fay said a dress would be nice, and Gail reached
for the white one Marvin's mother had sent Beth for
Easter. Fay opened a dresser drawer and held up socks
until Gail nodded at the pair with the cats on the toes.

        And then Gail couldn't stay in the room any longer.
The smells, the baby powder, the shampoo, the vaporizer,
the tennis shoes, the smells from the beginning, the
diapers, the milk, the baby food carrots she spit up for
so long, the smells, the smells. She had to get out
quick. She had to close the door to keep the smells in.

As they passed the bathroom, Fay stuffed Kleenexes into Gail's jacket pocket, and they met Peter at the front door of the apartment. It took both of them to get Gail down the stairs.

Once they were on the street, Fay said she would come along if that would help, but Gail said no. Then she reached out and Fay held her as long and close as she could, and then Peter took her arm and led her to the car.

As she watched them drive away, Fay prayed. For divine grace, for holy comfort, for the blessing of the pure in heart. And then she turned and walked down the street, toward her doorway, and the black Rolls Royce parked in front of it.

12:00 A.M.

* * *

Fay saw his languid arm first, draped out the open window of the satin Rolls, smoke curling lazily from the cigarette he held loosely between his fingers. She crossed the street about four cars ahead of him and stepped onto the sidewalk.

She knew she shouldn't stop, knew he wouldn't get out of the car, and knew that talking to him through the window would only make her feel worse. But she was going to do it anyway. From now on, there was nothing she wouldn't do to keep from losing Lizzie.

She walked in front of the car. He saw her, all right, but he didn't sit up, of course.

"Paul?" She tried not to bend toward him.

He gazed up at her, his voice as smooth and rich as an amber liqueur. "We wondered where you were," he said.

Fay straightened her shoulders. "If you're waiting for Lizzie," she said, "she's not coming with you."

Paul slipped further down in the seat, leaning his head back against the headrest. "If she weren't coming with me," he explained, perfectly pleasant, "I wouldn't be waiting for her."

"Where is the boat going?" Fay asked, wondering if any of her kitchen knives were sharp enough to puncture his radials.

"Wherever _Dad_ says," Paul said. "It's _his_ boat."

Fay nodded. "How long will you be gone?"

"Til we get back, I guess," he said, enjoying the elegance of the truth.

Fay stood there fuming, wishing she had a bottle of red nail polish to drip down the side of his car while she thought of what to say next.

But Paul was completely at ease. "I heard you found those other two boys," he said, flicking the cigarette butt past her into the street. "I wanted to congratulate you."

"Was it your father who put up the reward?" she asked.

"I think so," he said. "He likes to do things like that." He glanced out the window to Fay's front door. "He'd probably double it if you asked him to. Means nothing to him, one way or the other."

"Did you tell him it was me who was finding the children?"

"Maybe I did," Paul said. "I forget."

Fay had the whole picture now. "So he's buying Lizzie for you, is that right?"

Paul laughed.

Fay went on. "Just give the old lady a check, is that what you told him? So she won't miss her daughter?"

"Don't take the money, then," Paul said, still laughing. "Doesn't matter to me."

"What about your other girls," Fay asked. "Do you
just hand their mothers the money in cash?"

"Cash?" Paul choked. "Please." He still couldn't
stop laughing.

Fay had to get to Lizzie. Why had she wasted all
this time talking? Did she think there was something
else to learn? Did she think she might have imagined
all this? Did she think he wasn't really the Devil and
was maybe just a handsome Brazilian rogue of a boy?

She hurried around the car and across the sidewalk.
No way was he taking Lizzie away from her. No way.

* * *

Fay opened the door.

"Mom?" Lizzie called, "is that you?"

Please God, Fay prayed, help me. I have to make
her see who he is. See what's going to happen if she
leaves with him.

"It's _me_," Fay called back.

Lizzie came to the doorway of the hall, pulling a
silver slip over her head. "What's up?"

"Up?" Fay repeated. She started for the closet,
then decided to leave her raincoat on, for the moment.

"With the kidnapping," Lizzie said, smoothing the
slip down over her ribs and hips.

Fay pitched her purse into the chair. "It's not
good," she said.

"You didn't find Beth yet?"

Fay stopped. Her purse had knocked over the
needlepoint pillow. There was her mother's loaded
pistol, the one Fay had hidden there two hours ago when
she was afraid of those boys on the street.

"Whose gun is that?" Lizzie asked.

"It was mother's," Fay said, picking up the pistol
and stuffing it in her coat pocket.

"What did Granny need a gun for?" Lizzie asked.

"Snakes," Fay said. And she walked past the girl
into the kitchen.

Lizzie followed her. "Snakes?" she laughed.

Fay flicked on the kitchen light and stood there watching as a water bug scrambled back into the sink for safety.

"Beth is dead," Fay said, finally. "Arnie found her dead."

"Mother?" Lizzie asked from behind her.

"What?" Fay crossed the room to the refrigerator.

"What are you doing here?   Why aren't you with Gail?"

"Where do you think I've been?" Fay asked, jerking the refrigerator door open.

"I just asked," Lizzie said, leaning against the door frame. "You don't have to scream at me."

"I'm not screaming at you," Fay said.

"Yes, you are," Lizzie said. "Does Arnie know you have a gun?"

Fay bent down to look at the bottom shelf. "Yes," she said. "What happened to the rest of that pound cake?"

"I ate it," Lizzie said, and turned to go.

Fay whirled around. "You gave it to him, didn't you."

Lizzie sighed. "I ate it, Mom. Me, Lizzie. I ate it."

Fay saw Lizzie's patronizing look. "You have no idea, do you." She slammed the refrigerator door.

"I'm real sorry about Beth," Lizzie said. "I tried

to say that, but you. . ."

"No idea," Fay said.

"It's not your fault, Mother," Lizzie said. "You
did the best you could. You found all the rest of the
children."

Fay shook her head. "That's not what I'm talking
about." She opened the door to the pantry.

"I said I was sorry," Lizzie said. "I don't know
what else to say. I have to get dressed."

"You're _not_ getting dressed," Fay said.

Lizzie stopped in the doorway and took a deep
breath. "I have to get dressed, Mother. We're going
out on the boat again." She paused. "I thought I told
you that, but I guess with all this stuff going on
today. . ."

Fay closed the pantry door. There was nothing in
there that would help. "Do you know where this boat is
going?"

Lizzie looked away. "No, Mother."

"Well, I do," Fay said. "And I know who Paul is,
and who his father is, and you're not going."

"Not going?" Lizzie asked, her back stiffening in
surprise.

"No," Fay said.

Lizzie studied her mother a moment.

"I'm serious," Fay said.

No, Lizzie thought, you're tired and weird. And

she turned abruptly and walked back toward her bedroom.

Fay walked to the sink and picked up a not too
dirty glass and filled it with cloudy water from the
tap. The gun felt good in her pocket, the barrel long
and cold against her thigh, the handle grip hard and
round on her hip. Men knew about this, she thought, men
grew up playing with guns. They knew how good it felt
to have one on your side.

When Fay got to the doorway of Lizzie's room, the
girl was staring into her closet. But the good cheer
Lizzie had felt, anticipating the party, had left her.
Beth, across the street, was dead. And her own mother
was walking around the house with a gun in her pocket.

"You really _know_ where the boat is going?" Lizzie
asked, over her shoulder.

"Yes," Fay said, leaning against the doorframe, "I
do."

"Did Paul tell you?" Lizzie asked, stepping into a
pair of silver strip sandals.

"No," Fay said. "I saw it."

"Oh," the girl nodded. So it was a vision. One of
her mother's little trips. Well, no wonder she was
acting so strange.

"You go to California," Fay said.

Lizzie knew she had to be careful. "I see," she
said. She didn't want to insult her mother. "You think
he's kidnapping me. Is that right?"

"I know it," Fay said, "and it's not the first

time either."

"It's the first time for me," Lizzie said, admiring her legs in the mirror. "What else?"

Fay took a sip of water. "At the end of the trip Paul asks you to marry him," she said.

"What do I say?" Lizzie asked, disappearing into her closet.

"You say yes," Fay said.

"So what's the bad news?" Lizzie asked, pulling out a pale voile wisp of a dancing dress. "Does his daddy hate me?"

"He buys you a convertible," Fay said.

"His mother poisons me?" Lizzie asked.

"She has the Archbishop of Portugal bless the orchids for your wedding."

"You mean I actually marry him?" Lizzie grinned, stepping carefully into the dress.

"In San Diego," Fay said, finishing her glass of water.

"Do we have babies?" Lizzie asked.

"I only know of one," Fay said, watching as Lizzie struggled to zip the dress. "But there could be more, I guess. Want to know her name?"

"No," Lizzie said quickly. She turned around. "I'd like to think it up." She stopped. "If that's O.K. with you."

Fay bit her lip, and watched as Lizzie put on the

gold hoop earrings. Think it up. Did people actually think they _made up_ their children's names? Did they really believe that a creature as complicated as a child could arrive on the earth without a name? Could let someone else decide its name?

"I don't know why you're so worried about all this," Lizzie said, walking into the bathroom and opening the medicine cabinet. "Just because you saw it, doesn't mean it's going to happen."

Fay took a breath.

"But even if it does," Lizzie went on, "it sounds like a pretty nice life."

She found the wand of mascara and a tiny pot of cream blush and closed the cabinet door. "Did you tell me all of it?" Lizzie called out.

"I left out the part where you never call me and I never see you again," Fay said, walking up to block the bathroom door. "You don't invite me to your wedding, and you don't let me see," Fay stopped herself from saying Katie's name, "my granddaughter."

Lizzie applied the mascara carefully, slowly stroking both sides of her long lashes. "Why would I do that?"

Fay cleared her throat. "I don't know," she said. "Maybe you're ashamed of me. Maybe I'm not good enough for you any more."

Lizzie started to work on the other eye now.

Fay went on. "Maybe you find out I was right, only

you don't want to admit it, so you just don't call me."

"Right about what?" Lizzie leaned toward the mirror to inspect her work.

"That he's going to hurt you," Fay said. "He does something terrible, only. . ."

"So people hurt each other," Lizzie said. "They get over it."

". . only I can't tell you what it is," Fay finished, "because I haven't seen that part yet."

Lizzie had to laugh. "Well, maybe you could call me right before it happens. . ."

Fay didn't think that was funny. She tried to explain. "I want you to be married."

"Right," Lizzie said, opening the pot of pale pink blush.

"I want you to have a family," Fay pleaded. "But I want it to be your family. Not his."

"Mother," Lizzie said, dabbing the blush just under her cheekbones, "what if I like it?"

"You'll hate it," Fay said. "You'll hate how they live, you'll hate the way they talk. . ."

"If I hate it, I'll leave," Lizzie said. She was finished in the bathroom now.

"He won't let you leave, Lizzie," Fay said.

"No, Mother," Lizzie said, pointing to Fay's stance in the doorway. "It's not Paul who won't let me leave, it's you."

Fay backed up. "Lizzie, please," Fay said. "Have
I ever stopped you from doing anything?"

Lizzie walked toward her dresser.

Fay answered her own question. "No," she said, "I
haven't. I've given you everything you ever wanted."

"No, Mom," Lizzie said over her shoulder. "You
gave me everything you ever wanted."

Fay took a step toward her, genuinely confused.
"What did you want?" she asked.

"I don't know," Lizzie said, picking up her gold
evening bag. "Right now, I just want to go."

Fay's heart stopped. "Is that what you always
wanted?" she asked. "To leave me?"

"Maybe," Lizzie said, checking herself once more in
the full-length mirror. "I don't remember."

Fay couldn't breathe for a second. Could that be
true? All Lizzie ever wanted was to leave? No, no.
Lizzie had been happy here. All Lizzie needed was a
better explanation. "I had to keep you here," Fay said,
"so you could grow up."

"Well," Lizzie said quietly, putting a tissue in
the little purse, "you don't have to do that any more."
And she closed the clasp.

And they both heard the front door open.

"Lizzie?" Paul called.

"I'm coming," she sang out, starting toward Fay.

"No," Fay said, grabbing her by both arms. "I
can't let you go. I can't let you leave with him."

Gently, Lizzie pried her mother's hands loose, then held them in hers. "Mother," she said, "this is crazy. You're all worked up over nothing. It's just another party."

"Please," Fay said. "I wouldn't do this if I didn't think there was a real. . ."

"No," Lizzie said. "I promise. I'll be back in the morning."

And then Fay saw it. Looked right into Lizzie's pale green eyes and saw it. When Paul was finished with her, his father would hire the lawyers, bribe the judges, and take Katie away. Lizzie would lose her daughter not because Paul wanted to raise the little girl, but just because his father liked to win.

Someone knocked on the bedroom door.

"Lizzie?" It was Paul.

Fay froze as the door opened. She had to tell her.

"What's going on in here?" Paul asked.

"Lizzie. . ." Fay began.

"Mother thinks you're kidnapping me," Lizzie said, casting a careful sideways glance at Fay.

"That's not a bad idea," he said, opening the door even wider behind him. "You look wonderful."

Lizzie smiled at him. "Thanks," she said, then turned to Fay, and gave her a light kiss on the cheek. "I'll see you in the morning, Mother."

Fay looked up at her. How could she tell her?

What could she tell her? That she would lose her child?
Lizzie wouldn't believe it. Nobody ever did.

"Lizzie," Fay tried again, "if it's just another
party, then you don't have to go. There are lots of
parties."

"I'll be all right," Lizzie soothed.

"No," Fay pleaded. "You won't!"

Lizzie took Paul's arm. This was almost funny.
"You'll be O.K., Mom." She grinned and patted Fay on
the shoulder. "Arnie will be home soon."

And Paul and Lizzie turned together and walked out
the door.

Fay stood there listening to their footsteps down
the hall. She couldn't wait for Arnie. Paul was not
going to get away with this. Walk off with her
daughter? Walk off with her granddaughter? Just
because he was young and rich and always got what he
wanted? Not a chance in hell.

"Lizzie!" she screamed, and ran after them.

Paul was just opening the front door.

Lizzie stopped. "What?" she asked.

Fay drew the gun and braced herself against the
door to the hall. "Get out of the way," she said.

"Mother!" Lizzie screamed.

Paul bolted out the door, dragging Lizzie behind
him. "Get in the car!" he shouted, and pushed her
toward it, then ran around the front of the shadowy
Rolls.

Fay charged through the living room and out onto the sidewalk.

"Mother!" Lizzie cried, from the front seat, her hands pressed up against the closed window. "Don't do this!"

"Lizzie!" Fay screamed, but the engine roared to life. Fay ran back behind the car, but she didn't know where to shoot. The tires? The windows? What if she missed the tires and hit the gas tank? What if she blasted the windows and the broken glass hit Lizzie?

"Lizzie!" she screamed again, but the tires squealed, the car sprang forward and pulled away from the curb.

"Stop!" she screamed, and ran out into the street. But the car didn't stop. She raised the gun high above her head, fired two shots into the heavy black air, then ran up the street after them.

The Rolls ran the light at the corner. She couldn't see Lizzie inside it now.

Still, she followed, still screaming. "You don't know what he's going to do!"

And then she felt her legs slow down. They knew, even if she didn't, that it was useless.

"He's going to take. . . " She stopped. She had to stop.

"Katie!-----------------" Fay cried.

And then, in a desperate rage, she flung the heavy

pistol toward the tiny red taillights taking a left
turn three blocks away.

Lizzie was gone.

Fay didn't move. She stood over the yellow line
down the middle of the street, folded her trembling arms
around herself, and stared straight ahead. If any cars
came, they'd just have to go around her. If anybody had
heard the gunfire, they'd just have to get up, turn on a
light, and worry about it. Fay wasn't going anywhere
until she felt like it. Where was she supposed to go,
anyway? Home? Why? Because she'd left the front door
open? Who cared? So she could change clothes? Sleep?
Eat? Work? What was the point?

She closed her eyes. But there was nothing to see
there either. She already knew what would happen.
Arnie would come home, they would go to Gail's, then to
bed. Maybe he would quit the police force tomorrow,
maybe he wouldn't. Maybe they would go to Wyoming
tomorrow, maybe they wouldn't. But Lizzie would not
come home.

She wiped her forehead on the sleeve of her shirt.
She couldn't leave that pistol on the street. She
opened her eyes and started up the street to find it.
Behind her, somewhere down the block, a car screeched to
a stop. She assumed it was Arnie.

"Miss Morgan?" a young police officer called,
running toward her from the station on the corner.

"I'm all right," she yelled back to him.

"Fay!" It was Arnie's voice, as he chased up the
street.

"I'm all right!" she yelled even louder, angry at
both of them for finding her here.

"I heard the shot," the young officer said.

"I lost my mother's gun," Fay said, stooping down
to look underneath a beat-up Buick. "Let me have your
flashlight."

"Fay?" Arnie asked, coming up to join them now.

She stood up, took the young officer's flashlight
and turned to face Arnie.

"They got away," she said.

The young officer wanted to seem in charge. "Miss
Morgan called me about an hour ago," he said to Arnie.
"Told me there were some robbers watching her
apartment."

But Arnie guessed easily that Fay hadn't been
chasing robbers.

She walked on up the street.

"Where are you going now?" he called.

"She says it's her mother's gun," the young officer
said, as they followed her. "I guess they tried to
steal it."

"There it is," she said, pointing under the custom
Jeep.

"I'll take care of this," Arnie said to the young
man.

"It's Rodgers, sir," he answered.

"O.K., Rodgers," Arnie said. "Thanks."

"That's the lady who found all those kids, isn't it?" Rodgers asked.

"Yeah," Arnie said. "See you later."

"Any time," Rodgers said, deciding, reluctantly, that it probably wasn't a good idea to ask her for an autograph right now.

* * *

"I didn't hit them," Fay said, as soon as the young
officer was out of earshot.

"Good," Arnie said.

Fay wiped the gun on her skirt. "I wanted to,
though. I wanted to kill him," she said.

He shook his head. "It doesn't feel as good as you
think," he said. "The minute you know they're dead, you
start to wonder what else you might have tried."

She nodded, then shuddered to think how dangerously
close she had come to it. Dead in the street, the Devil
would have won for real.

"Want to walk?" he asked.

"I want to change clothes," she said, studying the
gun in the glow from the streetlight.

He stooped to pick up a soft drink can lying in the
gutter. "I want to throw this away," he said, "and go
in there and quit." He pointed to the station. "Then
I'll come down to your house."

"You're really going to quit?" she asked, but it
was more an echo than a question.

"I'm going to try," he said. "Want me to walk you
down to your house first?"

"No," she said, "I'll be all right." And she
walked off, carrying the pistol loosely at her side.

Arnie watched her go. If there were bullets left
in that gun, that was _her_ business. Maybe, if he were

an ordinary cop, he'd have taken it away from her. But
he could see it made her feel better. And after this
day, she deserved to feel better. Besides, he laughed
to himself, he'd like to see somebody <u>try</u> to take
anything else away from Fay Morgan tonight. She wasn't
going to shoot anybody. She was just going to put it
back in the closet where it belonged.

As Arnie watched Fay, she watched Paul and Lizzie
boarding the boat.

"Why did you do it?" Paul asked, taking her arm.
"Why did you save me?"

Lizzie spoke softly, privately, ignoring the crowd
that was waiting for them. "I wanted to be with you,"
she said.

"She wanted to kill me," Paul said, with no malice,
but a world of wonder at the actual fact of it.

"She loves me," Lizzie said, stepping onto the
gangplank.

"Is that what happens to people who love you?" he
asked, accepting a glass of champagne from the steward.

She laughed as the truth came to her. "If it is,"
she said, "does that scare you?"

"No," Paul grinned, tilting the glass toward her in
a silent toast. "It's a good thing to know, though."

Fay swallowed hard, and walked up to her door.
She felt the vacant chill as soon as she stepped inside
the apartment. Was it just Lizzie who was missing? No.
She closed the door behind her. It was everything

Lizzie had held in place just by living there. History, hope, the length of love, the promise of a child.

She walked to the closet, hung up her raincoat, then put the gun back in the box on the floor. Fay could just hear her mother clucking over this. You didn't believe me, did you, the old woman would say. I told you you would lose her. No, Fay would answer, you didn't tell me. Or . . . maybe I didn't hear you.

She closed the closet door, walked to the bathroom and washed her face. She looked awful, and felt even worse, like a cracked, cheap plastic carryall, abandoned in the back of somebody's closet.

She changed into faded trousers and a flannel shirt, then slipped on a pair of mocassins she and Lizzie had bought ten years ago on a trip to the Blue Ridge.

As she passed the closet, on her way back into the living room she stopped. She missed her mother, actually missed the nosey old hen. Missed her smell, her hair. Missed how she thought she knew everything, missed how mean she could be when she was right. Maybe, just maybe, way off in the distant future, way beyond where Fay could see right now, Lizzie would miss <u>her</u> that way.

No, Fay thought. That was hope. Fay didn't believe in hope. Fay believed in phone calls.

Arnie was standing on the sidewalk when she came out into the living room.

"I want to sleep at my house tonight," he said, opening the door. "Want to come?"

"I want to go to Gail's first," she said, running her hand along the back of the old upholstered arm chair.

"I just checked," he said. "They left the morgue about ten minutes ago. So they're not back yet."

He lifted the paper sack he held in his left hand. "I bought us a beer," he said.

"Good," she said, pushing her hair back away from her face. "A beer would be real good."

"I thought we could lock up," he said, "then sit out on the stoop and drink it."

"Good," she said.

He waited while she retrieved her purse from the chair, then closed the door behind her and locked it.

Fay sat down on the raised concrete stoop and stretched her legs out in front of her.

"How do you feel?" he asked, as he sat down beside her.

"I don't have any feelings left," she said.

"They'll be back."

"I can wait," she smiled, running her hand down his arm.

He set the sack between his legs, pulled out one of the cold beers and flipped the top.

"Thanks," she said, lifting the rush of cold foam to her mouth and licking the side of the can to catch the run off before it ruined her pants.

"I saw what was going to happen to Lizzie," she said finally, "but I couldn't tell her."

"It sounds like you did the right thing, Fay," he said. "It's over. Don't worry about it."

She stared into her beer. "How can it be over? Things don't ever end, Arnie. Tell me one thing, one thing that was ever over."

"Well," he pondered, then opened his beer. "For starters," he took a long drink, "this day is over."

He put the bag off to one side for the cans when they were empty, set the beer down on the stoop, and reached into his pocket for a fresh pack of cigarettes. Slowly, he unwound the gold strip around the top of the pack, tore off the folded foil square and tapped the pack against his hand.

"Did you quit?" she asked, wishing there were a breeze, or just one breath of air she didn't have to take by force.

He lifted the pack to his mouth and pulled one cigarette from the trio his tap had forced out of formation. Then he put the pack back in his pocket and reached into the other pocket for his lighter.

"I filled out the papers," he said, then shrugged. "Sooner or later, somebody's bound to find them."

Good, she thought. So at least they didn't have to leave for Wyoming _tomorrow_.

She pushed her hair back from her temples. "How can it still be so hot out here?"

He smiled as the thought hit him, then flicked the lighter, cupped his hands around the flame, lit the cigarette and inhaled. "You never did smoke, did you," he said.

"No," she said, gazing out into the darkness. "I never did."

He blew the smoke out in front of them in one long curl, reached for her hand and squeezed it.

"That's too bad," he said quietly. "Be just the thing."

THE END